Typewriter Pub, an imprint of Blvnp Incorporated
A Nevada Corporation
1887 Whitney Mesa DR #2002
Henderson, NV 89014
www.typewriterpub.com/info@typewriterpub.com

ISBN: 978-1-64434-183-4

DISCLAIMER

This book is a work of fiction. The characters, incidents, and dialogue are drawn from the author's imagination and are not to be construed as real. While references might be made to actual historical events or existing locations, the names, characters, places, and incidents are either products of the author's imagination or are used fictitiously, and any resemblance to actual persons living or dead, business establishments, events or locales is entirely coincidental.

AFTER THE INK

B.D. FRESQUEZ

For Serena, Emery, and Tony.
I love the laughs we share together.

PROLOGUE

In my nightmare, I know what is going to happen. It happens every night. The worst part is not knowing how to make it stop just for one second, so I can breathe.

The accident was three weeks ago, and I still haven't gotten that one second to breathe. It isn't some figment of my imagination that I can easily escape from. My parents are gone. That is my first thought when I wake up and my last when I fall asleep. I've been trying not to think about the car accident itself, but it creeps back into my mind anyway.

My family decided to have one funeral for the both of them, so I didn't have to go through everything twice. It didn't make things any better—seeing their closed caskets, everyone wearing black, and that stupid cemetery where they are now instead of work.

Like some cruel twist of fate, I still have to continue my life. I still have to worry about homework because school isn't going to stop and close shop due to a student losing both her parents. Instead, I've gotten some condolences, an extra day to turn in my work, and that is that.

The school counselor wants me to schedule meetings with her, but what will I even talk about? Them? Because that won't bring them back.

I already have a great support system anyway, people who actually know me and care about me. I have Aunt Jade, who is my guardian now; my best friend, Casey; and my boyfriend, Jacob.

Jacob is on my arm, babbling about an exam as we are walking to my journalism class. His exam is the last thing on my mind, but I still offer my advice to him anyway. All the talk about exams has me wondering about my own results. Junior year is ending in a week, and I wonder how it all went by so quickly.

When we reach my class, Jacob stops walking and I stand in front of him. With a gentle finger below my chin, he tilts my head so I am looking up at him. His light brown hair is swept up in his usual hairstyle. His warm brown eyes always make me feel safe and secure. I can get lost in them all day.

"Listen," he says. "I really want you to go with me to that party tonight. I won't even drink. I'll let you do your thing, you know, wind down a bit. I'll make sure you get home safe."

Since the accident, Jacob has put it in his head that I am afraid of driving or even being in a vehicle, which isn't true. He always has a way of deciding things for me, and I mostly blow it off.

I just don't want to be around a bunch of people at a stranger's house. Things are different right now, and I do *not* want to make my aunt anxious by being out late.

I chew on my lip and try to figure out a way to say no. "I don't know, Jake. I don't think my aunt wants me out late."

The disappointment is clear on his face, but he nods, seeming to understand. "I get it. I just want you to have some fun after everything that's happened."

He's been trying to get me to go to that party all week, and I keep brushing off the topic. He says he gets it, but I don't think he does. There are a million other things that I need to focus on right now.

"I don't think I'm ready to start going out yet," I tell him honestly. "Plus, I have a ton of homework and studying to do, not to mention all the boxes I still have to unpack at the apartment."

My home is no longer a house in a neighborhood with my parents but a two-bedroom apartment with my aunt.

Jacob takes my wrist in his hand and stares at my tattoo—our tattoo. He traces the heart and infinity symbol with his finger and brings it up to his lips for a sweet kiss. "I'm glad we got these together." His eyes meet mine. "I understand, babe. If you don't mind, I'm gonna go with the guys to that party tonight. This exam has me stressed the hell out, and I'd rather let loose than study."

Typical Jacob, procrastinating then hating himself later on. Instead of arguing with him about it, I let it go. His blasé attitude towards schoolwork is something I've learned to live with.

The first time I saw Jacob was in my Algebra class during our freshman year. I thought he was cute, and immediately felt butterflies every time he looked at me.

He liked to bother me and push my buttons. I always acted like I was annoyed, but I liked the attention he gave me. Our friends looked like they wanted us to go out, and when he finally asked me out on a date, I said yes.

The bell rings, and I'm brought back to reality. Jacob kisses my forehead and says he will see me after school before we both dash to our classes.

As Mrs. Thomas talks, I stare at my tattoo. I trace it in the same way Jacob did, and the memory of when my parents found out about it comes to mind.

They were pissed beyond belief, and even more so when they found out Jacob has the same one on his forearm. We got them for our two-year anniversary last September. I never told Jacob, but I regretted getting the tattoo immediately after the needle had touched my skin.

My parents didn't let me see him for nearly two months. They couldn't keep us apart at school, but outside of that, I couldn't see him at all.

Eventually, they forgave us and we were allowed to hang out again. They started trusting Jacob again, and that was when I let him meet my aunt and grandparents.

My mom liked him simply because he made me happy. My dad liked that he was captain of the soccer team and promised to continue liking him as long as he didn't hurt me.

Picturing my life with Jacob before the accident was a no-brainer. I wanted to be with him forever. We'd be the ultimate high school sweethearts, telling our kids and grandkids about our matching tattoos. After the accident, it suddenly felt like forever was a foreign idea.

After school, I meet Jacob in the parking lot like we usually do. He drives me to my aunt's apartment in his truck and parks in front of the building.

"Have fun tonight," I tell him.

He grins. "Let me know if you change your mind and I'll come get you."

"Whose party is it anyway?" He hasn't mentioned it being one of the soccer guys throwing it.

He shrugs. "Honestly, I don't remember."

Who knew everyone would be throwing end-of-the-year parties? I give him a kiss on the cheek before I let myself out of his truck. Once inside the apartment, I take a deep breath. The unpacked boxes in my room are enough to make me break down.

*   *   *

The weekend went by quickly, and I hardly heard from Jacob. I thought for sure I'd see him on Saturday, but he said he wasn't feeling good. I figured he was hungover from the party.

4

It's Monday morning, and I am not getting a text back from him about whether he is going to pick me up. I end up asking my aunt Jade to take me to school. She has the day off anyway, and I don't feel like bothering Casey.

Aunt Jade pulls up in front of the school and meets my eyes. Her nose is a bright pink, as it has been since the accident. Her short brown hair is done up in a lazy ponytail, with pieces of it coming out at messy points.

"I promise I'll help you get a car soon. I know it isn't exactly cool to be dropped off by your aunt," she says.

"I'll ride the bus if I need to," I tell her so she doesn't worry. I know she has a million other things to worry about too. "I'm sure Jacob will bring me home this afternoon."

She smiles. "Have a good day," she says as I step out and wave to her.

The atmosphere is different once I walk into the main building. I can't put my finger on it, but everything feels off. Maybe it is because we are in the last couple weeks before summer break.

I spot Casey in the hallway and she frowns.

"Where's Jacob?" she asks.

She knows that if I am not with her, I'll be with Jacob. Her face makes me think she doesn't really care where he is. She has never been a huge fan of him anyway.

"I think he slept in." I shrug. It won't be the first time it happens. "Today feels weird, right?"

"Probably because it's Monday. You know my philosophy, Monday's are bad for the skin." She moves her sandy blonde hair off her shoulders. "Hey, do you want to go shopping with me later? I literally have no good bras, and I can't ignore the wire sticking into my boob right now."

Casey has always been the candid one in our relationship. I don't know what I would do without her.

I agree to go with her, and we begin walking down the hall. I see some of Jacob's friends from the soccer team and wave to them, but they run off to the opposite direction, which I find a bit weird.

Soccer players aren't as glorified as the football players, so Jacob's popularity comes from being a social butterfly. Being in a relationship with him has boosted my own popularity, though I know I can only really trust Casey.

I feel eyes on me as I trudge into class. Heather, a girl who sits diagonally from me, is staring at me blatantly. She looks away once I sit down.

What is everyone's deal today?

Many review notes later, class ends. I shove my binder into my backpack and, in the corner of my eye, see Heather approaching me slowly.

"Hey, Heather." I decide to greet her first. We've only spoken directly a handful of times while working on class assignments, and she has always been friendly. I wonder what she wants to talk about.

"Hi." She smiles, though it looks forced.

She hasn't said anything else so I ask, "What's up?"

"I, uh, want to talk to you about something." She is holding a textbook tightly against her chest.

I pull my backpack over my shoulder and feel ready to talk until I notice her strange expression. Her brows are furrowed, and her entire body language is awkward and unsure. It makes me uncomfortable.

"Can we do it while walking?" I ask her. I don't want to be late for my next class. I start walking towards the door, hoping she will follow me and she does.

"Have you talked to Jacob?" she asks. "Since the party?"

"Not really," I admit. "Why?"

We make it just outside of the classroom when she suddenly stops. "He cheated on you," she blurts out.

Her words make me look at her dead in the eye. Cheated? "How the hell do you know that?" I demand.

6

"I saw it happen," she says quickly. "I was at that party last Friday, and I saw him flirting with Lauren all night. It didn't look good when they went into a room and came out thirty minutes later."

My heart is thumping rapidly in my chest. Flirting with Lauren? Did he sleep with her?

She has a pained expression on her face. "Listen, I'm not trying to start anything, but I know Jacob isn't going to tell you anything. I don't think you should hear it as gossip in the halls."

Tears threaten to spill onto my cheeks. Can I trust what she's saying? Is she telling the truth? I don't want to believe her, but inside, I know she is telling the truth. She has no reason to lie to me.

"I'm so sorry, Lacey," she says, backing away slowly. Then, she disappears into the crowd.

It feels as if everyone but me knows what Jacob has done. It is like everyone's eyes are on me, and they are waiting for me to react. I run to the nearest bathroom and try to calm myself down. My chest is heavy, and I am sure my head is going to explode. Thoughts of Jacob with Lauren enter my mind.

No, no, no, no, no!

This shouldn't have happened. Jacob is supposed to be there for me, to help me grieve, to help me laugh again, and to be my rock. Not cheat on me at some party.

I wipe my eyes and take a deep breath. I just have to make it through the rest of the day. I can meet Casey for lunch, and she will be able to help me get me through this.

*   *   *

After avoiding and ignoring Jacob all day, I have decided to take Casey's advice.

I need to end things with him.

A girl in my last class has no shame whatsoever, discussing the whole situation with another girl. She says Jacob looked unapologetic after someone brought me up.

The way they're talking about my personal life so openly only makes me angrier, and I almost snap at them to shut up. Instead, I hold my tongue and wait to talk to Jacob, who deserves my anger the most.

On my way to the parking lot after school, I come across Lauren. Her glossy appearance makes me think that she hasn't lost sleep over what she has done. As much as I want to call her every horrible name I can think of, I don't. It won't make me feel any better.

Her black hair is straight behind her shoulders, and it swings from side to side as she approaches me.

I speak before she can get a chance, "I don't have the energy to deal with you right now."

"Lacey, just listen—"

"No, you listen." I point at her. "Just leave me alone and we won't have a problem."

I'm in a relationship with Jacob, not her. What she has to say doesn't mean anything. It is Jacob's fault, and that is all that matters to me. I want to hate Lauren, but I can't. I need to focus my anger and hatred on Jacob.

I wait for him by his truck, with Casey parked nearby. I ignore call after call from him.

Soon enough, he's walking towards me, and I mentally prepare myself. I'm not going to let him smooth-talk his way out of the situation like he always does when we argue. I'm not going to let him change my mind. He has made me look like an idiot, and there is no way in hell I'm going to let him get away with it.

"What the hell? Why haven't you answered any of my calls or texts?" Jacob asks when he comes close enough.

I stare at him and try to detect if he's going to apologize to me. "Do you want to tell me what happened at that party, or do you want me to tell you what I heard?"

His face changes, but he recovers. He really is going to try to lie his way out of this. "What are you talking about?"

"I know you slept with Lauren." I try keeping my voice low as I say it.

"Where did you hear that?"

You've got to be kidding me. "It's all over the fucking school," I snap. "Everyone is talking about it like they're TMZ or something."

He opens his mouth but shuts it as soon as he glances around and sees people near us. "Can we get in the truck and talk about it?"

"Hell no. You made it everyone's business, so we're going to talk about it. Now, admit it."

"Why do you want to hear it? To make things worse?" He raises his voice.

"I want to hear it from you, so I can believe that you really are a piece of shit!" I yell. I'm losing my cool, but I'm fine with my anger boiling over. "Say it."

He throws his arms out to the side. "Okay, I slept with her. Happy now?"

People start coming closer to us after he says it. Hearing the words coming out of his mouth is a lot harder than I thought it'd be.

"Why?" I ask.

"I don't know why. I was drunk. I wasn't thinking." His eyes refuse to meet mine.

"You weren't thinking of me? Your girlfriend?" The tears start trailing down my face. "My parents just died, Jacob. You think I need this shit right now?"

I'm becoming a blubbering mess, and everyone is here watching us.

9

"Baby, please. Let's get in the truck and talk about it." He reaches out for my hand.

There is the sweet talk. "No."

His lips form a tight line, and his eyes scan around us. A partial circle of people is surrounding us now. If they are going to stick around, I'm going to make sure this is all Jacob's fault.

I can't stand looking at him any longer though. He's not the same person I've fallen for.

"Please don't do this," he pleads, getting closer to me.

"I can't trust you anymore." I wipe the tears from my cheeks. "I need you the most now more than ever, but you let me down."

"It was one mistake," he stresses. "I promise it'll never happen again. Just . . . get in the truck with me."

Casey appears by my side, signaling me that it is time to go. "It shouldn't have happened in the first place." I cross my arms. "We're done."

Before Jacob can say anything else, Casey takes my shoulders and guides me to her car while she shares some choice words with him. There is a ringing in my ears that won't go away.

When Casey and I are alone in her car, I lose it.

PART ONE

CHAPTER ONE

"You don't think this is too much for the first day?" I ask Casey, holding up the dark denim skirt she's picked out for me.

"Hell no!" She grabs the skirt from me and places it back on the bed with the rest of the outfit. The outfit consists of a denim skirt with buttons down the middle, a simple white cropped shirt, and some silver accessories. "It's just a jean skirt, Lace. It's not a formal gown or anything. Plus, you've got a killer tan. You have to show your legs off."

I've spent the summer with my grandparents at their lake house and have purposely gotten as much sun as I can get.

The time I've spent in the sun has given me time to think about this coming school year. I will start school without the support of my parents, without Jacob, and without a clue of what will happen.

My eyes trace over the outfit and I sigh. "Fine, but I'm wearing my cute white shoes with this." She originally has some platform sandals paired with the outfit, but I say no after having a vision of myself breaking an ankle in the hall. My white sneakers will make it a little more casual and more my style.

Casey rolls her eyes with dramatic effect. "I guess I'll let it slide this time."

Outfit searching is getting old. "Anyway," I say as I sit down with her on my bed, "what time are you getting there tomorrow?"

"My usual time," she says, shrugging. "Why?"

12

"I don't want to get there too early. I just want to get in and get out." And avoid certain people as much as possible.

She gives me a look I'm all too familiar with. "You can't avoid him forever."

"I can try."

"You can try, but it won't last." She scoots closer to me. "I know it's going to be hard, but you're going to have to face him sooner or later."

I haven't spoken to Jacob since I confronted him in the parking lot. Over the summer, he tried to text and call me but I ignored every one of his attempts. I even stayed off social media to avoid him. "I hate that you're right."

"Don't let him ruin your school life. Remember, this is your year."

The healing process is slow, but Casey has been a big help.

After that day in the parking lot, it was like everyone took his side, whatever side that was. Friends who I thought were my friends ditched me, except for Casey, which wasn't really surprising.

It's hard to accept that my first serious boyfriend has cheated on me. There were moments over the summer when I wanted to call him and forgive him just, so I could have him back in my life. When I caught myself trying to reach out to him, I remembered I couldn't trust him. The truth, no matter how hard it is to accept, is that I don't need him in my life. He's just a stupid boy.

"This is my year." I give an affirmative nod. "I'm not going to let Jacob or any other stupid boy ruin it for me."

"That's the spirit!" she exclaims, clasping her hands together. "You're going to be happier this year, Lace. I just know it."

That comment alone makes me happy. I'm tired of moping over Jacob. I want to be a happier, better version of myself. "You know what? Where are those sandals? I'm wearing those damn things tomorrow."

13

The first day of my senior year is going to be the start of a new era. The era of a Lacey who is single, happier, stronger, and isn't going to take any shit.

*   *   *

It is a restless night. I can feel myself tossing and turning, trying to find the cooler side of my bed.

When my alarm finally goes off, I'm already awake. I drag myself out of bed and go straight to the closet to grab my outfit. It's a really cute outfit, but the burst of confidence to wear the sandals is gone. I pull out my white sneakers instead.

After grabbing a towel, I jump in the shower to wash the sleep away. As much as I want to crawl back into bed and fall back asleep, I know I have to face the day head on. Jacob will be there surrounded by his soccer friends to back him up, and I'll have Casey to back me up.

I have to be tough. The new Lacey is ready to take on the day.

There's enough time after my shower to blow dry my hair and add a little curl to it. My brown hair has lighter pieces from how much sun I got over the break.

I brush on a light layer of foundation, fill in my brows a bit, and swipe on some mascara. I've learned to tone down my makeup routine. I always wore a full face when I was with Jacob. When I went makeup-less during my stay at my grandparents's place, I appreciated my natural self a little more.

I change into my outfit and stand in front of my full-length mirror. It was once littered with photos of me and Jacob; I ripped them off the day I broke up with him.

It is nice to see myself without all those pictures in the way. My room used to be covered in things that remind me of Jacob before I've cleaned it all out. It is a total transformation, and I'm happy for it.

14

Aunt Jade is bustling around the living room when I walk in. Her brown hair is in a bun already. She's wearing a pencil skirt with a light blue blouse. The only things missing are her high heels.

"Morning, sunshine!" she exclaims. "Have you seen my black heels?"

I shake my head. "They aren't in your closet?"

"I looked, but I'll go check again." She walks around the couch and points to the kitchen. "I made you some pancakes. Didn't want you going to school on an empty stomach."

"Thanks," I say as she runs into her room.

My stomach growls at the sight of the pancakes on the counter. After putting a load of butter and syrup, I start eating them.

"It's my first day, and I'm already late," my aunt grumbles as she rushes into the kitchen with her heels on.

She grabs her cup and fills it with black coffee. Her bun is coming loose, and she's juggling her black laptop bag and purple purse on her arm.

She teaches a business class at the community college and has been there for two years. She always complains about grading and such, but I know she loves it. "Alright, I gotta jam outta here. Cute outfit by the way. Casey knows what she's doing." She hugs me quickly and heads for the door. "I'll see you tonight!"

The past few months have been hard for both of us. She isn't as put together as my mom was. My mom always scolded her about her responsibilities.

I push those thoughts aside. The nerves are building up as I finish my breakfast. I grab my backpack, keys, and phone before heading out. The apartment is only about ten minutes away from school, which is perfect for a day like today when I want to get there just a few minutes before the bell rings.

In the school parking lot, I find Casey's white Ford Focus and pull in beside it. I gather my things and thoughts before

15

heading inside. My plan is to walk in, get my schedule, and head to class.

After waiting in a relatively short line at a table near the front office, I finally get my schedule. My first class is a general computer class. I make my way through the halls and walk into the computer lab. I find my name on the seating chart and sit down, recognizing a few faces in class with me.

My nerves are calming down finally. I relax into the chair and wait for our teacher to start class. Everything is going smoothly so far, and I hope the rest of my day goes like this.

Lunch arrives and I text Casey to meet me by our cars so we can head off campus. I'm walking to my car when I spot Jacob standing by his truck in his usual parking spot. A couple of his soccer friends are with him, and I pray they distract him from seeing me.

I start to speed walk past them and make it to my car with no problem. Casey's right behind me.

"I'm driving!" she exclaims, holding up her keys.

We get into her car and she starts talking about her day. "I have Psychology for second period, and there's this really cute guy in my group. His name is Travis or something."

"Or something?" I ask, laughing at her complete disregard for his name.

"I don't really remember." She shrugs it off. "I just remember his face, which is gorgeous."

Casey always pays more attention to faces. His personality could be complete shit, but she'd still like him for his looks. I change the subject when my stomach growls. I've been hungry since class ended. "Where are we heading? I was thinking a sandwich sounds good."

"The deli it is."

As she drives, I can't help but think about Jacob and how he looks. What he did was unfair. Last year, I was picturing how perfect our senior year would be together, and he decided to sleep with Lauren. I was ready for new adventures with him, and he was going on adventures with Lauren.

"You okay?" Casey asks.

"Yeah, I'm fine." I know she doesn't believe me, so I sigh in defeat. "I saw Jacob earlier."

"Did he talk to you?"

"No. I don't think he saw me."

"Good."

She pulls into the deli parking lot and shuts off her car after parking. "Listen, I know we've talked about this a million times since it happened, but I just want to make sure you know I'm here for you. I can tell when you're thinking about him."

I give her a smile. "I know you're always here for me. I don't really want to talk about it right now, though. I just need food."

The familiar scent of the deli hits my nose when we walk in, and my stomach starts growling again.

We're ordering our meals when Jacob walks in with his friends. I face the counter, just wanting to sit down already to avoid his gaze. Casey finishes ordering and I grab her arm.

"Speak of the devil," I tell her.

She glances behind us and her eyes widen. "Lace, we can get our food and go if you want."

"No, it's okay. Let's just find a table and sit."

We end up sitting in a booth in the back corner where we have a full view of the deli. My sandwich distracts me for a little bit. Casey's still going on about the guy in her Psychology class.

Jacob is sitting at a table near the front. He's laughing with one of his friends, and I feel guilty for missing his smile. I fell hard for that smile when I realized how happy he made me during our freshman year. That smile always made me weak at the knees.

He turns suddenly and our gazes lock. I'm the first to look away.

"We better be heading back soon," I tell Casey. The sooner we get out of here, the better.

She finishes her food and we throw our trash away. I know we have to pass by Jacob's table if we want to leave. I make Casey stand next to me, so I can't see him. While we are walking out, I feel his eyes burning into the back of my head.

When we get back to the campus, we only have a few minutes before the bell for the next class rings. We waste time by sitting in the car.

"What class do you have next?" Casey asks.

I pull my schedule from my bag. "Um, I have English next. jJournalism is my last class."

"I have math and some kind of science." She sighs. "We need to coordinate schedules next semester."

"Definitely. Our last semester should be the best one." I stare at her outfit for a bit. "You're gonna have to let me borrow that shirt at some point."

She's wearing a black and white striped button down shirt with a white tank top underneath it, and some black shorts to contrast her white Converse.

"I'll let you borrow it once you actually wear what I pick out for you." She rolls her eyes.

"I *am* wearing what you picked out."

"Not the sandals."

I'm the one to roll my eyes this time. "I didn't feel like wearing them."

"It would've made the outfit so much cuter."

"Thanks," I say sarcastically.

Casey and I go our separate ways in the main building. Jacob is walking not too far from me. I know where my class is, so I duck my head and start to walk faster. When I'm about to walk into class, someone taps on my shoulder.

I regret turning around when I come face to face with Jacob's familiar brown eyes.

18

"Hey, Lacey," he says as he gives me a smile.

I open my mouth to say something, but nothing comes out. My brain can't form a reply.

"I, uh . . . I just wanted to say you look great." He chews on his bottom lip.

My mind is racing. Do I ignore him? Say thanks? Tell him to screw himself? "Thanks," I say, not fully processing why I've said that. I take a step back and bump into someone. I quickly mumble an apology without looking at the person.

The bell rings and Jacob blinks. "Shit. I better get to class." He waves and disappears down the hall.

I walk into class and sit down at the first empty seat I can find. My mind is a jumbled mess. I mentally kick myself for saying thanks when he said I look great. Where was confident Lacey in that moment?

Our teacher walks to the front of the class. She's a tall woman with lines on her forehead. Her blonde hair mixed with streaks of gray lightly grazes her shoulders. Her cream sweater and black slacks don't really go together, but I'm not about to say that out loud.

"My name is Mrs. Beattie, and I'd like to welcome you to what will hopefully be your last English class of your high school career." Her voice is deep and slightly raspy, almost like a smoker's voice. "I have some papers I'd like you all to fill out before we get into the syllabus." She picks up a stack of papers and hands them out.

I hand the papers behind me and whoever is there isn't taking them. I shift in my seat, so I can put the papers on their desk. I blink when I see Dylan Parker sitting there.

Dylan is known to cause trouble wherever he is. He's been suspended before, but I don't know why. As far as I know, people either want to avoid him or sleep with him.

He takes the papers from me, and I face forward again to start filling it out. A tap on my shoulder distracts me. I sigh and turn around again. "Yes?"

"Can I borrow a pen or pencil?" Dylan asks, leaning forward in his seat.

"It's the first day, and you don't have anything to write with?" I ask incredulously. It comes out harsher than I've intended, but he doesn't look fazed at all. His green eyes are so captivating, it almost becomes hard to focus on what he's saying.

"I've been asking pretty girls like you all day." He winks. "And I believe you owe me for bumping into me earlier."

His green eyes are light, unlike any color I've seen on someone before.

I bumped into him earlier? I wrestle with the thought for a second. My good side takes over and I reach into my bag, pulling out a pen and handing it to him.

"Perfect." He smiles. "Thanks."

I go back to my paper. Other students are finishing up, so I rush through it. It's a bunch of basic questions about us. Nothing challenging. We turn them in to Mrs. Beattie, and she hands out the syllabus. It details what is expected of us in class and what books we will be reading.

Near the end of class, I guess Mrs. Beattie can tell we're getting restless and calls our attention. "For the last activity, I want you all to pair up and write down three facts about your partner. It'll help you learn a little more about your classmates."

Everyone seems to know who to partner up with. Another tap on my shoulder makes me turn around.

Dylan flashes a smile at me. "Partners?"

Since no one else is available, I sigh. "Sure." I turn my body all the way to face him. "You want to go first?"

"Let's see . . ." he trails off. "My name is Dylan Parker, if you didn't know, and I have two brothers."

"Their names?"

20

"Derrick and Ethan."

I scribble it all down. "What else? Any hobbies? Talents?"

"I can show you some of my talents later tonight. If you're not busy, I mean." He smirks as he says it.

Like I'd ever hook up with Dylan Parker. "Don't be gross. Let's just finish this." My cheeks feel a little warm, and I hate myself for it. Dylan is nothing but a flirt.

"Fine. I like to listen to music and hang out with my friends." He glances down at my notebook. "Can I have a piece of paper?"

I rip a page out and hand it to him before writing down the rest of his list.

"Alright, and your name is?"

"Lacey Reyes." He starts to write down my name, but he spells it wrong. "It's E-Y, not I-E."

He draws over it and rewrites it. "What about you? Any siblings?"

"Nope, I'm an only child."

He writes that down. "Any hobbies or talents?"

"Um." I think for a second. "I write for the school newspaper."

"We have a newspaper?" he asks, raising a brow.

That's always the reaction. People care more about sports than the arts. "Yeah, the Diamondback Chronicle."

"Okay . . ." He writes it down. "One more thing."

I'm drawing a blank. I don't even know who I am as a person. "I don't know. I like rocky road ice cream?"

"That works." He finishes writing and writes his name at the top. "So, Lacey . . . can I call you Lace?"

"Only a few people call me that—"

The bell rings and Mrs. Beattie announces that she wants the papers on her desk before we leave. Dylan stands up, grabs his backpack, and turns in his paper before walking out.

Never in my life would I think I would ever talk to Dylan Parker. The crowds we run with are totally different.

I start walking to my journalism class when I feel someone walking next to me. Dylan smiles and holds out the pen I let him use.

"Thanks again, Lace."

I take it, and before I can say no problem, he's already down the hall. I stuff the pen back into my bag.

Journalism being my last class of the day is actually a blessing. I can't wait to get writing again. When the classroom door comes into view, I see Jacob walk into the same room. I stop dead in my tracks and watch him as he sits down in the middle row of desks and pull out his phone. He seems anxious.

I know what he's up to. He knows journalism is my thing. He purposely chose that class to . . . what? Get back together with me? Spend more time with me? The anger is building in me.

I take a deep breath. Whatever plan he has for this class isn't going to work.

This class is meant to be my escape—somewhere I can relax by stressing over deadlines, as silly as that sounds. When I first took the class in my freshman year, it was so different from any other class I had. My love for reporting and writing heightened, and the editorial part of it grew to be my favorite.

Seeing Jacob sitting in my getaway class is a giant blow to my day. It's hard seeing him around, but it's going to be harder seeing him in a class I thought I could escape to.

Thankfully, my journalism teacher, Mrs. Thomas, greets me at the door.

"Lacey! I'm so glad to see you!" She wraps her arms around me and I do the same. When I had her in my freshman year, she met the shy, quiet, more reserved version of me, and I met the crazy, in-your-face version of her. While I have changed, she hasn't at all.

I've had her every year, and it's hard to accept that I won't have a class with her again after this. "I want to talk to you after class, if that's okay?" she says. Her short white hair and bright green blouse make her blue eyes stand out.

"No problem." I smile at her.

Inside the classroom, I immediately see the twins, Sophie and Seth, sitting in the front row. Both smile when they see me walk up to them.

"Lacey!" Sophie says, opening her arms.

I lean down and give her a hug. "You have no idea how great it is to see you guys," I say as I hug Seth. I sit down behind Sophie and purposely keep my back to Jacob. "How was your summer?"

Seth opens his mouth, but Sophie interrupts him, "Fantastic! We went to Oregon to visit our family, and it was so gorgeous. I got a lot of writing done, and Seth got some really great shots."

I truly love the twins. Sophie is an amazing writer, and not just for the newspaper. I've read a lot of her fiction and wanted more every time I finish one her stories. Seth is a great photographer with a knack for capturing nature stills.

Mrs. Thomas plants herself on her desk at the front of the room after the bell rings. "I'm glad everyone is settled. Hopefully there aren't any more stragglers coming in." She grins at the class. "Welcome to journalism, where I believe the pride of Foothills High School resides. The Diamondback Chronicle has been in production for almost twenty years now, and we'll continue that tradition this year."

She takes a paper and starts calling out everyone's names. Jacob, the twins, and I all seem to be the only seniors in the class.

She finishes taking attendance and clasps her hands together. "Let's get to business. I have a couple of familiar faces here, and I would like to recognize them." Her eyes flit over to me and the twins. "Seth Adams, will you stand up for me?" Seth stands

23

up and stays by his desk. "Seth will be our lead photographer this semester. For those of you looking to be a part of the photography part of the paper, move to the back of the class with him."

Seth gives me and Sophie an *oh-no* look, and we laugh. Being fraternal twins, they don't look too much alike. Both have brown eyes, but that's the only thing they really share. Seth's hair is a deeper shade of black than Sophie's, and he's taller than her. Sophie's short hair reminds me of a fairy.

Once the photography group is seated at the back, Mrs. Thomas looks at Sophie. "Sophie Adams, will you please stand up?" Sophie stands next to Mrs. Thomas. "Sophie is an excellent writer and reporter. If you're interested in reporting, sit in the front corner over here." She motions to the desks near the door. Everyone shuffles around and gathers their things.

"And finally, Miss Lacey, will you come up here?" My heart is racing as she says it. There's only one position left, and I know it's mine. I stand next to her, and she puts her arm around me. "Lacey has been around since her freshman year and has proven to be wonderful in every category. I'm naming her Senior Editor for this semester."

I can't stop myself from smiling. Being Senior Editor means the world. My mom always told me I would be an editor come my senior year. I wish I could tell her the news.

Mrs. Thomas's voice interrupts my thoughts. "If you're interested in editing, please come to this corner of the room with Lacey." She smiles at me before saying, "If you're unsure, come to the front with me and I'll help you decide where you'd like to start. The rest of you, get to know each other."

In my corner of the room, there are three people. Predictably, Jacob is one of them. The others are a guy and girl who look much younger than us. Maybe freshmen or sophomores.

I walk up to them and put on my best smile. "Small crowd."

"What exactly does an editor do?" the other guy asks. His short sand-colored hair and glasses make me think of Buddy Holly.

"An editor basically puts the paper together in the InDesign software. We assign you sections of the paper that you'll have to put together yourself. That means you'll have to be in contact with the reporters and photographers to format everything accordingly." He has a thinking face on as I spew all the information out. "You're not going to be alone. I know the software, so I can help you out. I hope I didn't scare you off."

He nods slowly. "No, we're good. I'm good. I can do it."

"Great," I say. "What's your name?"

"Will."

"Nice to meet you, Will." I turn to the girl who has reddish-brown hair and big doe-like eyes. "And your name?"

"Vicky," she squeaks out. Her cheeks are a slight shade of pink.

Definitely a shy one.

My heart pounds in my chest as I lock gazes with Jacob. I've spent all day avoiding him, and now he's sitting in front of me, waiting for me to acknowledge him. I clear my throat before saying, "Jacob, you want to be an editor?"

He shrugs. "It seems interesting."

"I see." I focus my attention on the other two. "What grade are you two in?"

"Freshman," they both say.

"Fresh meat." Jacob chuckles.

Who even says that anymore? I have to stop myself from rolling my eyes. "Well, I hope high school hasn't been too brutal."

Jacob shifts in his seat, so he's looking at them both. "You know," he starts, "Lacey and I met during our freshman year. You guys could turn out like us."

What exactly is he saying? I want to call him out, but I think twice about it. Unleashing drama will probably make things uncomfortable for everyone. "Or you guys can be your own person and be totally unlike us." This time, when I stare at him I don't look away. I need to prove a point.

"You guys hooked up before?" Will asks suddenly.

I don't really like the straight forward question. I squint my eyes at Jacob instead, and he smirks.

"We dated for two years," he says without breaking his gaze.

"Yeah, it's obvious." Will laughs. "Why did you guys break up?"

Nosy isn't a trait I like, even though I can be nosy myself, but that is mostly for reporting purposes. I focus on Vicky instead. "Do you have any class or school-related questions?"

She chews on her lip and shakes her head.

I sigh. It's going to be a long semester.

"Can I have everyone's attention?"

Mrs. Thomas's voice saves me from having to talk to my group some more. I lean against the wall and turn my attention to her.

"Tomorrow, we can brainstorm events that will be happening around the school and community to get article ideas. For the rest of class, you all can talk amongst yourselves. Keep the noise level low, please." She motions for me to go over to her.

I practically bolt towards her. We walk outside the classroom, and she shuts the door.

"I thought we were going to take up more time, but I was wrong." She laughs. "I'll talk to you now, so I don't keep you after class."

I nod, understanding.

"How are you?" she asks as she leans against the wall. "Is everything alright?"

Mrs. Thomas has been like my personal counselor. When my parents died, I went to her and told her what happened to them.

I bite my lip, not knowing how to answer. "Everything is okay. Not great but okay."

26

"You're with your aunt, correct?"

I nod. "Her apartment is close to school. It's a quick drive."

"Good," she says. She gives me the same sad smile people always give me when I say I've lost my parents. "If you want to talk more about it, I'm here. I know it isn't easy, but talking can be good for the soul."

"Thank you." I smile. "I also really appreciate the whole Senior Editor thing."

"You deserve it." Her smile turns brighter. "How's your group? Promising?"

I almost snort. "I think they will be." I've never told her anything about Jacob throughout my time in her classes. I don't know if she knows we were together. I figure I should just leave it alone.

"I have a good feeling about this semester," she says. "Hopefully I'm right."

Her response makes me think of Casey's comment about me being happier this year. Maybe that is a sign of a good year.

"Let's get back inside," Mrs. Thomas says.

We walk back in and I make my way to my group. The boys are chatting while Vicky sits back and watches. I sit down behind Jacob and next to Vicky. In the middle of pulling out my phone to text Casey, Will starts talking to me.

"So, are we going to have to write articles too? Even if we're editors?"

"It depends on how big we want the paper to be. We'll decide tomorrow when we're brainstorming."

"Is this class going to be an easy A?" Jacob asks me.

"That depends too," I tell him. "If you finish your work, yes."

The end of the school day is signaled by the bell, and everyone practically runs out of class. Vicky takes off and Will waves to me and Jacob. "See you guys."

I hurry to grab my things. Jacob catches up with me outside of class, which is what I desperately want to avoid.

"Hey, it'll be nice having a class together for once," he says.

That makes me stop in my tracks. He's really trying to talk to me like nothing has happened between us. The anger that has been building up before class is threatening to spill over. "Not if you're going to spew our personal lives to everyone."

"I was just trying to break the ice." He shrugs. "Honestly, I'm just glad you spoke to me at all in there."

"Why are you even in that class?" I snap. "You know journalism is my place. You have soccer, and I have the newspaper."

"You've ignored me for almost three months. I wanted to talk to you again."

I close my eyes and sigh. I'm getting heated, and I don't want to blow up. I try walking away from him, but he catches up again.

"I think I've been punished enough," he says, frowning. " It was one time, Lace. It was one mistake."

"I really don't want to talk about this right now." I shake my head. He's really pushing my buttons, and if I don't get out of here fast, I'm going to blow up and cause a scene. I push my way through the doors and walk out of the main building.

He grabs my arm and makes me look at him. "I thought we could bond over the newspaper stuff. That's why I'm taking that class. I need you back in my life, Lace, and if that's the only way, then so be it."

Why does he sound so confident about getting me back? This isn't a one-sided relationship where he gets to decide what's best for us. He's already done that.

I'm over this.

"What part of 'we're done' did you not understand?" I demand. "You cheated on me, and now you expect me to forgive you so easily? I don't need that bullshit in my life. I'll talk to you in class, but outside of that, I don't want you anywhere near me."

With that, I walk off.

CHAPTER TWO

The next few days go by quickly. Jacob keeps his distance like I've asked. We have to talk during journalism, but he doesn't try to be funny with our past again.

Vicky is starting to talk a little more, so I'm making some kind of progress with her. Will is still nosy and blunt. It's strange having polar opposites in my group, but it keeps things interesting.

Friday morning, everyone seems to be in a good mood. It's that Friday feeling getting to everyone. The football game tonight only adds to the buzz.

For lunch, Casey and I eat in the cafeteria. She's going on about that guy in her psychology class again.

"Why don't you just ask him out already?" I ask her.

"I want him to ask me out," she says. "I don't want to come off as desperate."

I roll my eyes. "It won't come off as desperate unless you're persistent about it. It'll just show that you're interested." She still doesn't look convinced. "Maybe suggest doing something as friends first."

"I can't do that." She shifts in her seat. "I can't just ask him to do something with me."

"Get to know him a little better and see what he likes. If you share something in common, then there's something to bond over. If he likes you enough, that's when he'll ask you out."

She picks at her fries. "How are you so good at this?"

"I guess getting my heart broken has opened my eyes," I say as lightly as I can. "I'm gonna throw my trash." I take my tray over to the trash cans, and as I'm tossing it all away, I feel someone behind me.

"Hey, got a pen I can borrow?"

I'm face to face with Dylan's smiling green eyes. "Not now, no." I laugh. "It's already Friday. Shouldn't you have learned to bring your own supplies by now?"

He shrugs. "I'm a slow learner."

He seems like he is pretty smart, so I think he's lying about that. "Whatever you say."

"I have a reputation to keep up. I can't bring my own supplies."

I raise a brow. "Reputation?"

"Yes." He smirks. He reaches out and throws something in the trash can. "I'll see you in class?"

I nod and he walks off. Casey is eyeing me suspiciously as I approach the table. "What?" I ask, sitting down.

"Were you just talking to Dylan Parker?"

"Yeah? Why?"

"You guys are friends now?"

"We have class together," I say, shrugging.

Lunch ends and I walk with her until we go into different hallways. I have two more classes to go before the weekend officially starts.

Mrs. Beattie isn't in yet when I walk into class with more students filing in behind me. Just as I sit down, Dylan casually strides in. I envy his relaxed, stress-free look. He sits down without looking at me.

I wonder what it's like in the mind of Dylan Parker.

A balding man with a white button up shirt rushes in and stands at the front of the class and sets some things down on Mrs. Beattie's desk.

"Can I have all eyes up here please? Thank you." His deep voice echoes through the room. It's hard not to pay attention. "You can call me Mr. Larry. Mrs. Beattie has some family matters to deal with, so I'll be your substitute for today's class. She left behind a reading assignment for all of you. In her instructions, she wanted you all to work on it separately, but some students had a hard time with it in the last class. Either work alone or in partners, just keep the noise level down."

Everyone whispers excitedly about working together. He hands out the papers, and when I turn to hand them to Dylan, he smiles at me.

"Why do I have a feeling you want to be my partner again?" he asks, obviously teasing.

I find myself laughing at his joke. "I think *you* want to be my partner again." Dylan's teasing makes me curious about him. We haven't really spoken since the first day in class, and now he suddenly feels like talking.

"Hey, if there's a chance for me to work with a pretty girl, I'll take it." He winks. "Now, do you want to just take over and I can copy the answers or . . ."

I ignore the pretty girl comment and shake my head. "We're working on this together, like partners are supposed to do."

He sticks out his bottom lip and pouts. "You're no fun."

That face is insanely cute. I feel butterflies in my stomach for a second, and now I want to kick myself. After what Jacob has done to me, I can't let myself start crushing on another guy. What if the next guy cheats on me too? Am I doomed to live alone forever?

"Let's get working," I say, pushing past those thoughts.

We read over the assignment, which is about a couple of short stories we read yesterday. We have to answer the questions with lengthy responses.

We're about halfway done when Dylan sets his pencil down. "This is tedious." He sighs. "Just busy work she probably won't even read."

"You never know," I tell him. I don't think Mrs. Beattie is the kind of teacher to just give us busy work. She's probably one to spend her time reading over every response.

When we're close to finishing, Dylan sets his pencil down again. He's probably the kind of student who needs a break ever so often to just mess around.

"You know, I saw you after school a few days ago," he says.

I feel myself frowning. "When?"

"The first day."

After school on the first day was when I blew up on Jacob. I pray that isn't what he's talking about. "Oh," I say.

"Looked pretty intense," he says, looking at me strangely.

So he saw it happen.

I think about telling him to mind his own business, but I don't get the impression that Dylan is a gossip. I've only ever seen him with his group of friends, and they seem to keep to themselves. They're a little intimidating, but that's it.

When I don't say anything, he speaks up, "That guy deserved to get yelled at, right?" He chuckles as he asks.

"He did." I nod. "He cheated on me last year, and I just don't want him near me."

"Damn. I think I've seen him around."

"Maybe. He plays soccer."

He practically snorts. "Soccer? Sounds like a real winner."

I'm over Jacob being my main topic of conversation all the time. I don't want that to be the case with Dylan too. "Yeah, um, let's just get this done."

We go back to work, but my mind still isn't off Jacob. Most of my time was taken up by soccer games and soccer tournaments when we were together. A few times after the games, instead of partying with his friends, we'd get something to eat and sit on the tailgate of his truck and talk about anything and everything. I catch myself missing those days.

33

Dylan takes our papers to the front to turn them in after we finish the assignment.

"Sorry about bringing up your ex," he says after sitting down again.

I wave it off. "Don't worry about it. I'm just . . ."

"Not over him?" he asks.

How can I explain what I'm feeling to Dylan Parker? We hardly know each other. "I'm still in the process of getting over him. I'm trying though." When he doesn't say anything, I say, "Sorry. I'm sharing too much."

"No worries." He leans forward in his seat. "I can be a great listener." He smirks.

I smile and look down at my hands. The tattoo on my wrist is becoming less and less important by the minute. I don't know what to do with it. It's small enough to cover up, but I'm not sure if I want a tattoo there at all. If I really want to, I can save up and have it removed.

"Nice tat," Dylan says, his eyes trained on my wrist.

I scoff. "Another reminder of him."

He raises his eyebrows. "Matching tattoos? Shit, must've been serious."

"I was serious. Him, not so much."

Class ends and everyone makes their way out of the classroom. As we're walking out, Dylan continues to walk next to me.

"I know a guy who does cover-ups," he says, motioning to the tattoo. "He can get you a pretty little flower over it if you want." His tone is teasing.

I try not to roll my eyes at the idea of getting a flower over it, but I smile anyway. "I don't know what I want to do with it yet. Thanks though."

He nods. "See you on Monday, partner." He winks at me before walking off.

I wave and watch him head down the hallway. Dylan is turning out to be a totally different person than I've expected, and that's a strangely good thing. Still a flirt, but he's nicer than I thought he'd be.

Sophie and Seth are walking into class just as I enter. We haven't gotten any time together in class since Mrs. Thomas has separated us into groups. I've been at the computers in the back of the class with the rest of my group showing them how to navigate the program.

"Lacey, you always look so put together and nice," Sophie says as we walk into class. "I can barely manage to fix my hair."

"Thanks, Sophie. And what are you talking about? Your hair is gorgeous," I tell her. Last year, I always found myself wearing nice clothes just to seem put together in front of Jacob and his friends's girlfriends, but now, I'm just trying to be confident and comfortable at the same time.

Seth and Sophie sit with their groups, and I trudge over to the computers with Will and Vicky. Jacob saunters in and plops down next to me.

Mrs. Thomas tells us to continue doing yesterday's work. My group signs into the computers and opens the files and the program book.

"Hey, Lacey, are you going to the game tonight?" Will asks. He's looking at me while he's beside Vicky, who is quietly opening her files.

"Probably not. Why?" Casey has mentioned going there, but I'm still on the fence about it. Football games are only so much fun.

"Just wondering if I'll see you there. My friends don't think I actually know any seniors," he says like it's the most normal thing ever.

I remember my freshman days. It did feel nice to know some seniors and have them accept little freshman me. "Well, if I do go, I'll make sure to say hi." Will is sometimes too nosy to tolerate, but I can do him a small favor if I go.

"What about you, Jacob? Are you going?" he asks Jacob, who's sitting at his computer silently.

Jacob shrugs. "I have other plans."

I almost ask him what he has planned, but I decide against it. I don't need him thinking I'm interested in what he's doing, even though I am a little curious. I wonder if they involve Lauren.

"Vicky?" Will looks at her expectantly.

"Oh," she says. "Football games aren't really my thing." Her eyes meet the keyboard.

"They aren't really my thing either," I say just to make her feel a little more comfortable.

Jacob makes a noise. "Lacey only ever went to my soccer games."

"Huge mistake," I say, looking back at Will and Vicky. "Anyway, let's get started."

Yesterday, I had them start some tutorials that I used when I was a freshman. They're fairly simple. The online tutorial goes along with the book, but has changed a bit so they have a couple of questions. All three of them seem to be getting the hang of it pretty quickly.

"Lacey, what is this?" Jacob asks. He's pointing to the book, but he isn't pointing at anything specific.

"Which part?"

"This whole section. Where is that tool?" He points to it in the book.

I understand his confusion. That tool is in a different spot than what the book says. I point to his computer screen. "Go to this drop down. No, this one. Then click that. I think it's . . . yeah, it's right here." I feel his eyes turn to me. Our bodies are closer than I want, so I sit back in my chair.

"What were you and Dylan Parker talking about in the hall a while ago?" he suddenly asks me.

36

Is he really asking me this? "Why?"

"You two looked pretty cozy. I was just wondering."

"It's none of your business," I say automatically. He doesn't have the right to question me about who I'm talking to and what we're talking about. I don't see what the big deal is about me talking to Dylan in the first place. Dylan isn't as bad as everyone makes him seem.

Jacob doesn't say anything and instead focuses on his computer.

For the rest of class, Jacob is in his own bubble while Will and Vicky ask me questions here and there. I feel a sense of relief when the bell rings. I need the weekend to start already.

While walking through the parking lot to my car, Casey is walking nearby. I almost make my way to her until I see her talking with a guy. She has her flirting smile on, so I leave her alone and watch instead.

It has to be that guy from her psychology class who she's always fawning over. It looks like he's interested in what she's saying, and I take that as a good sign. I wonder if she has gotten brave enough to ask him out.

I get to my car and act like I'm minding my own business while Casey and that guy are standing near hers. I try to eavesdrop, but I can't quite hear what they're saying.

Casey suddenly appears next to me with the biggest grin on her face.

"What was all that about?" I ask her, eager to hear the details.

"Well, we ran into each other in the hall and got to talking. I took your advice and asked him if he wanted to hang out sometime. I couldn't think of anything right then, so I was pretty vague, but I made sure he knew I was into him," she explains.

"Then he said we could hang out sometime this weekend, so I agreed and then he invited me to a party tonight. I know you're a protective ass, so I asked him if it was okay if you could tag along

37

and he said it was fine," she says it so quickly I almost don't catch all of it. "So, pretty please with a cherry on top, will you go to that party with me? He gave me the address and said he'd be there around nine."

A party? I haven't been to a party since last year, and that was when I was still with Jacob. I try to stay away because they never really feel like my scene. The idea of Casey going alone to a party with some guy makes me uneasy. It's my job as a best friend to keep her safe. As much as I don't want to go, I know I have to. "Um, yeah, I'll go."

It's a little strange for him to ask her to go to a party, but I'm not sure if this qualifies as a first date yet. I'll have to keep an eye on him.

She wraps her arms around me immediately. "Thank you, thank you!" She pulls herself away from me. "I have to get home to see what I'm wearing. Clear it with your aunt, then come over, so I can dress you."

Casey dressing me means a dress. "I'm not wearing a dress," I tell her.

She crosses her arms. "Fine. I'll see you at my place anyway, so we can take my car."

While driving home, a nervous feeling settles in my stomach. My lack of experience at parties makes it seem daunting and scary. Drunk teenagers aren't the best teenagers to be around.

At home, I make sure to finish the one homework I have. My aunt will be getting home soon, and I don't want her worrying about any work that I need to do.

She walks in as I'm grabbing a snack from the kitchen. "What afternoon snack have you prepared for me?" she asks as she smiles at me.

I lift my plate. "Apples with peanut butter."

"Yum." She picks up a slice and swipes some peanut butter on it. "Heaven," she says, laughing. "How was school?"

"Good." I nod. This is my chance. "Casey was invited to a party by some guy she likes, and she wants me to tag along in case it doesn't work out." I chew on my lip nervously. I've never had to ask her permission for something like going to a party, so I'm a little afraid of what she'll say.

She nods her head immediately. "Yeah, go ahead." Then she frowns. "Wait, what time are you going?"

"Nine, but Casey wants me to go over to her house to help her pick an outfit before we get there."

"Okay," she says slowly.

"Can I stay at Casey's, or should I be back by a certain time?" I ask.

I can tell she's uncomfortable. "Did your parents ever let you go to parties?"

"They let me go when I went with Jacob and Casey," I say. They trusted Jacob to take care of me, and they trusted Casey to watch over us.

"You can stay at Casey's. I know you're not dumb." She smiles at me. "But call me if anything happens. And I mean anything."

I'm glad she trusts me, so I give her a quick hug. "Thank you."

Next is trying to figure out what to wear. I want to control at least half of my outfit, so Casey doesn't make me look ridiculous. I want to be casual and comfortable. I pull out a pair of denim shorts that make my legs look good. There isn't anything wrong with showing off some leg.

Casey has cuter tops than me, so I'll let her pick the shirt. I pack my overnight bag and gather all my essentials.

Around seven, I say goodbye to my aunt and head to Casey's house. I hope the party doesn't turn into a disaster for her. She deserves to have a little fun with that guy. Hopefully, he's decent and treats her like a queen.

When I get to her house, I let myself in. Her parents aren't home, so I go straight to her room. In her room, the entire contents of her closet seems to be on her bed. She's standing in front of the closet with her hands on her hips.

"Having trouble?" I ask her.

She lets out a frustrated sigh. "You have no idea."

I set my bag down on the floor and start going through some shirts. "What kind of look are you going for?"

"I need to look hot. I know I don't have to look good just for him, but tonight, I need to." She blows some hair out of her face.

"I know my style isn't for you, but let me try to help," I tell her. I start rummaging through her clothes without a specific look in mind. She wants hot, which means it has to be something I would never personally wear.

Usually, when she wants to look hot she wears black or red. I remove all of the shirts that aren't those two colors. When I grab a handful of clothes, something catches my eye. "What's this?" I separate it from the others and lay it out. It's a black short-sleeve and sheer with large rose designs on it.

"I bought that over the summer," she says.

I stare at it until an idea comes to mind. "What about this shirt with your black bralette?"

She makes her thinking face, then quickly gets up and finds her black bralette. She picks up the sheer shirt and takes them into the bathroom to change. When she comes out, she's smiling. "Lacey, you're a genius."

"You're welcome," I say as I bow. "As for the bottoms, I'm not sure."

She picks up a pair of light wash jeans and holds them up. "These jeans make my ass look good."

"It's my turn now," I tell her. I reach into my bag and bring out my shorts. "I need a shirt to wear with these."

40

She taps her chin and looks at the mess on her bed. "Help me hang all of this back up? We'll see what we can find when we put it all away."

As we're hanging her clothes back up, there are a few shirts that catch my eye, but none of them really feel like party material.

Casey gasps suddenly. "This one!" She holds up an off-the-shoulder shirt in a pretty maroon color. It's flowy and seems comfortable enough.

I take it from her and put it on. The fabric feels soft on my skin. "I don't think I've ever seen you in this shirt," I say.

"I've only worn it once or twice." She shrugs. "You can have it. It's more your style anyway."

It's a little after eight when we start to get ready. I put the shirt and shorts together and glance over myself in Casey's mirror. Luckily, I brought a cute pair of sandals just in case. I put them on, and they pull the outfit together.

Casey and I share her bathroom mirror to touch up our makeup. I haven't really worn any makeup in the past couple of months, but I'll make an exception for the party. I draw on some winged liner and put on a darker lip color. Casey goes for a dramatic look with her eyeshadow and adds some fake lashes.

I borrow some jewelry to add to my outfit, and I start to feel myself a little more. Casey walks out of the bathroom with her complete look and my mouth drops.

Her makeup makes her eyes pop, and the outfit accentuates her curves, which is usually important to her. She smiles and does a happy dance. "I feel so hot right now."

I glance at my phone then back at her. "It's going to be nine-thirty. We should probably head out soon."

"I'm so excited!" she exclaims. "Thanks again for coming with me tonight."

"What are best friends for?"

We eventually get into her car and on the road, using my phone for directions to the house. It's near the outside of the city, an area I'm not familiar with, so it makes me nervous.

The house itself is smaller than I've imagined. It's on a big piece of land, so the cars are scattered all around. Casey parks and takes a deep breath.

"I can do this," she says.

"You can," I assure her but also reassure myself.

I rub my hands together nervously as we leave the car. I don't know what to expect, and it's making me more and more anxious as we walk up to the house. When the front door opens, I know I'm in for an interesting night.

A Kendrick Lamar song is playing in the living room. It isn't blaring, but it's loud enough to where you have to talk a bit louder than normal. Everyone seems to be in their own groups already. Casey says she has texted that guy, and she's waiting for his response.

"I told him we're by the door, and he says he's heading this way," she says.

I cross my arms and lean against the wall. I recognize a few people here and there. Casey's boy-toy then walks up to her and hugs her. I go into protective mode and stand by her side. Didn't Casey say his name is Travis?

"Tyler, this is my best friend Lacey," she introduces us.

He holds out his hand and smiles. "It's nice to meet you."

Tyler, not Travis, has dirty blond hair and a killer smile. He definitely looks like Casey's type. I take his hand. "You too."

"Can I get you guys something to drink?" He looks at Casey expectantly.

"Can you show us what there is?" I ask. I hate to sound like a mom, but I don't trust him enough to bring us drinks.

"Sure." He nods. "Follow me."

Casey gives me a look and I shrug. "We don't know. He could put something in our drinks," I tell her when he's out of hearing range.

We follow him to the kitchen, and there are cases of beer and a couple of liquor bottles along the countertop.

"I'll be the DD," I say to Casey. I know she wants to have fun.

She hands me the keys and smiles. "Thanks." She grabs a cup and starts making herself a drink while starting a conversation with Tyler.

I spot some water bottles and graciously take one. As I open it and take a sip, I glance out the glass door nearby and see some people outside. I tap Casey's arm and her eyes meet mine.

"I'll be around there. Call if you need anything," I say to her.

She waves to me and I journey outside.

CHAPTER THREE

I'm immediately impressed by the large pool outside. People are littered around it, talking animatedly. The music is faint, making it a little more peaceful. I make my way around a group and glance at the people to see if I know anyone. I'm also hoping Jacob isn't here because I know he'll only ruin my night.

My eyes are then drawn to Dylan, who is talking to two other guys near the edge of the pool. Seeing Dylan outside of class is odd. We aren't exactly friends, so I don't want to just walk up to him. Instead, I sit down on a small patio chair off to the side and pull my phone out.

Scrolling through Twitter keeps me entertained until I hear a familiar voice.

"Hey," Dylan says as he walks up to me, grinning. He's wearing a gray shirt and some black pants, with his brown hair pushed back.

"Hi," I say. I'm surprised he's even acknowledging me.

He makes himself comfortable in the chair next to mine. "Do you often sit alone at parties?"

"Parties aren't my thing, so no."

"There must be a reason for you to sit here alone then."

His small talk has me wondering what his motive is. "My best friend is on a date, and I'm here to make sure things don't turn sour," I tell him. I don't usually share my business so easily with someone, especially someone like Dylan, but there's something about him that I feel like I can trust.

He seems to understand. "A third wheel."

"I am, indeed, a third wheel." I laugh.

"Well, I wouldn't be a good host if I didn't offer you to join me and my friends," he says.

My eyes widen at the realization. "Host? This is your house?"

"Yes, it is." He smiles. "I can't have you sitting here looking like a loner. People will start to think you're bored with my party.

"But I'm not a loner."

"Currently, you are." He shrugs then stands up. "C'mon, I'll introduce you to my friends."

My stomach does a flip flop, but I agree. Why does he want me to hang out with him and his friends? Are they just like him or different? We walk to where he had just been, and there are now three guys instead of two.

"Guys," Dylan says to them, "this is Lacey. Lacey, this is Carlos, Reece, and my cousin Anthony."

Carlos has light sandy-brown hair and high cheekbones. Reece has dirty blond hair, like Tyler, and crazy blue eyes. Anthony has black hair and warm brown eyes, and it surprises me that he's Dylan's cousin. All of them are intimidatingly hot.

Anthony smiles at Dylan. "I didn't know you have a girlfriend."

I open my mouth to say I'm not his girlfriend, but Dylan speaks up before me. "Not my girlfriend, but we do have English together."

"Dylan has been my trusty partner in class," I say to them.

"I wish I had a pretty girl like you as my partner." Carlos winks at me.

Oh boy. I feel my cheeks warm, so I take a deep breath to calm myself. Being around four attractive guys can take a toll on a girl.

"Shut up, Carlos," Dylan tells him. He looks at me. "Ignore them if you want."

"Except for me." Anthony smiles. "Any friend of Dylan's is a friend of mine."

"Lacey was sitting alone, so I thought she could hang out with us," Dylan explains.

Reece steps forward and puts his arm around me. "Well, we'll take good care of you."

"I'm fine, really," I assure them. I want to check on Casey before she gets too engrossed in the party. I look at Dylan. "Actually, I should go check on my friend."

He nods. "Okay."

"It was nice meeting you guys." I wave to them. They wave back, and I turn around to go back into the house. Knowing it's Dylan's house makes this much more fascinating.

I focus on finding Casey and Tyler once I'm inside. They haven't moved far from the kitchen, as they are standing in the corner of the living room, talking. Casey sees me, says something to Tyler, then walks over to me.

"How's it going?" I ask.

"Great." She gives me an excited grin. "I think we're really hitting it off."

I feel happy for her, though I do notice her eyes look more relaxed than usual. The drinks are working a little too fast, I think. "That's great," I say instead of warning her about drinking too much. I step closer to her. "This is Dylan Parker's house."

Her mouth drops. "No way. Have you seen him?"

"Yeah, I just ran into him outside."

She opens her mouth to say something, but her eyes trail to something behind me. She then pulls me closer to the wall. "I don't want you to be upset, but I just saw Jacob pass by."

46

I blink, trying to process what she has said.

She bites her lip before saying, "And he was walking with Lauren."

My stomach drops, and my chest feels heavy. I'm angry that this is my first reaction. I need to get over him. He's clearly over me, and I can't torture myself any longer. "I'm over him." I wave it off. "I'm not going to let him ruin my night."

She doesn't look convinced.

"I'm going back outside," I tell her. "Don't worry about me."

I make a bee line for the glass door and open it. I bump into Dylan when I step out and instinctively pull myself away from him.

"Sorry," I tell him.

"Don't worry about it. Though, I think you're starting to bump into me on purpose now." He smirks.

I move away from the glass door and lean against the outside wall next to it.

"Is your friend okay?" he asks.

"Yeah, she's fine." *Is Jacob really with Lauren? Is that why he was always bringing up the past in class? Just to hurt me? Are they a couple now?*

I become aware of Dylan watching me with a strange face. "You look like you've seen a ghost."

Might as well tell him. "Remember that ex I told you about?"

He nods slowly.

"Well, he's here."

His mouth forms an "o" and he peeks around.

Before either of us can say anything, I hear my name.

"Lacey?"

Jacob's voice rings in my ears, and I'm dreading facing him. I finally force myself to look at him. There's no sign of Lauren around him. "Jacob," I acknowledge him. I angle myself away from him and pray that he goes away.

"I didn't know you were going to be here. This isn't your scene," Jacob says, getting closer and looking me up and down. I used to love how he looked at me.

"I invited her," Dylan interjects. He gives me a knowing look to play along.

Jacob's face changes immediately, almost like he's confused.

Dylan grins at him and suddenly puts his arm around me. "I thought Lacey could use a night out."

Jacob has already questioned me about Dylan, so Dylan's little lie will only add fuel to the fire. Why Jacob even cares about what I do bothers me. If he's still hanging around Lauren, there's no need for him to bother me.

"Guess some things have changed in the past couple months, huh?" Jacob asks me before staring down Dylan.

"Clearly not you and Lauren," I say without thinking. He opens his mouth, but I'm on a roll. "If you don't mind, we'd like to get back to the party."

Jacob doesn't have time to say anything because Dylan, with his arm still around me, steers me away from him and we end up inside again. When I feel we've walked far enough, I pull myself from Dylan's arm and take a deep breath.

"I think you handled that well. Mr. Soccer Player wasn't expecting that," Dylan says as he holds up his hand. "High five."

I give him a high five and let out a sigh. "Thanks. You didn't have to do that."

"You can pay me back later."

"I didn't know I had to pay for your services." I laugh. It sounds a little flirty, and I want to hit myself.

"Oh, sweetheart, these services never come for free." He winks, causing me to blush. When I don't say anything, he speaks up, "Actually, I know how you can pay me back."

Uh oh. "How?"

"Next Wednesday, I want to take you somewhere with me. Not like a date or some shit but just to hang out," he says. "The boys'll be there too, but I'll keep them in check."

"Where do you want to go?" I ask curiously. The thought of hanging out with Dylan outside of school makes me giddy and nervous. I only calm myself when I think about other girls he must have taken to the same place. That shouldn't bother me too much.

I'm not looking for another relationship right now anyway. If Jacob still affects me even after all that, then it's going to be a long process.

"It'll be a surprise, if you trust me enough." Dylan's voice breaks my string of thoughts.

I stare at him and contemplate what he says. Dylan hasn't given me a reason not to trust him. A friendship with Dylan isn't what I expected, but this is a new year. I need to do something different. "I trust you."

He grins. "Great."

"There you are, Lacey!" I hear Casey's voice. She's walking up to me, and I see her look suspiciously between me and Dylan.

He turns to me and says, "I'll be over there."

Casey and I watch him walk off, and she looks at me expectantly.

"What?" I ask her.

"What's up with you two?" I can tell she's trying to hide her smile. I can also tell she has another drink with her.

I shrug. "Nothing is up. Where's Tyler?"

"I told him I was going to look for you. He's playing beer pong right now," she says. "Did you run into Jacob?"

"Yup. Dylan helped me handle him, strangely enough." I know she isn't going to let me off the hook about Dylan. I have to make it clear that there isn't and never will be a thing between us.

She smiles. "Well, Dylan just sounds like a swell guy."

49

I ignore her comment and pull out my phone. It's just past eleven. "What time do you want to leave?" I ask her.

She looks in Tyler's direction. "Um . . ."

I sense that she doesn't want to leave right away. "Listen, just find me when you want to go. I'll be around. Also, be careful with the drinking."

She wraps her around me and squeezes me in a tight hug. "I will," she says. She walks back towards Tyler.

I wave and Dylan steps in front of me, almost like he's been waiting for Casey to leave. "You want a drink? I'll let you try my specialty."

Specialty? "I'm nervous to see what your specialty actually is."

He laughs. "Follow me." He gestures his head to the kitchen.

We go inside and he pulls out an unlabeled bottle from the cabinet under the sink. "That doesn't look sketchy at all," I say. The liquid is colored a light brown, so it can be anything.

He opens the top and takes a long sip. When he finishes, he wipes his mouth and holds it out to me. "Try it."

"What's in it?"

"I can't tell you." He chuckles. "It's a secret recipe."

"Yeah, okay, Mr. Krabs." He laughs again, clearly getting my reference, but I shake my head.

Rolling his eyes, he tries to hand it to me again. "Smell it at least."

I'm skeptical, but I grasp it and take a whiff. "It smells like tea."

He shrugs. "Guess you'll never know what it is."

I highly doubt it's roofied since he drank from it. It doesn't smell too strong, so I decide to take a sip. The liquid slides down my throat easily, and I'm surprised at how good it tastes. "That's definitely something with tea."

"It's my secret." He closes the bottle and puts it back in its original spot. He suddenly reaches into his pocket and pulls out his phone. Frowning at the screen, he puts it back in his pocket. He runs a hand through his hair and blows out a puff of air. "Let's go outside again."

We walk back to the patio chairs I was sitting on earlier. Dylan seems stressed about something, but I don't ask about it. I hope Casey doesn't want to leave soon. I'm actually having fun with Dylan. I wonder if he often throws parties.

"So, where are your parents?" I wonder out loud to him. They must be out of town or something.

"My dad is on a business trip," he says simply.

He doesn't say anything about his mom and it doesn't seem like he wants to, so I don't push it further.

"What about your brothers? You said you have two, right?"

"Yeah. Derrick only stays here sometimes, and my younger brother, Ethan, is at a friend's house."

A house full of boys. I bet that's interesting to see. "It must be nice to have brothers."

He shrugs, suddenly seeming like he doesn't want to talk, and I wonder if it has to do with me. Maybe I'm not exciting enough.

I bite my lip, not knowing what to do or say next. It's becoming increasingly awkward.

So I apologize, "I'm sorry if I'm boring you. You don't have to be out here with me."

He frowns and shakes his head. "You're definitely not boring me."

Still, that's not an explanation as to why he's being quiet. I want to say something, anything, when Carlos calls Dylan's name. Him, Reece, and Anthony are standing by the pool again.

Dylan seems to think for a moment before standing up. "C'mon."

I'm not sure why he wants me around his friends so much, but I follow anyway. I hope I don't come across as a lost puppy. That's the last thing I want.

"Dylan, we gotta talk to you. Alone." Carlos's eyes flicker to me then back to Dylan.

I take that as my cue. "I'll go over—"

"No, it's fine," Dylan interrupts me as he looks at Carlos. "We can talk about it tomorrow."

I, for one, have no idea what's going on. They are all so serious, and it feels like I'm intruding on something personal. I pull my phone out, so I can call Casey. "Actually, I should go find Casey now."

Right when I say her name, I hear her yelling for me. I quickly look over to the sliding glass door and see her crying face. Her mascara is running down her cheeks as she cries. She almost loses her balance. I can tell she officially had too much to drink. Shit, I should've stayed by her side.

"What's wrong?" I ask as I try to hold her up.

"T-Tyler says he doesn't like me," her words slur. "I w-wanna go now."

She's leaning too much on me, and I'm losing my balance. She tries to cry on my shoulder, but she loses her footing. I don't catch her in time and she falls to the floor, knocking herself against my legs. My foot goes over the edge of the pool, and before anyone can reach out to me, I fall into the cool water.

I come up from under the water and hear people calling my name as I cough out the liquid from my lungs. My hair is covering my face and I try to move it, so I can see where to swim to get out.

My cheeks burn with embarrassment when I clear the hair from my face and see people watching me. I wipe my eyes knowing I've probably smudged my makeup, but I just want to get out of the pool.

Of all people, it's Jacob who is standing at the edge of the pool where the stairs are, calling out my name and holding his hand

52

out to me. No one else is offering, so I swim over and stand up when it gets shallow enough. I take his hand, and he helps me out. Dylan, the boys, and a very unstable Casey rush over.

"Lacey, I'm so sorry," Casey cries harder.

Jacob reaches out and pushes some hair out of my face and suddenly, it felt like old times. "I have a hoodie in my truck. Do you want me to grab it?" His nice gesture almost has me fooled until I see Lauren not too far behind him, just staring at me.

"We have some towels inside," Dylan offers. "They aren't hoodies, but—you know."

"A towel is fine," I say, not looking at Jacob. The one night I want to show that I'm having fun without him and I end up embarrassing myself in front of him and Lauren. I just want to leave and not turn back.

Dylan looks at the boys. "Watch Casey while I take her inside."

I cross my arms and put my head down as I walk inside with Dylan. God, how embarrassing. It isn't like Casey pushed me on purpose, but it still happened in front of a lot of people, especially people like Jacob and Lauren.

Dylan directs me to their laundry room, away from everyone. He opens a cabinet, pulls out two towels, and hands them to me.

"Thanks," I tell him. I feel awkward and lame in front of him. Here I am, dripping wet from falling into his pool. Picking up a towel, I start to wipe my face. My eyes are stinging from the tears that want to come out.

Jacob is still hanging around Lauren, even though he just told me he wants me to be in his life again?

"You okay?" Dylan asks, interrupting my thoughts.

Without looking at him, I say, "I just want to go home now." My voice is quivering, and I hate it.

"I would offer the dryer for you to dry your clothes in and say some dirty jokes, but I don't think we're at that stage in our friendship," he says, trying to smile.

It's a nice gesture, but I'm in the mood to just go home and sleep. Or just lose some more sleep over Jacob. "It's fine."

"Is it Mr. Soccer Player that's bothering you?" he asks.

I take a deep breath and wipe down my arms and legs. "I really don't want to talk about it."

"Fine," he says as he crosses his arms and leans against the washer behind him.

When I look at him after wiping my legs, I notice his eyes are lingering too long on my butt. Anger builds up inside me, and I throw the towel at him. "Keep your eyes to yourself, asshole."

He visibly tries not to laugh, but it comes out as a full-on belly laugh. "Sorry, sorry." He holds up his hands.

My anger gets the best of me, so I reach out and punch his shoulder. "Stop laughing."

"Okay, sorry." He chuckles and covers his mouth. "I couldn't help it."

I roll my eyes and turn to walk out of the room. His hand clasps around my arm and spins me around. We're closer than I want, so I take a step back. His eyes flicker to my lips, and I feel my cheeks getting warm.

He lets go of my arm. "I'm sorry. That was the wrong moment to check you out."

"And any other moment is fine?" He's unbelievable.

He holds his hands up again and smirks. "I stare at the back of your head for an entire class period. I need something else to stare at."

I scoff. "I need to go now."

Casey is sitting with Reece, Carlos, and Anthony. She isn't crying anymore, but her makeup is a mess. I walk over to her and she stands up. "Let's get out of here," I say. I thank the boys for watching her, and we start to head inside.

54

Dylan comes up to us at the glass door and gives me a half smile. "Sorry about tonight."

"Don't worry about it," I tell him. "I'll see you on Monday."

We walk around him and go through the house. There's no sign of Jacob or Tyler, which is perfect. I get Casey into the car and drive back to her house, but when I get there, I decide that I need some time alone. I put her to bed, gather all my things, and leave.

With my windows rolled down, I feel the cool midnight air hitting my face as I drive home.

CHAPTER FOUR

It's not fair. I gave Jacob everything I had to offer, and he crushed it all to hell once he decided to hurt me. I was ready to move along in our relationship and have the best senior year with him full of new adventures.

Now I'm trying to get him out of my head and out of my life. Not seeing him over the summer made it easier to do that, but in school it's damn near impossible.

Seeing him with Lauren at Dylan's party was gut-wrenching. I thought he would at least feel guilty about cheating on me, but it doesn't seem like it.

The person who used to make me laugh and smile the most is now the person I dread seeing. Part of me wishes I could move past the cheating and be with him again, but the other part of me knows he would cheat again down the road somewhere.

It's like an endless cycle of hurt. No matter which path I choose, life is viciously laughing at me.

I wish my mom was here, so I can talk to her about everything. She was the one person I could talk to about anything, besides Casey. I know I can talk to Aunt Jade, but it isn't the same. I hate to think it, but she isn't my mom. I need my mom's advice, and no one else's.

Monday morning, it's like the weight that has been lifted off my shoulders is back on and is substantially crushing my will to do anything. I don't want to sit in class with people I don't want to be around anymore, and I don't want to study things that I have no interest in. School is getting tedious, and I just want to get the hell out of here.

For lunch, Casey tells me she has to talk to one of her teachers about a paper. I want to have lunch by myself anyway, so I'm not upset about it. While walking to the parking lot, I notice Dylan walking near me. Our gazes lock and he starts making his way towards me.

"We're seeing each other a lot lately," he says, stuffing his hands in his pockets.

I nod in agreement. I feel bad, but I'm not in the mood for people today. My car isn't too far away, so I hope I can escape soon.

He gives me a strange look. "You don't look as chipper as you usually do."

I usually look chipper to Dylan? "It's been a long day," I say. It's actually been a long few months, but I don't want to get into it.

"Hmm," he muses as he taps his chin. "You know what cures a long day?"

56

"What?"

"Ice cream."

"It's lunch though."

He stops walking and stares at me like I've just grown a third eye. "Don't tell me you're one of those people who only eats ice cream for dessert."

I laugh at his response. He must be serious about ice cream. "Because it is dessert."

He scoffs, looking offended. "Well, that's a habit we have to break." He starts walking again. "C'mon."

What is he planning? "You want me to come with you?"

"You know, you'll live a much happier life if you stop asking questions." He smirks. "And yes, we're having lunch together. Now let's go before we run out of time."

Half of my instincts is telling me not to go, but the other half is saying yes. I want to say no, but I remember what I told myself and Casey before the first day. This is the year of confident Lacey. I know if I eat by myself, I'll get too much in my head and it won't be good.

I follow Dylan as he approaches an old black motorcycle. My eyes widen, realizing this is our mode of transportation if I don't speak up. "I don't mind driving," I say.

"I'm selling it in a couple days. I have to spend as much time with it before we say goodbye," he says, handing me a helmet. "Look, you even get your own helmet."

Confident Lacey. I need to be the confident Lacey.

I force myself to take the helmet and hook it on around my chin. I probably look ridiculous, but Dylan gives me what I think is an assuring smile.

He hops on the bike with ease and starts it up. "C'mon."

I hesitantly swing my leg over and sit behind him, feeling awkward and not knowing where to put my arms and legs.

"You'll have to put your arms around me, you know."

His smirk almost makes me not put my arms around him, but when the motorcycle jerks forward, I do it out of instinct. He laughs at me as we drive off campus.

He weaves between cars and, instead of slowing down, speeds up at yellow lights. There's only one moment where I didn't find myself dying from anxiety. We pass by the bank where my dad worked and, for a split second, it feel like I might cry.

My heart rate calms down once we pull into the parking lot of a local ice cream shop. I've driven past the shop numerous times but have never actually been inside.

Dylan parks and I unhook the helmet. My legs are shaking slightly when I step off the bike, and I laugh at myself.

"You're a terrible driver," I tell him.

He appears unbothered, only shrugging while flashing his usual smile. "I doubt you're a better driver than me."

We walk to the front, and Dylan holds the door open for me. Upon entering, I see the front counter has endless tubs of ice cream in different flavors. I've told Dylan ice cream is only for dessert, but my mouth starts watering when I see how many flavors there are.

"Which one are you getting?" I ask him.

"I usually get cookies and cream."

Cookies and cream isn't my favorite, so that's a no. I glance over the tubs, and my eyes immediately spot the rocky road ice cream.

Once Dylan orders his cone, I order mine in a cup. We then find a spot at a small table. I immediately dig into my ice cream.

"I knew you couldn't resist ice cream." Dylan laughs at me.

"You're right," I say, laughing along with him. The ice cream is definitely lifting my spirits. "Thanks for bringing me here."

"No problem. You looked like you were having a bad case of the Monday blues."

It isn't actually the Monday blues, but I don't want to get into it. It's too much to explain, and there's not enough time to talk about it. Besides, I don't want to dump my life story on Dylan yet. Who knows if we'll even get to that point. We might stop talking for whatever reason in class and go on with our semesters as strangers.

It's weird not knowing what will happen, if hanging out with him will turn out to be a regular thing or not. I admit, it is weird talking to him in the first place. The idea that I'd be getting ice cream with Dylan Parker never came to mind last year.

"Yeah, the Monday blues," I agree anyway. "What about you? No lunch plans with your friends?"

"They skipped class and went for an early lunch."

"They didn't invite you?"

"Oh, they did. I just didn't feel like skipping," he says as he takes another bite off his cone. "I save my skip days for when it's necessary."

I don't think I'll ever skip a class. There's too much work to be done to skip. "When is it necessary to skip?"

He squints his eyes at me, but in a teasing manner. "Are you judging me? I thought you were better than that."

"I genuinely want to know when a necessary time to skip is," I say, covering my mouth while I laugh.

"Maybe you'll figure that out by the end of the semester," he muses. "Oh, and can you tell your ex not to stare me down in the hallway unless he wants to get punched?"

Jacob probably thinks there's something going on between me and Dylan. Why does he feel threatened by Dylan? It's ridiculous. As long as we're not together, he needs to keep his nose out of my business. "Sorry, but I don't have control over what he does."

"I'm just telling you right now, if he's going to start shit, he's going to get socked," he says matter-of-factly.

"I don't even know why he's trying to insert himself back into my life. He cheated on me, so that means he shouldn't care about me anymore, right? He obviously didn't when he slept with—" I'm speaking my thoughts out loud. I sigh instead of finishing my rant.

I want to know why he did it, but that means talking to him. That's something I can't do. "Sorry, I don't know why I'm letting this all out right now."

"Maybe it needs to come out."

It probably does. I find myself tracing over my tattoo, and once again, I'm frustrated over it all.

"It's like—I feel so stupid for even getting a matching tattoo with him. And getting it done by his amateur cousin, of all people."

His eyebrows raise. "You didn't get it done in a real shop?"

I shake my head. "It was after one of his soccer games last September. His cousin was having a party and we ended up going. His cousin was learning how to use his tattooing equipment and was giving free tattoos to whoever wanted one.

"Jacob convinced me that getting matching tattoos for our two year anniversary would be a good idea. I didn't want to seem like a party-pooper, so I went through with it."

Dylan seems impressed but confused at the same time. "Your parents must've been pissed."

"They were." I nod. I don't want to talk about my parents, so I steer the conversation away from them. "Not one of my finest moments. I try not to tell this story. I don't want people thinking I'm insane."

Dylan smiles. "But you told me."

I don't tell him this, but he's easy to talk to. Maybe because I know our friendship won't last long or maybe because I know it will. I don't know. "Maybe I'm trying to see if I can scare you off," I tease him.

He shrugs. "I've heard scarier stories than your matching tattoo." He suddenly leans forward. "Do you really want to scare me off?"

His voice is low, almost sultry, and my heart starts to beat a little faster.

"No . . .," I say slowly.

"Good." He nods. "I mean, you fell in my pool, so I have to befriend you out of pity, right?"

He's teasing again, so I laugh and he laughs with me. "We'll never speak of that night again, Parker."

I expect him to keep teasing me about it, but instead he says, "Deal." Then he gets serious. "Sorry the party didn't end well for you."

It wasn't his fault, but my heart warms at the fact that he is the one apologizing. "That's just been my luck lately."

"Shitty luck." He gives me a half smile.

"Tell me about it."

His eyes stay fixed on me, and I instantly feel self-conscious. *Do I have ice cream on my face?*

"What?" I ask finally, wiping my mouth with a napkin just in case there is ice cream on me.

"Nothing," he says, smiling. "Are you still coming with me on Wednesday?"

I thought he would've forgotten about that. It's amusing to think he remembers so easily. "As long as you're not going to kill me."

"Not yet." He winks and glances at his phone. "We should get going."

Dylan is charming and extremely attractive, both of which are not a good mix for me right now. I can't go catching feelings so quickly after what Jacob has done, and falling for Dylan can only end badly for me. I know his reputation. He's a major flirt, which suggests that he isn't ready for a relationship any time soon.

The ride back to school isn't as scary. Dylan doesn't weave through cars like he did on the way to the ice cream shop. When he parks on campus, he looks back at me and grins.

"Better driving?"

I nod as I take my helmet off. "A lot better."

When I hand the helmet to Dylan, I spot Jacob in the distance with his friends. If he sees me with Dylan, I'll never hear the end of it.

"Let's get to class," I say to Dylan.

We're about to start walking, but in the corner of my eye, I see Jacob approaching us. I try to ignore him by walking faster, but he speaks up.

"Hey, Lacey."

"Hey," I say, not meeting his eyes, hoping he'll get the hint that I don't want to talk to him.

Dylan is watching us. I just want the both of them to go away.

Jacob presses on though. "I have a question about that program we're using in class."

"And I'll gladly answer it. In class."

He walks ahead of me and makes me come to a stop. "I actually need to talk to you about something else."

Dylan also stops to watch him. Jacob won't get off my back if I don't talk to him, so I look at Dylan. "I'll meet you in class."

He doesn't do anything at first, but he then strides off towards the main building.

"What do you want, Jacob?" I know he only wants to talk to me because I am walking with Dylan. Whatever he has against him needs to stop now.

"He your bodyguard now, or what?" he asks, referring to Dylan. I only put my hands on my hips instead of answering. He takes a deep breath. "My parents are separating."

Separating? The last I saw of them, they seemed happy together. Other than my parents, they are the couple who gives me faith at the idea of soulmates. As much as I hate to think about it, it must be hard for Jacob.

"I'm sorry." Separating parents isn't nearly as bad as losing them in an accident, but I give him somewhat a benefit of the doubt.

"Not your fault. They just decided they needed some space. They haven't said anything about divorce, but they haven't shot the idea down either." He runs a hand through his hair, which I know he does a lot when he's really stressed. "I just felt like I had to tell you."

I sneak a look at the time on my phone and realize we'll be late if we don't get a move on. "Can we walk and talk?"

Jacob sighs as we walk in the hall. "Listen, I know you've made it very clear that you don't want to get back together, but would you reconsider being friends?"

"Friends?"

"I just—" He stops and lets out a frustrated sigh. "I can't talk to the guys about shit like this. If I can't talk to them, then I have no one else."

I want to ask about Lauren, but I decide against it. Jacob ruined our relationship, but I guess I can talk to him without bringing up more drama. I need to put all of it behind me.

We're coming up to my class, and he comes to a stop. "If you hate me that much, then tell me to fuck off and deal with it on my own. You were there for me, for everything else, and not having you now sucks. I just want your friendship."

The look in his eyes tells me he's sincere. The feeling I used to get while looking in his eyes is returning, and I hate it. I need to learn to control my emotions more. I should tell him to forget about it and leave me alone, but that doesn't feel right.

Becoming friends with Jacob might not be the smartest thing to do, but it is better than leaving him by himself to deal with it alone. Maybe I need to be the bigger person. "Okay," I say hesitantly. "But, there has to be some boundaries."

"Is a hug within those boundaries?"

"Yes," I say before I could stop myself.

He engulfs me in his arms, and somehow, everything is okay and not okay at the same time. The bell rings and he lets go of me.

"I'll see you later," he says, smiling.

I rush into class and quickly sit down. I can feel Dylan's eyes burning into the back of my head. Mrs. Beattie has us doing individual work, so Dylan and I don't talk the whole class period.

When class ends, I glance over at Dylan. "Thanks for the ice cream again."

"Don't worry about it." He waves it off.

Leaving class together gives me the urge to tell him about what Jacob has said, but I keep my mouth shut. He doesn't care about Jacob. He just wants Jacob to get out of his face.

"See you later," he says before walking off.

I wonder where Dylan wants to take me on Wednesday. His vague answers make me nervous, but weirdly enough, I'm eager to see where we will go.

Once I'm in journalism, Jacob is sitting at the computers already with Will. Vicky is missing.

Will smiles when he sees me. "Hey, Lacey. How was your weekend?"

"It was okay. How was the football game?" I don't want to go into details about the party. I'll save myself from reliving the embarrassment.

"Sucked. My friends and I didn't even get good seats in the student section. Plus, we lost." He logs into his computer then sighs. "Were you busy Friday night?"

"Just hung out with some friends at a party," I say.

Jacob leans towards me when I say it. "So you *are* friends with Dylan Parker."

"Yes, we're friends." I shift so I'm facing him completely. He wants to be friends, so I'm going to ask friendly questions. "What about you? What's your problem with him anyway?"

"I don't have to explain myself."

I want to push his buttons. "You know, Dylan doesn't appreciate the dirty looks you give him in the halls."

He smirks. "Dirty looks? Is he scared, or what?"

"I doubt it."

"Well, if he's intimidated, tell him to talk to me about it. Not use you as a messenger."

Mrs. Thomas starts talking to the class. Vicky is already sitting next to Will, and I realize I didn't even hear her sit down.

Mrs. Thomas talks about the photography group and how she wants everyone to be somewhat trained in taking photos relevant to the articles.

She then tells Seth to take people out in groups to teach them how to use the cameras. She ends up sending Will and Vicky with the first group, leaving me and Jacob alone.

When they leave, Jacob speaks up again, "How did you and Dylan even start hanging out?"

"Why does it bother you that we're friends?"

"Because he's not good for you."

That gets my blood boiling. "And you are?"

He shuts up, allowing me to continue working on my computer. He stays silent until Will, Vicky, and the rest of the group come back. Mrs. Thomas then sends out the next group, which includes me and Jacob. We take some cameras and follow Seth. Instead of walking with Jacob, I fall in line with Seth.

"How's it going so far?" I ask him.

"There are a couple people who've been really good. The others might need more help." He chuckles. "What about your group?"

"We're getting there," I say. "I just want this issue to turn out okay."

He nudges my arm. "Don't worry. It will be."

We arrive at the main hall, and Seth announces that he wants us to partner up and take pictures of the things around us for five minutes.

"Partners?" Jacob asks. The word seems like it belongs to Dylan, not Jacob.

"Sure."

Jacob takes pictures of the posters on the walls, only pointing and shooting without actually taking the time to get a good photo. I'm trying to take an artsy picture of the vending machine when Jacob motions to a specific poster on the wall. "Homecoming is coming up already?"

"Guess so."

Jacob and I had gone to the homecoming dance together for our freshman, sophomore, and junior years. I have no intention of going with him for my senior year. I don't even know if I'm going at all, but if Casey wants to go, I'll go.

"You going with Dylan?"

"Are you obsessed with Dylan or something? You can't seem to go five minutes without talking about him." Friendship with Jacob isn't going to work well if he's constantly asking about Dylan.

He doesn't get to answer. Seth brings the group back together and tells us to delete all the photos we took, except for our favorite two to save them. Jacob keeps his distance as we walk back to the classroom.

Once we're back inside, we go back to work on the computers. Jacob ignores me, putting in his earphones, and Will and Vicky seem to understand the sections they're working on in the program book.

My mind drifts to a friendship with Jacob. Maybe becoming friends with him is what I need for closure.

Or not. Becoming friends with him could also lead to unearthing feelings I have buried over the summer. I know if I don't try to be friendly with him, he'll never leave me completely alone. Strict boundaries need to be set in place if this friendship is going to work

After class, I catch Jacob's arm. "Let's talk."

We walk out of the class together, and he puts his earphones away. "What's up?"

"Because of our past, us being friends will only work if we set boundaries." I know I'm not going to get back together with him, but I have to clear the air in case he gets any ideas.

He wears a skeptical look. "What boundaries then?"

"I'm making it crystal clear right now, we are not getting back together," I stress the last few words. "I'm not in this to be your girlfriend again. You need a friend to talk to while you're dealing with whatever, and I'll be that friend."

"Okay," he says, nodding quickly. "Understood."

"Good. Just—please understand, I don't want to hear about anything else other than what's going on with your parents. This friendship will only work if we let go of everything in the past. I'm trying to move on, and I can't do that if you're constantly bringing up old memories. Let's start fresh."

"Start fresh . . ." He nods slowly. "I can do that."

I'm going to finish with that, but one more thought comes to mind. "And leave Dylan alone. We're only friends."

He doesn't look happy about it, but he says, "Fine."

"It's settled then. I'll see you tomorrow."

He steps in front of me. "One more thing."

What can he possibly say now? "What's that?"

If it's something about Lauren, I don't care. As much as I dislike her for going after my boyfriend, I can't do anything to stop them from getting together again. We've broken up, so I can't say a damn thing about it.

Jacob's mouth opens, but nothing comes out. He shakes his head instead. "Nothing. Never mind. Thanks for clearing up the boundaries."

CHAPTER FIVE

While getting ready on Wednesday morning, everything falls into place perfectly. My hair is cooperating with me, my outfit is coming together nicely, and my skin allows me to be light on my makeup.

Everything is fine until I walk out to my car and see a flat tire on the driver's side. In a panic, I call Casey, who manages to pick me up on time.

"You're a lifesaver, you know," I tell her once I'm buckled in.

"Tell me something I don't know." She glances at me and smiles. "You look cute today."

To make her mad, I say, "As opposed to other days?"

"Oh, you know what I mean."

I have been listening to Nirvana all morning, so it is only appropriate to wear my Nirvana tank top. I've matched it with a red and black flannel, a pair of distressed light-wash shorts, and red Converse.

Casey, on the other hand, is wearing a black and white striped dress with a lightweight army-green jacket. Stylish, as usual.

"Hey, I know I've apologized a million times for the pool incident, but I still feel awful," she says.

"And I've forgiven you a million times," I stress.

She doesn't remember exactly what Tyler said to her to make her upset that night. I tried to help her remember, but she was too tipsy to remember the details. She's been avoiding him since then.

"I think I'm going to talk to Tyler today. I've just been so embarrassed by all of it."

"If he turns out to be a jerk, then don't bother giving him a second chance."

She parks in her usual spot. "Let's get today over with."

I haven't told Casey about Jacob and I being friends yet. He hasn't really talked to me much, so I figure there isn't a whole lot to tell her.

"You want to go see a movie or something tonight?" Casey asks as we're walking inside the main building.

I am about to say yes until I remember that Dylan wants to take me somewhere tonight. We haven't talked much either, so I don't even know if those plans are still on. "Um, let me get back to you on that one."

We part ways and head to class.

For lunch, Casey and I eat in the cafeteria again. The salad I've bought looks great until I see Casey's cheese fries on her tray. In an attempt to put off the craving, I load more ranch on my salad.

"I didn't talk to Tyler," she says as she pokes at her fries.

"I thought today was the day to do it?"

"Well, we usually talk when we have to do partner work, and we haven't done any. He didn't even look at me. I think I was the one who made a mess of things at the party."

There's no way of knowing what has really happened. "Maybe this will just have to settle on its own."

"It's frustrating," she says before shoving a forkful of fries into her mouth.

That's it. I push my salad aside and stand up. "I'll be right back."

I wait in line for the cheese fries and pray they won't run out before I get to them.

My mind wanders to Jacob. There's a food truck downtown that sells pretty good cheese fries along with some other great food. Jacob and I would stop by on some Friday nights to pig out. I hate myself for it, but I miss those times.

"Couldn't resist the cheese?"

Dylan is standing next to me, wearing a broad smile. His green shirt makes his light-green eyes pop. I blink before I can respond.

"Who can?" I ask, laughing along.

"No more Monday blues?"

"Not anymore, no."

"Good." He nods. "Are you still coming with me tonight?"

The way he says it makes me more excited than nervous, but I don't want to come across as too excited. "Sure."

He looks me up and down, and I'm about to scold him for checking me out so obviously when he says, "Did you figure out where we're going?"

"No?"

"Well, it's safe to say that you don't have to change before we go."

That's when it hits me. "Um, my car has a flat tire, so I got a ride with Casey this morning. I don't know if you want me to meet you there, or . . ."

The line moves and we both move forward. "You don't know how to change a tire?" he asks.

I shake my head. My parents talked about teaching me, but neither of them got around to doing it.

He stays quiet for a second before he says, "I can change it for you. I mean, unless your dad or someone else wants to."

The word dad stings. I try not to get visibly upset. "Actually, if you could do it, that'd be great."

"Let me get your number so you can text me your address later," he says instead of asking questions.

I smirk at him. "Dylan Parker wants my phone number?"

It's clear that he's trying to hide a smile, but it breaks through anyway. "Do you want my help or not, Lace?"

Not too many people call me Lace, and I admittedly like the way he says it. "Okay, okay. Let me see your phone." He surrenders his phone, and I type my number in. "Here." I hand it back to him.

"I'll see you in class," he says.

"Wait, you aren't getting cheese fries?"

"Unlike you, I can resist the cheese." He winks at me before walking away.

After obtaining my precious cheese fries, I happily sit back down with Casey and she eyes me.

"Dylan Parker was totally flirting with you," she says immediately. "And he gave you his phone, which could only mean you gave him your number."

Casey watches me like a hawk sometimes. On one hand, it's a good thing, but on the other hand, it's not. "If you must know, I gave him my number so he can change my tire later."

My little Dodge Neon has been getting me where I need to be since my aunt helped me buy it over the summer, and I don't need anything else happening to it. That'll just be one more thing on her plate, and I don't need her to worry.

"And he's doing this out of the goodness of his heart?" she teases.

"I have something else to tell you," I say, knowing I need to fess up. "Me and Dylan are going somewhere tonight."

"Somewhere?" She raises a brow. "Where is this somewhere?"

I feel myself blushing because of the lack of details. "I don't exactly know."

"You're going with Dylan somewhere tonight, but you don't know where," she says it slowly, and I can tell she's hardcore judging me. "Doesn't sound safe to me."

"Dylan hasn't given me a reason not to trust him." I want to make it sound like it isn't a big deal because it isn't.

She presses her lips together, making her unapproving face. "This isn't some kind of rebound thing, is it?"

"Rebound? What do you mean?"

"You shouldn't rebound from Jacob with Dylan. Not so soon."

I have to clear the air. I've made things clear to Jacob, and now I have to do the same thing with Casey. "There is nothing going on between me and Dylan, I promise." On that note, I know I have to tell her about Jacob. "I also have something else to tell you."

She looks at me expectantly.

"Jacob and I are friends now."

The frown on her face deepens, and I instantly regret telling her.

"I'm starting to think you shouldn't make decisions without consulting me first," she says. "Jacob does *not* deserve any kind of second chances, Lace."

"It's not a second chance. His parents are going through some stuff, and he needs someone to talk to. I already told him we're not getting back together."

She rolls her eyes. "He was barely there for you when your parents passed. Does he really deserve your help during his parents's rough patch?"

Deep down, as much as it hurt, I know she's right. Jacob can be selfish at times, and that was clear when he cheated on me after I lost my parents.

One thing I pride myself on is being caring, and if caring for Jacob when he needs it most helps me to feel better about myself, then so be it. "I'm not doing it entirely for him. I think I need this. I need to see him move on without me, so I can move on without him."

"And being friends is going to do that for you?"

73

"I guess we'll find out."

She shakes her head in disapproval. "I like the idea of you hanging out with Dylan more than you being friends with Jacob."

"Just know that I think I know what I'm doing." I laugh at myself after saying it. I don't know what's going to happen, but hopefully I'll learn something in the process.

My stomach erupts into butterflies when lunch ends, and I realize I'm excited to see Dylan. I calm myself down before more feelings build up.

Dylan isn't in class when I sit down. As more people file in, he still isn't amongst them. Class starts, and he doesn't show. I wonder if this is one of those necessary times to skip class.

My phone buzzes in my pocket, and I discreetly pull it out to see who it is. An unknown number is on the screen with two text messages.

Had a slight emergency and can't make it 2 class. I'll pick u up after school.
It's Dylan btw

I'm not going to fight him about picking me up. It will probably be easier for him and Casey. I wait until after class to text him back.

Sounds good.

As soon as I send it, I want to hit myself over how lame I sound. I put my phone back in my pocket and walk to journalism.

Dylan doesn't text me back after my message, and I find myself checking my phone almost every ten minutes. Will clearly notices.

"Is the Queen of England going to call you or something?" he asks me.

I ignore him and text Casey to tell her she doesn't need to take me home. Once again, she tells me to be careful, so I assure her I'll be fine.

Another message from Dylan comes in.

Meet me where I usually park.

I don't have time to text him back. Class ends, and I want to get my stuff together as quickly as possible.

"Where's the fire?" Jacob asks me. He ends up walking out of class with me.

"No fire. Just wanted today to end," I say.

He stays quiet as he walks along next to me. When we step outside, he speaks up again, "Are you busy this weekend?"

Oh no. "I'm not sure. Why?"

"We have a game on Saturday, one o'clock. I was just wondering if you wanted to go, you know, just like old times . . ."

He slows down once he sees the look on my face. He's overstepping one of the boundaries.

"Jacob—"

"Forget that last part. We're friends, right? Friends go to each other's events." He sounds hopeful.

"Um . . ." I trail off once I see Dylan waiting by his motorcycle. "We'll see."

I start to walk away until Jacob stands in front of me. "Please, Lace. It'll mean a lot if you go. I don't care if I'm ignoring the boundaries, I just want to see you at my games again."

He's already disregarding the boundaries. Before I can speak, Dylan appears by my side. He stares at Jacob before looking at me. "You ready to go?"

I know that irritated expression on Jacob's face all too well. "Can I finish talking to her? Alone?" Jacob asks Dylan.

"It doesn't look like she wants to talk to you," Dylan says, getting closer to him.

75

The situation is only going to escalate if I don't try to mediate. "Dylan, it's fine, really." He helped me with Jacob at his party, but I feel like I can handle this on my own. I turn towards Jacob. "We can talk about this tomorrow."

He doesn't look satisfied. "Fine." He then pulls me in for a hug. It's tighter than I want it to be, but once I breathe in his familiar cologne, I ease into it. For a split second, it really is just like old times. Before I can get in too deep, I pull away.

"I'll see you tomorrow," I tell him.

Dylan takes long strides to his motorcycle and hands me a helmet. "Gotta make sure you don't get a head injury before your important conversation with him tomorrow."

He's acting petty, but I put the helmet on anyway. "Not funny."

"I thought you said he was your ex?" he asks as he sits down.

"He is."

He's about to start the motorcycle when he looks back at me. "Address?"

The engine roars after I give it to him, and we're off to the apartment. I immediately think about whether or not he'll want to go inside and how clean the place is at the moment. He only has to turn once before we arrive to the complex. I direct him to our building.

Dylan parks next to my car, giving a clear view of the flat tire. I stare at it as I take the helmet off. We walk up to my car and I sigh. "This is it."

"Can you pop your trunk open?"

I reach for the keys in my bag, unlock the car, and press the button to open the trunk for him.

He takes a look inside and taps his chin. "Okay, I should've known you wouldn't have anything to change it. I'm going to call Anthony."

"I'm going to take my stuff in. Do you want to wait for him inside?" It feels weird asking him to go into the apartment with me.

"Uh, if you're sure it's okay," he says as he glances around.

"Yeah, it's fine." I can't tell if he's frustrated or if he feels just as awkward as I do as we climb the stairs and walk inside.

I set my things down on our small dining table as Dylan shuts the door behind him. I quickly glance over everything to see if we have any laundry laying out or if anything is obviously cluttered.

"I'm gonna call Anthony to see where he's at," he says, pulling out his phone.

I nod and watch him go back out the door. I then turn to the kitchen to see what snacks we have. *What does Dylan like? Is he a cookie or cracker kind of person? Does he snack on fruits or vegetables?* I'm going through the pantry when he walks back in.

"Anthony isn't too far from us, so he'll be here in a minute." His eyes scan over the numerous snacks I have sitting on the counter. "What are you doing?"

"I don't know what you like, so I brought out some options." I scratch the back of my neck nervously. "Sorry, we don't usually have people over." As I say that, I immediately think about when my aunt is going to be home. The clock on the stove reads four-fifteen, meaning she'll be home very soon.

"Are these all of your snacks, or do you happen to share with your parents?" he asks, sounding amused.

"I snack a lot." I shrug, ignoring the part about my parents.

To my horror, the front door opens and in walks my aunt. She's wearing a black blazer with a white button down underneath, jeans, and her favorite pair of leopard print heels. "Lacey, I was just looking at your car and you have a flat tire!"

She walks into the kitchen and stops when she sees Dylan. Her eyes flash between us, and they finally settle on Dylan. "Oh, hi there."

"Aunt Jade, this is my friend Dylan," I say quickly. "Dylan, this is my aunt, Jade."

Dylan holds out his hand and smiles at her. "It's nice to meet you."

She takes his hand hesitantly. "Likewise. I didn't know we were having company." She looks at me for answers.

"Dylan is actually going to change my tire," I explain. "Then we're going to hang out after."

Her eyes brighten slightly. "Oh, that's sweet of you. Where are you two going?"

I look at Dylan. Time to give up the spot.

Dylan seems cool and collected. "It's a place called Raven's, downtown. There's a band I want Lacey to see."

Raven's? I've seen the building before, but I've never given it much thought. It doesn't look like much from the outside. I just think it is an old building.

"Sounds fun." She smiles at me.

Dylan briefly looks at his phone. "My cousin just got here to help me change that tire. We'll be downstairs." He excuses himself and walks out.

I let out the breath I have been holding since my aunt entered and she gives me a look.

"He seems nice," she says. She grabs a bag of Goldfish and starts eating from it. "Cute too."

"We're just friends."

"Nothing wrong with having cute friends. Your dad started off as friends with your mom."

"It's not like that. I swear we're only friends," I assure her.

"I don't know a lot of guys who would go out of their way to change my tire." She seems like she's in deep thought for a second. "I'm trying to think of how your parents would've handled this."

I sigh. "Mom probably would've been on her millionth question towards him while dad would've sat there and watched him."

She laughs. "Were they that way with Jacob?"

"Yeah, but he handled it like a champ," I say. "If dad were around to hear what he did to me . . ."

She shakes her head. "I think Jacob would have been more afraid of your mom."

"True." My mom would have immediately hunted him down and demanded answers from him.

"Listen," she says as she leans against the counter. "I'm not like your mom. I know that. I was only supposed to be the cool aunt who slipped you a drink of wine at family gatherings. I love being your guardian, I really do, but I'm still trying to figure all of this out. I guess your mom handled the hard part with the first boyfriend. I know you're smart. I guess—I mean, what I'm trying to say is—"

"I understand," I say. "I should've told you he would be here. I'm sorry, but trust me, I'm not ready to jump into something after what happened with Jacob . . ."

She takes my hand. "Okay, I'm just going for the cool aunt part here. Guys suck, and you don't need one to feel complete in your life. You're young, and you're allowed to have fun. If some silly high school boy tries to ruin that, then he's not for you." She squeezes my hand. "Just as long as you're careful and you make smart choices."

I can't help but wrap my arms around her for a tight hug while my eyes start to water. "I think mom would've said the same thing."

She pulls away and puts her hands on my shoulders. "You look more and more like her every day."

"Maybe we should have heart-to-heart like this every month. I feel a lot better," I admit. We've talked about my parents before, but it feels different this time.

"Deal. And babe, if you ever feel like crying, let me cry with you. It sucks crying alone."

I give her one more hug and sigh. "I think I'll go check on the boys."

"Okay. I'm going to get out of these heels," she says, jogging into her room.

I wipe my eyes and take a deep breath. I practically skip down the stairs to find Dylan and Anthony messing with the spare tire.

"Hey, Lacey." Anthony smiles at me. "You look different without pool water all over you."

"Ignore him," Dylan says as he positions the spare in place.

I laugh. "Is that my reputation now?"

"Better that than something else," Anthony says, helping Dylan with the tire.

It's incredibly nice of them to do this for me, especially when I've only known them for a short time. "Thanks for coming to help, Anthony."

"No problem."

After the spare is on, their hands are black from the tire and Dylan has a black smudge on his neck. Anthony wipes his hands with a rag from his car before handing it to Dylan.

"Well, I better get going," Anthony says. "Am I seeing you guys tonight?"

"Yeah, we'll be there," Dylan tells him.

Anthony waves and says his goodbyes before he drives off in his car.

"What now?" I ask Dylan.

"Well, you should only use your spare for so many miles, so you'll have to deal with getting a new tire soon."

Not what I mean, but that's good to know. "Oh, okay. Are we going to head to Raven's now or . . .?"

"Oh." He pulls his phone out of his pocket and checks it. "Yeah, we can go now. We'll go on my bike, so you won't have to use your spare yet."

We jog back up the stairs and find my aunt sitting on the small couch grading some papers. She smiles at us when we come through the doorway. Dylan explains the situation with my tire, and she thanks him for everything.

"I'm gonna go wipe all this black stuff off of me," Dylan says. "Is it alright if I—"

"Sure, no problem. The bathroom is the first door on the left," my aunt tells him.

He thanks her before walking away. My aunt raises her eyebrows at me.

"A handyman," she says, smirking.

I ignore her comment, and when Dylan comes back, I rush the goodbyes. I love my aunt, but she has a habit of talking with no filter.

Dylan steps out the door and waves to her. I'm about to step out when she catches my attention.

"Remember, always use protection," she says, giving me a thumbs-up.

I have to stop myself from smacking my forehead. I quickly shut the door behind me and pray Dylan didn't hear her.

As we approach his bike, Dylan hands me my helmet. "Gotta use protection," he says, trying to stifle a laugh.

"Very funny. I thought you were going to sell the bike?" I ask, remembering what he said the day we got ice cream.

"We're parting ways on Friday. I'm actually trading it off for a car."

"Something less dangerous. I like that idea," I say as I pull the helmet on.

He smirks. "You care about my safety?"

I ignore his cheeky comment. "Let's go."

We arrive at Raven's and park in a small lot behind the old building, where a few other cars are already parked. I follow Dylan to the front of the building where we walk in.

"Dylan!" someone exclaims as soon as we enter. People are sitting at different sized tables around us. In a far corner, there's a small stage set up with amps and cords littering the floor.

The walls around us are a rusty red color and are covered with posters of old bands such as Led Zeppelin, Nirvana, Pink Floyd, The Rolling Stones, and a whole lot of others.

Dylan and the guy who has said his name do the man hug thing guys usually do when they see each other. "Look who decided to show up," the guy tells Dylan. He doesn't look much older than us, maybe in his early to mid-twenties. He has black hair and brown eyes, and is wearing a black and maroon flannel with a pair of faded black pants. He has that 90s grunge look going on.

"Why wouldn't I?" Dylan asks.

Grunge guy scoffs. "You haven't been here in a while, man." His eyes flicker to me then back to Dylan. "And I can see why."

"Right," Dylan says. "Max, this is Lacey. Lacey, this is Max, a family friend."

Max holds his hand out to me, and I shake it. "It's nice to meet you," I say politely.

He smiles. "Brought a girlfriend here with you, huh? You're growing up so fast." He messes with Dylan's hair, and Dylan shoves his arm.

Well, that needs to be cleared up. "We're not—"

"She's just a friend," Dylan tells Max, cutting me off.

Max chuckles. "Whatever you say." He says something about having to go to the back before leaving me and Dylan.

Dylan heads towards a table and motions for me to follow. We sit down on stool-like chairs around a tall circular table near the middle of the room.

"So," Dylan says as he motions around us, "what do you think?"

"I think my shirt matches that poster." I point to the Nirvana poster behind him.

He looks at my shirt before turning to look at the poster. "Told you you're dressed appropriately. I thought you had figured out where we were coming. Are you really a fan?"

"Not at all. I just thought the shirt looked good on me." I try to hold back a smile, but I can't.

He holds his hands up in defense. "Sorry. I didn't think you'd be a Nirvana fan."

"There are a lot of things you don't know about me," I point out. It sounds flirty when it leaves my mouth.

Dylan bites his lip and leans forward. "Is that a challenge?"

There's a commotion behind us and we both turn. Anthony, Reece, and Carlos walk in through a different door, and their attention is quickly focused on us.

"Dylan!" Reece yells.

I smirk. "Well, aren't you Mr. Popular."

Dylan rolls his eyes but grins. "Shut up."

The guys join us at the table. Anthony sits to my right and Reece sits to my left.

"Good to see you again," Carlos says to me, smiling.

"Yeah, you guys too." They all looked intimidating when I first met them at Dylan's party. They don't seem as intimidating sitting here at the table.

"Have you ever been here?" Reece asks me.

I shake my head.

"I thought she'd be a fan of the place," Dylan says.

I'm not sure what to think. There are only a couple other people in the building besides me, Dylan, and the guys. Oldies are playing in the background, making it somewhat peaceful.

"Are you guys staying for the performance?" Anthony asks, mostly to Dylan.

Dylan has mentioned there is a band he wants me to see. I wonder if that's who they're talking about.

"Not sure yet," he says. His attention is on his phone.

"Did you see Max?" Reece asks him and Dylan nods. "Did you see Derrick?"

Dylan shakes his head and puts his phone away. "No. Is he in the back?" This time Reece nods. Dylan stands up and starts walking away. I don't know what to think, but then he stops and points at me. "Don't let these guys be a bad influence on you."

Carlos sounds amused. "No promises."

Dylan goes through the door where the guys came from, and the guys turn their attention to me.

"You two have a class together?" Carlos asks me.

I nod.

"Hmm." He taps his chin while glancing at the other guys.

"Dylan doesn't just bring any girl around, you know," Anthony pipes in.

Why does everyone assume that something must be going on between me and Dylan? Can't we just be friends?

"Listen, Dylan and I became friends in class. That's all." If I have to make it clear to one more person, I'm going to explode. "Besides, I'm not exactly looking to be in a relationship right now."

"Guys suck. Don't date us." Reece smirks.

"Trust me, I know guys suck." I haven't had the best of luck with guys so far.

"Girls are the ones who suck," Carlos objects. "My first girlfriend in middle school dumped me in front of her friends, and they all laughed at me."

"You were the dumpee?" Anthony laughs at him.

Reece cracks up as well. "I remember that!"

"Then my next girlfriend cheated on me, so yeah, I think I can say girls suck," Carlos crosses his arms.

"My boyfriend cheated on me at the end of last year, and now he's taking a class with me to reconcile," I blurt out. If we're

84

going to talk about sucky relationships, I have to throw mine in there.

"Reconcile? Fuck that. Why didn't you try to get out of that class?" Carlos makes a face as he asks.

"It's my favorite class." I can't let Jacob be in my favorite class while I take another one that doesn't even interest me.

Anthony shakes his head. "I would never take a class with my ex. Hell no."

"Oh hell." Reece's shoulder's droop. "If Lacey can get cheated on, then there's no fucking hope in this world."

I take it as a compliment. Talking to them turns out to be easy. They aren't the scary guys people make them out to be at school. They're relatively normal.

"That's why I don't believe in that love bullshit. I'm going to stay a bachelor forever," Carlos declares with a shrug. He's definitely the more carefree one of the group.

Anthony and Reece break out into the song *Love Stinks* while Carlos and I laugh at them. I'm having a better time than I thought I would. My stomach is hurting from all the laughing.

"What the fuck is going on here?" Dylan asks with a smile as he stands next to me.

"We're talking about how relationships suck," Anthony tells him.

"Right." Dylan shakes his head and rubs his temple.

Anthony points to me. "We're all going to sing. You know the song, right Lacey?"

I'm going to respond, but Dylan interjects, "Actually, I want you to meet someone."

"Okay." I nod.

He holds his hand out to me and I take it as I stand up from my seat. As we're walking away, Anthony and Reece continue to sing the song.

Dylan is still holding my hand as we walk through a doorway. I attempt to push the feeling of butterflies in my stomach. We walk down a long corridor until we reach an old wooden door.

"You're not going to kill me, are you?" I tease him.

He smirks and says, "Not yet."

He knocks on the door and we hear someone behind it say, "Come in."

Once we're in, Dylan shuts the door behind us.

There are two guys in the small room—one is stretched out on a couch, strumming a guitar, and the other is looking at some papers at a table in the corner. They both look up and smile when they see Dylan.

The one strumming the guitar has brown hair that hangs in front of his face and big brown eyes.

The guy at the table has blond hair, similar to Reece. In fact, they look a lot alike, blue eyes and all. Both are extremely attractive as well.

"Well, shit, Dylan, if you told us we were going to meet a model, we would have worn something decent," the blond guy says as he smiles at me.

The brunette guy stands up from the couch and glances between me and Dylan.

"This is Lacey," Dylan tells them.

Blondie continues to smile. "Nice shirt." He winks at me.

"Thanks." My cheeks feel warm, and I casually place my hand on my cheek to cool down.

"That idiot," Dylan points to blondie, "is Reece's older brother, Jared." That explains why they look almost like twins.

"And this," he wraps an arm around the other guy, "is my brother Derrick."

CHAPTER SIX

Seeing Derrick and Dylan standing next to each other helps me point out the features they share. The only striking difference is their eyes; Dylan's are a mischievous green, and Derrick's are a warm brown.

Derrick smiles at me and says, "Lacey is a beautiful name."

"Are you guys ready?" Dylan asks them before I can respond to Derrick.

Jared claps his hands. "Hell yeah, man. I've been waiting for this all week."

"What time do you guys go on?" Dylan asks, leaning against the wall beside him.

This time Derrick speaks. "Around nine. There are a few bands ahead of us."

Dylan twists his mouth. "I don't know what time Lacey has to get back home, but we'll be able to catch some of the other bands."

I hope I can see Derrick and Jared perform. It feels like the whole purpose of Dylan bringing me here is to hear them, but why? It's strange to think he wants me to meet his brother. I don't even know why Dylan thought about bringing me here in the first place.

"No problem. There are always other performances," Derrick assures me.

Dylan places his hand on the small of my back, making my heart beat faster. "Ready?" he asks me.

"Sure," I say. The way he grabs my hand and holds my back make me question whether he has some kind of feelings for me or if he is just being his regular, flirty self. I've never taken Dylan to be a lovey kind of guy, so I go for the latter.

"It was nice meeting you, Lacey." Jared smiles at me as he says it.

Derrick is staring at Dylan, but he tears his gaze away and focuses on me. "Yeah, we hope to see you around here again."

That comment sounds like it should be directed towards Dylan.

I wave to them as Dylan ushers me out of the room and into the corridor.

"How long have they been performing here?" I ask Dylan.

"They've been playing here since they formed their band in high school."

"How old are they?"

"Jared is twenty, and Derrick is twenty-one."

"I hope I can stay to watch them." I wonder what kind of music they play or how good they play.

I text my aunt and ask her what time she wants me home. When she responds, she says she doesn't want me out past nine, especially since it's a school night.

"That's okay. Maybe next time," Dylan says after I tell him what she has said.

The light in the sky is fading and more people show up, developing a good crowd. A band made up of two guys and a girl go up on stage and start to play covers of what sound like songs from the 90s.

Carlos rubs his forehead. "Fuck this music."

"It's not too bad," Anthony says. "At least it's not what that band was playing a couple weeks ago. Remember that shit? I don't know what Max was thinking of, booking a bunch of complete amateurs."

"That'll never happen again," Dylan puts in his two cents, even though he's been on his phone since we've sat back down with the guys.

"So, Lacey," Anthony turns his attention to me, "what do you think of Raven's so far?"

Everyone waits for my answer, and I immediately feel self-conscious. "It's pretty nice."

"Shit, is it raining?" Reece suddenly asks us as he stares out the window near us.

This makes Dylan look outside and frown. "Hope it stops before I take Lacey back."

I hope so as well. I'm already nervous enough driving around with Dylan on a motorcycle. Driving in the rain would put me even more on edge.

Two more bands go on as we sit and watch them. The boys listen to the music and laugh along to each other's jokes.

Just from observing them, I'm right about my impression of Carlos being the more carefree type of the group. There are moments when he makes comments about someone or something that makes me think of him as an ass.

Dylan seems as if he tries hard to keep up his cool guy facade. He laughs at something but catches himself and turns serious again.

Anthony and Reece are like a playful, comedic duo. Reece is the comedian, and Anthony tries to outdo him. It's just back and forth banter between the two of them, almost like they feed off of each other.

It's a little after eight, and the rain hasn't let up. Dylan's gaze would occassionally shift to the window, and I can tell he's watching the rain carefully. He finally speaks to me about it. "If it were just me, I'd drive in this. I'm getting the impression you don't want to, though."

I don't want to cause a fuss over some rain. Maybe I'll have to tough it out and ride in the rain with him.

89

"We're gonna head out of here in a minute," Dylan announces to the guys.

"Aren't you on your bike?" Anthony raises a brow.

"We'll tough out the rain," I answer for Dylan. I don't want them to think I can't handle it.

"Fuck that. Take my car," Anthony says, pulling out his keys. "Just don't wreck my baby."

Dylan takes the keys and the anxious pit in my stomach instantly goes away. After standing up from his stool, he stretches. I can't help but sneak a peek at his stomach when his shirt lifts.

Mentally kicking myself has become a trend when I hang out with Dylan. I can't believe I just tried checking him out.

"Let's go," he says, not knowing I've just eyed him up.

The guys all say their goodbyes to me. Dylan and Anthony smirks. "No fooling around in my car, you two."

"Please, Dylan could never get a girl like Lacey anyway." Carlos lets out a laugh as he says it, making the others laugh too.

"You guys are going to be sorry when I get back," Dylan tells them. I can see a smile wanting to spread across his face.

I didn't think I would need a jacket this morning, so I pull my arms through my flannel and cover my head with it. Dylan and I dash out to Anthony's car and quickly slide inside.

Dylan takes a look in the backseat after he shuts his door. "I'd give you a jacket of his, but it doesn't look like he has one."

"It's fine. I'm not cold. I just feel like a wet dog." My flannel did nothing to protect me from the rain, so my hair is sticking to my face. I run my fingers through it to get it back to normal.

Dylan smirks for a split second, but I don't ask him what he's thinking. He starts driving towards the apartment, and I find myself staring out the window and watching the traffic.

"Your aunt seems pretty cool," Dylan says suddenly.

I have a feeling Dylan is wondering why I'm with my aunt and not my parents. I hope the conversation doesn't head in that direction. "Yeah, she's great."

"How long are you staying with her?" he asks.

And my instincts are right. "Until I move out, I guess."

He stays quiet for a minute. "I promise I'm not trying to be nosy."

It might just be easier if I tell him the truth. That way, I don't have to dodge any more questions. "My parents died back in May. My aunt is the closest relative, so she took guardianship of me."

The conversation takes an awkward turn for both of us when he doesn't say anything. I don't blame him for not knowing what to say. How do you respond to something like that?

"You don't have to say you're sorry or anything. I've gotten enough of that since it happened." Hearing it from Dylan will probably drive me mad.

"Fuck," he starts, "that has to be hard."

I don't want anyone's pity, though I know that's hardly ever someone's intention. Talking about it will help, but sometimes, I'd just rather not. It's different with Dylan, for some reason. Part of me wants to tell him about my parents and how great they were, but the other part of me wants to shut it down.

"It is." It's hard to express how hard it really is, but I don't want others to know this pain. It's rough, it's not okay, and no one else should have to know how it feels to lose both parents. "I don't want to sound mean or anything, but can we talk about something else?"

"Yeah, for sure." He nods. "But listen, I know you have your friend to talk to and everything, and I know we haven't known each other long, but I just want to—you know, I don't mind if you want to talk about it at some point."

Dylan's softer side is coming out, and I can't stop the smile from spreading on my face. "Thanks, Dylan. And thanks for inviting me tonight. I had a lot of fun."

His mouth twists, like he wants to smile. "I'm glad you had fun. The guys can be a fucking trip sometimes."

"I like them. Maybe I'll come to Raven's more often." I don't know if I actually will, but it's nice to think about.

"What makes you think I'm bringing you back?" he smirks as he asks.

I decide to play along. "What makes you think I need you to bring me?"

He lets out a laugh. "Be my guest."

"I don't need to be your guest, remember?" I say it just to be obnoxious and it makes him laugh louder, which makes me feel weirdly good.

"Okay, okay. Just shut up." He laughs. "Does your friend ever get annoyed with you?"

"Casey and I have been friends since elementary, of course she gets annoyed with me." I shrug. "That's the great thing about having her as a best friend. She's used to me already." When he doesn't say anything, I ask, "What about you and the guys? How long have you all known each other?"

He blows out a breath. "Well, Anthony I've known my whole life because we're cousins. We didn't meet Carlos and Reece until freshman year. When my brother formed his band, Jared would bring Reece around and we'd hang out. I think Carlos was Reece's friend in middle school, so there's also that history."

"Very exclusive."

"It is. You have to go through an initiation to get in."

I let out a nervous laugh. "I don't think I want to know what the initiation is."

The apartment complex comes into view, and Dylan pulls up in front of my building.

"Thanks for driving me. I'll get out of your hair, so you can catch the performance," I say.

"Don't worry about it. I've seen plenty of their shows."

The rain is steady outside the car. I take a deep breath and prepare myself to run. Hopefully, I don't slip and fall and have Dylan laugh at me for it. "I'll see you tomorrow," I tell him as I put my flannel over my head again.

Without falling, I manage to run up the stairs and get out of the rain. Dylan leaves in the car as soon as I walk inside.

*   *   *

It is Friday afternoon, and all I can think about is the deadline to get a large portion of the newspaper done. I'm not in journalism yet, but it has been occupying my mind the whole day.

Jacob distracted me during class yesterday, and instead of helping, he decided he couldn't figure out how to format the articles with the photos.

When the bell rings for fourth period, I quickly gather my things. Hopefully, getting to journalism early will help, so I can finish formatting that specific section. I don't totally mind helping him because I'm mostly a perfectionist. Formatting makes me extra picky, but it does set me behind.

I sit at a computer as soon as I enter and log in. Mrs. Thomas walks over to me.

"Everything okay?" she asks, sitting on the desk next to the computers.

"I'm a little behind on formatting," I tell her.

"Don't worry. Stay after school to finish if you need to."

I hope I don't have to, but I'm grateful for her leniency. "Thank you so much."

Jacob sits at the computer next to me as she walks away. He casually sits and takes his time logging into the computer, like we don't have a big deadline to meet.

My work depends on him and the other two, and if they take their time, then it sets me back even more. Plus, even if they finish on time, I still have to go in and make sure everything has the right size, the right fonts, and more.

"Hey, friend," he says. It's how he's been greeting me for the past couple days. I don't particularly like it, but I let it be.

"Hey," I say as I pull up the newspaper template. "Have you finished pages four and five yet?"

"I'm almost done. I just have to—"

"Can you just put them on the drive? I'll work on them. In the mean time, you can finish page eight. I think it just needs a picture."

I think he can tell I am stressing over the deadline, so he does as I ask and doesn't really talk to me for the rest of the class period. While I take on the bigger workloads, I assign Vicky and Will to smaller workloads like I've done with Jacob. Not only will this get them out of my hair but it will also help get things done faster.

"Lacey, does this picture look better on this side or this side?" Will asks me.

I really don't have time to teach him which way pictures should face, so I say, "Just put it however you like and I'll fix it if I have to."

Jacob turns to me. "Someone's stressed out. Need a back rub?"

If we were still dating, it would've been perfect. "Not now, Jacob."

"Hey, I know we didn't get to talk about my game yesterday, so can we do that here for a bit?" he asks.

Will pokes his head out. "Are you guys getting back together soon?"

Their questions and comments are making me lose my focus. I ignore Will and address Jacob instead. "Jake, this is the

94

worst time to talk about anything else right now. I have to get this done, and I can't if I lose my focus."

His eyebrows raise in surprise. "You just called me Jake."

I only ever called him Jake when I was upset with him, but didn't want to hurt his feelings by snapping at him. He used to like when I said it because he said it made him feel like I loved him a lot more than I let on.

I didn't even realize I just said it. "Sorry, it slipped," I tell him. I don't even know why it has slipped. Old habits coming back to haunt me, I guess.

"Right," he says, going back to his computer screen.

They leave me alone, and right before class ends, they put their portions of the paper in the drive so I can put them in the template. Just as I'm placing the first two, the bell rings.

"You need any help?" Jacob asks.

Instead of making a snarky comment about him helping me days ago, I shake my head. "Nope, I'm good."

"Okay. About my game tomorrow, I don't know if my parents are going, so that's why I want you to go."

It isn't like he's asking me to give him my liver. However, going to his game might bring back certain memories.

Maybe I can push them out.

Before I can answer, there's a knock at the door. Dylan is standing at the doorway, but he's looking at Mrs. Thomas.

"Ah, Mr. Parker," Mrs. Thomas says. "I'm glad you showed up."

"I don't know what else I'd rather do after school on a Friday," he says with a deadpan face.

Jacob is obviously annoyed and rolls his eyes. "Is this guy ever not around?"

Dylan seems surprised to see me. His eyes travel to Jacob, then back to Mrs. Thomas.

She's going through her desk, but she stops and sighs. "Just stay here, Mr. Parker. I need to go to the office, so I'll be right back. Sit in the front row, please."

He does as she says, and she steps out of the classroom.

Jacob gives me an expectant look. "Anyway, it'd be great if you could go tomorrow."

"Um, sure, I'll go," I say, mostly to get him off my back.

His arms wrap around me before I can dodge them. Once they're around me, I feel a sense of comfort and instantly regret saying yes to going to his game. "Awesome. I'll see you then."

As he's walking to the door, he glances at Dylan and a smirk appears on his face. It bothers me slightly, but it's best if I focus on finishing the paper and not on either of them.

As I'm formatting the second to last page, I hear Dylan's voice next to me.

"What's this?"

His chair is close to mine, and his attention is on my computer.

"The school newspaper. I have to finish this before I leave," I say. "What are you doing here?"

"Detention." He shrugs.

Mrs. Thomas is a freshman English teacher as well as the journalism teacher. I can't imagine how Dylan got detention from her.

"What class do you have with Mrs. Thomas?"

"Advisory. Apparently, she doesn't like me and Reece talking."

"Why isn't Reece here?"

"I guess I was doing more talking than him. That bastard owes me."

I shake my head, not really surprised. "Mrs. Thomas is the nicest teacher in this school, and you managed to get detention from her. Really, Dylan?"

96

"Gotta keep up my reputation somehow," he says with a wink.

I start to format again, and I can feel Dylan watching my screen as I move articles and pictures around. An article Jacob has written, predictably about the soccer team, is on my screen as I put it with the other articles in the sports section.

"What's up with you and Mr. Soccer Player? You two back together?" he asks suddenly.

That's what he wants to talk about? "No. We're just friends."

"Didn't look like you guys were just friends."

His comment annoys me. Could neither boy go one second without making comments about the other, and why do I have to be caught in the middle? I'm being judged by Jacob for hanging out with Dylan, and I'm being judged by Dylan for talking to Jacob.

It's like I'm being interrogated for doing something wrong. "Jesus, Dylan, you're sounding an awful lot like Jacob right now."

That seems to strike a nerve in him. "I'm not like that asshole. I just don't see why you would get back together with a guy who cheated on you."

"We're not even back together. He's going through a rough time, so I'm helping him out." Why is he getting so upset over nothing?

He scoffs. "I can put two and two together, Lacey. He doesn't deserve your help. What kind of piece of shit cheats on his girlfriend after her parents die?"

Anger boils over. "Why do you even care? It's my fucking business, not yours," I snap. Why is everyone suddenly concerned about what I am doing in my life?

We stare each other down for a moment before Mrs. Thomas walks in.

"Mr. Parker, leave Lacey alone. Get back to the front," she says.

He continues to stare at me before pushing the chair back and walking to the front again.

I continue working on the paper once I push the argument out of my mind. I put the finishing touches before I log off and pick up my things.

"Done, Lacey?" Mrs. Thomas asks me.

"Yeah, I just emailed it to you," I say, putting on my best smile and ignoring Dylan.

"Great, have a good weekend."

I'm not sure what made me snap at Dylan the way I did. I feel a sense of protectiveness over Jacob. I don't like that those feelings returned so quickly. It's like I was defending him; that's the exact opposite of moving on.

I let Jacob get to me when I called him Jake. It's like I can't control my own emotions when I'm with him. What's wrong with me?

While I'm in my car, I put my bag in the backseat and notice a red car pull up near the front of the parking lot.

A girl steps out of the car and leans against it. She has long brown hair that's curled at the ends. She's wearing a pair of high waisted shorts with a crop top tee that's tied in the middle. She crosses her arms, seemingly waiting for someone or something.

I ignore the girl until I see Dylan walking out of the main building and head straight for her. She smiles when she sees him, and when he's close enough to her, he pulls her in for a kiss that's long enough to make me look away. I know I shouldn't be watching them, but I can't help it. Dylan having a girlfriend is news to me.

Her flirty smile gives away why Dylan likes her. She's beautiful. He's holding her waist while they talk, before he kisses her again. They part and he jogs around to the passenger's side to get into the car with her. They drive off, and I finally tear my eyes away from them.

My mind drifts to Dylan and his girlfriend as I try to fall asleep that night. It makes sense as to why he's on his phone so much. He's probably been texting her this whole time.

I miss the times when Jacob would text me cute messages in the mornings and at night. I miss the giddiness I felt before we went out on a date. I want what Dylan has.

Happiness.

I miss everything I had before all the bad things happened. Hating the universe for taking my parents from me put me in a dark place over the summer. I don't want to go back there. Part of me feels like I wouldn't have gone there if I had Jacob, but the other part of me feels it was better for him not to be there.

I don't know what to think.

*   *   *

It's Saturday, and I feel the need to go to Jacob's game. I won't tell Casey where I'm going because I know I won't hear the end of it. It's probably going to be a stupid choice, but something drives me there.

When I park in the dirt lot near the soccer fields, I take a deep breath and get out. A rush of memories hit me like a truck, and it feels both soothing and discomforting. The game has already started, so I make my way to the bleachers and sit near the spot I used to sit at.

I glance over the other fans and spot Jacob's mom sitting in the same row as me. She has her hands clasped together as she watches the game intently. I wonder if I should say hi or if I should stay in my own bubble. I don't know if he has told his parents why we've broken up. If he has lied and blamed it all on me, she might be upset with me.

Making up my mind, I walk over to her. She does a double take when she sees me and a smile spreads across her face, which is a good thing.

99

"Lacey!" she yells in her high-pitched voice. "Come over here! Look at you, you're stunning!"

I feel myself blushing and give her a quick hug. "It's good to see you again." I almost call her Mrs. Fields, but then I remember the separation and I'm not sure if she wants to be called that. She pats the spot next to her and I sit.

"I wasn't expecting to see you here." Her eyes glimmer. She always gave me that look while Jacob and I were together.

"Jacob invited me."

"Well, I'm glad you're here. These games always make me a nervous wreck, especially against city rivals."

"Yeah, they're tough."

She gives me a serious look. "Oh, honey. How are you holding up? We didn't see much of you after the funeral . . ."

Do we have to talk about it? I keep it short and simple. "Yeah, I'm fine. I'm with my aunt right now."

"Well, if it weren't for her, I would've taken you in myself." She smiles. "When Jacob told us you two had broken up, I was so shocked. I wasn't expecting it."

"Yeah, I wasn't either," I say. Him not telling them why we've broken up just shows how cowardly he can be.

"What happened, honey? Did you two grow apart?"

One of my pet peeves with her is her constant questioning. She has to know everything about anything about everyone. I'll be honest with her. "Not really. Jacob cheated on me."

Her eyes nearly pop out of her head.

"I was the one who ended it. People were talking about it at school before he admitted it. I didn't want to stay with him after that."

"I had no idea, honey," she says, opening and closing her mouth. "I'm sorry."

I shrug in response.

She scowls instantly, and I think for a moment that she's going to call me a liar. "I'll talk to him. Clearly, the apple doesn't fall far from the tree."

That's a hint as to why his parents are separating. Did Mr. Fields cheat on her? That would be incredibly ironic.

We drop the subject and try to cheer Jacob on. Mrs. Fields doesn't cheer as much as she usually does, and I wonder if it has anything to do with what I've told her.

The game goes by fairly quickly, with Jacob scoring to win the game. We walk down to wait for the team. When the team finishes their meeting, Jacob makes his way to us.

"My best girls," he says.

More memories come to mind.

"She didn't talk your ear off, did she?" Jacob asks me, laughing.

She points a finger at him. "Don't get on my bad side. We have some things to talk about at home."

I smirk and he instantly diverts his attention to me. When he gives me the death glare, I shrug casually. His mom deserves to know the truth, since he clearly hasn't told her.

She sighs and checks her watch. "I still have to go grocery shopping. I'll see you at home." She wraps her arms around me and squeezes. "Honey, you can stop by anytime you want. You're always welcome."

"Thank you." I hug her back.

Jacob looks less than pleased after she's gone. "You told my mom why we broke up?"

"You didn't? What did you tell her all these months?" I shoot back.

"I avoided the conversation as much as possible." He rubs his face. "I guess she had to know sooner or later."

It isn't really my problem.

"How was the game? You still remember all the rules?" He nudges my arm.

"Please. I taught you the rules." I played soccer in middle school, but it didn't interest me beyond that. Without rose-colored glasses on, he's an average player.

He laughs, and I can't help but laugh too. It feels good to hang out with him again.

"What are you going to do now?" he asks.

"Probably head home. Do some homework."

"Oh, okay," he says. "I'll walk you to your car."

As he waves to his friends, some of them wave to me and I feel like I belong again. It makes me wonder why none of them asked if I was okay after everything that happened with Jacob. I guess it shows where their loyalty truly lies with.

While walking to my car, Jacob is noticeably quiet.

"What's up with you? You guys won, you should be happy," I tell him. He's usually pumped up after a win.

"I am." He nods. "I'm just thinking."

"About?"

"You."

"Oh." This conversation is starting to go downhill.

He scratches the back of his neck. "It was awesome seeing you in the stands again."

I let out a nervous laugh. "Well, what are friends for?" This conversation is going in a direction I'm not sure I want it to go.

"Yeah," he says as we walk up to my car. He puts his hand on it, and I know this conversation isn't over yet by that gesture. "I gotta talk to you about that."

Uh oh. "Okay."

"It's so fucking hard to be just friends with you. Like today, for a split second, I forgot we weren't together because it felt like old times," he says. "I don't know what to do."

I don't know what to do either. Old feelings are resurfacing from the memories I have sitting in the bleachers, no matter how hard I try to push them away. There's a part of me that is wary

102

about being with him again. Will he cheat on me again if I give him a second chance? Can I trust him again? "Jacob . . ."

"I know, I know. You're never getting back together with me. It's just damn hard to accept." His eyes are deep into mine, and I feel my knees go weak slightly.

"I don't know what to say." Looking into his eyes is difficult. When I look into them, it's like nothing has changed between us.

His hand is soft on mine as he flips it over to look at the tattoo on my wrist. "What I said to you after we got these probably means shit to you now, but I'm glad you didn't cover it up."

We're treading in a territory that is not good for my health right now. I need to get out of here. "I have to get home." I take my hand away from him.

"Do you still have feelings for me?" he asks suddenly. "I feel like you do. You called me Jake yesterday, which you haven't done in a while."

"That was a slip up. I don't know why I said it." I need to leave before I do something stupid.

"Bullshit. I know you, Lace. Just let me back in."

"Let you back in?" I repeat, shaking my head. "So you can hurt me again?"

He holds my hands to his chest. "Look at me."

I try not to, but I can't help it. His eyes remind me of the day he asked me to be his girlfriend and I fall for them again.

He leans down and presses his lips on mine. The familiar feeling of his lips takes me back to the first time we kissed and all the times we kissed after that. For a minute, everything is okay again.

CHAPTER SEVEN

I'm not sure how to go about the rest of my life knowing I kissed my ex who cheated on me right after my parents died. How do I do it? How do I recover?

My mom, if she's watching over me somehow, is probably pissed at me.

I've managed to successfully avoid Jacob for the rest of the weekend. Monday will be a different story. I'll have to face him in class, and I don't know what I'll say to him.

He's sent me text after text over the weekend, and I've ignored every single one of them. He wants to talk about what happened, and I'm not ready. I'm angry at myself for kissing him back. Even though it didn't feel like it at that moment, what I've done is still a big mistake.

When I park in the campus parking lot on Monday, I remain in my car, gripping the steering wheel. Maybe this is one of those necessary times to skip like Dylan said. Is it acceptable to skip more than one class? I need a whole day off just to think things through. This is a problem I can't deal with while seeing Jacob.

A knock on my window makes me jump out of my skin. Dylan is standing behind the window, and I try to calm myself as I roll the window down.

"You're staring off into space, and it looks like you might break your steering wheel off," he says. I wonder if he has decided to forget the argument we've had on Friday.

"I—" I don't know what to say. He looks at me expectantly. "It was a long weekend."

"I can tell." He puts his arm on my car and peers in. "We should probably head in before we're late."

"Right." I roll the window back up, shut the car off, and grab my bag. Dylan waits for me as I get out and lock my car. I don't wait for him though, as I walk ahead of him.

I hear him laugh behind me. "Is your dress inside out, or is the tag supposed to stick out like that?"

My red striped t-shirt dress looks the same inside and out. Did I really put it on wrong this morning? I reach for the tag instantly, which is sticking out, then feel the seams, which are facing out instead of in. "Perfect," I mutter.

"I guess it really was a long weekend." Dylan chuckles.

"I have to go change."

"You're welcome to change right here." His smile turns mischievous.

I narrow my eyes at him. "Aren't you mad at me?" It's strange that he's acting normal again.

"About that," he says. "It wasn't my place to butt in. After the things you've told me about him, I guess I was trying to look out for you, and it didn't come out how I wanted."

I raise a brow. "Are you apologizing?"

He scoffs. I should've known better than to ask. "I never apologize. I still think he's a piece of shit."

"Fair enough." I shrug. I can't help but also feel guilty for the things I said to him. "I'm sorry for snapping at you. Friends?"

"Friends."

The image of him and that girl enters my mind and I want to ask him about her, but we're already in the main building and I need to fix my dress situation. "I'll see you in class."

"Later," he says, walking off.

I meet up with Casey in the cafeteria for lunch. I have to tell her about the incident with Jacob. I dug myself into a hole that I can't get out of, and I'm in desperate need of her help. She won't be happy with the choices I've made without her again.

Casey sits down with her food across from me and smiles. "I feel like I haven't seen you in forever."

"It has been forever, and a lot has happened that I need to tell you." As soon as I say it, she leans in closer.

"I'm all ears."

I start by telling her about me accepting Jacob's invitation to the soccer game. She makes a face of disapproval but stays silent as I tell her about the events that happened after the game. Then comes the part about the kiss and how I kissed him back.

She smacks her forehead. "What the hell have you done?"

"I know!" I say, pushing my hair out of my face. "I got caught up in the moment!"

"That clearly means this friendship, which you said would help you move on, is not working. It's obvious he wants to be more than friends again."

"I have class with him later. I don't even want to see him," I say, picking at my food that no longer looks appealing.

"You gotta make a choice now." She shrugs. "Either you admit to yourself that you still have feelings for him and go back to him, or you delete him from your life completely and move on." She leans closer to me. "Like you should've done in the first place."

"Well, you clearly aren't biased," I say sarcastically.

"He broke your heart after you lost your parents," she says, giving me a deadpan look. "Of course I don't want you to get back together with him."

I can't make a choice right then. It's too sudden, too daunting of a task. I want to explain yet again how I feel, but it's redundant. We'll repeat this conversation over and over, and I still wouldn't make up my mind.

We finish our lunch and head for class. I'm eager to get to English, so I can see Dylan. I feel a sense of relief that we're on good terms again.

106

He's in his spot already when I enter the classroom. He smiles as I sit in my seat. "Good lunch?"

"Very good," I say. "Nothing like eating high-quality cafeteria food." Even though I didn't really touch it.

"And here I thought your new favorite thing was going to get ice cream for lunch."

"Obviously, I can't get ice cream without you." I laugh.

"You're a quick learner." The smirk on his face makes my cheeks warm.

I suddenly feel guilty when that girl he was with comes to mind. What if he's taken and I am being flirty? An icky feeling takes over me.

Class starts and I face forward, but my mind is still wandering. Dylan seems to be a private person, not exactly an open book. Will he tell me he has a girlfriend if I get too flirty with him, or does he have a serious disregard for the fact that he's in a relationship?

We don't talk much in class. Mrs. Beattie has us doing individual work again and it's more reading than actual activities. Towards the end of class, my phone buzzes in my pocket. I sneakily pull it out and scan over the message that's on the screen. It's from Dylan.

Skipping next period to go to Raven's. U wanna go?

My heart flutters a bit when I read it. Do I really want to miss journalism to go with him? I text him back.

Maybe. Idk.

If I miss journalism, that means there will be more work on my plate. If I don't skip, I'll have to deal with Jacob.

Everyone shoots up to leave when the bell rings. Dylan and I walk out of class together, and he waits for me to give him an answer. "Well?"

"Hold on," I say as I peek inside Mrs. Thomas's classroom from a distance. Jacob is already sitting in his spot along with Will and Vicky. Dylan peers in as well.

"You wanna see him?" he asks.

"Not really. Let's go." Seeing Jacob will only make things worse for me. I can't see him without replaying the kiss in my mind, and I want to forget it ever happened. I don't know if I can trust him again, and that's the only thing that's stopping me from being with him again.

A smile forms on Dylan's face, and he motions for us to go. "We gotta hurry."

We're speed walking towards the exit and Dylan slows. "Fuck," he mutters.

"What's wrong?" If we're in a hurry, then we need to leave right now.

"I got dropped off this morning. I can't drive us."

I have the feeling that girl dropped him off. I yank my keys out of my bag and flash them in front of him. "I can. Now let's get going."

"You better be an impeccable driver. I don't want to die a teenager," he says as we approach my car.

"I guess you'll find out."

While driving, I notice Dylan looking around my car. "Glad to see you're not one of those people who has random shit in their cars."

"I don't like clutter." I wish my life is as organized as my car. That would make things a whole lot easier.

Dylan is silent the rest of the way to Raven's. I wonder what's on his mind. Is he thinking about that girl? Should I ask about her?

Only a couple of cars are in the parking lot at Raven's as I park in the front.

"Are Derrick and Jared playing?" I ask as we near the entrance.

"Yeah, but a little bit later. Maybe you'll get to see them," Dylan says as he holds the door open for me. "After you."

I immediately see Reece, Carlos, and Anthony sitting at a nearby table. We make our way over, and the boys all smile when we're close enough.

"Look who decided to join in," Anthony says, opening his arms. "I think this calls for a hug."

I go in for the hug, and Anthony lifts me off the ground. I can't stop myself from laughing as he puts me down. "What was that for?" I ask him.

"You've officially joined our group," he says, looking at the guys with a look I can't decipher.

"I give her 'til the end of the night." Carlos smirks.

"Well, as long as you don't fucking scare her off." Anthony rolls his eyes.

Dylan shakes his head as he sits next to me. "You guys are already scaring her off."

"I'm surprised you haven't yet," Anthony says, shoving his shoulder then looking at me. "How can you stand him?"

"He has his moments." I smile at Dylan.

A smile plays at his lips, but he doesn't meet my eyes.

Reece squeezes Dylan's cheek. "Aw, what a sweetheart," he says with a high-pitched voice.

"Oh, fuck off." Dylan pushes Reece's hand away, though he's smiling. "Are Derrick and Jared in the back?"

Reece nods. "I think they're rehearsing."

Dylan stands up. "I'll be right back," he tells me.

As soon as he disappears behind the door, Carlos speaks up. "Dylan's in a good fucking mood."

"It's because Lacey's here." Reece smirks as the others snicker.

There's no way I put Dylan in a good mood. "Dylan's mood has nothing to do with me. Maybe it's someone else." I only say it to see if they know about that girl. Maybe I can get something out of them.

Anthony scoffs. "I highly doubt it."

Just when I think I'm not going to get any juicy information, Reece says, "What if he hooked up with that one chick?"

The conversation takes an interesting turn. I grab my phone to make it seem like I'm uninterested, but I'm all ears.

"I hope not," Carlos says. "Fuck her."

"Maybe he already did?" Anthony scowls and I can't help but wonder what's so bad about this girl?

It isn't quite where I thought the conversation would go. I'd rather not hear about Dylan's activities outside of school. "You guys are gross," I tell them.

Anthony smirks and nudges my shoulder. "Jealous much?"

"Not at all." I cross my arms. Whatever Dylan does with that girl is his business, and we don't need to make assumptions about what they do together. Even if I'm slightly curious about who she is.

"Who's jealous?" Dylan asks, sitting back down.

Anthony just gives me a look and ignores Dylan. The guys start talking about bands that have played at Raven's in the past. Somewhere along the conversation, Dylan starts checking his phone constantly. He is clearly texting someone, but I try not to be too nosy.

The afternoon continues, and more people show up. A band starts to play, but they don't seem well-rehearsed. They look about our age, maybe younger.

"When are Derrick and Jared going on?" I ask Dylan.

"Probably after the next band," he says, not looking away from his phone.

He's preoccupied with whoever he's texting to, so I turn to Anthony. "What do you think of Derrick and Jared?"

Anthony angles his body towards me. "I think they're pretty good. They mostly cover other songs that I don't really listen to, but yeah, they're cool."

"What do they play?"

"Rock, classic rock, and some alternative." He leans in closer. "The alternative sucks, but Derrick is my cousin, so I have to support the shit he likes."

I let out a laugh. "And Jared?"

"Yeah, I guess I support him too." He chuckles. "A record label looked at them about a month ago, but they haven't heard anything back."

"That's amazing." They must be great if someone from a record label came see them. My interest is piqued, and I'm growing more and more excited to see them perform.

"Hey, boys." An unfamiliar voice reaches us.

We all whip our heads to see who's talking. Standing behind Dylan is the girl who picked him up on Friday. Her long hair is pin-straight, and her makeup is flawless. She places her hand on Dylan's shoulder and smiles down at him.

"Guys, you remember Kay, right?" Dylan asks them and seems to avoid looking at me.

None of them really respond, just a couple of nods. It's almost like they don't want to acknowledge her at all. Reece and Carlos immediately strike up their own conversation, and Anthony zeroes in on his phone.

Kay noticeably looks me up and down. "And you are?"

Her tone doesn't sit well with me, but I understand where she's coming from.

Dylan speaks up before I can say anything. "This is my friend, Lacey."

111

She doesn't look impressed, but I smile at her anyway. "It's nice to meet you."

"You too." She smiles back. There's something about her that's sweet, but a sickly kind of sweet. Like when you eat candy after candy and get a stomach ache afterwards.

She plops down on Dylan's lap and puts her arm around him. "I missed you," she says to him.

He gently pushes her off his lap and stands up. "Let's get out of here," he says, trying to keep his voice low.

"Leaving so soon?" Anthony asks him.

"I'll be right back," he says, then turns his attention to me. "Don't wait up on me if it gets late."

"Wasn't going to," I say. It comes out a bit harsh, but I don't care. Why did he invite me if he is just going to leave with her and miss his brother's performance?

I mean, if she's his girlfriend, then it makes sense, but it still irks me.

They walk out of Raven's and Carlos whistles. "Does Dylan not fucking think sometimes?"

What does he mean?

Anthony pats his hands on the table. "It's Dylan we're talking about. Does he ever?"

"What's wrong with her?" I ask, wanting to be in on the gossip.

They all give each other weird looks before Anthony says, "Kay just isn't the best person for Dylan to get mixed up with."

I want to ask why, but I figure I'll only get another vague answer.

"You're not going to leave now that Dylan is gone, are you?" Anthony asks me.

Dylan doesn't dictate how I spend my time. His friends have accepted me, at least I think they have, so there's no harm in hanging out with them. "No, I'll stay to watch Derrick and Jared."

"Atta girl." Carlos grins.

112

We watch the next band play and they're pretty good. They got the crowd to sing along, and singing idiotically with the rest of the guys is more fun than I thought it would be.

Max gets up on stage and introduces Derrick and Jared. We all cheer for them, the guys whooping and hollering more than they did for the other bands.

Derrick sits on a stool with his guitar and Jared stands in front of the microphone. He adjusts it before smiling and speaking. "I hope everyone is in the mood for some Black Keys tonight." Everyone cheers and they start to sing and play.

Jared's voice is so nice it surprises me, and Derrick's voice pops in at the right moments to resonate beautifully with him. They're clearly more rehearsed than the other bands, which to me shows their maturity and seriousness.

They finish their set, which is about five songs long, and jump off stage excitedly. They say hi to a few people then walk over to our table.

"Great show, guys," Anthony tells them. I can tell that he's a lot more supportive of them than he let on.

Derrick gives them all high fives before looking at me. "Hey . . . Lacey, right?"

"That's me."

"No Dylan? Did you get rid of him?" He laughs as he sits down. Jared pulls up a chair next to him.

"Fuck him. He missed a hell of a show," Anthony says.

Jared downs a bottle of water before putting the cap back on and setting it down in front of him. "I think this is my favorite set we've played. The place is pretty alive for a Monday show."

When he says Monday, I look down at my phone and see that it's nearing eight o'clock. I'll have to head home.

"I should be going soon," I say to Anthony.

Reece hears me and perks up. "You're leaving, Lacey?"

I nod. "I gotta get home."

113

"Thanks for staying to watch us," Derrick says. "I know Dylan disappeared, but we're glad you're here."

At that point, I really do feel accepted. This gives me confidence to hang out with them more without Dylan. "No problem. Who needs him anyway?" I joke.

"I'll walk you out," Derrick says after I say my goodbyes to everyone. "There are too many weirdos around here."

He watches me get into my car and waves when I drive away with a smile on my face.

After I get home, I eat a quick dinner, which consists of leftovers, then hole myself up in my room to do homework. In the middle of listening to music and finishing my English homework, my phone starts buzzing. The only person who calls at nine in the evening is Casey, so I immediately answer it.

"If you're going to ask if ice cream is an appropriate meal at this time, then the answer is yes," I say, sitting up in my bed.

"So, it's okay to eat ice cream right now, but not for lunch? That's some backwards logic you have there," Dylan's voice comes through instead.

His voice surprises me. I didn't expect him to call. "I thought you were Casey," I say, smiling. Why is he calling me so late?

"If that means I'm labeled as Best Friend on your phone, then it's definitely okay." He chuckles.

"Sorry to burst your bubble, but you're not." I pause. "So, what's up?"

I hear shuffling on the other side before he says, "I was just wondering what you thought of Derrick and Jared's performance. The guys said you had fun."

It's a little upsetting that he left me by myself at Raven's, but that didn't completely kill the vibes that Derrick and Jared sent off while performing. "I had a great time. Derrick and Jared killed it," I say. Being around a bunch of guys was a little intimidating, but they made sure I was having fun and wasn't uncomfortable.

"Yeah, they always put on a good show."

"What about you? How was your night?" It's an innocent question, but I hope he tells me about Kay. The guys say Dylan shouldn't get involved with her, but I wonder why?

The line is quiet before he speaks. "It was alright."

Not the answer I wanted. Maybe if I open up to him more, he'll do the same. We're friends, and friends tell each other personal things. I debate with myself over telling him about Jacob, and ultimately I think he can help me decide what to do. It's a bit of a reach to try to get him to open up, but it's worth a shot. "Can I tell you something?"

"Yeah, sure."

"I've talked to Casey about this, but it's gotten to the point where we've talked about it too much and her help isn't helping. Not that I don't appreciate her help, because I do. This might be too girly of a topic to talk about with you, but I kind of need an outside opinion." Hopefully that makes sense to him.

"Okay. Continue."

Here goes nothing. "So, you know Jacob cheated on me after my parents . . ."

"Right," he says.

I take a deep breath. "It's just . . . everything was so sudden. I didn't expect to lose my parents, and I definitely didn't expect to lose the one person who I thought would help me through it all, you know? I dumped him as soon as I found out he cheated and didn't talk to him at all until the first day of school.

"I thought I could put everything behind me and move on. Instead, it was like everything I thought I pushed away came right back. I figured becoming friends with him would help me move on."

"That isn't working, is it?"

"Not exactly." I can't believe I'm about to tell him this. "I went to his soccer game last Saturday. His parents are having issues, so he wanted some extra support. I didn't think it'd be a big deal. I saw his mom and we got to talking like it was old times. After the game, Jacob said he still has feelings for me and one thing led to another and he kissed me—and I kissed him back."

Dylan's end is quiet, and for a second, I think he fell asleep. "Why did you kiss him back?" he finally asks.

I let out a long sigh. "I guess I got caught up in the moment." A feeling of frustration comes over me. "I know he cheated on me, but it pisses me off that he could just switch off his feelings long enough to sleep with that girl. As if I wouldn't find out or care.

"I know I should be completely done with him, but in a way, he makes me feel closer to my parents somehow. He used to come to my house all the time, and my parents loved him. It sucks that they'll never know what he did to me, and it sucks that it's never really over for me."

Letting it all out feels nice, and I hope Dylan sees where I'm coming from.

"I know I was upset with you last week about being friends with that douchebag, but I think I understand," he says.

"Casey has been telling me to drop him, obviously because she hates him. It's not that simple or easy for me. I can't hate him or forget him, but I also feel stuck in an endless cycle with him."

A sigh comes from him. "Listen, Lace, I'm not good at this kind of stuff. Me and the guys don't talk about our relationship problems regularly."

My heart drops and disappointment washes over me. I shake my head. "Right, yeah. I didn't mean to dump all of that on you."

"No, no. I didn't mean it like that," he says quickly. "I'm trying to say that we aren't poster boys for perfect relationships. We've all done some shitty things to girls. I just want to tell you that while I'm not the best person to take advice from, if I were you, I'd still try my best to move on."

It would all be so easy if I didn't crumble everytime I see Jacob. "I'm trying, but nothing seems to be working."

"Well, for one, you need to stop being his friend. That was a horrible idea."

"Fine, fine."

"And he wasn't the only one who knew your parents. I'm assuming Casey knew them pretty well. Your aunt can probably help too when you're missing them."

The thought of Dylan meeting my parents crosses my mind and part of me wishes he got the chance to meet them.

"You're right," I tell him. I can't believe I never noticed how much I depended on Jacob for these things. The way I was connected to everything through him.

"I'll help you as much as I can, but only if you're serious about it. I don't want to waste my time if you're just going to run back to him, only to get hurt again."

It's going to be hard, but I need to move on. Jacob is clearly not the right person for me. "I'm serious."

"Okay. Mission Move-the-Fuck-On is a go."

I laugh. "Thanks, Dylan. It means a lot." Somehow, I know he will make me feel better about the whole situation, not that Casey hasn't because she absolutely helped me feel more confident.

"No problem."

I'm getting ready to say goodnight when he speaks up again. "Hey, since we're having a moment or whatever, I just want to tell you that girl Kay and I aren't dating or anything. It's more of a friends with benefits kinda thing."

So she isn't his girlfriend. Noted, but I'm still curious about why the guys don't like him being with her. That's clearly a conversation for another day. "You know, a friend with benefits situation usually results in someone having feelings for the other, right?"

"Yeah, well, we'll see about that."

"Just be careful, Dylan Parker. I don't think the world can handle a mini-Dylan right now," I tease him.

He lets out a laugh. "Oh, trust me. I know."

"Good." The conversation is dying down, and I don't know what else to say. I want to know more about Kay, how they met, and why he's in this situation with her, but I stop myself.

"I'll let you get back to whatever you were doing," he says.

"Just English homework."

"Shit, we have homework?"

"Get working, Dylan. I'll see you tomorrow," I tell him, laughing.

"Goodnight, Lace."

CHAPTER EIGHT

Tuesday morning goes by fairly quickly. I'm sitting in English with a knot in my stomach, knowing I'll have to face Jacob. I'm still not ready. However, the newspaper needs to get done, and I'm not going to let him stop me from finishing it. I'll focus on that and stand my ground.

I'm hesitant to leave when class ends. Dylan walks out with me and nudges my arm.

"Just do your best to ignore him," he tells me like it's the most obvious thing in the world.

"I'm going to focus on the paper and nothing else," I declare, mostly to myself. I inhale a deep breath when I see the classroom before turning to face Dylan. "I can do this."

His eyes are on something behind me. "You better be. He's about to walk in."

Just as I turn around, I catch Jacob's eye before he walks into Mrs. Thomas's classroom. His eyes flutter between me and Dylan before he stalks inside.

"He always looks so happy to see me," Dylan jokes. "I'm pretty sure I make his day so much better."

I laugh but I know Jacob will only get irritated by Dylan's presence. "Yeah, you put him in a real great mood."

"Well, I gotta get to class. You got this." He gives me one last encouraging nudge.

119

I can't help but feel butterflies in my stomach. I'm not sure if they're caused by Dylan or by my nervousness to see Jacob. As I walk in, Sophie appears in front of me.

"Hey, we missed you yesterday," she says as her eyes brighten. "Luckily for you, I was done with all of my work, so I worked on your stuff for a bit. It's not much, just a couple of pages."

I breathe a sigh of relief. "That's the best news I've heard all day. I really appreciate it."

"No problem." She shrugs. "My editing skills aren't as good as yours, so you'll probably have to fix a couple of things, but I tried."

"That's perfectly fine with me." I smile at her. "How much is left?"

She twists her face as she thinks about it. "Three pages, if I'm remembering correctly. Then one more ad needs to be put in."

"One step closer to publishing this one." I hold up my hand and she gives me a high five. "You're a lifesaver, Soph."

She smiles. "It's no big deal."

I make my way over to the computers in the back and sit down. Ignoring Jacob, who is in his usual spot next to me, I log in.

"Well, hello to you too," Jacob says. He's looking at his computer screen instead of me.

Will and Vicky are sitting down and I smile at them. "Hey guys." Dismissing Jacob will only make him angrier, and I'm hoping if I make him mad enough he won't want to talk to me at all.

Will looks at me strangely. "Hey, Lacey."

"Ha-ha, very funny," Jacob says behind me. "Why are you ignoring me?"

"I don't want to talk about it, so let's just get to work," I reply. I open my files and find the pages Sophie formatted for me.

Jacob actually listens to me for once and stays silent. I finish the pages Sophie didn't get to before formatting the pages Will did. I insert one last quarter page ad and realize Will has inserted an ad from a company that doesn't even exist anymore. I shake my head and instead of scolding him over it, I just take it out and restructure the page it has been placed in.

Once I have everything done, I scroll through one last time before emailing it to Mrs. Thomas.

"So, what now?" Will asks me.

"Now we wait for Mrs. Thomas to proofread it. If it's perfect, then we'll place it on the online website for the paper. Then, we send it to the printers and distribute them throughout the school. After that, we start the whole process over again for the next issue," I explain. I'm excited to see it all come together, especially since it's my turn being Senior Editor.

Will seems to be excited too and he begins talking to Vicky about how it'll come out.

At the end of class, I pick up my things and start to follow everyone out into the hallway. I try to rush out of there before Jacob tries to talk to me, but he catches my arm and tugs me back.

"We need to talk," he says.

I jerk my arm away. "We really don't." I need to be firm. Be firm.

His face twists into a frown. "You don't even want to talk about what happened last Saturday? Or the fact that you've obviously been avoiding me?"

Instead of answering, I push past him and make my way down the hallway. There's so much I want to say to him, but everything is getting jumbled in my mind. Nothing is making sense; nothing is clear.

He ends up following and walking alongside me. "You can't just stop talking to me. I know you still feel something for me because you would've pushed me away if you didn't," he says, stepping in front of me. "I know you're pissed at yourself because you kissed me. I know that, but there are feelings there. I just need another chance. Things will work out this time around."

Things will work out? "I was at your game to support you, like friends do," I stress. "You broke the simple rules I gave you. I told you I didn't want you back, and you still overstepped that boundary."

"What boundary? You're clearly still in love with me," he says, raising his voice. "I don't see what the problem is."

I know in my heart that I still have feelings for him, no matter what I try to do to stop them from resurfacing. The plan I've formulated to stop my feelings is crumbling. If I get back together with him, I will always doubt his feelings. I don't want to be manipulated into getting hurt again.

"The problem is, you did this after I just lost my parents," my voice raises in response. "You don't even seem to care about that."

I can see the hurt in his eyes. "I do care. I loved your parents," he says before sighing. "I know you better than anyone else. We can help each other get through all the shit in our lives. Just push past that pride of yours and give me another chance."

Pride? "This has nothing to do with pride, Jacob. My words are not getting through your thick skull."

"Everything okay here?" Dylan asks, appearing next to me. I can see the frustration behind his eyes, and I know he's heard most of the conversation.

Jacob crosses his arms. "Of course, you'd be here. Can you just fuck off for once?"

Dylan moves in front of me and faces Jacob head on. "Lacey doesn't want to talk, so why don't you run along. Don't you have a ball to go kick around?"

Jacob smirks. "You have a crush on my girl, Parker? You think you actually have a chance with her?"

Both boys have their jaws clenched, and I chew on my lip nervously. Things are escalating quickly.

"You better back off before I punch those teeth out of your loud mouth," Dylan's voice goes low.

Just as I think things are going downhill, Anthony comes from behind me and stands next to Dylan. "We don't have a problem here, do we?" he asks, directing it to Jacob.

Jacob laughs at both of them and backs off. He peeks around them and says to me, "I thought you could fight your own battles, Lace. I know you're better than these two." With that, he turns around and starts walking down the hall.

Anthony scoffs. "What an ass."

Dylan has a strange expression on his face. "What happened to ignoring him?" he asks me, clearly irritated.

Maybe I'm not as strong as I thought I was. Even after the pep talks that Dylan and Casey have given me, I still can't do it. Will I ever let go of Jacob? "I know. He got to me," I say, avoiding his eyes.

"Am I missing something?" Anthony asks, glancing between us.

Dylan shakes his head. "Let's get out of here."

The three of us exit the building together, not talking. My mind is still trying to process what happened back there. I've never seen Jacob fight anyone. Could he take on Dylan? Part of me doubts it.

The familiar red car is sitting in front of the main building. On the driver's side, I can see Kay sitting there with a smile on her face.

Dylan's eyes scan over me and Anthony. "I'll see you guys later."

Anthony waves as Dylan gets into the car with Kay. Almost as soon as he shuts the door, the car takes off.

I wonder how Dylan really feels about Kay. Friends with benefits never works out, so I wonder if he'll end up developing feelings for her.

"Is it really just a friends with benefits thing?" I ask Anthony before I can stop myself. I didn't mean for it to come out, but my curiosity gets the better of me. Dylan and Kay are spending more time together than I originally thought.

Anthony smirks and shoves his hands into his front pockets. "Jealous much?"

"How many times do I have to say that Dylan and I are only friends? I'm just curious about her."

"Well, Dylan clearly told you they aren't dating, which is more than what he's told any of us."

I practically snort, though it's interesting that Dylan would tell me something he hasn't even told the guys. "You know just as well as I do that a friends with benefits situation never works out. Feelings happen."

Anthony is quiet for a second. "Her feelings will get in the way before his do."

"Why don't you guys like her?" I want more information and asking directly seems to be my best bet since I haven't gotten anything from being vague.

He doesn't give me a quick answer. "Dylan just has his priorities fucked." He starts walking to the parking lot, and I follow him.

Anthony's unclear answers are getting me nowhere. What does that even mean? What is Dylan not prioritizing?

"What's going on with you two?" he asks suddenly.

He says it like we're hiding something. "What do you mean?"

"If he's not with Kay, he's usually with you, which is a majority of the time."

I think about the times Dylan and I have hung out. I guess he's right. Dylan and I have only known each other for two weeks, but it feels like so much longer. "He's just trying to help me get over Jacob." He raises a brow. "Not like that." I don't think Dylan would ever like me anyhow. His type is definitely not me, judging by how Kay looks.

"You two are weird." He shakes his head as we reach my car. "Don't worry about Dylan. Kay is just a distraction."

"From?"

"A lot of things," he says hesitantly. "I gotta get out of here. I'll see you sometime this week. Maybe."

Anthony is very cryptic. He's like Dylan in that way, never giving full explanations of things and keeping secrets. I guess I have to be in the group longer to be let in on everything.

I want to know more about them. To outsiders, they seem to be the type of guys who go to underground fights or are involved in dangerous gang-related situations. I don't get that vibe from them, but I could be wrong.

*   *   *

When I met Casey in the third grade, I thought she was weirdly outspoken. She told everyone when she had to pee, talked about bugs that she'd seen outside her house, and wore jean overalls constantly.

In the fifth grade, a boy she liked told her she acted too much like a boy and said she even dressed like one. When middle school started, Casey had completely changed her look. Gone were the overall days and in were the sparkly skirts and curled hair.

The jean overall days were where some of my favorite memories happened. Once I learned to accept her weird tendencies, we became inseparable. I was upset when she changed her look just because a boy gave his stupid opinion about her. It still makes me upset whenever she feels heartbroken over some lame boy.

She finally talked to Tyler about the mishap at Dylan's party. It turns out that Tyler only invited her to the party to make his ex-girlfriend jealous. He was buzzed when he tried making a move on his ex, with Casey watching the whole thing. He explained that he didn't like her more than a friend, and that's when the chaos started.

125

She's leaning against the wall between her bedroom and bathroom as she tells me what they've talked about.

"I mean, I get the whole 'I'm trying to win my ex back' thing, but don't hurt another girl in the process, you know?" Casey says as she crosses her arms.

"He's clearly not worth your time," I tell her, making myself comfortable on her bed.

It's Friday night, and we don't know what to do other than talk about what's going on in our lives. I've already explained to her what happened with Jacob. Thankfully, he hasn't spoken to me in class since then.

I find myself thinking about what he has said to me about fighting my own battles. In this case, it makes sense. I've completely lost my self-control.

When he and I were together, there was no reason for me to fight my own battles because I never made choices for myself. It was always him who decided things. In the end, he still chose to cheat on me and I was forced to end the relationship.

"Well, we can either stay here, watch Disney movies, and cry or we can go out, do something, and still cry," Casey says. "You're staying over either way, right?"

I nod. "We can stay in, but I'm getting the feeling you don't want to."

She grins. "Do you know of any parties going on tonight?"

I give her a deadpan look. She knows better than to ask me about parties. I'm the last person to know.

"Right," she says. "Well, I'm going to pee, so you think about some options and I'll do the same." She closes the bathroom door behind her.

There's only so much to do in town. We could get ice cream, but we always do that.

My phone buzzes next to me, and an unsaved number pops up on my screen. It's a local number, so I answer.

"Hello?"

126

"What are you doing right at this very moment?"

I know that voice. "Anthony? I don't remember giving you my number." What is he calling me for?

"I stole it from Dylan the other day, and I'm glad I did."

He stole my number? "Why?"

"There's a rumor going around that someone from the record label is coming back to see Derrick and Jared play tonight."

I sit up against Casey's headboard. "No way."

"What did you say?" Casey asks from the bathroom.

Ignoring her, I listen to Anthony. "Yeah, so we're trying to get them more support than usual for their show, and Reece told me to call you."

Dylan didn't want to call me? Maybe he isn't there. "I'm at Casey's right now," I say just as she's coming out of the bathroom. She sits in front of me on the bed and gives me a quizzical look.

"Bring her. The more the merrier."

I look at Casey. "Are you up for some live music?" I can't see how she'll turn down live music, but I ask anyway.

She's intrigued. "Sure."

"We'll be there. What time?" I ask Anthony.

"They go on at nine."

"We'll see you there," I say before hanging up.

Casey makes herself more comfortable on her bed. "Where are we going?"

"Remember that place I told you about? Where Dylan took me?"

She nods.

"There. His brother's band is performing and someone from a record label is going to be watching them, so they're rallying more support for them," I explain. My mind drifts back to Dylan, and I wonder if he's with Kay. I have a strong feeling he is.

"That was Dylan?" she asks, raising her eyebrows.

"No." I shake my head. Instead of explaining, I glance at the time on my phone, which reads eight-fifteen. "We should probably start getting ready. They go on at nine."

Of course, I didn't know we'd be going out, so I don't have any nicer clothes to wear. Casey and I start digging through her closet for something to wear.

She's pulling out girlier options, and I'm trying to stop her. Girly is not the right attire for Raven's. She doesn't have any band t-shirts other than a One Direction shirt her cousin got at one of their concerts.

She ends up in a plain shirt with simple stripes and a jean skirt. I settle for some ripped jeans and an olive-green tank top. I throw my hair into a messy bun and call it done.

The parking lot is full when we get to Raven's, so I have to park somewhere along the street. I anxiously rub my hands together as we walk up to the door. If Derrick and Jared are getting looked at by a label for the second time, then it must be a good sign for them.

"This place is . . . different than I expected," Casey says as we walk through the door. "It's a good different, I think."

Before I can answer, I hear my name being called. I scan the room and see the boys sitting in the corner. I grab Casey's hand, so I won't lose her in the crowd. "C'mon."

We make our way over to the boys's table, and they smile as we approach them. It's the typical group sans Dylan.

"Look who made it!" Reece says excitedly. "And you brought a friend."

The only time they met Casey was at Dylan's party, when they watched over her while Dylan helped me dry off after falling into the pool.

"Casey, maybe you remember, but this is Reece, Carlos, and Anthony," I introduce her.

They wave to her and she waves back. Casey and I get comfy on some stools Anthony pulls up for us, and I look at him. "Are Derrick and Jared nervous?"

He shakes his head. "No way. They're ready to put on a good show."

"Where's Dylan?" Casey asks him. "I mean, it's his brother playing, right?"

Anthony's face changes. "I'm not sure if he can make it."

How can he not be here to support his brother? If I had a sibling pursuing something they dreamed of, I'd be there to support them one hundred percent of the time.

I guess Dylan doesn't have the same mindset as I do. He didn't even mention their show in class. He's hardly spoken to me all week.

I don't bother asking if he is with Kay. I know they're together.

More people enter the building as it's nearing nine o'clock. The noise level goes up, and Casey leans closer to me so I can hear her talk.

"What kind of music do they play?" she asks.

"Alternative, rock, and classic rock. They're really good."

Reece catches my attention. "Are you going to be singing along again?" he asks me.

"If you guys are, then yeah." I chuckle. I'm all for singing obnoxiously with them again.

Casey gives me a questioning look, and I only smile at her. It's fun introducing her to something new. She's usually the one getting me to go out and try new things; I take pride in knowing it's the opposite this time.

"Great, we get to hear Lacey sing offkey again." Carlos smirks.

I don't want to be the subject of jokes, so I shake off any uncertainty and say, "I don't know, Carlos, you might scare people off with your vocal chords."

Everyone snickers and Carlos seems to take the challenge. "Don't start what you can't finish, Lacey."

"I can finish. Can you?" I ask him, raising my eyebrow.

"You should hear Carlos sing *Love On the Brain*, that Rihanna song? He sings it pretty well when he's drunk," Reece snitches on him.

Casey and I laugh. I can only imagine what that must be like, especially coming from Carlos. "I bet I can do better," I can't help but say.

Anthony holds up his hands. "Okay, okay. Just kiss and make up."

Pushing on in my confidence, I blow Carlos a kiss. Reece whistles, and Carlos and Anthony laugh.

"That's all the action he's getting tonight," Anthony says and Carlos punches his arm.

"Who's getting action tonight?"

We all turn and find Dylan standing behind me. Next to him is Kay in a tight white crop top and slim jeans.

Anthony smirks at me before turning back to him. "Carlos is getting action from Lacey."

Carlos flips all of them off. "Yeah, more than any of you bastards."

There's no point in disputing. It's fun to play along.

Kay gives Casey a strange look and Casey does the same. "Hey, Kay," she says.

"Casey," Kay acknowledges her. "Didn't expect to see you here."

"I brought her with me," I speak up. How do they know each other? This is a twist my brain isn't ready for.

"You two know each other?" Dylan asks, practically reading my mind.

Kay takes his hand in hers. "Casey and I go way back."

How did I not know this? Casey is avoiding my eyes as more questions come to mind. I know I've never told Casey about

130

Dylan and Kay, but this is still a surprise. She's the last person I would expect to know Kay.

"Well, are you guys going to sit down, or what?" Anthony asks Dylan and Kay, changing the subject.

Dylan looks around, and I wonder if he's purposely not addressing me. "We'll grab a seat over there."

They walk over to a smaller table behind us, and I stare at Casey. "You know Kay?" I need answers now.

"Her family are friends with my family." She shrugs. "Why is she with Dylan?"

"I'll tell you later." I want to ask her why she got anxious around Kay, but it isn't the time for questions. I put it to the back of my mind for now.

Reece makes a funny face at Carlos before addressing the rest of us, "Anyway, the show is going to start soon."

"What does this record label person look like?" I ask all of them. Maybe we can watch their reaction to the performance.

"No idea," Anthony says. "Maybe he'll be in a suit."

"Or maybe a she," I point out. *Or they if we want to journey into the nonbinary realm.*

"Or maybe he'll look like some scrub off the street," Reece says. "It's hard to tell."

"Which could be anyone in here," Casey says to me, glancing around.

Max climbs onto the stage, announces Derrick and Jared, and everyone claps for them. I sneak a glance at Dylan and Kay. Kay is on her phone while Dylan is watching the stage intently.

His eyes meet mine, and instead of looking away, I smile at him. His serious expression breaks and he smiles back.

Carlos watches me teasingly before I focus my attention back on the stage. He winks at me before shifting his gaze.

These boys will probably be the death of me. I have a feeling their strange stares and crazy personalities are only the tip of the iceberg.

The music starts and it doesn't sound like anything I've heard before. It's upbeat and energetic, with Derrick doing a little more singing this time around. It fills me with some kind of joy that they're being pursued by a label who likes their style. It's huge.

"I think they wrote this song," Anthony interrupts my thoughts.

It makes sense that they would break out their original songs. Proving they can write their own music is probably a plus.

Casey is dancing in her chair and seems to be enjoying their set. They do a couple covers of other songs, and the boys and I sing along. It feels good to have Casey there having just as much fun as I am.

Towards the end of their set, Kay stands up from her spot with Dylan. She says a few words to him before she walks towards us. She walks directly to Casey and flashes her a smile.

"I'll tell Xavier you said hi," she says. It sounds innocent, but who the hell is Xavier?

Casey ignores her and watches the set instead. Kay smirks before she walks towards the exit and leaves Raven's.

Dylan positions himself next to Anthony and puts his arm around him, nodding his head along to the song.

When Derrick and Jared finish, they walk off stage, managing to get through the thick crowd. They give people high-fives and hugs, and they seem really pumped. Instead of coming to our table, they go through the door to the back of Raven's.

Reece nearly jumps out of his seat with excitement. "That was awesome, man. They were great tonight."

Anthony nods. "They get better and better every time."

"They are so amazing!" Casey is at the edge of her seat. "I'm definitely coming more often to watch them."

Dylan finally sits between Casey and Reece and shoves his phone in his pocket in the process.

"Look who's finally joining the party," Carlos teases him.

"Shut up." Dylan rolls his eyes.

The next band goes on stage and plays some more upbeat songs. They start to play a slower song and Carlos stands up suddenly, causing everyone to watch him. He holds his hand out to me.

"Let's dance," he says.

Carlos wants to dance with me? I look around to see if it's a joke. Everyone else seems just as surprised as I am. Dylan doesn't particularly look impressed.

It's an unexpected gesture, but I take Carlos's hand anyway and he whisks me to where everyone else is dancing. He's actually a great dancer, and I can't help but laugh as he spins me around multiple times. He dips me just as the song ends.

"Where did you learn to dance like that?" I ask him while we're walking back to the table.

"I'm self-taught." He smiles proudly. He grabs my hand and spins me around one more time, but this time bringing me in closer to his body. "In a lot of things actually." He's close enough that his hot breath tickles my ear. I let out a laugh. He then smirks and walks back around to his spot at the table.

Casey is gone from her seat, so I turn to Dylan for answers.

"Where's Casey?" I ask him.

"Bathroom."

He's acting strangely, not meeting my eyes when I talk to him. I move into Casey's seat and nudge him. "Why didn't you and Kay dance out there?"

"Kay doesn't like to dance."

"Kay or you?"

He stares at me. "Fine, you caught me. I'm not Carlos."

The way he says Carlos's name makes me twist my mouth into a frown. He sounds . . . bitter? Does he have something against Carlos? "Didn't you see me out there? I'm sure I looked like a rag doll being dragged around."

A small chuckle escapes from him and I smile, knowing I'm making progress with him.

"I'm not a good dancer, but I still like doing it." I shrug.

"Well, you didn't look so bad with Carlos."

"You kind of have to learn fast with him, I guess. Don't tell me you're jealous of his skills?" I make it so I'm teasing him and so he knows I'm joking around.

"Hardly." He rolls his eyes. "I thought you were getting over that fuckhead? Are you into Carlos now, or what?"

"Carlos and I were just having fun," I say quickly. "What's your deal?" His change in attitude doesn't sit right with me.

"Did he invite you tonight?"

"What? No, Anthony did. What does that—"

"Hey, you seat-stealer." Casey bumps my shoulder playfully.

Dylan shifts his body away from us. "Never mind."

What is his problem? Is he assuming there's something going on between me and Carlos? Why would that bother him anyway?

I move from Casey's seat, and her brows knit together.

"Are you ready to go?" I ask her. Dylan's attitude ruined the vibe, and I feel like it's time to go.

"Uh, sure," she says.

I turn to Anthony. "Casey and I are heading out." Thanks to Dylan.

"You're leaving already?" Reece says, hearing me.

"Yeah, we should probably get out of here."

Dylan's tall figure suddenly towers over me. "I'll walk you guys out."

Not what I want but I don't say no. We wave to the guys before Casey takes my hand. We make our way through the crowd with Dylan closely behind. We get to the door, and Casey eyes me and Dylan. "I'll go start the car." She holds out her hand.

I hand her the keys, and she disappears out the door. I cross my arms and Dylan runs a hand through his hair.

"I hope you had fun tonight," he says, leaning against the wall next to the door.

"I had a lot of fun. I think Casey did too." I'm anxious to talk to her about Kay, how she knows her, and to find out who Xavier is.

"Listen, I didn't mean to get all crazy on you about Carlos." His eyes drop to the floor. "He's just irritating the shit out of me."

"We were only having fun." To tease him, I say, "Besides, if I were even a little bit interested in someone new, you'd be the first to know."

He smirks. "Before Casey?"

"Sure, just don't tell her." I laugh. She'd kill me if I told Dylan first about liking someone new.

It's like he wants to say something else, but he shuts his mouth quickly. Instead, he pushes himself off the wall and says, "Get home safe."

When we get back to Casey's, we go straight to her room. We didn't talk much during the ride back.

"That was fun," I say just to get the conversation going. "Did you have fun?"

"I did. I see why you like hanging out with them." She laughs as she kicks off her shoes and throws them into her closet.

The boys are an interesting group but mostly entertaining. "Things got kind of awkward when Dylan and Kay showed up," I say, hoping she'll spill some kind of tea.

"Yeah, a little."

And that's it.

She walks or escapes into the bathroom and shuts the door.

As I'm putting on my pajamas, I think about Dylan and Carlos. Are they fighting? Why did Dylan get so upset when I danced with Carlos? Plus, Casey and Kay know each other somehow. How did I not know this?

When Casey comes out of the bathroom in her pajamas and a fresh face, I ask, "So, you and Kay were friends?"

Her eyes don't meet mine. "I wouldn't say that."

"What would you say then?"

She sits on the bed and brings her legs close to her chest. "Kay has a brother named Xavier. They used to live next to us when we were in middle school. My parents wanted me to be friends with Kay, but she didn't seem to like me. Xavier and I got along really well though."

Really well? "Did you like him?"

"A little." She shrugs.

"What happened? Did you guys grow apart or something?"

"Something like that. The age difference was weird."

Age difference? "How old is he?"

"He's twenty-one."

I sit on the bed in front of her. "Why didn't you tell me about them?"

"Well, Xavier and I didn't really hang out until freshman year, right around the time you and Jacob got together. When you guys did your thing, I'd hang out with him and Kay," she explains. "An eighteen-year-old hanging out with a fourteen-year-old looks weird, but we were just friends. I developed a crush on him, and he figured it out.

"I tried to stop liking him because he got mixed up with a bad crowd. We argued about it, and I haven't talked to him since last year."

While I was soaked up in my personal soap opera with Jacob, Casey was silently dealing with her own boy drama. There's an uncomfortable pit in my stomach. "Case, why didn't you tell me?"

"You had your own stuff going on, and I didn't want to dump my drama on you. I figured it was best for me to just forget it all."

136

I'm a horrible best friend. I didn't even notice she was going through something. "And you haven't talked to Kay since then?"

"I always had the feeling Kay hated me, but I don't know why. She never bothered talking to me. That's why I liked Xavier better. He was actually nice to me."

She says he got involved with some bad people. I wonder if that has anything to do with why the guys don't like Kay. Is she in with bad people too? What about Dylan?

Instead of pestering on, I say, "My drama isn't the only drama that matters. Tell me when you're going through something next time."

She smiles. "I will."

I then go to the bathroom to wash my face. As I shut the door, I place my hands on my face and sigh. Casey managed to provide a lot of information, yet there are still questions I need answers to.

I've gotten a little more background on Kay, but there's so much more behind what Casey has said. What crowd is Xavier mixed in? Is Kay in a bad way too, and did she get Dylan sucked into all of it?

We stay up a little longer, and Casey ends up falling asleep before I do. My mind swirls with a million thoughts, but one sticks out. August is ending, and that thought alone makes me anxious.

September used to be my favorite month because not only is it my birthday month but it's also when mine and Jacob's anniversary was.

I need to be more proactive when it comes to handling Jacob. I know he's going to try something on our anniversary, and I have to be prepared for whatever curveball is coming at me.

CHAPTER NINE

A giant banner strings from wall to wall in the main hallway on Monday morning. In bold red letters it says, "HOMECOMING WEEK."

Dread washes over me. Homecoming week is festive and all, but it's the last thing on my mind. I have a feeling Casey will want to go to the dance on Saturday, and that involves dress shopping. Not that I mind dress shopping, it's just going to be different this year. If I were still with Jacob, I'd be coordinating with him.

At lunch, she proves my suspicions right. She brings it up casually and starts imagining what she would hypothetically wear to fit the theme, which is Lost Down the Rabbit Hole; in other words, Alice in Wonderland.

"No one ever wears anything to fit the theme," I point out.

"Some people do."

"Yeah, the student government."

She frowns. "Why are you raining on my homecoming parade?" When I don't say anything, she says, "I know you've been going with Jacob as your date, but this is a new year. We can go together. Or if we can find dates in five days, that works too."

She's right, but I hate having to be constantly reminded that it's a new year. I'm becoming too dependent on people to give me a pep talk before I do something. I still need reassurance when it comes to avoiding Jacob, but I have to start making decisions for myself without asking the advice of others.

"You're right," I say.

Her face lights up. "Does that mean . . ."

"We can go to homecoming," I finish for her. "Just me and you though."

"Yay!" she exclaims, earning a few looks from the people around us. "It's going to be so much fun, I promise. If it's not, you can banish me from our friendship forever."

We finish our lunch and exit the cafeteria. As we're walking, Casey is suspiciously quiet. She only speaks up when we near my English class.

"What?" I ask, knowing she's scheming something already. I know that look.

"You should ask Dylan to go to the dance with you." She raises her eyebrows suggestively.

I almost choke. "Dylan doesn't seem like the school dance type." My heart flutters at the thought of going to homecoming with him, and I try to ignore it. Dylan is not interested in me, and I shouldn't be interested in him.

"I bet he'd go if you asked him."

"What does that mean?"

"He has a soft spot for you." She shrugs. "I saw the way you two were around each other on Friday. He was definitely jealous when Carlos was dancing with you."

Dylan couldn't have been jealous. He was just annoyed by Carlos, which I can understand because Carlos was more outgoing than usual. Maybe that side of him has always annoyed Dylan a little.

I then roll my eyes at the thought of Dylan being jealous of Carlos. There's just no way.

"Think about it," she stresses. Then she gasps. "Maybe you should ask Carlos to the dance."

"Okay, that's where I draw the line. Why can't me and you just go together?" I ask, hoping she'll drop the subject.

"Fine," she huffs. "I'm just saying, Carlos would be a great candidate to make Dylan jealous." Her eyes go behind me and seem to watch something.

I brush it off. "I don't need to make anyone jealous, and I'm sure Carlos wouldn't go to the dance with me anyway."

Her eyes grow bigger and I finally turn to see what has her attention. Right as I look, Dylan is passing by me to go to class.

Did he hear what I said about Carlos? Once I realize what she's done, I flash a glare at her. "You knew he was walking over here. You knew he'd hear me."

In return, she gives me an evil grin. "Have fun in class." She then twists around and practically skips down the hallway.

I inhale sharply before walking into class. Dylan is sitting coolly in his seat as I sit down in front of him. I have to be honest with him and explain what just happened. "Did you hear me and Casey talking just now in the hall?"

His face doesn't show any emotion. "I'm no eavesdropper, but you're thinking of going to the dance with Carlos?"

Oh, great. "That was just Casey throwing the idea out there, which I'm not considering. She's insisting we find dates instead of just going together."

He leans forward in his chair. "You're really going to that lame dance?"

"You aren't?" I ask just to see if there's a possibility of him going.

"It's a waste of time."

"Why don't you take Kay?"

He scoffs. "That would be a waste of money." Then he smirks. "Why do you always bring her up anyway?"

"I'm just curious about her."

"She's not my girlfriend, Lace."

"It kind of seems like it."

140

"Well, she's not."

"Okay." I back off. She may not be his girlfriend, but he has to have some kind of feelings towards her. I mean, he brought her to his brother's performance. That has to count for something.

Dylan reclines in his seat and crosses his arms. "Probably won't be seeing much of her anyway."

This interests me. "Why?"

"I need a break from her."

Is he giving me more of an insight into his life? This is a major breakthrough in our friendship. I feel like I'm included now. "Trouble in paradise?"

"Paradise my ass," he says.

Mrs. Beattie calls everyone's attention, and I face the front of class before I get in trouble.

Throughout class, I keep thinking about the dance, no matter how hard I try not to. Memories from the past three homecoming dances are flooding my mind, and I can't stop them.

Jacob and I went to homecoming together for the first time during our freshman year. He texted me the whole day, wanting to see what my dress looked like but I didn't give him any hints. Thinking back on it, that dress was a hideous blush pink that should've never seen the light of day.

I'll have to start dress shopping soon. Maybe Casey will want to go after school. She's the picky one with her dresses, so it'll take her longer to find one.

After class, I text her and ask her if she wants to go shopping. Obviously, she doesn't turn down the offer.

During journalism class, since the paper is already finished and sent to Mrs. Thomas for proofreading, she gives an easy-going lesson on grammar within news writing. I sit with Sophie and Seth while Jacob sits near the front of the class, completely ignoring me.

I watch the back of his head, which sports a fresh haircut. I never really liked when he cut his hair. It's better when he grows it out a bit.

There he is, the once love of my life, sitting in the same class as me for the first time since freshman year. How ironic. During freshman year, he was trying to woo me. Now, I'm trying to cut him out of my life completely.

"Lacey, are you going to the dance?" Sophie asks me as we finish our assignment.

I nod. "What about you two?"

"Well, Seth has a date so I was thinking of third-wheeling." She shrugs.

I immediately look to Seth. He isn't as talkative as Sophie, probably because she doesn't give him the chance, but he didn't say anything about a date. "Who's your date?" I ask him.

I can tell he's bashful about it. "Her name is Heather. We have History together."

Heather? "Heather James?" As in, the Heather who told me about Jacob.

"Yeah, that's her," he says.

Heather and Seth would actually make a cute couple. I don't know if they're going as friends, but I'm definitely rooting for them. "Oh, she's cute." I smile at him.

He only smiles and looks down at his paper.

After school, I tell Casey to meet me at the apartment so we can go to the mall together.

When Casey and I get there, she has an oddly specific look in mind.

"I want to look like a glowing flower," she says firmly.

A glowing flower. That's what she wants to look like, and I don't want to fight with her about it. If my best friend wants to look like a glowing flower, then so be it.

There's a store we wander into that has a lot of formal dresses, so we give it a go. Casey finds a peach-colored dress but decides it doesn't go with her hair and doesn't give her the glowing flower vibe she wants.

As we're searching the racks, a certain dress catches my eye. I pluck it from the other dresses and instantly fall in love with it. At first glance, it's silvery-gray, but once I move it in my hands, I notice that it shifts from a light blue to a light pink in a duochrome fashion.

There's a gasp next to me, and I glance at Casey. "That's it," she says.

My heart drops a little. I don't want to be selfish, but I like the dress for myself.

"You think?" I ask her, trying not to let the disappointment show.

"Lace, that's definitely your dress. It'll look stunning on you," she says with a smile.

Relief washes over me, and I pull the dress completely from the rack. I check the tag, and it's exactly the size I need.

"Try it on. I have to see it," she says excitedly, practically pushing me towards the dressing rooms.

In the dressing room, I scan over myself in the dress. It has thin straps over my shoulders and a v-neckline that shows a little more cleavage than I usually allow. It's tight on my waist but flows nicely down to just above my knees. It's a simple fit, but the colors are absolutely gorgeous.

I step out of the dressing room to show Casey and she drops her jaw.

"Lacey, that dress was practically made for you." She clasps her hands together. "You have to get it."

Finding a dress so quickly surprises me. Maybe I should do some more shopping. "You don't think I should look around more? Maybe I'll find something—"

"No, no. I don't want to hear it." She shakes her head. "I think you know that this is your dress."

It really is beautiful, and the price is right. "Okay, I'll get it."

After a couple more stores, Casey gives up on finding her dress. "I know it's out there. I have five days to find it."

"There are still plenty of stores to look at. Don't worry," I reassure her.

When we get to my car, I put my bag with my dress in the backseat before jumping in on the driver's side.

I'm excited to put the whole look together for homecoming. It's my last homecoming as a high schooler, so it has to be epic somehow. Of course, prom will be a night to remember, but I can still get psyched for homecoming.

After Casey leaves the apartment, my aunt opens the door and immediately takes her heels off. She smiles when she sees me.

"It was a hell of a long day. Do you mind takeout today?" she asks, setting her purse on the dining table.

"That sounds perfect."

"Great." She strolls to the kitchen, picking up a cup to get water from the sink. She takes a sip before saying, "How was your day?"

"It was alright. Casey and I went dress shopping earlier."

"Find anything?"

I hold a finger up before jogging to my room and pulling the bag off my bed. In the kitchen, I gently reveal the dress, holding it up for her to see.

She puts her hand over her mouth. "Lacey, that is beautiful."

"I think Casey would have killed me if I didn't get it," I explain. "She didn't find one, but she's going shopping again tomorrow."

"Are you two going to the dance together?"

"Yeah, she's set on finding dates by Saturday, but I just want to go with her. I don't want any boy drama for once."

She has a look on her face that I can't quite decipher.

"What are you thinking?" I ask her.

She says while shrugging, "I wouldn't be opposed to you going with your friend that came over."

"Are you talking about Dylan?"

"So that's his name." She gives a sly grin.

I shake my head. "Oh, no. Definitely not. We're just friends. Nothing more."

She gives me a look like she doesn't believe me. "I've noticed you hanging out with him more than you hang out with Casey."

"We do what friends do: talk and hang out."

"Well, I sure wish I had friends like Dylan" She doesn't look convinced, but she drops it. "We should order our food soon. I'm starving."

While waiting for takeout, I ignore my homework and go on social media. I'm scrolling through Instagram when a thought strikes me. I wonder if Dylan has any social media.

I go to the explore page and search his name. A few Dylan Parker's come up, but none of them are him. Dylan doesn't seem like the Instagram type anyway. I search on Snapchat and Twitter and the results are the same.

I lock my phone, lay back on my bed, and stare at the ceiling. There's an urge to look up Jacob. I unfollowed him on everything after the break up and I've been trying to stop myself from stalking his social media, or even Lauren's.

Just as I pick my phone up, the doorbell rings, signaling our takeout has arrived. I silently thank the delivery person for stopping me from making a stupid decision.

*   *   *

I perfect my eyeshadow in the mirror and admire my work before I realize I have to do the exact same thing on my left eye. Sighing, I glance over at Casey who is taking out a bun she's spent about thirty minutes finalizing.

"These stupid YouTube videos are useless for creating a decent hairstyle," she rants. "Homecoming is canceled."

I laugh at how overdramatic she can be. "Just wear your hair down."

"But my hair will cover part of the dress if I wear it down. It has to be up in order to get the full effect."

I hold my hands up in defense. "Okay, okay."

Casey's kind of stressing me out over all this homecoming stuff. Earlier, she told me to be here at her house so we can get ready for the dance together. Then she said won't show me her dress until she gets ready. Now, she wants me to let her know when it's a certain time so she can pace herself.

"Everything has to be perfect," she says as she starts to put her hair up into a ponytail.

I focus on my eyeshadow again. With careful precision, I blend the shadows into my crease. It's not a perfect eye look because I haven't worn eyeshadow in ages, but I'm still happy with how it's coming out. Once I finish, I lean back and inspect my eyes to see if they are evenly matched.

"Good enough," I say to myself.

The rest of my makeup comes together nicely. I walk over to Casey, who has settled on an elegant updo.

"Very nice," I tell her.

"I have so many bobby pins in my hair right now. One wrong move and it might come crashing down," she says, standing up carefully from her chair. "Time to switch."

I take her spot and turn the curling iron on. I'm going to curl the ends of my hair, then pull half of it up into a plain half-up/half-down style. I don't know if I'll be able to split my hair evenly, so I might have to ask Casey for her help.

"So, I have something to tell you," Casey says suddenly.

Whenever Casey says something like that, it's usually about something she's done that I've asked her not to do. "What did you do?" I automatically ask.

146

"I got us dates for tonight."

"You what?"

"Don't worry. They're perfect for one-time dates."

I should've known she'd do something drastic on a day like today. I haven't been feeling stressed out over a date, but after learning about her little setup, an enormous pressure presses down on me.

I style my hair, which doesn't take long, just as Casey finishes her makeup.

She waves her hands in front of her face, probably to cool herself down. "Now for the dresses." She opens her bathroom door carefully. "When I come out, I'm going to be a glowing flower."

While I still don't know what a glowing flower is meant to look like, I laugh as she shuts the door. I slip my dress off the hanger and start to shrug off my clothes. Slithering my way into the dress, I pull it over my chest and zip it as much as I can.

"Case, I need you to zip up the rest of my dress, please," I call out to her.

The bathroom door opens and she steps out. Her dress is a deep violet color, the top is a halter-style, and the bottom spreads out in tulle. There are sequins and beads covering the top. When she twirls around, I see the back opens into a keyhole shape.

"What do you think?" she asks me, putting her hand on her hip to pose.

"That color looks fantastic on you." I smile.

She twirls again. "I feel exactly like a glowing flower."

"Okay, glowing flower, can you help with my dress, please?" I say, turning so she can finish zipping it up for me.

Once my dress is zipped up, we step into our heels—hers nude and mine silver. I admire the dress in Casey's full-length mirror. Confident Lacey is coming out, and it feels so good.

"It's been a while since I've felt this good," I admit. My dress fits well, my makeup is great, and I feel cute. I feel beautiful.

147

"Your date won't even recognize you," Casey teases.

Well, there's one clue. "So it's someone I know?" I have a feeling our dates will be two of the guys, but which two I'm not sure. There's a part of me that wants my date to be Dylan just because I know him a little better, but I know it's not likely. He called the dance lame and wasn't interested in going.

"I wouldn't make you go with a stranger, Lace," she says as she swipes on some lipstick. "I'm not going with a stranger either."

The doorbell rings and Casey hastily puts her lipstick away. "C'mon, I don't want them to be with my parents for too long."

She practically runs out of her room, almost falling in the process. Mrs. Taylor, Casey's mom, is sitting upright on the couch. Casey is graced with her mom's beautiful features.

She's a former pageant queen, something she would talk to my mom about constantly. Mr. Taylor, who can be strict and straight-forward, has already walked to the front door, which is out of view from where we're standing.

"Well, you girls look beautiful," Mrs. Taylor compliments us as she stands up. "Stunning, the both of you." She puts her arm around Casey and kisses the top of her head.

"Thanks, Mom," Casey says, smiling while hugging her back.

I thank Mrs. Taylor and try not to feel envious of Casey. Her mom is around to see these moments in her life, and both of my parents aren't. It's unfair, but I know it's not Casey's fault. It just sucks because I know sometimes Casey takes her parents for granted.

Pushing those thoughts out of my mind, I focus on the rapid beating of my heart. I'm anxious to see who walked into the living room. I can hear Mr. Taylor's voice along with two others.

Mr. Taylor walks into the living room with Anthony and Carlos trailing behind him. Carlos seems cool and collected, while Anthony has his hands clasped together.

"Which one belongs to you, Casey?" Mr. Taylor asks her.

She points to Carlos and approaches him. "This one right here." They smile at each other. I wonder when this friendship happened.

Carlos flashes his brilliant smile and offers a hand to Mrs. Taylor. "It's nice to meet you, Mrs. Taylor. I'm Carlos." His attire includes a white button-up shirt with black pants. His hair is somewhat combed, more than usual.

She takes his hand and smiles. "It's so good to meet you, Carlos."

Anthony, who's wearing a dark gray button-up with black pants, bows his head at me. "Lacey."

I can't stop a laugh from coming out. "So proper, Anthony. Save it for prom."

"Will do." He winks before turning his attention to Mrs. Taylor and introducing himself.

Anthony's mannerisms are similar to Dylan's, and it becomes easier to see the other similarities between them. If Dylan didn't introduce Anthony as his cousin to me, I would've thought they were brothers. They're more in sync than Dylan and Derrick.

"Maybe we should all sit down and chat for a bit." Mr. Taylor eyes the boys, especially Carlos. "Lacey, I know your dad would want me to straighten out the boys in your life."

Not knowing how to respond, I say, "Um, thanks, Mr. Taylor."

Casey visibly rolls her eyes. "There's no time for that, Dad. We have to go." As strict as her dad can be, she often ignores him. He'll give her a curfew of eight o'clock, but she'll stride in one minute past just to tick him off.

Mrs. Taylor puts a hand over his chest. "We can't keep them too long, hun. We're cramping their style."

"That's exactly right," Casey says.

"Wait! Let me at least get a picture before you go. Lacey, your aunt wanted me to take plenty of pictures of you," Mrs. Taylor says, grabbing her phone.

I give Casey an apologetic look and she sighs. "Okay, fine."

The guys are silly with the photos. They pose more together than they do with me and Casey, and even manage to get a laugh out of Mr. Taylor.

Casey clutches Carlos's arm and starts pulling him towards the front door. "We have to get going. Now."

"Remember, Case, midnight is the curfew," Mrs. Taylor calls out to us.

"I know!" she says, opening the front door and ushering the rest of us out.

Carlos, Anthony, and I say our quick goodbyes before we step outside.

"I'm driving." Anthony holds up his keys. "Let's get this party started."

I'm heading to the backseat when Carlos cuts in front of me. "Sit in the front with your date, Lace. C'mon," he says teasingly.

In the same tone, Casey says, "Yeah, Lace, what's wrong with you?" She smiles at me before opening the door and slipping inside.

Anthony opens the passenger side door for me. "After you," he says.

Before I can say anything, Carlos smacks his forehead. "Shit, Casey, I was supposed to open the door for you."

Sticking to the theme of the dance, the entrance of the gym is decorated with giant artificial leaves and brown butcher paper lining the walls, mimicking the rabbit hole. A small painted rabbit is next to the door with a sign above the leaves that says "Lost Down the Rabbit Hole."

We make our way through the makeshift "hole" and enter the gym, where enlarged playing cards are splayed on the walls, along with the Cheshire cat sitting near the DJ. White paper flowers with red paint adorn the tables surrounding the dance floor.

Casey leans to me and says, "I give them a seven out of ten for decorations."

"Let's head to that table over there," Anthony says, pointing to a table off to the side.

There's a large group of people on the dance floor already, and I recognize a few faces. I even spot Sophie dancing away with a guy and I wonder if she ended up with a date after all. My heartbeat picks up once I realize that Jacob could be here. I just hope I don't run into him.

"You guys want anything to drink?" Carlos asks us.

I say no, but Casey says she's thirsty. She and Carlos make their way to the drink table while Anthony and I make ourselves comfortable.

"Casey told me not to tell you that she was inviting me and Carlos to be you guys's dates. I hope it's cool with you," he says.

"I'm cool with it. I'm honestly glad it's you guys." It would've been uncomfortable with strangers.

His attention is on the dance floor and I wonder if he's a dancer like Carlos. What about the other guys? Are Reece and Dylan dancers?

"And the other two? What are they up to tonight?" I ask curiously. "I mean, I wasn't expecting Dylan to show up, but I wasn't sure about Reece."

"Reece is out of town for the weekend, and I'm not sure what Dylan is up to. Staring at a wall maybe." He shrugs.

Staring at a wall? "Why do you say that?"

"He's currently not seeing Kay and you're here, so yeah, he's definitely staring at a wall." He smirks.

He's implying things and I need to settle them. "You guys are here too," I say, giving him a look. "Doesn't he have any hobbies to keep him occupied?"

"Yeah, but like I said, he's currently not seeing her."

Okay, too much information.

"I would tell you more about Dylan's life, but I don't think he'd appreciate me spilling all of his dirty secrets."

That intrigues me. "Dirty secrets? Does he live a double life? A secret hobby?" Imagine that. Dylan Parker: brooding teenage boy by day, quilter by night.

"That's a no," he says, laughing.

Maybe I can learn more about Dylan by asking Anthony about himself. I mean, they are related. "You and Dylan are cousins, right?"

He nods. "His mom is my mom's sister. And yes, Dylan has been a troublemaker since birth."

We both laugh and I try to envision what Dylan was like when he was younger. I bet his parents have a lot of cute baby pictures of him. Now that I think about it, Dylan has never really said anything about his mom. I wonder if she's in the picture.

Anthony looks at the dance floor then back at me. "You wanna dance?"

"I thought you'd never ask," I say with a grin.

We jog onto the dance floor and start dancing along to the upbeat song that's already playing. Carlos and Casey join us soon after. The boys are making me and Casey double over in laughter with their ridiculous moves and obnoxious singing. We earn a few looks from the people around us, but I ignore them. We grow tired after a couple more songs and decide to sit.

"These heels are already killing me," Casey complains, loosening the strap around her ankle.

"We'll go get some more drinks," Carlos says as he and Anthony stand up. They disappear to the refreshments table.

Casey grins and leans towards me. "See? Having dates isn't so bad."

"It's actually pretty fun," I admit. "Good choice."

She pretends to bow. "Thank you, thank you. I know."

The boys join us, and as Anthony puts a drink in front of me, he says, "Look what the cat dragged in."

Dylan, who's standing next to Anthony, is in an all-black ensemble, with a black button-up and black pants; the outfit definitely suits him. I try to stop my heart from beating so quickly, but nothing works. I have to admit he looks really good.

Dylan shoves his hands into his pockets and smirks. "It was a big ass cat."

"Must've been." Anthony sips on his drink after he says it.

They sit at the table, with Dylan between Carlos and Anthony. It doesn't last long. Carlos twists his body towards Casey. "Do you want to dance again?"

Of course, she doesn't turn him down. The two practically run to the dance floor.

I lean forward, so I can talk to Dylan. "I thought you weren't going to come to this lame dance?"

"Well, Anthony convinced me it wouldn't be so lame," he says, leaning forward also.

"Lacey's made it not so lame, but fuck, I'm hungry," Anthony says as he glances around. "I think I'm gonna go eat all those cookies at the table. You guys want any?"

I shake my head and Dylan replies, "I'm good."

After Anthony leaves, I take his spot next to Dylan. He gives me a teasing side-eye before he faces me.

"I never thought I'd see Dylan Parker wearing something other than a t-shirt," I tease him. He pulls off his outfit so well that I'm actually mad at how great he looks.

"Wait until you see me without a t-shirt," he says, winking. "But I'll take that as a compliment, since I know your pride won't let you actually compliment me."

An image of Dylan without a shirt flashes in my mind, and I immediately shove it out. That's something I don't need to visualize right now. Instead, I focus on how he looks now and appreciate how he still feels like himself. A few slight curls in his hair fall on his forehead, leading me to his light-green eyes.

"How's Anthony as a homecoming date?" he asks me.

153

"Anthony is a perfect gentleman with some not-so-smooth dance moves. Just don't tell him." I laugh.

"You should see him dance while he's drunk."

"What about you? Are you a good or a bad dancer when you're drunk?"

He tilts his head and grins. "What's your obsession with me and my dancing?"

I shrug. "I'm only curious. I can't pinpoint you." I've had to gather information about him from others. He's a private person, but I find myself wanting to know more about him. I want him to let me in.

"Pinpoint me?"

"Yeah, I can usually figure certain things out about people, but with you, I can't. You're a tough cookie to break."

His body moves closer to mine as he speaks, making my heart race. "Maybe that's a good thing."

"That sounds ominous," I say slowly. "Do you have any dirty secrets that you're hiding?" Being a quilter perhaps?

"I might have a few skeletons in my closet."

Dylan could be hiding something, but I don't know what. What could be worth hiding in his life?

Casey and Carlos plop back down in their seats and are practically sweating from dancing. Anthony sits down as well, and we all talk about school and more school until it reaches about ten-thirty. Anthony gets strangely quiet after a while, and I put my hand on his shoulder.

"You okay?" I ask him.

"Those cookies might've fucked me up." He clutches his stomach. "I'll be right back." He stands up quickly and speed walks towards the restrooms.

Casey and I give each other a look of concern while Carlos and Dylan crack up at him.

"I don't think we'll see him for another hour if it's that bad," Carlos says.

154

I watch Carlos and Dylan talk, and everything seems to be fine between them. There doesn't seem to be any bad blood.

After the Homecoming king and queen are announced, a slow song plays for them. Once they get a bit of a dance in, all the couples flood the dance floor. Carlos and Casey look at each other before he grabs her hand and take off again. They stay at the edge of the crowd.

I watch them carefully. I wonder if they're starting to like each other a little more than friends. They go along with whatever the other wants to do. It's actually kind of cute.

"Do you think Carlos likes Casey?" I ask Dylan, wanting to get some kind of insight.

He puts his hand on his chin and studies them as well. "Hard to say."

Carlos's hands are on her waist while hers are hanging loose around his neck. He's saying something to her and she smiles, nodding along. I find myself envying her.

Last year, I thought I was going to homecoming with Jacob. Instead, I'm watching my best friend dance with her date while I'm sitting by the sideline. If Anthony weren't in the bathroom, I'd ask him to dance.

"You don't look like you're having fun now," Dylan comments.

I stop myself from sighing. "I am," I assure him. "It's just . . . a lot of things have changed since last year." Too many things have changed, in fact. It's like my life completely shifted 180 degrees.

Dylan gazes off into the distance for a few moments. Then he shifts his body towards me and inhales loudly. "Okay, listen up. I know you like shit like homecoming, and by the looks of it, this night has turned to shit because you keep thinking about your douchebag ex.

"I'm not going to let you sit and mope over that dickhead when you should be having the night of your life. I told you I'd

155

help you get over him, and I'd like to think I'm a man of my word. So," he says, holding out his hand to me, "do you want to dance with me?"

There are butterflies in my stomach, and I can't say anything. It's such a nice gesture, especially by him, that I've been rendered speechless, so I nod.

We awkwardly walk over to the dance floor just as another slow song starts. I've been curious about Dylan's dancing skills, but I didn't think I would actually dance with him. We pause in front of each other, and suddenly, it's like everything I know about dancing is gone from my mind.

"I thought you were the dancer of the group," he jokes, relieving some of the awkwardness. He takes my hands and puts them around his neck before putting his on my waist. "Like this, right?"

"Right," I say, smiling and easing into it.

We begin to sway back and forth before picking up our pace a bit, and he spins me around. His rhythm isn't bad at all. I suspect that he knows how to dance better than Carlos.

"I think I've discovered one of your secrets," I tell him.

A grin appears on his face. "What's that?"

"You know how to dance very well."

"Maybe that's one of my many talents you have yet to learn about." His voice is teasing, but I don't think he's entirely joking. What other talents is he capable of?

It hits me. I finally got him to dance with me. I bite my lip to stop myself from smiling. I find myself leaning my head on his shoulder, feeling like it's the most natural thing in the world. I'm glad he lets it happen.

The butterflies are back, and I don't do anything to cause them to scatter. Dancing with Dylan is different from dancing with Jacob. Jacob was clumsy and didn't quite know how to work his feet. Dylan, on the other hand, knows exactly what he's doing.

It's crazy how Dylan swept into my life and managed to turn things around, and for the better. I didn't expect for things to move so fast in our friendship, but it feels . . . right? It scares me, but I try not to dive into those thoughts. I focus on the positive for now.

"Can I tell you something?" I ask him before I can change my mind.

"Hmm?"

"I'm glad you're here."

He chuckles. "The guys are pretty good at putting peer pressure on me."

I pick my head up, so I can look at him. "No, I mean like, here in my life right now. I'm glad we became friends."

His lips curve at the ends, and I know he's trying to stop the smile from spreading across his face, but it peeks through. "Me too, Lace," he says finally.

CHAPTER TEN

My phone plays soft background music as I clear out some clothes from my closet on Monday night.

The amount of clothes I hardly ever wear is growing, and I have to clear them out before my closet explodes. I'm not interested in wearing half of my wardrobe, so I like to see it as a shedding of the skin.

Out with the old and in with the new. Since they are all in good shape, I'm shoving them into a large bag so I can donate them.

My music stops suddenly, so I figure it's an incoming call. Dylan's name is on the screen, so I grab it.

I smile as I answer, "Hey, Dylan."

"What are you up to?" he asks.

"Just hanging out here at home. Mostly cleaning my closet."

"Sounds very fun on this lovely Monday night. What would you say if I told you I have something even better for you to do?"

I fold my legs under me as I sit on my bed. "Well, I would ask what that could be?"

"There's a diner downtown that has bomb ass cheese fries that I've been craving, and I know you can't resist the cheese."

How sweet, he remembers. "That's a tempting offer."

"Who said it's an offer?"

The doorbell rings throughout the apartment. "What do you mean?" I ask him, but the line goes dead.

Aunt Jade walks past my room to open the door. She begins talking to whoever has rang the doorbell. I toss my phone onto the bed and saunter around the corner. Dylan is standing at the threshold of the front door.

"Lacey, you have a visitor," Aunt Jade says, smiling knowingly at me.

Dylan smirks when he meets my eyes. "Surprise."

Before I can say anything, my aunt cuts in, "We love surprises! I mean, she loves surprises." She opens the door wider for him. "Come in, come in."

"If it's okay, I'd like to take Lacey to a diner downtown. We won't be out for too long, I promise," he says as she closes the door behind him.

"Well, that sounds like a great idea." She grins.

Dylan looks at me expectantly.

I trail my eyes down my body and realize I have to change out of my comfy shorts and old t-shirt. "I guess I'll go change."

Rushing into my room and shutting the door behind me, I search through my clothes to find something decent to wear. The task is only slightly difficult considering my clothes are a mess but already out. I try not to take too long. I'm afraid of what Aunt Jade might say to him if I don't hurry.

I quickly put on some jean shorts and a loose navy blue shirt. I throw on my sandals and toss my keys and wallet in my purse. I think about putting on makeup, but it'll take too much time, so I only brush on some mascara. I tousle my hair before walking out.

Dylan is sitting on our small couch, and Aunt Jade is walking out of the kitchen with a water bottle in hand. She hands it to him, and he thanks her.

"Are you ready?" I ask Dylan.

He towers over me as he stands next to me. A hint of cologne hits me that doesn't smell familiar, but it smells heavenly.

"Have fun and be careful," Aunt Jade says in a singsong voice as we make our way outside the apartment.

Descending the stairs, I turn and look at him. "You're sneaky."

A smirk is on his face. "I'm never sneaky. I plan things very well."

"What a sweetheart." I nudge him.

"Yeah, yeah." He waves it off. "Don't let it get to your head."

It hits me that Dylan has sold his motorcycle, and I've only ever seen him drive in Kay's car.

"Do you want me to drive?" I ask. I have no idea how he even got here in the first place.

"I'm parked right here," he says, pointing to a black car next to mine.

"When did you get this?"

"This past Saturday. My dad knew a guy who wanted to get rid of it, so I bought it with the money I got from the bike." He walks over to it, and I follow him. "It's a little rough looking, but it runs."

That's exactly what I say about my car.

We hop in and I feel strangely comfortable in the soft seat.

"Is that your bedroom window right there?" he asks, gesturing to my window. He's parked directly below it.

"Don't tell me you were parked here the whole time we were on the phone," I say, trying to see if it's possible to see into my room.

"I guessed that one was yours. I can't see inside though."

"Thank God."

I know he wants to say something, but he just laughs. "Let's go."

We don't talk much on the way to the diner, but it's a silence I'm content with. Only when we arrive at the diner does he speak up.

"They serve breakfast all day, if you're into that."

"Are you telling me you eat ice cream for lunch and breakfast for dinner?" I tease him.

He grins. "That's exactly what I'm saying."

He gets out of the car, and I follow inside the diner.

I'm blown away by the neon signs that line the walls, each splashing a different color. The vibe of the diner is hard to distinguish. It's like a 50s diner but with a modern, almost futuristic twist.

Not many people occupy the booths. There's a group of people in a large booth in the back and an older couple off to the side.

I follow Dylan to a booth next to a large window. I make myself comfortable as a waitress walks up to us. Her black hair has pink streaks and is pulled into a side braid. Her baby blue shirt and black pants have stains on them. She looks like she could be about a year or two older than me and Dylan.

"Dylan Parker, you haven't shown your pretty little face here in a while," she says to him before setting our menus down on the table. She's standing very close to him.

Dylan is clearly uncomfortable, and I raise my brow in amusement. "Yeah, it's been a while, Esme."

Her eyes trace over me. "And you brought a girl with you. That's new."

They have apparent history together, and it's funny to watch Dylan squirm under her. "Sure is. Uh, I'll just have some water. What about you, Lace?"

"Water is fine too," I tell her.

She walks away without saying anything, and Dylan rubs his face. "Great," he says.

"You're into pink streaks?" I ask him, trying to get a reaction.

He shifts in his seat. "She didn't have those when we hooked up. It was one time, and I thought they fired her after they caught us in the parking lot."

That's a lot to take in. "The parking lot? Really, Dylan?"

"My summer was interesting, to say the least," he says, scratching the back of his neck.

My curiosity gets the best of me, so I ask, "Was this before or after you met Kay?"

His face changes. "I don't want to talk about Kay. Anyway, Anthony must've caught something because he's been sick all weekend."

I don't mind Dylan changing the subject, and I try not to laugh about Anthony. "My poor date."

"You're lucky I was there to step in." He winks at me.

"I guess I was." I wondered all weekend what had driven Dylan to the dance. He said Anthony and the guys peer pressured him into going, but I don't really believe that.

Dylan picks up his menu and glances over it. The way he reads over the menu reminds me of Jacob. For a second, I see Jacob's face in place of Dylan's and I blink to make it go away. Mine and Jacob's anniversary would have been on Wednesday, and thinking about it is making me lose my mind.

"I'm afraid to order anything. Esme might spit in my food," Dylan says, interrupting my thoughts.

"Great," I say, trying to shake Jacob from my mind. "I think I'll take your advice and try the cheese fries."

Esme comes back with our drinks and sets them in front of us. Dylan and I both order the cheese fries, and once she finishes writing the order down, she takes off without saying anything again.

"Is this your luck with most girls?" I ask. It seems like he doesn't have a great track record. I've never seen him with a girl at school—not that I can remember anyway—yet when people talk about him, they talk about how much of a flirt and player he is.

"That's a conversation for another day." He laughs before looking out the window next to us.

My mind goes back to the conversation I've had with Casey about Kay and Xavier. I wonder if he asked Kay how she knew Casey. "Do you know Xavier? Kay's brother?"

His head whips back towards me. "How do you know his name?"

"Casey knows him and Kay." I want to say more about her history, but I figure it isn't my business to share.

"Oh yeah." He frowns, seeming to think hard about something.

Dylan's mind appears to be working hard every time I see him. I don't know what thoughts are swirling around in there, and that only makes me more curious about what they could be.

Esme brings our cheese fries out. They're on a plate larger than I expected. Dylan laughs when he sees my reaction to the size of the meal.

"I probably should've warned you," he says cheekily.

It won't be too hard to eat, I think. "I can take it," I say mostly to myself. I pick up a fry drenched in cheese and bite down on it. I almost moan, but I catch myself. "Good choice," I tell Dylan.

It's nearly impossible to eat without getting the cheese everywhere. I end up with cheese on my arms, and I almost feel embarrassed for being so messy until I see Dylan with cheese on his eyebrow. I can't help but laugh and point at him.

"What?" he asks.

"You have—" I can't even finish without cracking up. I only motion to his eyebrow and he touches it slowly. When he sees the cheese on his finger, he grabs a napkin and starts wiping furiously.

"These damn things are messy as hell," he says, tossing his napkin off to the side.

There's cheese on his cheek now, and I cover my mouth to stop myself from laughing harder. "You still have some."

He tries to act mad but smiles when I keep laughing. "Shut up and help me," he says, handing me a clean napkin.

I lean over the table and wipe off the cheese from his face. It's strange to touch Dylan and be so close to him. He's staring at me with an expression I can't read, and I quickly finish and sit back in the booth.

"You're cheese free," I tell him, feeling butterflies in my stomach.

It's a familiar feeling. Jacob and I had a handful of moments where we found ourselves laughing until our stomachs started to hurt. It's odd experiencing it with Dylan.

His plate is a little emptier than mine. I start to feel full, so I slow down a bit. Dylan notices.

"Quitting already?" he asks.

"I don't think my stomach is as big as yours."

He laughs but stops when his eyes focus on something behind me. "Oh, fuck."

He starts wiping his hands, and before I can turn to see what he's looking at, a voice reaches us.

"What the fuck, Parker? You running around behind my sister's back?"

Appearing next to our table is a tall guy with arms bigger than my head. He plants his hands on our table and stares directly at Dylan. His black hair is gelled up, and his eyes are so dark they could be black too.

"You've got it all wrong." Dylan holds his hands up in defense. "Your sister and I ended things. I'm just here with a friend."

With the context clues I've been given just now, I'm betting this is the infamous Xavier. I study him as Dylan talks to him.

I thought Dylan and his friends were intimidating when I first met them, but Xavier is on a whole other level. I wonder what led to Casey having a crush on him. He's different from her usual type.

Xavier's eyes suddenly meet mine and they narrow. "I know you." He takes his hands off the table and crosses his arms, making him seem larger. "You're Casey's friend."

I don't know what to say, but luckily he speaks again.

"You tell her I've been trying to reach her," he says in a tone that isn't threatening, but it still sets alarm bells off in my head. He looks at Dylan. "I'll deal with you this weekend, Parker."

With that, he stalks off to a booth in the back where a bunch of guys are, and I feel like I can breathe again. Dylan glances to the booth in the back and I see him tense up.

"Should've known they'd be here," Dylan says, shaking his head. "Has Casey said anything else about him?"

"Nope," I tell him.

He taps his fingers on the table before saying, "Don't tell her you saw him. She's ignoring him for a reason, and I think I know why."

I don't like being left out of the loop, but I agree to not tell her. If Xavier has a problem with Casey, then I'll figure it out. If she doesn't want him around, I'll make sure he doesn't. I wasn't there for her when she was going through her drama with him, but I will damn sure be here for her this time.

"What an asshole," Dylan scoffs. "He thinks I can't kick his ass by myself. I can take him and his dumbass friends."

I sneak a peek at the guys Xavier is with, and they're just as big as he is. "No offense, but I'm not sure about that."

165

He picks at his fries. "Don't tell the guys anything about Xavier either. They think they know what's best for me, but I can handle myself. I know what I'm doing."

"Is that why they don't like Kay? Because she has a scary brother?" I ask him.

"It's a little more complicated than that."

"Well, they're your friends and family. I'm sure the guys are just looking out for you."

"I don't need anyone looking out for me." He pushes his fries away from him. He crosses his arms and stares out the window.

He's acting like a child. I don't know why he's refusing everyone's help. I don't know the whole situation, but I want to help him too. I'm going to figure out what's going on one way or another.

"You've been helping me with this whole Jacob thing and I really appreciate it, but just so you know, I can help you with whatever you need too," I say.

He sighs. "This is more than just relationship drama, Lace. I don't need your help."

I'm not going to take no for an answer. "Listen here, Parker. This isn't a one-sided friendship. If you need my support for anything, I'll give it to you. I don't know what Xavier is mixed up in or if you're getting mixed in too, but I'm here. I know the guys will back you up, but I'm here too whether you like it or not."

"Lace—"

"I'm not done." I put my hand up before he can object. "Casey had a rough time with Xavier last year, and I didn't even know because I was sucked up in everything with Jacob. I'm going to help her this time around if he causes any more trouble. So if I'm going to help her, I'm going to help you too."

It's still hard to process that Casey had a whole other life outside of our friendship that I didn't know about all because I paid too much attention on myself.

Dylan stays quiet. He runs a hand through his hair before looking at me. "So if I call you to come kick Xavier's ass, you will?" His eyes are teasing, which makes me relax a bit.

"If I have to, yeah." I nod before smiling. "You think I can take him by myself?"

"No doubt," he says with a grin. He reaches into his pocket and pulls out enough cash to cover the bill and a tip. "Let's get out of here."

Once we're in his car, he doesn't start it right away. "The reason I'm keeping you in the dark about all this stuff with Xavier and Kay is because I don't want you dragged into shit that has nothing to do with you. I might know his situation with Casey, so I'll try to get him off her back. I just don't want him near you guys."

The way he says it scares me. What is Xavier sucked up in? How bad is he?

"Are you sure you know what you're doing?" I ask hesitantly.

"I know you can't help it, but don't worry about me," he says, winking. "And if Xavier even thinks about you, I'll beat his ass."

That comes out as flirty rather than reassuring, and the butterflies in my stomach come back, making me smile. "You would protect me?"

He rolls his eyes but smirks anyway. "Just put your seatbelt on."

While I do what he says, I notice his eyes are stuck on my wrist. I clear my throat and turn my hand, so the tattoo isn't visible. Maybe I should take Dylan up on his offer for a cover-up. Covering it would really be the beginning of a new era. Am I ready to give up my matching tattoo?

Dylan remains quiet as he drives back to the apartment. I'm a little uncomfortable with the silence this time, so I decide to voice my thoughts to him.

"If I were to cover up my tattoo with something else, what do you think I should get?" I ask.

He shrugs, eyes staying on the road. "It would have to be something big enough to cover it."

"Like a flower, maybe?"

"If that's what you want."

A flower sounds a little basic. I trace the heart and sigh. "I don't know." I don't know what I want anymore. Choosing a tattoo with Jacob was easy. Covering it up is a completely different story.

Dylan speaks up again, "Or turn it into something else. Add a quote to turn the meaning around, you know?"

That's possible. "I'll have to think about it. Maybe that'll be my graduation present to myself." It makes me curious about Jacob. Is he ever going to change his or cover it, or will he keep it that way forever?

"Don't tell me you're thinking about that dickhead," Dylan says.

"It's hard not to when thinking about the tattoo," I admit. It's hard not to think about him, period. Everything was fine until I saw him the first day of school. It's been downhill ever since then.

He stays quiet for a second. "I know I'm supposed to be helping you get over him or whatever, but you don't seem ready to."

What? "But I am."

"It doesn't seem like it sometimes. I can tell you get in your head and you start thinking about him and it messes with you," he stresses. "Look, I'm here to help, but I'm also here to tell you that if getting over him seems impossible, then don't."

What is he saying? That I should get back together with Jacob? My heart starts pounding in my chest, and not in the good way. Instead I feel angry that he's even suggested that. "Are you saying I should go back to him?" My voice rises as I speak.

He doesn't look at me. "I'm not saying that—"

"But you're implying it."

168

"Fine, I'm implying it," he says, his voice rising also. "But I'll say it too. Get back together with him if you're that miserable without him."

Am I miserable without Jacob? The possibility of getting back together with him makes me lightheaded, and I don't know if that's a good thing.

I'm not sure why Dylan is putting all these thoughts into my head, but whatever he's doing is really screwing with me. "Do you think he would cheat on me again?"

He looks deep in thought, like he's choosing his words carefully. "Yeah." He nods decisively. "I think every word he spews out to you is a fucking lie. With the way he's been sweet-talking you? There's no way."

I don't know what to say. I don't know what brought Dylan to these conclusions. It feels like he's giving up on me. Appearing weak and all for a boy doesn't settle well with me. I can't be that miserable without Jacob.

When he parks at the apartment, Dylan grabs my arm. His warm hand feels feather-light, and his eyes are trained on my wrist again. "Sorry I said all of that. I just had to get it off my chest," he says, casting his eyes away from my tattoo.

I nod mostly because I want this conversation to be over with. "It's fine. I'll see you tomorrow, okay?"

Before he can answer, I open the door and step out.

In my room, I stare at the ceiling wondering what the hell I should do. Can I trust Jacob again? Am I willing to run back to him because I can't imagine my life without him?

I feel like I'll lose everything I've worked hard for in these past few months if I get back together with him. I might lose Casey in the process, and even Dylan, and that just doesn't seem right. But even as I'm falling asleep, I see Jacob's warm brown eyes.

CHAPTER ELEVEN

I wake up with a nervous pit in my stomach.

Getting ready and driving to school didn't help with that feeling, and I'm stuck anxiously waiting for journalism so I can talk to Jacob, or at least tell him I want to talk to him. I know what I want to ask and say to him, and hopefully it will go smoothly.

As it turns out, I don't have to wait long. As soon as I park, I see Jacob's truck pull into the lot. I hurriedly gather my things and catch him before he leaves his truck.

"Hey," I say, approaching him.

I haven't really spoken to him since he and Dylan almost fought, so he gives a confused look. "Hey," he says hesitantly. "What's up?"

Everything I want to say is suddenly jumbled in my mind. I take a deep breath and try to focus. "I need to talk to you."

I can tell he's suspicious. He glances around before looking at me again. "Your new friends aren't going to gang up on me, are they?"

"Why? Are you afraid of them?" I ask, amused. Dylan would get a kick out of that one.

"Hell no." He shakes his head. "What do you want to talk about?"

I bite my lip. "I want to talk to you about, um, us."

"Us?"

Us. It sounds different when it comes out of his mouth. I lean against his truck. "Did you ever think about covering your tattoo?" I ask him, pointing to his arm.

His eyes trail down to it. "I've thought about it," he says slowly. "Just don't know what I would cover it with."

"Me too," I admit. "Part of me doesn't want to cover it though."

"What do you mean?"

I have to get it off my chest. Dylan is right. I am miserable without Jacob and it makes me feel gross, but I can't help it. "Have you been with Lauren since we broke up?"

"What? No." He shakes his head but hesitates. "I mean, I took her to Dylan's party, but that's it."

Jacob isn't a great liar, but he isn't the worst. There are moments when I know he's lying and others where he surprises me pretty well. I try to detect any trace of fabrication, but I think he's telling me the truth. "Do you mean it when you say you want to get back together with me?"

"I mean every word," he says firmly. "What's with all these questions? Are you okay?"

My heart is beating quickly in my chest. "I don't know." I shake my head. Visions of when we were together flash in my mind, and the kiss from his soccer game plays over and over. It's like every part of my being craves his touch, and I can't stop myself from feeling that way.

Screw it. "Don't make me regret this."

Before he can answer, I take his face in my hands and pull him in for a kiss. His lips meet mine eagerly, and in a single second, everything I've tried to build up to protect myself from him comes crashing down.

His hands cup my face before they trail down to my waist to bring me closer to him. Every second feels like an hour, then time disappears. I know it's wrong, I know he'll hurt me, but I need to feel his lips against mine again.

Neither of us speak when we pull apart. We only stare at each other and catch our breath.

Jacob smiles and wraps his arms around me for a hug. "Jesus, Lacey."

I instinctively put my arms around him too, but I still feel like I know I've just made a huge mistake. I can't deny that I still have feelings for him. I woke up today wanting to get back together with him, but this is not how I wanted to feel after kissing him. I thought getting back together the day before our anniversary would be romantic, but this is all wrong.

"Let's go before we're late to class," he says, stepping away from his truck.

I'm not ready to walk with him, so I say, "Actually, I think I forgot a textbook in my car. You can go ahead."

"You sure?"

I nod and he kisses my forehead before jogging off.

A loud clap behind me makes me jump, and I turn to see where it is coming from. Then, I see Carlos walking towards me.

"That was like a movie scene. The drama, the angst. Great performance," he says as he approaches me. "I give it a seven out of ten."

"What do you mean?" I ask him, feeling breathless. Carlos isn't the last person I want to see, but his presence still irritates me.

"To think all of this wouldn't even be happening if he hadn't cheated on you," he says, shaking his head. "I wonder who gave him that idea in the first place?"

What's he talking about? Who gave Jacob the idea to cheat on me? Lauren? "Do you know Lauren?" I ask him.

He waves it off. "It doesn't matter. I gotta get to class."

The bell rings just as he says it and I trail behind him, wondering what that was all about.

*   *   *

172

I feel like I'm practically sprinting towards the cafeteria for lunch. I thought I was going to die of embarrassment when my stomach growled loudly in class.

Someone grabs my arm suddenly and pulls me into a dark room. Whatever door I've just entered closes quickly, and the darkness consumes me.

My heart is pounding in my chest. "What the hell?"

"Don't panic," a voice tells me.

I freeze. "Jacob? Are you crazy?"

He chuckles and I can tell he's close to me. "Crazy for you."

"What are you doing?" I ask, my voice barely above a whisper now. There's only one reason he wants to talk to me again, and I'm not ready for this conversation. I thought I wanted him back, but now I know that'll do more harm than good.

"I need you back with me, and judging by that kiss earlier, you want this too," he says.

I should stop this before we go too far, but his hand presses against my face, his thumb tracing over my cheek.

I'm breathing heavily before his lips connect with mine. I'm taken back to the old days when we were still together and all this drama never happened. My morals might be shot to hell now, but I don't care. His hands slide down to my waist, pinning me to the wall.

My heart is going crazy in my chest as his mouth leaves mine and trails kisses down my jawline. He nuzzles into the soft spot in the crook of my neck and slowly sucks on the skin as my hands get tangled in his hair.

I don't even realize what he's doing until my phone starts buzzing in my back pocket. I push Jacob away slightly and grab my phone. I see Casey's name and answer it.

"Hello?" I say breathlessly.

"Where are you?" she asks.

I gulp, trying to catch my breath. "Um, I'm walking down the hall. Why?"

"Are you okay? You sound like you've been running around."

"I'm fine."

She sighs. "Well, at least you're not dead. I was sitting alone until Carlos and the guys came over. Dylan left a while ago to look for you."

Oh no.

"I'll be there in a sec," I tell her before hanging up.

I take a deep breath and grab my bag. Shit, this is not how I wanted things to go. I'm stupid, stupid, stupid.

"Are we going to talk about what just happened?" Jacob asks, and I feel his hand on my arm.

"I gotta go," I say, opening the door and stepping out into the hallway.

I instantly see Dylan walking in my direction.

He gives me a small smile. "There you are. Casey was convinced you got kidnapped."

I try to laugh. "Not kidnapped. I was—" A door closes behind me and dread washes over me. I can't help but turn around to look at Jacob, who is fixing his jacket and hair. I cringe when I think about what I look like.

Jacob shoots a smirk at Dylan before taking off in the opposite direction. Dylan is glaring at him then locks eyes with me. They widen a bit and narrow.

"Did you even realize he left a hickey on your neck?"

His words cut into me, and I instinctively cover my neck.

Rolling his eyes, he says, "It's on the other side."

"It's not what it looks like." I hate the way those words come out of my mouth. It is as bad as it looks, and I want to kick myself for using such a shitty line with Dylan.

"You're telling me you didn't just make out with your douchebag ex?" he asks, crossing his arms. The disappointment on his face kills me.

"Things were really confusing for me, but I know what I want now—"

"Yeah, it's pretty damn clear what you want," he snaps.

I get that he's angry, but he's not innocent. "You're the one who put it in my head," I shoot back. "You're the one who told me to get back together with him."

"Don't put the blame on me. I only told you what you wanted to hear." He steps closer to me, and the expression on his face scares me. "Why do you still want him anyway? He doesn't care about you, Lace. He made that pretty clear by cheating on you."

The words are coming at me from all directions and they're stinging. In my mind, I can see the disappointment on my parents's faces.

"You're still buying into his bullshit," Dylan's voice brings me back to reality.

What does he want from me? He tells me he'll help me get over Jacob, but then he turns around and tells me to get back together with him. "You're not helping me like you said you would. If anything, you've made things even more confusing for me. Maybe I should've never asked for your help."

"Maybe you shouldn't have," he says, raising his voice. There's hurt in his voice too, and that stings more than anything else. "God forbid I care about you, but if you want to go crawling back to him, then go ahead. He's going to treat you like shit again, and I don't want to stand by and watch it happen because you don't deserve that."

"You don't understand," I say, my voice cracking. I try to calm down, but my eyes are stinging. Why am I crying?

"I guess I don't." He holds his hands up. He turns to walk away but stops himself and looks at me. "When I told you to go

175

back to him, I wanted you to realize how shitty he actually is, but you did the exact opposite." He shakes his head, almost in disbelief. "I thought you would be stronger than this."

Before I can explain myself any further, he strides down the hallway while I try to blink the tears away.

*   *   *

It's Thursday, and I haven't told Casey what happened with Jacob and Dylan that Tuesday. Dylan didn't speak to me—or even look at me—yesterday, and I made Jacob mad so he wouldn't talk to me.

I meet Casey for lunch in the cafeteria, though I wish I could eat alone. I'm afraid to tell her about what happened, and I know she knows something is off.

"I just think my dad is overreacting," she continues her story.

"Right." I nod, even though I have no idea what she's been talking about.

She gives me a deadpan look. "Are you even listening?"

I'm caught. "I'm sorry. I just have a lot on my mind right now." Instead of going into it, I say, "What were you saying?"

"My dad thinks Carlos is my boyfriend and that we're trying to sneak around behind his and Mom's backs." She rolls her eyes. "I mean, can you even imagine me and Carlos dating?"

I've had that impression during homecoming, but I wonder if there really isn't anything going on. "No way," I say, almost too sarcastically.

She doesn't seem phased, so I glance around to look for Dylan. Just as I'm looking around, the cafeteria doors open and I see the guys walk in with Dylan trailing behind them. Carlos, Reece, and Anthony are joking around with each other while Dylan looks less than interested with his hands in his pockets.

The other guys don't look our way, but Dylan happens to meet my gaze. We lock eyes and I try to silently plead to him that I'm sorry, but with a cold turn, he brushes me off and keeps walking with the guys to a table in the corner.

"Uh oh," Casey says, catching my attention. "What's up with you guys?"

"Nothing."

She scoffs. "Doesn't look like nothing."

I know she'll disown me as her best friend if I tell her about Jacob. I just need to make it clear that it has been one huge mistake. All the hard work we put into me getting over him will be flushed down the toilet, if it hasn't already.

"I can always ask Carlos, you know," she says.

That's the last thing I want. "I made a mistake, Case," I give in. I hope she doesn't give up on me after I tell her. I won't have anyone else to confide in.

She raises her brow. "What happened?"

She sits quietly as I explain everything from what Dylan suggested after the diner, to what I said and did with Jacob. I pull the neckline of my t-shirt down to show her the remnants of the hickey. I've been able to hide it with my hair, but I've been wearing shirts with a higher neckline for good measure.

"I see," she says in a monotone voice.

"Dylan saw us and now he's pissed at me," I say. I completely betrayed our agreement, and he was right. I needed an excuse to run back to Jacob and completely screwed myself over. I put my head in my hands and sigh. "I don't know what to do."

Casey doesn't say anything at first, seeming deep in thought. "I don't know what to tell you," she finally says.

No scolding, no blowing up? "You aren't going to yell at me?"

"Lace, you knew what you were doing. At this point, you're only doing it to yourself. You can't blame anyone else. Not me, not Dylan, and not Jacob. Jacob hadn't been bothering you, and I think you missed him being in your life." She shrugs. "You initiated everything."

Casey's carefree response is upsetting. I know it's my fault, but hearing it from her makes it hurt more.

"It's up to you what your next move will be," she says.

"If I choose Jacob, then you and Dylan might not forgive me. If I choose you guys over Jacob, it'll be like starting from square one all over again," I stress.

"I'm not going anywhere. I might be angry if you choose to go back with Jacob, but you're my best friend. I can't just leave you in the dust." She glances toward the table in the corner. "However, I don't know about Dylan."

Dylan said he doesn't want to watch me get hurt again if I get back together with Jacob, but does that mean he wouldn't want anything to do with me? The thought of never speaking to him again doesn't settle well with me. "I have to talk to him," I say.

"You have to decide what's going to make you happy in the end. Just remember that," she says, giving me a small smile. "And I'm here whenever you need me."

When I walk into English, Dylan isn't there yet. I go to my seat and try to think of what I can say to him and if he'll even listen to me at all. He told me he cares about me. Does that mean he has feelings for me, or is it caring on a friendship level?

Right before the bell rings, Dylan stalks into class and hastily sits down behind me without even so much as a glance my way.

I don't have time to talk to him because Mrs. Beattie starts the lesson. She wants us to do some silent reading for a few minutes, so we all reach under our desks and pull out our textbooks. When I reach for mine, I can't feel it. I lean over and peer under me. Sure enough, the book isn't there.

Dylan already put his book on his table. The empty desk behind him has one, so I take a chance.

"Can you hand me the book from the desk behind you?" I ask him quietly since others are already reading.

He gives me a blank stare.

I try not to get flustered. "Please, Dylan."

He sighs and turns to reach for the book. While handing it to me, I don't have a good grip, so it slams on the ground with a hard thud.

I whip around to find Mrs. Beattie giving me a death glare. I sheepishly pick up the book, set it on my desk, and quickly find the pages we should be reading.

A couple of lines in, I feel my desk start to shake. I glance under my desk to see Dylan's foot on the bars that hold the textbooks. He's shaking his leg, causing my desk to move around. I try to ignore it as best as I can.

It stops and I internally sigh in relief. I can focus on reading now.

Something hits my desk, and I look down again to see Dylan's foot repeatedly hitting the leg of my desk.

"Stop," I say quietly over my shoulder.

I can't see his reaction, but the hitting doesn't stop. Then it starts to shake again.

"Cut it out," I whisper harshly.

The hitting and the shaking don't stop. It's irritating me to no end, and I can't focus. I can't take it anymore.

"Knock it off," I say loudly, twisting in my seat so I can see his reaction, which brings everyone's attention to me and Dylan.

Great. I've caused a scene. I slowly turn back around, and Mrs. Beattie is staring right at me.

"Is there a problem, Ms. Reyes?" she asks, seeming unamused.

I shake my head. "No."

"What about you Mr. Parker? Is something wrong?" She uses the same tone with him.

"I don't know, Mrs. Beattie. She just turned around and yelled at me," he says, trying to sound innocent.

My jaw drops. There's no way he's pinning this on me. I sit up straight and try to explain myself. "He kept kicking my seat, which prevented me from concentrating. I kept telling him to stop."

She narrows her eyes at me. "You could have ignored him."

Before I can stop myself, I roll my eyes. "That would've worked well," I say sarcastically. There's a few snickers around me, and I know I'm in trouble.

"Way to go," Dylan's amused voice says behind me.

"Ms. Reyes and Mr. Parker, may I see you out in the hallway?" Mrs. Beatie asks, standing up.

More snickers follow as I stand up and follow Mrs. Beattie with Dylan right behind me.

We step outside of the classroom, and Mrs. Beattie shuts the door. She's clearly irritated, and I know I'm in for it.

"For disturbing my class, I'm giving you both detention today after school," she says, crossing her arms.

Detention? "But Mrs. Beatt—"

She holds up her hand and I stop. "No buts. For the remainder of class, I want you to sit out here. I advise you not to interrupt my class again." With that said, she goes back into the classroom.

I glare at Dylan as soon as she's gone. He holds his hands up in defense. "Don't look at me."

"You were the one shaking my desk," I point at him, "and I got detention."

"Maybe you shouldn't give our teacher attitude." He shrugs before leaning against the wall.

"What's your problem?" I demand.

"I was just sitting there. You're the one who flipped out in front of everyone," he says, glancing down the hallway instead of looking at me.

"You're impossible, you know that?" I ask him, putting my hands on my hips. "I've never had detention before." My aunt won't be too upset, but I hate knowing that it's Dylan's fault that I've ended up in this situation.

Casey's voice echoes in my ears, and I know I shouldn't blame him. I probably could have ignored him, but I let my anger get the best of me.

"It's not like you got suspended," he says.

What have I gotten myself into? This past month has been hell. I can't believe I've dug myself into such a deep grave that even Dylan doesn't want anything to do with me. A friendship I didn't think I would ever be a part of is now on the rocks when I don't want it to be.

Defeated, I lean against the wall and sink to the ground. "Can you sit for a second?" I ask. I need to apologize to him.

He hesitates but sits next to me. I can feel the warmth coming from his arm even though it's barely touching mine. Dylan and I have never been this close.

"I'm sorry." I shake my head. "When we talked about this the other day, it just brought back so many old memories I shared with Jacob, and I missed those days. You were right. I was looking for an excuse to go back to Jacob."

I sigh. "I know you don't want to hear this, but I need to explain myself. On Tuesday, I came to school wanting to be with Jacob again. I kissed him twice, and after the first time, I knew it wasn't what I wanted anymore. I still have feelings for him, but now I know for sure it won't work out again."

Dylan doesn't say anything. He is eerily silent, so I look at him to make sure he hasn't fallen asleep or checked out. Instead, he's staring at the ground.

"This might be too personal, and you don't have to answer, but have you ever been in a long-term relationship?" I ask for the hell of it. If he has, then he can try to relate to my situation. If not, then I don't know how to make him understand where I'm coming from.

I don't expect him to answer, but he does. "No, I haven't."

"What about wanting a person that you know you shouldn't want? Has that ever happened to you?" Wanting Jacob is one thing. Wanting him knowing he'll hurt me again is another thing.

Dylan stretches his legs out and picks his head up, so he's looking straight ahead. "I guess so."

"Yesterday would've been our three year anniversary. Can you believe it?" I scoff. "I know he would hurt me again if we got back together. I just don't know why he cheated on me in the first place, you know? And I still don't. Was I not good enough for him?" I'm just rambling now, but I have to say it out loud. Not being enough for him kills me. What else could I have done to keep him happy?

Dylan faces me instantly. "It isn't your fault he's a piece of shit. You just realized it too late." He runs a hand through his hair and sighs. "I don't think we should talk about him. Once he's in your head, you're off dreaming about what could have happened if he didn't cheat."

He's right, but I'm afraid of what will happen if we go back to plan A. What if no plan works?

"Listen," he says. "Let's get through detention today, and later on, I'll take you to someone who I think can help."

Who else can possibly try to help me? I'm a lost cause. "Who?"

"It'll be a surprise," he says, letting a small smile peek through. "If he can't help you, then you're hopeless."

My heart warms when I see his smile, and I can't help but nudge his shoulder. "Thanks," I say sarcastically. "Are we friends again?"

He rolls his eyes but grins anyway. "I don't think we stopped being friends."

*   *   *

Detention is torture. I can go without my phone for a long period of time, but not being able to do anything absolutely sucks. I'm never getting in trouble again.

The clock on the wall behind her reads four-thirty when she tears her gaze away from her computer and says, "Mr. Parker, you're free to go."

I frown. Why is he being let go earlier than me?

"What about Lacey?" he asks from his desk, which is five seats in front of mine.

"Ms. Reyes can leave when I say she can," she says before returning her attention back to her computer.

This is so not fair.

Dylan stands up, facing my direction. He then points and fakes a laugh at me.

"Good day, Mr. Parker," Mrs. Beattie says sternly.

I want to argue over why he gets to leave earlier, but I figure it won't do me well. I'll end up with detention for the next three days.

At about four forty-five, Mrs. Beattie looks at me. "No more disturbances in my class, Ms. Reyes. You can go now."

I ignore her and practically sprint out of the classroom. I wonder if Dylan waited for me or if he left. I wouldn't be surprised if he left.

Just as I'm walking out the front doors and pulling my phone out to call him, I run into a tall figure and stop myself from losing my balance.

"Don't go falling for me that easily. I like to play hard-to-get," Dylan says, smirking down at me.

I laugh it off. Falling for Dylan? Yeah, right. "In your dreams, Parker. I thought you left me."

He shoves his hands in his pockets. "I thought about it."

"But you didn't, so what's the plan?" I ask. "You mentioned you know someone who can help me?"

"Ah yes." He nods. "You wanna follow me in your car? We won't be too long."

"Sure," I say slowly. He's being vague about who we're going to meet and where. If it's going to be Anthony, Reece, or Carlos, then I don't want to hear what they have to say. I'm not one hundred percent sure if I even want anyone's help.

I think he senses my hesitation because he says, "Don't worry. You'll feel better when you see him."

I follow Dylan's little black car and recognize the streets he leads us down. I haven't been this way since Casey and I went to his party. When we pull up to his house, I can't help but feel more anxious about the situation.

Why did he bring me to his house? There is one other car sitting in the driveway. Does that belong to the guy who is going to help me?

"Don't say anything yet," he says as he walks towards me after parking our cars. "Just trust me."

The nervous pit in my stomach hasn't left for a couple days, but I trust him. Dylan can be a bit of an ass, but he hasn't given me a reason not to trust him.

He unlocks the large wooden door and opens it. The sound of a TV is playing in the background. Everything seems to be neat and tidy, compared to the mess it has been during the party. It definitely looks different without a bunch of teens scattered around the place.

"Mary Helen, I'm home!" Dylan calls out.

Even though I've been here before, it feels more intimate when it's nearly empty.

A short woman with short brown hair comes into view, and she gives Dylan a stern look. "You aren't home on time," she says, putting her hands on her hips.

"Sorry, I got detention."

"Do I have to tell your dad?" she asks. "You know he—"

"I know, Mary Helen, I know." He sighs. His eyes meet mine, and he looks at Mary Helen again. "This is my friend Lacey. Lacey, this is Mary Helen."

I offer my hand to her. "It's nice to meet you."

She shakes my hand and smiles back. "You too, Lacey. Beautiful name." She glances at Dylan. "Are you sure it was detention that kept you?"

Oh God.

"She's a friend," he stresses.

It doesn't seem like she believes him, but she grabs what looks like her purse from the small table near us. "I gotta go. It's nice to meet you, Lacey." She put a hand on my shoulder before pointing at Dylan. "No funny business."

He chuckles at her. "Goodbye, Mary Helen."

She hustles out the door, and I realize I don't know who she is to him. "Is she a relative?" I ask.

"Her? No," he shakes his head. "She cleans up and watches over—"

"DYLAN!"

The sound of someone else yelling makes me jump. I hear footsteps running in the distance until a young boy comes to the area near us. His hair is the same color as Dylan's, only a little longer. His eyes are chocolate brown, and they light up when he's in front of Dylan.

"You're home finally," he tells Dylan. "Can you make me a grilled cheese sandwich?"

185

I look at Dylan and he smiles. "Lace, this is my brother Ethan. Ethan, this is my friend Lacey."

Ethan scans over me and waves. "That's a weird name."

Dylan gives him a flat look while I laugh. I like this kid already.

"I'll make you a grilled cheese sandwich. Just give me a minute," Dylan tells him.

Ethan nods and runs off into the living room.

Appearance wise, he's just like Dylan. Even the way he stands is exactly like Dylan. "Cute. How old is he?" I ask.

"Ten," he says. "And he's going to help you with your relationship problems."

CHAPTER TWELVE

Dylan and I are standing in the kitchen while Ethan is at the small dining table near the kitchen, waiting for his grilled cheese sandwich to be finished.

I've accepted the fact that a ten-year-old can give me relationship advice. He's probably wise . . . right? I mean, I'm willing to accept any kind of help at this point, and if Ethan wants to help me, then so be it.

Once the sandwich is in front of Ethan, Dylan looks at me. "You want one? It might be a long afternoon of love advice."

I can't turn down food. "Sure." I'm already emotionally drained. Some comfort food might do me some good.

Ethan is intensely staring at the TV when I sit with him. He tears his gaze away from the TV to look at me.

"So, you're friends with Dylan?" he asks, biting into his sandwich.

"I am."

With a full mouth, he asks, "Are you guys new friends?"

"Finish chewing the food in your mouth, you sicko," Dylan scolds him as he's placing bread on the small pan in front of him.

I let a laugh escape my mouth. "Yeah, you could say we're new friends," I answer him.

"Cool," he says as he takes another bite. He swallows his food before speaking again. "Dylan isn't that cool, you know."

"He's not?" I ask, amused. Ethan is quickly becoming my favorite person. Maybe I can get dirt on Dylan through him.

He shakes his head, causing his hair to swish on his head. "No. I'm way cooler than him. He only acts cool, but I am cool."

Playing along will get Ethan to trust me more. "I bet you have way more friends than Dylan," I try to say it quietly.

Either Dylan doesn't hear me or he's ignoring me because I don't hear any comments from him.

"He has three, and Anthony doesn't even count. He's our cousin." He taps his chin. "Do you know Anthony?"

I nod.

"Anthony's pretty cool too," he says before lowering his voice. "He's nicer than Dylan."

"I don't like all this whispering you two are doing." Dylan appears next to me with a plate of grilled cheese, which he sets in front of me. "Are you guys conspiring to take over the world?"

Ethan and I smile at each other. "Just making small talk," I say.

He slides into a seat next to Ethan at the dining table and clasps his hands together like we're in a business meeting. "Lacey needs your help," he says to Ethan.

Ethan raises his eyebrow. "With what?"

Dylan gives me a knowing look so I speak up, "If you're up for it, I could really use some relationship advice."

"I'm listening." He nods.

The whole situation seems bizarre, but I tell him everything. Well, almost everything. I don't tell him about Jacob sleeping with another girl, only saying he kissed someone else. I tell him I don't know what to do about Jacob.

"This Jacob guy sounds like a real jerk," Ethan says after listening to me rant.

Dylan smirks. "That's what I've been saying."

"Let me speak, please." Ethan holds his hand up to Dylan. "I think you should stop talking to him. He's trash. He's done."

How can I explain to a ten-year-old what loving someone else is like? It's hard getting over someone you were once in love with. "It's just hard to forget him," I say, hoping he'll understand.

"I'm imagining him to be pretty ugly, so maybe you should find a guy who's better looking to help you forget him," he says before taking a last bite of his grilled cheese. "I think I'm pretty good looking, for example."

Dylan and I try not to laugh. "You know, I think you're right," I say, mostly to feed his ego. I can already tell he is going to grow up to be just like Dylan, and I'm not sure if that's a good or a bad thing. "So, I need to find another guy to date?"

"It's an option." He stands up. He walks into the kitchen and puts his plate in the sink. Before he can walk back, Dylan stops him.

"Your dish. You wash it," he tells him.

Ethan lets out a long sigh and turns on the faucet.

Dylan then turns his attention to me. "You better finish that sandwich. Making that thing was hard work."

I roll my eyes. "Do I have to wash my own plate too?"

"Unless you can get Ethan to wash it for you," he says, chuckling.

Ethan comes back after washing his plate and sits down in his spot. I'm just about finished eating my grilled cheese.

I consider Ethan's option, but I'm not sure how well it will work. How can I give my heart to someone when I don't have all the pieces to give? I also don't want to be dependent on a guy again. I need to be my own person.

"I'm not sure if I'm ready for another boyfriend," I say to Ethan. "I'm beginning to think all guys are garbage, except for you, of course."

Ethan grins. "Well, maybe another boyfriend isn't the right option. You can try hanging out with friends? Or maybe punch Jacob in the face. Just to show him he's a jerk."

Dylan, who has been listening silently, suddenly stands up with a smirk on his face. Probably imagining me punching Jacob. He grabs my plate and walks into the kitchen where he starts the water in the sink. Before I can tell him I'll wash my plate, Ethan speaks up again.

"You could date Dylan. That'd be kinda cool, I guess."

My eyes feel like they might bulge out of my head. I glance at Dylan, who is busy with the dishes. I turn to Ethan. "Uh, I don't think so. We're just friends."

"Dylan's never had a girlfriend before. He's gonna need one eventually." Ethan shrugs.

I want to laugh from how nonchalant he is about it. Me and Dylan dating? There's no way that will ever happen. Becoming friends has been a pleasant surprise, but I don't think it will go further than this. It probably won't work out between us. Dylan doesn't seem like he wants anything serious anyway.

"Now, Ethan, I know you're not talking about me," Dylan says behind me.

Ethan laughs before he says, "Gotta go." He runs to the living room, leaving me and Dylan alone.

Did Dylan hear the whole conversation? I hope not. I don't want him to think I'm weird for talking about dating him.

Pushing those thoughts out of my head, I stand up and walk into the kitchen. "Funny kid," I say, chuckling a bit.

"He's a trip. Sometimes, he hangs out with Anthony too much," he shakes his head. "Anyway, did you get the answers you need from the almighty Ethan?"

My single takeaway is getting rid of Jacob. I'm only trying to see the good in him and not realizing how much more he could hurt me. "Not all the answers, but some."

"Ten-year-olds." He shrugs. "They know more than us."

"So, what now?" I ask, not really wanting to leave just yet. Hanging out with Ethan is fun. Plus, we get to talk about Dylan behind his back.

He picks up his backpack from the ground in the hall. "You can hang out with Ethan for a second while I throw my bag in my room. We can go sit by the pool in a bit."

There's something that makes me curious about his room. Dylan is good at putting up barriers, and seeing his room might break some of those. "I want to see your room," I say before I can stop myself.

He raises his eyebrow before smirking. "I didn't realize that's what you wanted."

I roll my eyes, but my cheeks burn from embarrassment. "That's so not what I meant. I just want to see what you have."

He seems hesitant, but he nods. "Okay, weirdo. Follow me."

I trail behind him, and while we pass the laundry room, I remember standing in there with him to dry myself off after falling in the pool. That day seems like it happened forever ago.

Dylan opens a door at the end of the hallway, and instead of it opening to a regular room, there are stairs that lead to darkness.

"What's this?" I ask him.

"My room," he says, reaching in and switching on a light. "You scared?"

"No, but you can go first."

He laughs and descends down the stairs. I follow suit, practically jogging to keep up with him.

"Is this supposed to be a basement or something?" I ask.

"Yeah. This way I get some kind of privacy."

I wonder if his parents will show up. Dylan and I are only friends, but I still want to make a good impression if I have to meet them. I'm not sure how they'll react to us being in his room alone, though.

Dylan's laugh brings me out of my thoughts. "Don't look so scared, Lace. It's just my room. You've been in a guy's room before, haven't you?"

191

My cheeks warm. Jacob and I usually hung out in his room while I was at his house. "Well, yeah, but it's your room," I point out.

As we reach the bottom of the stairs, I take a deep breath, preparing myself.

His room is like any other guys room, I guess. His bed has a dark blue comforter with matching pillows. Of course, it's unmade. I glance around and see a shelf with CDs piling up, which interests me because not a lot of people have CDs anymore. A few items of clothing are strewn across the floor. The walls have a few band posters. Names such as Chevelle and the Red Hot Chili Peppers are mixed in with posters of Kendrick Lamar and J. Cole. Dylan's taste in music is interesting.

"What do you think?" he asks me.

"I think it's like any other guy's room," I tell him. "I'm not sure if I expected it to be so . . . typical." I didn't exactly expect a dungeon, but I didn't really expect it to look . . . normal.

He crosses his arms. "What were you expecting?"

"I really don't know."

"Well, this is my lair, and it's exactly how I want it." He smiles to himself as he throws his backpack on his bed.

"It's good to know you cleaned up beforehand," I say, gesturing to the clothes on the floor.

He waves it off. "Don't worry about it," he says, smirking. He's serious for a second and seems to be thinking hard about something.

"What?" I ask.

"I'm gonna show you something," he says, walking toward the steps.

A nervous pit settles in my stomach. What's he going to show me?

He starts walking up the stairs and disappears from my sight. "What are you doing?" I ask him.

"Just trust me."

And I do.

There's a small click, and the lights go out. I'm about to ask what's going on, but a small light above me flickers, catching my attention. Like stars, tiny lights cover the ceiling. They're everywhere, flickering on and off while others stay on.

"Pretty cool, huh?" I hear Dylan's voice behind me. I've lost all sense of sight, but he sounds close to me.

"It's beautiful," I say, my eyes scanning over the lights. "Why can't you see them when the lights are on?"

"That's for me to know and you to find out."

Figures. "Who knew Dylan Parker would have twinkling lights in his room?" I tease him. "But wow, this is gorgeous."

"One word about this to the guys and I'll—"

"Yeah, yeah, I know," I interrupt him. I laugh, and he chuckles with me. "Let's just enjoy the lights."

The guys don't know about these? Well, I can imagine them giving him hell for it, so I see why it's a secret. I feel giddy knowing something about Dylan that they don't know. My birthday is next week, and this feels like an early gift to me somehow.

My eyes are still adjusting to the dark, so when I turn around, I bump into his torso. An oomph escapes my mouth. "Sorry. I didn't realize you were this close."

"If you want to be close to me, all you have to do is ask." I don't have to see his face to know that he's smirking.

My eyes adjust to the dark, and I can see Dylan's outline next to me. My heart starts beating faster. Suddenly, this moment feels different from every other moment I've had with him.

He's sharing something private with me in the most peaceful and beautiful way he can. It's like seeing a unique side of him without him being completely out of touch with himself. This moment feels intimate and almost romantic, and the butterflies in my stomach make their return.

"If you're trying to seduce me, it's not working," I joke, mostly to keep the awkwardness at bay, though I'm probably the one making things awkward.

"I think you're the one trying to seduce me. Did Ethan tell you going out with me is the best option?"

So he did hear our conversation. My face feels hot, and I'm dizzy for a split second. "What Ethan and I talk about is between us," I say, trying not to get into that conversation. "Unless you told him to tell me that." Imagine that; Dylan convincing his younger brother to persuade me to date him. I just can't see Dylan going to those lengths to ask me out, though.

Would I even say yes?

"What Ethan says or does is completely his own doing," he says.

Even in the darkness, I can see his facial features from the faint glimmer of the lights above us. His sharp jaw, the bridge of his nose, and his dark eyebrows. The curve of his lips go on forever, and I blink to cast them from my mind. Oh god, I shouldn't have looked at his lips.

"Are you having dirty thoughts about me?" He lets out a small laugh as he says it.

"No," I say defensively. "I'm just . . ." *Thinking about your lips*, I almost say. I can't come up with a lie quick enough.

He's looking at me, and I feel insecure even in the dark. It's as if he's really seeing me, really studying me. To make it worse, he's not saying anything. I don't know if I'm imagining it, but he seems to be getting closer and closer to me.

When I realize he is, I start to breathe faster. I can feel the warmth of his body near me and it's almost intoxicating.

"Dylan—" I instinctively put my hands on his chest. His heart is beating rhythmically in his chest, and it only makes mine flutter more.

"I'm going to kiss you, Lace . . ." His voice is raspy and barely above a whisper.

My heart feels like it might leap out of my chest. The moment is perfect. The way it all falls into play, like it is meant to happen. A part of my brain is telling me to stop before we get carried away, but every other part of me is saying go for it.

His hands rest on my waist, tugging me so I'm closer to him. My body is tingling from his touch. He then brings his hand up to trace over my lips. I can't help but close my eyes and melt into him.

Our lips lightly brush against each other's and more shocks go coursing through my body. He presses his lips firmly against mine, and my mind swirls. For a moment, I forget where we are.

The lights suddenly flicker on. "Dylan, where—oh my God! My eyes!"

Dylan and I instantly jump away from each other. I nervously clutch my chest before running my hands through my hair.

What the hell just happened?

Ethan is standing there covering his eyes. He then peeks through his hands. "Okay good. Dylan, where's the vacuum?"

"Why?" Dylan asks, sounding breathless.

Ethan's eyes widen. "No reason."

Dylan rubs his face with his hands. "Whatever mess you made, I'll clean it up in a minute."

Ethan nods before bolting up the stairs.

What is probably only a couple of seconds of silence feels like hours. "Um, I should probably get going before my aunt starts calling me," I say, wringing my hands together and not really knowing what to do with myself.

"Yeah, I'll walk you out," Dylan says, not meeting my eyes.

I walk up the stairs first and almost trip on the top step from my lack of concentration. I go to the kitchen and grab my keys before meeting Dylan at the front door. We saunter out to my car. I can't help but think our friendship is ruined because of that kiss, even though it felt right in the moment.

195

I stand next to my car, and Dylan shoves his hands into his pockets. I can't take the silence anymore so I say, "Thanks for bringing me to Ethan."

"No problem." He pulls his hands out of his pockets and scratches the back of his neck. "I'll see you tomorrow?"

"Yeah, sure," I say without thinking. I slide into my car, though it takes me a few seconds to actually buckle myself in. I wave to him as I drive off, and he goes back inside the house.

Focusing on the road is a challenge. When I finally get home, I release a breath that I've probably been holding since I left Dylan's house.

Leaning against the front door, I replay the kiss in my head over and over again. It didn't last too long, but it all seemed to happen in slow motion. As much as I try not to think about, I compare that kiss to every other kiss I've had with Jacob.

With Jacob, everything was fast and more lustful. With Dylan, everything slowed down and there seemed to be more . . . emotion? Does Dylan have feelings for me, or did he get caught up in the moment?

Was I caught up in the moment?

I'm not sure how Dylan is feeling, and I don't even know how I'm feeling. I admit, I always feel that there is some kind of connection between me and Dylan, but I've never been sure what kind. I figured we'd have a great friendship, but a relationship? I don't know.

What the hell are we doing?

CHAPTER THIRTEEN

Fridays are supposed to be fun, buzzing with energy. On the contrary, I feel anything but energetic this morning.

I forgot to turn on my alarm last night, so I woke up extremely late for class. By the time I've gotten myself to campus, my computer class is already in session. After giving my teacher a late pass and ignoring her evil eye, I hurriedly sit down.

Second period is mostly boring until I'm suddenly called out of class. Mrs. Thomas has asked for me, Sophie, and Seth. Because I don't know how long I'm going to be out for, my teacher gives me the textbook to finish my work. Of course, it has to be a giant textbook that isn't the easiest to carry around, so I don't feel like putting it in my backpack.

Last Wednesday, we were supposed to get our newspapers, but the printers had some issues with the press and were backed up on their orders. Now, Mrs. Thomas wants us to distribute the papers around the school after they've come in later than planned.

We take our time putting papers in all the teachers mailboxes. We finish the job just as the bell rings for lunch.

"Should we take the rest back to class?" Sophie asks me.

The twins have a bundle each and I have two. I figure it will be best if we get rid of most of them as quick as we can. "Might as well finish setting them out. Sophie, you can take yours to the office where the secretaries are, and Seth, you can take yours back to class so everyone can get their own copy."

I pick up my two bundles and balance them on my textbook. I'll probably take mine to the library and to some of the English teachers.

Seth sees me juggling the bundles, and he holds his hand out. "I can take one of those."

I shake my head. "I'm okay, really. I'll get rid of them in no time."

He doesn't look convinced, but he and Sophie say their goodbyes and take off. I start walking down the hallway and try my best not to run into people. I think of where I want to go first. I should probably split one bundle between some English teachers. They always like to show off student writings.

I round a corner and one of the bundles falls and busts open, scattering newspapers all over the ground.

"Great," I say to myself. I drop to the floor and set my things down to start picking up the papers.

"Should I ignorantly walk past you like everyone else, or should I stop to help?" Dylan asks.

My heart flutters at the sound of his voice, and my mind immediately goes to our kiss.

"I got it," I say as I finish putting the stack back together, purposely avoiding his eyes. I grab the stack, the other bundle, my backpack, and my textbook, then try to stand up.

Dylan instantly takes my textbook from me. "You clearly need help," he says, taking that and my backpack from me.

"In many ways, but that helps, yes," I say, half-heartedly joking, finally peering up at him.

He lets out an airy laugh. Then he gestures to the papers in my hands. "Is that your finished product?"

I nod. "I just have to distribute them for now. I'm sure everyone is eager to glance over them, then proceed to weaponize the pages as spitballs."

"You mean, you're actually supposed to read these?" He smirks before tilting his head. "You seem like you have the Monday blues, but it's Friday, so I'm a bit confused."

I thought he would avoid me because of the kiss, but here he is, striking up a conversation and easily carrying my things for me. It's a pleasant surprise. "Just anxious for the weekend to get here," I say instead of telling him it's been a long morning. "Can you follow me? I need to get these off my hands."

We walk in silence to some of the classrooms of English teachers I know. With one bundle down, we head to the library to leave the other bundle. The librarian graciously lets me put them on his desk.

He starts reading over it and tells me how excited he is to see students writing about school issues and blah blah blah. I feel bad for barely listening, but I'm ready to be done with this.

With the bundles gone and my fingers stained from newspaper ink, I turn to Dylan as we return to the main hallway. "Thanks for carrying my stuff." I hold out my hands, so he isn't carrying them everywhere.

"No problem," he says, handing my things back to me.

I look at my phone and find it strange that Casey hasn't blown it up with messages or calls asking where I am. "What are you doing for lunch?" I ask him.

"Just gonna meet up with the guys in the cafeteria."

"Can I tag along? Maybe Casey is with them," I say. Things only feel a little awkward, though not unbearable enough where I can't be around him. I know the conversation will come up eventually, and I don't think I'll be ready.

"Yeah, c'mon," he says. As we start to walk, he speaks up again, "Ethan said he likes you."

That makes me smile. "I've only met him once, though." I must've made a good impression on him.

Dylan shrugs.

"I guess my natural charm got him," I say, feeling a little more comfortable now.

He shoves his hands in his pockets and grins. "I guess so."

In the cafeteria, we find Casey sitting with the guys. We approach the table, and Anthony grins at us.

"Well, look who finally decided to show up," he says.

I sit next to Casey, who gives me the "where have you two been" look. I didn't tell Casey about the kiss between me and Dylan. I wonder if he has mentioned it to any of the guys.

"You two seem very secretive," Reece says, leaning forward.

"Dylan was helping me deliver newspapers," I say, hoping that'll clear the air. I don't want things to be any more awkward between us.

Reece puts his arm around Dylan and smirks. "Is that what they call it nowadays?"

Dylan rolls his eyes and shrugs off Reece's arm. "Shut up." He doesn't meet my eyes, so I look away.

Should I tell Casey about the kiss? She's always suggesting that Dylan likes me, so telling her might add fuel to the fire.

"Someone's on edge," Anthony says, shoving fries into his mouth. "I say we head to Raven's after school, just to take the edge off."

"No way." Carlos shakes his head. "There are some shitty bands playing tonight. When do Derrick and Jared play again?"

Reece steals some fries from Anthony. "Next Wednesday."

Anthony smacks his hand when he tries to get more. "Get your own food, fucker."

Next Wednesday? That's my birthday.

"Well, isn't that perfect," Casey says, grinning broadly at me. "That's Lacey's birthday," she announces.

Dylan finally looks at me. "Your eighteenth?"

I nod. My birthday has always been great. My parents would throw me the best birthday parties when I was younger, and they always took me out to dinner once I started getting older. They made my birthday a special day every time it came around.

And this year, they're gone.

"Holy shit, Lacey is older than me," Reece says. "Mine is in December."

"Way to make me feel old," I say, trying to cheer up. It makes me wonder when Dylan's birthday is. Anything to distract me from thinking about my parents.

"Mine is all the way in February," Carlos says before looking at Casey. "When's yours?"

"Not until March." She shrugs.

I sense a bit more chemistry between them. Carlos seems to like her, but I want to know for sure.

Bringing me out of my thoughts, Anthony says, "October baby, right here." He points to himself.

Dylan hasn't contributed to the conversation, and I'm curious about his birthday. "When is yours?" I ask him.

He appears hesitant but answers anyway. "August."

His birthday already passed? "What day?"

"The thirteenth."

That was the day before the first day of school. Was the party at his house that week meant to be a birthday party?

Anthony grins at me. "You should come to Raven's for your birthday. I mean, if you don't have plans already."

Knowing that I'll be spending my eighteenth birthday without my parents is really weighing down on me. The thought is finally hitting me, and the feeling I felt when I found out they were gone returns. My eyes sting from the tears that want to come out.

"I'll be right back," I say, not wanting anyone to see me cry. I need to get out of here.

I feel like I'm suffocating and dizzy at the same time as I push through the cafeteria doors. My hands are shaking, my face is warm, and my jaw is clenched out of frustration.

Everything crashes down on me. My parents should be here to see me turn eighteen, to see me graduate, and to see me go to college, but they aren't.

I'm walking down the hallways when I see Jacob walking in my direction. He's the last person I want to see. I glance around for an escape route, but before I can go anywhere, he zeroes in on me.

"Hey," he says as he gets closer. "Do you have time to talk?"

I try to walk past him, but the anger inside me takes over. "I do actually," I say, balling my fists at my sides. The urge to hit him comes over me, but that won't make me feel any better. "Why did you do it?"

His expression changes. "Do what?"

"Cheat on me." Tears spill onto my cheeks. "After my parents died."

His mouth gapes open, like he doesn't know what to say. "Lacey, I told you I wasn't thinking—"

"You sure as hell weren't thinking. Come up with a new excuse because I'm tired of hearing that one. While I was trying to cope with the fact that I would never see my parents again, you were fucking Lauren at that party." I wipe my eyes as I say it. "And you want me to take you back?"

"Just listen—"

"Don't." I hold my hand up. "I'm sick of all the shit you put me through. I'm done with you. I don't want you in my life."

Jacob's face is unreadable for once, but he bows his head and turns away from me. He stalks off into a different hallway, and I let out a long sigh.

I stand there for a second before I feel someone watching me. Dylan is leaning against the wall by the cafeteria doors with his arms crossed. I suspect he has seen most, if not all, of my outburst on Jacob.

I can't talk to him though. Not yet. I head to the opposite direction and walk straight into the bathroom to collect myself.

202

*   *   *

Casey is sitting on my bed with me, processing what I've just told her. Saturday nights should be the nights we cry and complain to each other because we feel a lot better after letting it all out.

I can't keep the kiss with Dylan a secret any longer, and I have to tell her about my episode with Jacob. I needed to lash out in that moment, and Jacob was the unlucky one to feel my fury. Rightfully so.

I hold my head in my hands, afraid to look at her. "Say something already."

"I can't believe you and Dylan kissed." She clasps her hands together. "I feel like that should make everything right in the world."

"It's so confusing." I shake my head. "I don't know how he feels about me, and I don't know how I feel about him. I think we just got caught up in the moment."

I've omitted the part about the lights in Dylan's room because that's a secret he only wants certain people to know about. I feel lucky to know about it, and I'm not about to ruin his trust in me.

She tilts her head. "Clearly, there are feelings there. I think it's hard for you to start liking someone after getting out of a long relationship, but I think you're getting there."

"Is it too soon, though? I'm barely getting over Jacob. Is it even smart to move on so fast?"

She shrugs. "I don't think there's a right answer to that. Maybe you'll just know if it's too soon or not."

Even so. "I don't think Dylan is looking for anything serious. Him and Kay didn't even last, and they weren't really dating," I point out.

"Or maybe he dumped her because he likes you."

That just doesn't seem likely.

She lies on her stomach and looks at me. "You blew up on Jacob for many reasons. You're sick of him, you miss your parents, and you might like Dylan. All of those emotions building up were bound to come out somehow."

If my mom was here, I would ask for her advice. She always knew the right things to say. "Is it weird that things are suddenly feeling finalized with Jacob?"

"You're taking steps in the right direction, so I don't think so." Then she sighs. "I still can't get over you and Dylan. You two would actually make a great pair."

"What makes you say that?"

"I don't know. You two just seem to fit together." She smiles.

I'm overtalking about my drama. "Like you and Carlos?" She hasn't said anything about him, but I'm dying to know if there's chemistry there.

"I don't know what you're talking about." She turns so I can't see her face.

"Oh, c'mon," I groan. "We've been talking about my boy drama this whole time. Tell me some of yours."

Now she's staring at the ceiling. "There's nothing to talk about because I have no boy drama in my life."

Denial, of course. "Yeah, sure."

"Let's watch a movie," she says, sitting up from the bed and clearly changing the subject. She picks up my laptop from the shelf. "I need some Netflix in my life right now."

I drop the Carlos talk and let her choose a movie. She chooses a Keira Knightly film, and we sit in silence as we watch it. She's lying on her stomach with her head on her arms while I lean against the headboard. I'm hardly watching the movie. Being in my own head is the better option for the moment.

My phone buzzes and my heart skips a beat when I read Dylan's name. He sent me a text.

Ethan and his friends have taken over the house. I'm going mad.

Trying not to laugh, I text him back.

You're the oldest. Take control.

I imagine Dylan being tied up by Ethan and his ten-year-old friends as they take over the house and wreak havoc. Now that would be a sight to see.

He texts back within the minute.

I have a feeling you've never been around five little brats at the same time.

Before I can type back a response, another message pops up.

Are we good?

It's a vague question. Is he talking about the kiss? I'm not sure what else he could be talking about. I mean, he saw me blow up on Jacob, and he didn't talk to me in class. That doesn't mean we're on bad terms or anything, I just don't know what terms we're on exactly. My reply is short and sweet.

Yeah, why?

If he wants to talk about the kiss, then this is the opportunity to bring it up. I'm scared of bringing it up myself. Scared to start having real feelings for him and maybe scared I won't ever be good enough for someone again.

My phone buzzes and I take my time looking at his response.

Just don't want things to be weird between us.

I don't want that either, and we don't have to talk about it right away. Maybe we can see how things play out. Putting that conversation on hold might be better for us.

We're okay. I promise.

I wonder if he regrets kissing me. I mean, he initiated it, but maybe he got caught up in the moment and is worried he gave me the wrong idea. I don't know what's going on in his mind that time, and it's frustrating.

Ethan and his friends must have caused mayhem for him, I assume, because he doesn't text me back.

*　　　*　　　*

The next few days go by in a blur.

Dylan seems to be in his own world every time I see him, which is only in English. During class, he appears occupied by something else in his mind. Once class is over, he walks me to journalism, gives me a smile, then disappears without a word.

Jacob hasn't bothered me since I blew up at him. He doesn't even look at me in class. He's angry and it shows clearly on his face. The good thing is he doesn't lash out and keeps his distance from me. I wonder if his anger is directed towards his parents or me.

Tuesday night, Dylan texts me that he'll pick me up in the morning. No ifs, ands, or buts.

I can't help but wonder what he's up to. Tomorrow is my birthday after all. If him, Casey, and maybe even the guys have something planned, they've done a good job at hiding it. Part of me hopes they haven't done anything, so I can spend my birthday alone with my aunt.

The next morning, after my grandparents call to say happy birthday, Casey FaceTimes me to see what I'm going to wear on what she calls "the best day ever." Every outfit I pull out, she dismisses.

"I'm losing hope and time here," I say, sifting through my closet.

She gasps suddenly. "Remember that red skirt you bought and still haven't worn?"

I know exactly what skirt she's talking about. I haven't worn it yet because it's a little shorter than I like. I was supposed to return it but never got around doing it. "Yes," I say hesitantly.

"Wear that and your solid black shirt. You still have those black boots I left at your house, right? The leather ones that go up past the ankle? BOOM. Outfit right there."

The look she's going for is a little edgier than what I usually wear when it comes to clothes. "I don't know, Case . . ."

"Please, just do this for yourself. Remember our talk at the beginning of the year? Confident Lacey is in there somewhere, and she's ready to come out again," she says.

When I don't say anything, she sighs. "I know today is a little glum, but it's my job as your best friend to make sure you're always going to be okay. And today, you will be okay. You're going to put on that outfit and make today your bitch because you're eighteen!"

She's right. It absolutely sucks that my parents aren't here to celebrate with me, but they wouldn't want me to mope the whole day. I know, wherever they are, they're watching and celebrating with me.

I walk over to my drawer, pull out the skirt, and yank my black shirt from the closet. "Okay. Outfit picked."

Casey's smile practically takes up my entire phone screen. "Great! And if you're feeling really badass, I have my leather jacket you can borrow."

The leather jacket will undoubtedly boost my confidence, as it usually does when I wear it, so I nod. "Perfect."

I tell her I'll see her at school and hang up. While getting ready, I feel the pain slowly easing away. It won't ever go away, but for a moment, I feel undeniably happy.

A badass, confident ensemble deserves some winged eyeliner. Once I finish it, I look myself over in the mirror. Even if it is just for the day, gone is the girl who has been broken by Jacob's unfaithfulness. It's my birthday, and no one is going to ruin it.

Dylan texts me, saying he's on his way to pick me up, making my heart pound a little faster in my chest. I saunter into the kitchen, where my aunt is doing a little dance at the stove.

When she sees me, her jaw drops before she grins broadly. "You definitely got my sense of style." She walks up to me and grabs my hand. "But you look so much like your mom."

It makes me tear up.

"Don't cry. I don't want you to ruin your makeup," she says, tucking a piece of my hair behind my ear. "I just want to say happy birthday, and you look amazing."

"Thank you," I say, trying not to get choked up.

"Your parents are watching you grow into a beautiful young woman, you know. I know they aren't missing a single beat of your life." She smiles and I can see her eyes watering. She blinks them away and takes a deep breath. "I made chocolate chip pancakes for you. I remembered you really liking them when you were younger."

"The perfect birthday breakfast," I say, leaning against the cabinets. "Dylan is on his way to pick me up."

"I'll make a couple more for him too." I can see her smirk as she flips a pancake. "He really is a gentleman."

He's more than he likes to admit, probably. I just nod.

"Are you two going out tonight?"

"Not if you have anything planned," I tell her. I don't want to ditch her for my friends if she is planning some birthday dinner.

"I'm ashamed to say I don't," she says, turning to look at me. "I'm never good at planning parties like your mom and dad, but I hope my present will make up for that."

She walks out of the kitchen and disappears into her room. I flip the pancakes she left on the stove before she waltzes back into the kitchen. "Here." She holds out a small gift bag as I put the pancakes on a plate.

"You didn't have to get me anything," I say, taking it from her.

"I know, but this is something I really want you to have."

Inside the bag is a small box. When I open the box, there's a dainty silver ring with a teardrop-shaped gem in the middle. It looks a little worn, but it's perfect.

"This is gorgeous," I say, looking at her.

"Your grandma gave me that ring for Christmas one year, I think before you were born. She gave your mom a necklace. Your mom was always mad because she liked my ring more than she liked her necklace. She would try to trade me with one of her other rings, but I always said no," she explains, smiling. "I hardly ever wear it. I wish I would've given it to her when she asked, but I'm going to give it to you. I know you'll take care of it the way she would have."

Her story makes the ring so much more valuable, and I slip it on a finger on my right hand. "I love it. Thank you."

"And it goes perfectly with your outfit." She winks.

I take a seat and start eating breakfast.

There's a knock at the door while I'm chewing on some pancakes. When I open it, Dylan has his back faced to me. He looks different; I notice he isn't wearing his usual t-shirt. He's wearing dark denim jeans, a casual navy-blue button up with the sleeves rolled up to his elbows, and a pair of gray shoes.

When he faces me he says, "Hey, happy birth—" He doesn't finish when his eyes trail down my body shamelessly. I don't feel the need to call him out on it. I smirk knowing he just checked me out. "Happy birthday. You, uh, you look great."

"Thanks," I say, smiling. "Come in."

He steps inside and my aunt is already opening her arms to hug him. "It's good to see you, Dylan."

"You too," he says, hugging her. "Smells good in here."

"My aunt's famous chocolate chip pancakes," I tell him.

"I wouldn't say famous," she waves her hand, "but I did make enough for you, Dylan."

We walk into the kitchen. I move my gift bag out of the way on the counter. I continue to eat while Dylan eats next to me.

"I'm gonna have to jet out of here for work," she says, putting the dishes in the sink. She points at us. "No skipping school."

I smile and Dylan nods.

When she leaves, Dylan looks at me. "She's really nice."

"If you like her, you would've really liked my mom," I say, twisting the ring on my finger.

"I'd like to know about your parents sometime," he says. His eyes flicker to my ring. "That new?"

I nod. "Birthday gift from my aunt." The way he says he wants to know about my parents has my heart swelling. Talking to him about my parents might not be that bad.

"Well, enjoy it. That's the only present you're going to get today." He nudges my arm and smirks.

"Whatever you say." I nudge him back. I finish what's on my plate and put it in the sink. "I just have to grab my bag."

I walk into my room and grab my backpack. A picture of my parents on the wall catches my eye, and I stop to look at it. My aunt says I look just like my mom, but everyone always tells me I have more of my dad's features.

Grabbing the photo off the wall, I study it carefully. My aunt took the picture when my parents first bought our house. In the photo, my parents are standing on the front porch with me on my dad's shoulders. I haven't been to the house since me and my aunt moved everything out. My aunt can't afford the mortgage, so I couldn't stay there after my parents have died. I'm always tempted to drive by it, but I don't have the heart yet.

"You ready?" Dylan asks, peeking his head into my room. He glances at the photo in my hands. "What's that?"

I hand it to him. "These are my parents."

His eyes scan the picture and he smiles. "Your mom is pretty. You look like a daddy's girl in this one, though."

My dad was a pushover. He acted tough, but he was a huge softy.

"I guess I was." I don't sound like myself, and when I blink, a tear slides down my face. I try to wipe it without messing up my makeup and without Dylan seeing me.

"You okay?" he asks.

"Yeah, I'm fine. I'll be right back." I walk into the bathroom in the hall and make sure my makeup is fine before walking back out. I pick up my bag from the floor and nod at Dylan. "I'm ready."

I hang the frame back on the wall and leave the apartment.

When we're at the bottom of the stairs, Dylan puts his hand on the small of my back. "No more tears today, okay?" he asks, giving me a small smile.

My heart flutters when his hand leaves my back. I take a deep breath and walk to his car. It's going to be a long day.

When we arrive at school, Dylan parks where I usually park, next to Casey. She jumps out of her car excitedly. She practically mauls me when I get out of the car.

"Happy birthday, best friend!" she exclaims. "Here's to being another year older and another year of being my very best friend."

I hug her tightly and she pulls back excitedly. "Oh, I almost forgot." She opens the door to her backseat and yanks out the leather jacket. "For you."

At the sight of the jacket, I straighten my back. Confident Lacey is the mood for today. I've cried for my parents, but I now need to get it together.

I put on the jacket and grab my bag from Dylan's car. Him and Casey both look at me expectantly and I nod. "Let's go."

Upon entering the main building, I instantly spot the guys. Anthony, Reece, and Carlos are standing near the end of the hallway and we walk towards them. Once we're close enough, Reece does a double take when his eyes land on me.

"Damn," he says, looking me up and down. "Happy birthday to you."

"Thank you." I smile at him. I usually don't feel comfortable when people examine me, but Confident Lacey is loving it.

"Edgy. I like it." Anthony nods in approval. "Do you like Lacey's outfit, Dylan?"

Dylan shoves his hands in his pockets and clearly ignores Anthony.

Carlos casually, or not so casually, puts his arm around Casey. "Why do I have the feeling you had something to do with this outfit?" he asks her.

She grins and shrugs. "Well, this is definitely a look I'll have to steal."

My first two classes go by quickly. When I walk to the cafeteria, I notice Jacob walking in the same direction. His eyes nearly pop out of his head when he sees me. He strides ahead and opens the door to the cafeteria for me.

I look past him and stalk towards the table with my friends. While walking up to them, they seem to be whispering about something, but quickly go quiet when I sit down between Dylan and Anthony.

"Uh oh, am I interrupting plans for my surprise party?" I tease them.

Reece lets out a laugh. "What? No? No."

Turns out Reece is a terrible liar.

"There are two parts," Casey says, trying to cover for him. "One tonight, and one this weekend."

It's like a birthday week. "Okay, so what's happening this weekend?"

"Well, we'll at least keep that part a surprise," Anthony says.

"However, we're going to Raven's to watch Derrick and Jared perform tonight," Casey explains.

That sounds perfect. I haven't seen them in a while. I feel a little guilty that they're planning things for me. I don't know if I deserve all of this.

"You guys know you don't have to do anything for me, right?" I ask them.

Anthony scoffs. "What fun would that be?"

*   *   *

I feel like I'm in a haze for the rest of the day. In journalism, Mrs. Thomas makes a big fuss over my birthday, and I can tell by the look on Jacob's face that he's annoyed.

Will gives me a hug. "Happy birthday to my favorite senior," he says.

Vicky flashes me a quick smile and quietly tells me happy birthday. Sophie gives me a charm bracelet with some of the beads spelling out Senior Editor, and Seth gifts me a framed print of my favorite pictures that he's taken. I hug them both and make sure they know how much I appreciate their friendship.

After class, I rush out to meet Dylan at his car. I manage to avoid Jacob and make it to the parking lot without any problems. When I'm close enough to Dylan's car, I notice a familiar red car parked next to his. There he is, talking to Kay. I slow my stride and watch them.

Kay is giving him her best lip bite, while he has his arms crossed as he's talking to her. She smirks at something he says and loops her fingers around his belt loops and pulls him closer to her.

It looks as if they're going to kiss, but he pulls back and shakes his head. But he does reach out and brushes some hair out of her face. An intimate gesture that leaves me wondering how he really feels about her.

I can't watch anymore, so I start walking normally and approach them carefully. Dylan sees me and swiftly looks back at Kay. He says something to her before turning to me. "Ready to go?" he asks, walking up to me and blocking my view of Kay.

"Don't let me interrupt," I say, crossing my arms.

"You're not interrupting anything." He shakes his head.

Kay appears next to him and wraps her hand around his arm. "Hey, Lacey." Her sweet voice is practically dripping with venom. "Heard it's your birthday." She looks me up and down. "Nice boots."

"Thanks." I flash her a smile. Her presence throws me off, and Confident Lacey is receding.

"I'll catch you guys later." She smiles at Dylan before she gets in her car and drives off in a blur.

"So, Kay is back," I say more as a statement rather than a question.

Dylan doesn't say anything as he walks to the driver's side and unlocks the car. I step inside and wait for him to respond.

"She wanted to talk about Xavier," he says, not looking at me.

I have the feeling he's lying. I also have the sneaking suspicion that Kay is trying to slither her way back into Dylan's life, and her timing is impeccable. Here I am, trying to figure out my feelings for him and she suddenly appears. I wonder if he asked her to come back.

"Derrick and Jared won't go on until seven, but we can head to Raven's now and hang out if you want," Dylan says.

"Yeah, that's fine." I nod. I'm hoping being at Raven's will lift my mood. I really need this night to go smoothly.

CHAPTER FOURTEEN

At Raven's, a band whose name I can't remember is playing some upbeat music, and people are standing in front of the stage cheering for them.

It's nearing seven o'clock, and more people show up as the light in the sky darkens. I'm sitting with Dylan at a giant table where all of us have been sitting. The other four have disappeared to wherever and haven't returned.

"So, where did the others run off to?" I ask him.

He chuckles and avoids my eyes again. "I'm not supposed to say."

I've figured out that Dylan cannot look me in the eye when he's trying to lie about something. Obviously, something is up with the other four, and obviously Kay is back in his life.

"Ominous." I laugh with him instead of getting upset.

His eyes flicker behind me and a smile spreads on his face.

Before I can turn around, a monstrous bouquet of flowers is placed in front of me.

"This is gorgeous, you guys." I cover my mouth and marvel at the colors.

"Surprise!" Reece exclaims.

Anthony gestures to the bouquet. "Here, you are looking at peach roses . . . um, someone's breath, and—"

"Anyway, there are a lot of flowers and they're beautiful," Casey says. "We all pitched in to get these for you."

"Some more than others," Anthony says, glancing at Dylan.

It isn't some small simple bouquet of flowers. It's a quality arrangement with a glass vase and everything, meaning it must've cost them a lot to get it. I instantly feel bad. "Not to sound ungrateful, but you guys didn't have to do this," I tell them.

"You deserve it." Casey shrugs while smiling.

I hug her first. I don't know what I'd do without her. Then I move to Reece, Anthony, and Carlos. I walk up to Dylan and he waves it off.

"Save the hug," he says with a smirk.

"Well, I'm giving you one anyway," I say, going in for the hug.

He stops me halfway and holds up a finger. "Let's go to my car first."

He lets everyone know we'll be right back, and I flash a confused look at Casey. She only shrugs.

We get to his car and he reaches into the backseat to pull out a purple gift bag with a decorative curly ribbon on it. "From me to you."

I can't help but smile as I hold it in my arms. I stare at it, not believing he got me a present along with pitching in for the flowers.

"Well, are you going to stare at it or open it?" he asks impatiently.

"Calm down, I'm opening it." I laugh as I pull out the tissue paper and peer inside. My heart soars when I see a big box in the bag. I draw it out of the gift bag, studying it until I figure out what it is. "Dylan . . ."

"You seemed to really like the lights in my room, so I got you some of your own. They're not exactly like mine, but I hope you won't mind."

They're plain white Christmas lights, and I'm already picturing where I can put them in my room. "I don't mind at all." I practically hug the box. "This is so sweet. Thank you."

217

He shrugs but an airy laugh escapes him. "I try."

We stare at each other for a moment, and it's like I forgot how to speak. Dylan has proven to be caring, sweet, and incredibly fun to be around. I can't believe he has such a huge impact on my life, and I'm so glad he's there for me.

His eyes flicker to my lips and licks his own, making my palms sweaty. My mind goes to our first kiss, and I briefly wonder if there will ever be another one.

He clears his throat and scratches the back of his neck. "Listen, I've been wanting to talk to you about something for a couple days now."

I nod, not trusting my voice. Whatever he has to say is making him nervous. He's fidgeting with his hands until he puts them in his pockets.

Before he can say anything else, Anthony's voice interrupts us. "Hey, Derrick and Jared are going on." He's standing at the door, poking his head out.

Dylan's jaw tenses up. "Thanks, Anthony," he says, almost sarcastically.

Anthony smirks and goes backs inside.

"You were saying?" I ask, desperate to know what he wanted to say.

He inhales deeply and his shoulders rise. "I'll tell you later," he says, letting out the breath. "Let's get back inside."

I put the box of lights back in the bag. "Can I leave this in the car?"

He nods and I put it on the passenger seat. When we walk back inside, I can't help but notice my flowers are about the most colorful thing in the building, and I smile to myself.

We all wait for Derrick and Jared to go on stage. Reece and Anthony are talking quietly to each other, and Carlos and Casey are having an animated conversation.

People start cheering once Derrick and Jared finally emerge. They sit down and get everything situated. Derrick stands

218

in front of the main microphone and grins. "How is everyone tonight?" he asks the crowd. They all cheer some more, and I realize how much of a great stage presence they have. "Well, we're going to slow it down for a few minutes. Why don't you all grab that special someone and bring them onto the floor?" His eyes flicker to me, and he gives me a big but mischievous smile.

Carlos immediately jumps up and looks at Casey. He doesn't even have to ask her to dance. They lock hands and pull each other to the dance floor.

I feel Dylan move next to me, and I glance at him. My eyes are blessed at the sight of his smile. "Care to dance?"

My heart thumps hard in my chest as he leads me to the floor where everyone is, and the music starts to play. Jared strums the guitar and Derrick's voice fills the room. The familiar chords of *This* by Ed Sheeran run through my ears.

Dylan has his arms wrapped around my waist, and I put mine around his neck. He's smiling down at me, and I can't help but smile back. I then lean my head against his torso, just like at homecoming, and we sway to the sound.

My mind is swirling with thoughts that scare me. Everything is so right with Dylan,—the way we laugh with each other, the way he listens to my rants, and the way he lets me into his world just a little more each time we're together.

His heart is beating fast in his chest as his hands trace patterns on my back. Derrick's voice joins Jared's, both singing as Dylan pulls away from me and we lock gazes. His eyes are so dreamy and so mesmerizing, I can't bring myself to look away from them. His cool hand cups my cheek, and I feel exactly how I felt when we first kissed.

The butterflies in my stomach are erupting as he leans down and kisses my cheek lightly. This is a small glimpse of what life would be like if we were together, and I like what I see.

Before either of us can say anything, he's ripped from my arms, tearing the fantasy I've conjured in my head. Beyond him is

219

Kay pulling him away. He finally stops and yanks his arm away from her. I'm frozen in my spot, just watching them and waiting to see what will happen.

Just when I thought I have him all to myself, she comes in, as if trying to intentionally hurt me by taking him away. She's grabbing him wherever she can, trying to pull him towards the exit. Derrick and Jared start another song, something more upbeat, so I can't hear what Dylan and Kay are saying to each other.

"Come here," Casey suddenly says next to me. She spins me around, so I'm not looking at Dylan and Kay. "Are you okay?"

"I don't know," I say, finding my voice. My feelings for Dylan hit me like a truck at full speed, and I think he's returning those feelings, but not with the help of Kay.

"Kay is such a bitch. She's just jealous because Dylan obviously likes you," she says, crossing her arms and looking behind me. Her eyes widen and her arms drop to her sides. "Oh no."

I turn around again. Dylan and Kay are still standing by the exit, but Xavier is with them, standing dangerously close to Dylan's face.

I'm not sure what Casey is feeling when she sees Xavier, and the look on her face is unreadable. I'm anxious to see how he'll react to seeing her.

"What did I tell you about running around behind my sister's back?" Xavier asks Dylan, poking his shoulder roughly.

"Don't fucking touch me." Dylan shoves Xavier away from him.

Xavier looks as if he is about to lunge at Dylan when Casey jumps between them. Xavier stops in his tracks and frowns at Casey.

"What the hell are you doing here?" he asks her.

"That's none of your business. You're not going to lay another finger on Dylan. You're going to take Kay and leave," she says in a voice that scares me.

He doesn't look happy to see her at all. "You don't even care what he's doing to Kay?"

"I don't give a shit about Kay. You were my friend, not her." She crosses her arms.

The way she carries herself in front of him surprises me. Xavier is a big and scary guy, but Casey makes him look so small.

Dylan is quietly standing by. His fists are clenched at his sides, but he's clearly interested in how Xavier and Casey are interacting.

"I see." Xavier nods, but there's a look of disgust on his face. "After everything we've talked about these past couple weeks, you still won't take my side."

"You left my side last year. You don't get to say that." Casey points at him. Her voice is tinged with pain.

Even Xavier's face holds a slight twinge of hurt. His eyes are focused on Casey, and it's like something clicks. Finally, he looks at Kay and says, "Let's go."

"But—" she starts.

"We're done here," he tells her. "For now." He pushes past her and walks out the entrance.

Kay shoots a glare at all of us before she follows Xavier out of Raven's.

Dylan clears his throat, breaking the silence between the three of us. "Thanks, Casey."

She lets out a long sigh. "No problem. I don't know if I'll be able to pull that one again, so you're on your own next time," she says, nudging his arm and smiling. "I'll leave you crazy kids alone."

I didn't miss the part where he said they've been talking for a couple weeks now. That's news to me. Casey hasn't said anything about him, meaning she's hiding something. I've left the Carlos situation alone, but I need to know what she's been talking to Xavier about.

After she heads back to the table, things feel particularly awkward between me and Dylan. The Xavier and Casey situation disappears from my mind. My emotions catch up with me, and I realize I like him a lot more than I've allowed myself to admit.

"I think we should talk," Dylan says before I can say anything. "Wanna go outside?"

I nod and we walk out into the cool air, which feels good on my warm cheeks. The rapid beating of my heart makes me feel like I'm going to pass out. Dylan walks to his car and leans against the hood. I hesitantly sit next to him and wait.

"There's something I have to tell you," he says, meeting my eyes. There's a part of me that thinks he's more nervous than I am. "I became your friend because I wanted to get to know you."

A smile plays at my lips. "Isn't that why people become friends in the first place?"

"Well, yeah," he says, scratching the back of his neck until he laughs. "You're making this impossible."

If he's going to say what I think he's going to say, then I need to ask him something before it drives me mad. "What was going on in your head the other day in your room?"

He hesitates. "I didn't want you to get the wrong idea about me after it happened."

"The wrong idea?"

"I didn't want you to think I brought you to my house and my room just so I could kiss you," he explains.

I haven't thought about his intentions. I guess I know Dylan well enough to know all of that isn't a part of some grand scheme to get me to fall for him. All along, it has felt like he just wants to be my friend.

"I never thought that." I shake my head. "I just felt confused."

"Me too," he says. He hesitates again and I wait for him to speak. "I liked you at the beginning of the school year, and I wanted to get to know you better. I also still liked Kay at the time

222

you were still figuring things out with Jacob, so I assumed things would never work out between us."

So, he did like Kay. Does he still like her? "How do you feel about Kay now?"

"I haven't felt anything towards her since homecoming. When she came to me after school earlier, I told her to fuck off." He smirks. "I thought I wanted her, but then I met you." The smirk turns into a small grin.

"A bit cliché, don't you think, Parker?" I nudge his arm to break some of the tension.

"Maybe, but that's how I feel. I left her, and now she won't leave me the fuck alone, as you saw in there." He lets out a frustrated sigh and runs a hand through his hair.

Kay is a nuisance, but she can be dealt with. Once again, everything is happening so quickly. I don't have feelings for Jacob anymore, and my emotions towards Dylan have only gotten stronger, though I'm not sure if I should be jumping into another relationship when I've barely gotten over my last one.

Dylan speaks up again. "It was selfish to help you get over that dickhead. I wanted you to realize that you could do way better than him."

"And you're better for me?" I smile.

"I like to think so."

It's a lot to process. Dylan is basically admitting that he likes me. He's being honest with me, so I need to be honest with him.

"I just wanted to get all of that out, and now I feel kinda weird because you're not saying much," he says, shoving his hands in his pockets.

"I feel the same way." I give him a small smile. "I don't want to rush anything, though."

He nods. "I get it. We don't have to talk about it right now. We can go inside, if you want."

"Okay," I say.

As we make our way to the door, I stop him. Questions appear in his eyes, and I know what I want to do. I know I said I didn't want to rush into everything, but I want to do this.

A little ungracefully, I press my lips to his. His soft lips move against mine, and I feel his hands grip on to my waist. With his back against the wall, I bring myself as close to him as I can. There's a part of me that feels insecure and unsure about where we're headed, but I push those thoughts out. When I pull away, our foreheads rest against each other.

"Let's keep that one a secret," I say, breathlessly.

He grins but nods in agreement.

Casey and Carlos are on the dancefloor again when we walk back inside. Derrick and Jared are no longer on the stage. I feel bad for missing most of their set. A new band is on, and they're playing more upbeat music.

When Dylan and I sit down at the table, Anthony and Reece give us suggestive looks. "Where have you two been?" Anthony asks, raising a brow and smiling.

"Just talking outside," I say before Dylan can speak up. He's a terrible liar too.

Reece has a smirk on his face as he says, "Long talk."

Dylan and I swap glances, and I smile to myself. "It was."

CHAPTER FIFTEEN

Friday afternoon, the school seems to be buzzing with excitement. I meet up with Casey in front of the main building after school and ask, "What's going on today? Is it because of the football game?"

She smiles at me. "Maybe, but probably because Dylan practically invited the whole school to his party later."

A party? At Dylan's house? "Is this the other surprise you guys were talking about?"

"I thought we were all going to tell her?" Dylan asks next to me.

He winks at me when we look at each other, and I stop myself from smiling like an idiot. Yesterday, we couldn't stop grinning at each other during lunch and in class, and the same happened today, only he snuck in a kiss on my cheek before I went to journalism class.

"You're lucky she didn't hear from someone in class." She gives him a stern look as we begin walking to the parking lot. "Is inviting everyone really necessary?"

He holds his hands up in defense. "I invited some people, and it just took off from there."

"What about Ethan?" I ask him. I'm still curious about his parents. Dylan hasn't said much about them, but surely they know about all the parties their teenage son is throwing?

"He's staying at a friend's tonight, which makes this the perfect day to have a little fun," he says, raising his eyebrows.

"What time is everyone going over?" I ask. If it's going to be a big party, I want to be prepared and perhaps wear waterproof makeup just in case.

"Ten o'clock maybe. A lot of people are going after the football game."

Casey hooks her arm onto mine. "That gives us plenty of time to doll up."

We get to our cars, and I throw my bag into the backseat. Dylan and Casey meet me at my driver's side door.

"So, ten o'clock?" Casey asks him.

He nods.

She glances between me and him and smirks. "I'll just go over here for a second," she says as she walks away. When she's out of his eyesight, she puckers her lips mockingly at me.

I roll my eyes and focus on him.

"She knows." His voice is low as he says it.

Casey is sitting in her car, but she's still within earshot.

"She knows a little bit," I say, shrugging. After the party at Raven's, she tried to get me to tell her what happened between me and Dylan. I only told her we talked about our feelings toward each other. I can't jump the gun because we're technically not together and Kay is still lurking around.

"Well, I'll see you tonight," he says, tracing his finger along my arm. "Try not to fall in my pool again, okay?"

Not falling in the pool? No problem. Not falling for Dylan? Impossible. "No promises." I laugh before peeking at Casey and making sure she isn't looking our way. I go on my tiptoes and swiftly kiss his cheek. "I'll see you tonight," I say, giving him an innocent smile.

There is a look of desire in his eyes, and it makes me weak at the knees. He shakes his head, but the smile remains on his face. Without saying a word, he walks to his car.

226

Casey stands next to me and watches him leave the parking lot. "You didn't tell me the whole story the other day."

"I'll tell you when there's a full story to tell," I say. "For now, we should focus on what time you're coming over to get ready."

*   *   *

Before I can tell my aunt about the party, I'm surprised to hear that she's going out on a date.

"Who is he?" I ask curiously. As far as I know, she doesn't go out too much. Maybe he's someone from work.

"He's a genetics professor." She smiles as she wanders into her room, with me following her. "I always see him in the mornings getting a cup of coffee at the food court. He asked me to have a drink with him, and I said yes."

A genetics professor? "He sounds like a smart guy."

"An equal match for a smart woman, don't you think?" She laughs. "I have no idea what to wear. I haven't been on a date since . . . Well, it's been a while."

It clicks. "Casey is going to be here in a minute. She's my stylist, so I'm sure she can help you too," I offer.

"This might be embarrassing to admit, but I'll need all the help I can get." She sits on her bed.

Casey casually walks into the room and puts her hands on her hips. "Sorry to barge in. The door was unlocked, and I can totally help you."

Casey has always been one to walk into my old house without knocking. My parents had no problem with it, since she practically lived there too.

"Where are you two going?" she asks, eyeing us both.

"Dylan is throwing somewhat of a birthday party for Lacey," Casey beats me to the punch. She even does a little hop in her place.

227

"A party?" My aunt raises her brow.

Once again, Casey speaks, "I promise I'll look out for Lacey. Hell, Dylan will look out for Lacey too. He's totally got a thing for her."

My aunt grins. "I knew it."

"Moving on," I interject. "Let's get you ready and then talk about a curfew, young lady."

My aunt's closet is full of fun outfit pieces that Casey is dying to have. At one point, she even makes a pile of clothes that my aunt doesn't want anymore for her to take home.

My aunt, similar to when Casey styled me, turns down every outfit she puts together. Casey is just too daring for our tastes. My aunt expresses that she feels like she is too old to wear what Casey picks out.

"If I had my eighteen-year-old body, I'd definitely wear everything." My aunt sighs. She tells Casey what kind of look she wants to go for, since it is basically just a drink date.

Casey taps her chin and looks around at the clothes. "Let me dig a little deeper."

After about five minutes, Casey emerges from the closet with a huge smile on her face. "These are perfect!" In her hands are a pair of black knee-high boots.

"I forgot I even had those. They were part of a costume I wore for Halloween many, many moons ago." My aunt shakes her head. "What are you thinking?"

"A pair of dark denim skinny jeans, a black v-neck shirt, the boots, and your olive-green blazer," she says. "The blazer says 'professional,' but the boots say 'let's have a good time,' especially if worn on the outside of your jeans."

My aunt looks a little hesitant, but Casey urges her to try everything on together before turning it down.

As she's changing in her room, Casey and I wait in my room and think about what we're going to wear to Dylan's party.

My aunt walks in with the outfit on. Me and Casey's jaws drop.

"Holy—"

"Shit, you look amazing!" Casey finishes for me.

Casey was right about the outfit. It's sexy but mature. My aunt smiles, and I know Casey has gotten it right with the outfit. "I feel great." Aunt Jade glances at the clock on my night stand and sighs. "Well, I have just enough time to accessorize and fix my makeup."

By the time she's getting ready to leave, she looks stunning. I can tell she likes the guy because she's really anxious.

"What time should I be home, Mom and Dad?" she jokingly asks me and Casey. "Are you girls having a sleepover here after the party?"

Casey smirks. "Do you want the apartment empty later on?"

My aunt blushes and shakes her head immediately. "No, no."

"What time do you want us back here?" I ask her.

"Well, let's make it one." She nods. "You girls have fun, and be safe."

"You too," we reply as she walks out the door.

Casey takes a deep breath and puts her hands on her hips. "Let's focus on you now," she says, ushering me back into my room. "We have to make you look good for Dylan."

I hold up my hands. "If I'm going to look good, it's going to be for myself."

She claps. "Atta girl!. I brought some options for you, for whichever road you're looking to go down. I have sexy, casual, fun, you name it."

I'm afraid of what she has brought for a sexy look, so I say, "Let's see your fun outfit."

She reaches into her large bag and pulls out all the clothes, laying them out on the bed. One outfit catches my eye. It's a

229

cropped, strapless top that is red with white and black stripes. With it is a pair of black high-waisted pants.

"I like this." I point to it.

She raises her brows. "That's a little casual. I was expecting a different option from you."

"I think I'll feel great but comfortable in it." I shrug.

She looks like she's about to object, but she nods. "Okay, done. The straight neckline makes the boobs look fantastic, so good choice."

She glances over the other outfits and chooses a black romper with a low v-neckline.

While we're getting ready, there's a nervous feeling in my stomach. I can't tell if it's a bad nervous or a good nervous. I ignore it and continue to straighten my hair.

It's nearing ten o'clock when we have finished our looks. I haven't realized how long my hair has gotten until I finish straightening it and see that it's reaching my lower back. I put on the same boots from my birthday and complete my look with a simple gold necklace.

Casey curls her hair and slips on some nude gladiator sandals that go up her calf. She is definitely dressing up for the night.

I decide to drive us because of what happened the last time at Dylan's party. The nervous feeling in my stomach grows as we draw nearer to his house. It's a good thing he doesn't have close neighbors because the road leading to his house is lined with cars. I find a spot along the road and pray no drunk teenager hits my car.

Casey and I are walking up to the house when she wraps her arm around mine. "Tonight will be fun, I promise."

"Let's hope so," I say.

We wander into the house and see that there are more people than the last party. I take Casey's hand before I lose her in the crowd.

We search for Dylan and the guys, but see no sign of them. Casey and I walk into the kitchen and try to talk over the music and chatter. The kitchen is different without Dylan standing by the stove making grilled cheese sandwiches.

"Should we call them?" Casey asks.

Before I can answer, I feel an arm go around my shoulders. My stomach flips because I think it's Dylan, but it isn't. Anthony grins at me instead. "There you are," his words slur slightly.

"Hey, Anthony." I smile back at him. "Where is everyone?"

"They're outside." He points to the glass doors. "Let me grab a drink, and I'll take you to them. You guys want one?"

We shake our heads, and he doesn't pester us. He grabs a beer then looks at us. "Let's go!"

We walk through the glass doors and images from the last party flashes in my mind.

Dylan, Reece, and Carlos are sitting in some plastic chairs. Dylan is laughing along with them, and I smile when I see him having a good time. When his gaze lands on me, he immediately stands up from his chair.

"Hey," he says as he walks up to me. "You look amazing." His eyes quickly flicker to my chest.

I smirk. Dylan really has no shame when it comes to checking me out. "Thank you, and my eyes are up here."

He lets out a laugh and puts his arm around me. "I know they are."

Carlos takes Casey's hand and spins her around. "Look at my hot date. Damn!"

She only laughs and hugs him, but I can tell something is off. I wonder if it's Carlos making her uneasy or if it has something to do with Xavier again, which I still haven't asked her about.

"You guys want anything to drink?" Dylan asks us.

Casey shakes her head instantly. "No drinking for me tonight, and I think we should stay away from the pool."

231

Everyone laughs and Dylan nods. "Smart," he says before he glances down at me.

The guys brought more chairs, so all of us can sit in a circle. Dylan's chair is close to mine, and he keeps his arm around me, with his thumb rubbing circles on my shoulder. I feel at ease, the nervous pit in my stomach slowly going away.

A guy I recognize from my computer class walks over and asks Dylan and the guys if they want to play beer pong. It seems like Dylan wants to play, but no one else wants to. Before he can say no, I say, "I'll be your partner."

He smirks. "Have you ever played before?"

"Well, no."

He stares at me before nodding. "Okay. Let's go play then."

The nervous feeling is amplified. I'm afraid of looking stupid in front of everyone, but once Dylan grabs my hand, it subsides. We walk over to the table in front of the pool, and two other guys are already waiting.

"Oh shit, Parker's come to whoop our asses," one guy says.

"Nah, he has a chick with him, not Anthony." The other laughs.

My competitive side comes out and I cross my arms. "Dylan and I will still kick your asses."

Everyone around us snickers, and Dylan has a huge grin on his face. "That's what I like to hear," he says. "Now, just sink the ball into their cups. If one lands in the cup, they have to drink it. And don't worry, if one lands in our cup, I'll drink it."

I peer into the cups, and it looks like plain beer is inside it. I don't like beer, but I don't want Dylan to have to drink all of it by himself. "No, I can drink too."

"You sure? I don't want another incident like last time to happen." he laughs.

"I'll be okay," I assure him.

We've had a rough start. The guys we're playing against are pretty good. I have to drink two cups, and Dylan drinks another two. Then, I get a groove going and sink three balls in a row.

Dylan gives me a high five. "That's my girl," he says excitedly.

Being called "my girl" has the butterflies in my stomach going crazy.

In the end, our team and theirs have one cup left and it's our shot. Dylan misses and looks at me like his life depends on my shot. I throw the ball, and for a second, I think it's going to sink, but it bounces off the tip and falls on the ground.

The first guy throws the ball effortlessly and sinks the ball, winning the game. Dylan goes to grab the cup, but I beat him. The already warm beer slides down my throat, and I slam the cup on the table.

"Shit," I swear. "I'm sorry."

"My fault, my fault," Dylan says, waving it off.

The guys ask to play another game, but Dylan waves them off. We walk over to the glass doors, and I shake my head at the fact that we've lost to them. "We were so close," I say. I hate losing, and especially to drunk idiots.

"Not bad, though." He chuckles. "You're cute when you're competitive."

I can't say I'm not competitive, so I shrug.

He puts his arm around my waist and smiles down at me. "You know, you look beautiful in red."

My cheeks warm. "You're just saying that." Jacob always told me I looked better in blue, so it's strange that Dylan likes me in red.

"No, really. I think red looks really good on you."

His smile is so genuine. It's still crazy to think that Dylan Parker actually has feelings for me. He takes my hand and leads me to the side of the house, where no one can see us.

His eyes drop to my lips, and he dips his head so his meet mine. Everything around us disappears as we perfect our kiss. I'm completely aware of my hands tangling themselves in his hair and him pushing me up against the wall to feel as close as possible. He's trailing kisses down my neck, and I can't help but think that things are only going to be just fine with Dylan in my life.

"Oh shit, I totally called it," Anthony's voice interrupts us.

Dylan breaks away and I breathe heavily. Anthony is staring at us with a large grin on his face and his arms crossed. "I found them," he calls out.

Casey, Carlos, and Reece walk up to us. Dylan runs his hands through his hair, clearly frustrated that we've been interrupted.

"They were making out, dude," he slurs to Reece before they both start giggling.

Casey gives me an *a-ha* look. "You little liar. There is a full story!"

"Can you guys give us a minute, please?" Dylan asks them, sounding impatient.

They all laugh and giggle as they walk off. It's hard not to laugh too. "Guess we don't have to sneak kisses in now."

He sighs and wraps his arms around me. His forehead rests on mine, and his eyes peer into mine. "Good. I don't want to hide them anymore." Before I can say anything else, he says, "Come with me inside? I need some water."

I nod and take his hand as he leads me inside. All the beer is going right through me, so I need to find a restroom before I pee and start a tradition of embarrassing myself at Dylan's house.

"Hey, where's the restroom?" I ask Dylan once we're in the kitchen.

"It's the door right before my bedroom on your left," he says. "Want me to wait for you outside the door? I don't want any assholes bothering you."

"No, I'll be okay," I say. I kiss his cheek before walking toward the restroom.

After I finish, I quickly wash my hands to rid them of the smell of beer and fix my hair in the mirror. I take a deep breath before opening the door and stepping out.

Down the hall are two girls talking. One looks like Lauren, so I face away from them, but their conversation catches my attention.

"And Jacob? He didn't want to come or what?" the other girl asks.

I pause my walking and pretend like I'm on my phone while listening in. I know I shouldn't, but I do it anyway.

"He said he was going to come. I mean, coming to Dylan's parties is like a tradition for us now," Lauren says. "This is where we first hooked up."

"Here?"

"Dylan's the one who offered me and Jacob a room." Lauren lets out with a laugh. "I felt bad for Lacey, but Jacob said they hadn't even slept together yet. It couldn't have been that serious."

My heart remembers the pain I felt when I found out Jacob had cheated on me. I knew Jacob had cheated at a party, but he did it at Dylan's party? Jacob has blatantly lied to Lauren too when he told her we never had sex.

"I mean, I'm not complaining now. We don't have to sneak around anymore. He was just at my house yesterday," she continues.

I can't listen anymore. My mind is racing with the information I've just heard. I don't know if what she's saying is true, but I have to find out.

Dylan is still in the kitchen, standing with Reece. Seeing him hurts so bad because I want to blame him for Jacob cheating on me, but I know it's not his fault. "What's wrong?" he asks.

"Can we talk? Outside?"

235

He nods, and I pull him through the glass doors to take him to the side of the house again.

"Seriously, Lace, what's wrong?" he asks me.

"It happened here, didn't it?" It's a test, of course. I need to see if he'll be honest with me, like he always has.

His face shows confusion, but it quickly crumbles. He looks away, and I know Lauren told the truth.

"Why didn't you tell me?"

"I didn't know how—"

"You saw how much it hurt me," I say, feeling the strings of my heart being tugged in all directions. "And you didn't say anything?"

Dylan pinches the bridge of his nose. "What good would that have done? It would've made you feel worse, and I didn't want to do that to you."

Is that why he talked to me on the first day? Did he know about me and Jacob before I even told him? "What else have you not told me?" I demand. "The truth. Now."

Dylan's expression is pained, but he nods. "That party got out of hand and everyone was wasted. I met Jacob when we played beer pong against each other. He'd been all over that girl the whole night, and when he beat me, I told him he could take Derrick's room to sleep with her. He told me not to say anything to his girlfriend, but I thought he was bullshitting me."

I feel anger course through me all over again. Dylan knows this the whole time and chooses not to tell me.

"That Monday, I saw you arguing with him in the parking lot. I blew it off because that was his business, but when I remembered you on the first day of school, I—"

"You, what? Thought you'd be my friend out of guilt? Pity?" I ask. "That's a shitty way of starting a friendship."

Anger crosses his face. "Yeah, I felt guilty for about two seconds. I got over it when I realized what a huge asshole Jacob was anyway. He's the one who cheated on you. He's the one who

236

did it after you lost your parents. And you were still crawling back to him."

My head hurts as I process everything he has said. Jacob cheated on me here at Dylan's house. Maybe I shouldn't have found out. It hurts that Dylan, who has been honest with me since day one, hasn't been honest with me about *this* from the beginning.

"You should have told me," I say, feeling the heaviness on my chest. "I should have heard this from you, not from the girl he cheated with."

"Don't blame me." He shakes his head. "Don't blame me when it was that douchebag's fault."

I need to get out of here. I don't know if I need to cry or scream or both, but I don't want to see Dylan right now. I need to think everything over.

"I have to go," I say. I try to leave, but Dylan catches my arm.

"Lace, I'm sorry—"

I pull my arm away and push past him. I search for Casey and find her by the patio with Carlos. The tears are starting to come out, and I try to wipe them away before I stand in front of her. "Can we go now?" I ask her.

She looks at my face and frowns. "Hey, what's wrong?"

"I'll explain in the car. Can we just go now? Please?" I plead. I want to get out of here before Dylan tries to talk to me again.

"Um, yeah, sure." She looks at Carlos, still frowning.

"Where's Dylan?" Carlos asks me before he glances around.

"I don't know, and I don't care," I tell him. I wonder if the guys know about Jacob cheating on me at Dylan's party. *Did everyone know but me?*

Casey takes my hand in hers. "Okay. Let's get out of here."

It isn't even midnight when Casey and I get back to the apartment. I don't speak until we actually get inside. In the

237

bathroom, I wash my face and watch the makeup disappear down the drain. When my face is fresh, I walk into my room and see Casey typing away at her phone, probably texting Carlos to find out what happened.

"You can wash your face, if you want to," I tell her. I want to delay the talk as much as I can.

But she doesn't. "I want to talk first," she says, patting the spot next to her on my bed. "Tell me what happened."

As I'm telling her everything I've heard and everything Dylan and I have said to each other, it all sounds so silly. Maybe I have overreacted. It isn't Dylan's fault that Jacob cheated on me. All my old emotions hit me, and they are mixed with my anger towards Dylan for not telling me in the first place.

Casey doesn't express any emotion, even after I finish telling her.

"I don't think," she says hesitantly, "Dylan was trying to hurt you."

"I know," I nod, "but it still hurt to find out from Lauren first." Dylan's intentions might've been good, but he has taken too long to tell me what he knows.

Casey casts her eyes away and seems to be thinking hard. "If Dylan was the one who offered the room to Jacob, why didn't Jacob tell you when he saw you getting close to Dylan? He clearly doesn't like Dylan, why not try to separate you guys with that?"

The thought hasn't crossed my mind. Jacob easily could've revealed Dylan's part in all of it. Why hasn't he? Does he not remember?

"I think I have to talk to Jacob. I'll be officially done with him once I have this talk," I tell her. "I promise."

She takes my hands and holds them. "All I want is for you to be happy. Seeing you with Dylan makes me happy because you two are so right for each other."

There's hesitation from her. "But?" I ask.

"But like you always tell me, you don't need a guy in your life to make you happy," she says. "If Dylan really cares about you, then he'll respect your decision to do your own thing for a little while. And if you do want to be with him, then I'm sure he'll be happy with that too."

This is a lot to think about, especially about Dylan. Before I can make any decisions, I need to talk to Jacob.

*   *   *

Jacob was wary when I texted him on Saturday. He didn't want to meet up with me at first, but I convinced him that it's important for both of us and he finally agreed. We've decided to meet at the food court in the mall.

When I get there, I find a small table off to the side and sit anxiously in the chair. I watch people pass by while I wait for him to arrive.

This morning, I threw on some denim skinny jeans, a loose t-shirt, and my old Converse. Jacob, however, looks like he's ready for a business meeting. His brown hair is gelled up, for once. He's wearing a light-blue button up shirt that is rolled up to his elbows and a pair of navy dress pants. He's like a whole new person.

"Before you make any comments"—he holds a finger up as he sits across from me—"I had a job interview before this."

A job? "Where did you apply for? The secret service?"

"Very funny." He gives me a deadpan look. "Anyway, what do you want to talk about?"

I'm still stuck on the job part. Jacob's parents are well off moneywise. They always make sure he has his weekly allowance. Are they trying to humble him by making him get a job? "Wait, why are you getting a job anyway?"

He shifts in his chair. "Well, my parents are divorcing and my dad is taking everything. My mom's job pays well but only enough to cover certain things. I have to step up to help her."

"I'm sorry," I find myself saying.

"My dad is such a prick. He left my mom for some new chick who started working at the firm, then he left me and my mom with nothing," he practically spits. "After all my mom has done for him."

I want to say karma is a bitch, but it won't make me feel any better. His mom doesn't deserve that.

"I know what you want to say. Nothing like a taste of my own medicine, right? Maybe I deserve it, but my mom doesn't." He sighs. "You didn't deserve it either."

"Which leads me to what I want to talk to you about," I say. "I saw Lauren at Dylan's party last night."

"She was pissed at me for not going." He rolls his eyes. "How did that go?"

"I overheard her saying Dylan offered you guys a room."

He just nods before taking his glance away from me.

"Why didn't you tell me?" I ask him. "You saw me getting closer to Dylan, why didn't you tell me he played a part in all of this?"

He puts his hands on his face and drags them down. "His part was tiny."

I put my hands on the table. "You could've easily used that against him, but you didn't."

"I thought about it," he says. "I didn't tell you because I thought he was going to tell you what I said about you. I told you I wasn't thinking when I did it, but I was. I said some bad things about you while I was there, things that shouldn't have been said."

Now that I think about it, I'm glad Dylan spared me from those details. Maybe it is for the best that I've found out now and not early on.

Jacob rubs his temple. "I was in a bad place when it happened, Lace. I cared about you, but I got to know Lauren in class. I tried not to like her. I mean, me and you have matching

240

tattoos. We were supposed to be end game, but I started liking her, no matter how hard I tried not to."

"And then?" I urge him to continue.

"And then the accident happened," he says, looking down at his hands. "Your parents were practically a second pair of parents to me. I know I still have my parents, but losing yours was hard. They were always good to me, and knowing they wouldn't be around anymore . . ." He shakes his head. "It sounds shitty, but I couldn't take it."

I never thought about how losing them affected him. I never thought to even ask.

"Anyway, I went to Dylan's party to get my mind off of everything. Lauren was there. We were drinking, and it was all downhill from there. I figured it was just a one time thing, and if I didn't tell you, then it was like it never happened."

Everything is jumbled in my head. Jacob fell for Lauren before my parents's accident and I didn't even suspect it.

"So, what happened over the summer? Did you really want me back?" I ask him.

"I missed you over the summer. I felt like shit for doing what I did and wanted to fix that. That's why I signed up for journalism. To get close to you again. But then you started spending time with Parker. I felt like an idiot for signing up for a class I didn't even care about just to see you with another guy. I thought I wanted you back, but then I'd see Lauren and I wouldn't stop thinking about her."

It doesn't make sense. There are still so many questions that are unanswered. "What about the times you kissed me?"

"Trying to convince myself I wanted you." He shrugs. "Bad idea, I know."

"You have no idea how much you screwed with my head." I rub my temples. Jacob has been unsure about his feelings this whole time. All of this information would have been helpful to me about a month ago.

"I didn't expect all of this to happen." He shakes his head. "I got this tattoo with you because I thought we'd be together for a long time. I'm sorry."

It feels like a weight has been lifted from my chest. Jacob and I are finally letting go of each other after months of heartbreak.

"How are you and Lauren now?" I ask him.

"I think we're okay." He nods. "She's been helping me with the divorce stuff. She even met my mom the other day."

Interesting development. "How did that go?"

"My mom doesn't like her. She sees her as the other woman, thanks to you." He sighs. "I told my mom everything, like everything everything. She isn't happy with me, probably because it's exactly what my dad has done to her."

"Understandable." I nod. "She'll forgive you. Just don't cheat again, okay?"

"I think I've learned my lesson." He gives me a half smile. "You know, I miss your friendship. It reminds me of when I first met you."

"That was definitely a long time ago," I say, letting out a sigh. Those days are simpler. "But the last time you wanted to be my friend, you kissed me."

He holds his hands up. "No kissing this time. I'm a loyal man now, remember?"

I laugh a little and wonder why it couldn't have ended easier for us.

"What about you?" He raises a brow. "You and Parker together now?"

One door is closed, but another has opened. "No." I shake my head. "I argued with him because he didn't tell me everything."

"Listen, Lace, I still don't like him, but don't punish him for something I did."

My head is clear now, and I know Dylan is only trying to protect me from a painful truth. I need to apologize to him, but I also need to clear some things up with him.

*   *   *

Later that day, I meet up with Dylan at the ice cream shop and tell him about my conversation with Jacob. I apologize for getting so angry, and luckily, he forgives me.

I also tell him about my decision not to jump into another relationship. Casey is right. I don't need to be in a relationship to be happy. I just need to see how everything plays out if me and Dylan continue our friendship.

"I want to be with you, but I need to be happy on my own for a little while," I explain. And there's also the issue with Kay. She's going to keep inserting herself into Dylan's life. "And I don't know if I can deal with Kay right now."

"Is that what this is really about? Kay? Because I can get rid of her," he says urgently. "I don't care if Xavier kicks the shit out of me for breaking her heart or whatever the fuck. I can get her to leave us alone."

I shake my head. "It's not only that. I need my head to be clear. I need some time to myself, to actually grieve over my parents, and be here for my aunt."

"I can help you, Lace." He grabs my hands. "I didn't know your parents, but I'd like to know about them. Talking sometimes helps with the grieving process, right?"

It's a sweet gesture, and my heart is filled with happiness knowing Dylan wants to help me through it.

"If I keep depending on other people to help me, then I'll never be able to do anything on my own."

Nothing comes out of his mouth for a minute. He runs a hand through his hair and nods in understanding. "Okay. I'll give you the time you need," he says. There's a moment of pause before he says, "But if you're happier on your own, then let me know as soon as you figure it out. I don't want to wait for you, only to find out you're over me."

243

"I won't lead you on. I promise." I give him a smile.

When we walk out of the ice cream shop, he spins me around and plants a sweet kiss on my lips, then he is gone in a flash.

PART TWO

CHAPTER SIXTEEN

The last week of September is upon us, and the cool air has me ready for fall. I breathe in the fresh Monday morning air and feel happy and sad at the same time. Happy because fall is my favorite season, but sad because one of the last conversations I've had with my parents was about the possibility of throwing a Halloween party at our house.

I don't want to be too down from it, so I get the idea that Casey and I go to the movies. We haven't been to one in ages, and there are a couple of good movies out. I ask her during lunch and she agrees.

After school, I head home and tell Aunt Jade about our plans. Around five o'clock, I leave for the theater.

I see Casey's car already in the lot, so I get out and walk to the entrance. As I'm rounding the corner, I spot Casey talking to a familiar tall figure nearby. I back up before Casey sees me and watch her as she talks to Xavier.

I catch part of their conversation.

"You can't keep showing up, expecting me to talk to you," she stresses. "I don't want you coming to my house unexpectedly, I don't want you finding me at school, and I don't want you around Lacey. Why is that so hard to understand?"

"It's always about her," he says. "Who was there for you when she wasn't? Me."

"Things are different than they were last year." She crosses her arms. "I'm done talking about this. I don't want you coming near me anymore."

"You're making a mistake," he tells her.

She turns away from him. "I really don't care." She walks away into the entrance, and he stands there with his fists clenched. It's a scary sight, so I hide behind the wall when he walks away. He was talking about me, and it doesn't sound like he likes me very much.

When I see that he's out of view, I walk into the entrance and find Casey. I wonder whether I should bring him up or wait to see if she does.

"I think we should see that movie with Bradley Cooper," she says as soon as I walk up to her. "That one starts in twenty minutes."

She doesn't bring up Xavier, which doesn't surprise me. She hasn't told me that he's been around, but I don't want to push her to talk about it if she doesn't want to.

"Yeah, that's fine," I say instead.

I pay no attention to the movie. Her conversation with Xavier is the only thing on my mind. Why is he always trying to meet up with her? What have I done that has made him hate me so much? By the time the movie ends, I'm at home just thinking about what to do for Casey.

The next day, I figure I should tell Dylan about Xavier. Maybe he can give me some more insight into the situation. I don't see him until lunch when I spot him talking to a brunette girl as they're coming out of the main building. He doesn't look interested in the conversation, but she looks like she's trying her best to keep it going.

I catch his eye and wave him over. He immediately tells the girl something and separates himself from her. The disappointment on her face is clear.

"Hey," he says, walking up to me.

247

"Hi," I say, realizing I haven't talked to him since I told him I just wanted to be friends for now. "I need to talk to you about something."

I start walking to the parking lot, and he follows me. "I saw Xavier talking to Casey last night, and I kind of eavesdropped in on their conversation."

At the mention of Xavier's name, he listens to me more attentively. "Okay . . ." he trails off.

"It sounds like he's been following her. She told him to stop showing up where she was, and he wasn't happy about it," I say. I decide not to tell him about Xavier not liking me. That detail can be left out for now.

"I noticed he hasn't been giving me as much shit lately." He taps his chin. "I don't like that he's following her around."

"She doesn't know I know all of this, so don't tell her I told you," I quickly say. "I just want to make sure nothing bad is going to happen." Xavier could be a psychopath for all I know.

"I'll keep an eye on him." He nods.

We're quiet and I don't know what else to say. I've been worried this would happen. That things would be awkward when I don't want them to be.

"I should get going," Dylan says, his eyes on his shoes. "I forgot my damn book for English at my house."

"Oh, okay."

He starts walking to his car, and I let out a long sigh. I'm doing this for me.

*   *   *

Time moves slowly after that day, each second longer than the last. October begins, and Casey moans and groans about hating fall and winter outfits, but her mood turns around when we discuss our Halloween plans. I want to do as much as possible to keep my spirits up.

248

She doesn't say it explicitly, but I know she's been seeing Carlos a lot more. I haven't seen her much for lunch, and she says it's because she's working on homework, but I know she's with him.

It's the first week of October, and Anthony has invited us to his birthday party at Raven's on Friday, which is his actual birthday. I'm excited to do something normal with everyone again.

I've bought Anthony a birthday card before I head to Raven's. I wished him a happy birthday when I saw him earlier in the day, but I felt empty handed. I write a quick message in the card before getting out of my car. Casey wanted to drive me, but I might go home early. I also don't want to depend on her to take me home.

Tonight, Raven's seems to be particularly busy. I wonder if it's because of Anthony's birthday or if it's a coincidence. I spot everyone at a table in the back, and they all greet me warmly, except for Carlos, who barely waves to me. Anthony opens my card and grins when he reads what I've written.

"Thanks, Lacey." He hugs me. "You're the only one who's given me a card today."

I sit at the only open seat between Dylan and Carlos. Carlos blocks Casey from me, so I don't get to talk to her much.

Dylan doesn't say much, only speaking when Anthony or Reece talk to him directly. I see Derrick and Jared making their way to the stage, and everyone claps for them. Things are better when they perform, getting everyone to sing or dance along. Their set is short, only being four songs long.

After they finish, I find myself missing my bed. Maybe I should've stayed home. Casey is preoccupied with Carlos. I wonder if this is how she felt when I was with Jacob. The feeling sucks.

Dylan's legs suddenly swing towards me, and he leans on his elbow to look at me.

"Have you finished the project for English?" he asks.

A wave of relief washes over me. I really don't want things to be weird between us. "I finished it in class today."

He scratches the back of his neck. "I'm barely finishing the book."

Our project is on the book *Crime and Punishment*, which is a fairly large book. "Dylan, the project is due on Monday."

"That's why I'm going to work on it on Sunday." He chuckles.

Anthony suddenly appears between us and slings his arm around Dylan. "Are you guys having fun?" he asks us.

Dylan and I both nod.

Anthony twists his mouth like he's thinking. "I'm losing interest in this place. You guys wanna go catch the rest of the football game?"

The football game? "I didn't know you were into football," I say to Anthony.

He smirks. "I'm into one of the cheerleaders at the football game."

Makes sense. I've never seen Anthony around any other girls. I wonder if he's had a girlfriend before.

We all end up driving to the game. Once we make it into the stadium, we find spots in the stands where the student section is.

"Fuck, we're actually winning," Anthony says, squinting at the scoreboard.

I look at the scoreboard and see that we've made it just before halftime is due to start. I know very little about football, so this should be interesting.

"You want anything from the concession stand?" Dylan asks as he stands next to me on the bleachers.

Dylan looks good in his gray shirt and dark jeans under the Friday night lights. His green eyes seem brighter.

It takes a moment for me to answer. "Um, no, thanks. I'm okay right now."

250

"Guess I should've asked when we passed by it." He scratches the back of his neck.

"It's fine." I laugh slightly. Things feel awkward again, especially since Dylan is somewhat shy. It's a side of him I've never seen, and it's throwing me off. He's always been a confident person, and now he seems nervous.

Carlos is explaining something to Casey about the game, so I turn to talk to Dylan, but a girl makes her way over to us. Her eyes are a crystal clear blue, and the blonde hair on her head shines beneath the lights.

"Hey, Dylan." She slides between me and him. "I never see you here at the games."

Dylan and I aren't together, but I feel particularly irritated by this girl and the way she pushes herself between us. I have to remind myself that Dylan can talk to whoever he wants.

"Football isn't my thing," he says, not looking at her and watching the field instead.

"Me neither. I just come for the after parties," she says, standing closer to him. "I heard you aren't seeing anyone."

"Nope," he says. "But I've got my eye on someone."

"Who?"

My heart is beating quickly in my chest.

"You don't know her, Zoey."

"Lucky girl. You sure you don't want to explore some more options?" she asks, staring up at him with flirty eyes.

I've never mastered that look. Jacob always said I wasn't like other girls, and I always hated when he said that. There's nothing wrong with being like other girls with flirty eyes.

"Not really," he says.

It's like a weight has lifted from my chest as soon as he says that. I don't know why I'm nervous about him saying something else. Dylan has always been genuine with his feelings.

"Well, if you change your mind, you know where to find me." She winks at him before walking further down the bleachers.

251

Dylan doesn't say anything as he stands close to me. This time, he doesn't leave room for anyone to come between us.

*   *   *

October seems to flash before my eyes. It's filled with strained conversations with Dylan, talks with my aunt about her genetics professor boyfriend, and not seeing Casey because she's with Carlos.

Neither Casey nor Dylan bring up Xavier, and I'm starting to think he's going to leave everyone alone, unless they're not telling me everything.

As October nears its end, I manage to finally make some plans for me and Casey to go to the Fall Festival. What is supposed to be something for just the two of us ends up being an outing with the boys. It is fun, but I'm still a bit miffed that me and Casey don't get to have our alone time. It especially gets a bit awkward by the end with me and Dylan.

Halloween arrives, but my plan to watch horror movies all night with Casey changes when she catches the flu. Usually, we'd stay at my house to hand out candy to trick-or-treaters while my parents went to work parties. I've been looking forward to spending time with her, but I can't blame her for getting sick.

My aunt watches horror movies with me for the rest of the night. She hasn't asked about Dylan, or why I'm spending more time at home rather than out and about. Luckily, she doesn't have plans with her genetics professor, though they go out pretty often. I haven't met him yet. I only know his name is James and that he drives a Mercedes.

When November reaches our grasp, my aunt is freaking out over where to host the Thanksgiving party. She's been trying to decide whether she wants to have Thanksgiving here at the apartment with my grandparents or at their house. Either way, she's planning to bring James over.

After a few anxious fits, she finally decides to host it over at my grandparent's house.

I finally meet him for Thanksgiving at my grandparent's place. My grandparents seem to like him. He fits in with the family, but I can't help but feel left out.

Everyone strains to stay happy since my mom and dad aren't there. Their constant asking of whether I'm fine or not bothers me. I'm not fine, but I don't want to spend the whole holiday season thinking about it.

These are the times when I feel like calling Dylan just to hear his voice. He'd listen to me then give me encouraging words to help me get through all of it, but I don't give him a chance to.

At school, he's started to avoid me. We don't talk in class. He always comes in at the last second and is always the first one out. I'm not sure whether he's already trying to get over me or if it hurts too much to see me. I'm causing conflict in his mind, and I feel horrible for it.

As much as I hate to admit it, I feel lonely. Casey spends a lot of time with Carlos and in turn spends a lot of time with the guys. There's a feeling of jealousy rising inside me, but I know I'm only doing it to myself.

I'm the one who wants solitude. The idea of being with Dylan so soon is scary to me, and I don't want to mess up what we has going. I need to be completely ready to jump into a relationship with him, and that means learning how to be by myself for a while.

As the days grow colder and the loneliness grows into the most agonizing monster, I'm beginning to question my sense of reasoning.

On the first day of December, a Saturday, Casey comes to the apartment. When I open the door for her, her eyes are red and teary.

"I need your help," she says.

"What's going on?" I ask as soon as we are in the comfort of my bedroom.

She instantly takes her usual spot on my bed, and I sit next to her. I watch as she wipes her eyes and smears a bit of her mascara. I don't know what to think. Has something happened between her and Carlos?

"It's Xavier," she says, looking down at her hands. "He's pissed at me because I've been seeing Carlos."

I've been hoping Xavier just disappeared. Looks like he hasn't.

"He thinks he can just burst back into my life and tell me who I can and can't talk to. He says he'll send guys after Carlos if we keep seeing each other." She has a disgusted look on her face. "That's why I didn't want to talk to him anymore. He's just too weird now."

Before I can say anything, she keeps going. "I don't know why he's even bothering me now. I mean, I was fine without him in my life. I got over my crush, and Carlos swooped in at the right time. Now all of sudden, he wants Carlos to stay away from me and Dylan to make things right with Kay."

That's news to me. Xavier is pushing Dylan back to Kay? I feel the anger rising in me, and Casey sees it in my face.

"I wasn't supposed to say anything about that," she says, avoiding my eyes.

"Why?"

"Dylan didn't want you to worry."

It's frustrating. I don't need people dictating how I should feel, and it irritates me to no end. Even the way Casey says it bothers me. I know she's hanging out with the guys more. Knowing that she's spending more time with Dylan makes me upset.

I'm her best friend, and I haven't even seen much of her since Halloween. "You and Dylan are best friends now?"

I regret saying it as the words leave my mouth. It isn't her fault that I've isolated myself, but it still irks me. I mean, she's my best friend, yet she's been with the guys more than she's been with me. She's been with Dylan more than I have.

It isn't just about Dylan. I feel like I'm losing her to Carlos. I'm getting the same sense of loss I've felt when I lost my parents and Jacob in the same month.

It's almost as if I've completely lost everything close to me. Here I am, being angry over Casey putting herself out there and having fun while I've purposely shut myself out from everything and everyone.

"What is that supposed to mean?" she asks, straightening herself.

"Nothing." I stand up from my bed. Arguing about it won't do any good. Instead, I cross my arms and stare out my window.

"If you're going to say something, then say it, Lace," her voice rises. "I've given you plenty of opportunities to rant about how I'm spending time with the guys, and you haven't taken any of it."

Did she really just say that? "I just—yeah, I'm jealous, okay?" I snap. "You have Carlos, you have Xavier, you have the guys, and you have both of your parents."

It's coming out and I can't stop it, no matter how bad it all sounds. "Being without my parents for the holidays sucks, Case, and I can't do anything to fix that. Being without them is hard, period. I don't want to play the victim, but I can't help it this time."

I'm sick of seeing a parking lot outside my window instead of the landscaped yard of my old house. I miss waking up on the weekends to my parents singing along to music in the kitchen as they cook breakfast together. Or hearing my mom scold my dad for drinking straight from the milk gallon. Or even just hearing their voices. What if, one day, I can't remember what they sound like?

"Lace, I'm sorry—"

I stop her. "You said sorry when I told you about the accident, and you said sorry at the funerals. I don't want to hear it again."

"I wish you could've told me this sooner," she says quietly.

255

Tears are forming in my eyes, and I know I won't be able to stop them if I look at her. I don't want that. I clear my throat and try to settle myself. "I can say the same thing. There are a lot of things I wish you could've told me." She's barely told me she's with Carlos now, and I haven't even known about Xavier until a couple months ago.

"You're already dealing with all the stuff going on in your life, and I didn't want to dump my problems onto you," she says.

"Case, I would've gladly thought about something else these past few months." I finally look at her. "You could've told me about Xavier. You could've told me about you and Carlos."

"I didn't want to make you feel bad about me and Carlos—"

"Why? Because Dylan and I aren't together? I don't care about that."

She stands up and walks over to me. "Fine, I should've told you."

"I'm over this conversation." I shake my head. Being in an argument with Casey isn't going to do me any good. If I'm not able to talk to her, then I'll go crazy. "Let's just move on."

"Deal." She nods immediately.

"What are you going to do about Xavier?"

"I don't know. He's being psychotic about this whole thing."

"Maybe you just need to sit and talk to him."

Her nose scrunches up. "There's no way I'm going to sit and talk to him. I still haven't forgiven him for ditching our friendship. Plus, he's kind of freaking me out."

"Honestly, I wish I knew what to say," I tell her. Xavier seems like a scary guy, but he doesn't look so scary next to Casey. It's like she's his Achilles heel in the worst possible way.

Casey leaves soon after. Things don't seem to be completely resolved between us, but I let it be. Everything will work out, as they usually do with us. We're just hitting a bump in our friendship.

That night, I stare at my phone and wonder if I should shoot a text to Dylan. I'm anxious to hear what he has to say about Xavier pushing him and Kay together.

But I can't bring myself to text him.

*　　　*　　　*

People are buzzing this Monday morning. Student government is doing their usual candy cane grams and the *Mean Girls* references are never-ending. Hearing the chatter in the hallways is giving me a headache. I want nothing more than to go home, get under a cozy blanket, and watch Christmas movies.

It's crazy to think that we only have a couple more weeks of school before winter break. My senior year is nearly half finished, and I don't know how fulfilled it has been so far.

"Hey, that sweater is cute," Casey says as she starts walking with me to the cafeteria.

I found this colorful, striped sweater at the thrift store. It's super soft, and it's warm enough to be comfortable in it. "Thanks. I see you're going for a Kurt Cobain-like look."

She's wearing a striped dark-gray shirt under a flannel. "Who?" she asks.

I shake my head. "Never mind."

We walk into the cafeteria, and my eyes scan the room for Dylan and the guys, but they are nowhere in sight. Casey doesn't mention their whereabouts, so I don't ask.

Instead, we get our lunch and sit at a table together. We haven't done this in a while, and it feels good.

"I would die for these cheese fries," I say, moaning as I shovel them into my mouth.

"I wouldn't go that far." Casey laughs. "They're just cheese on top of fries."

Dylan would understand. He gets the cheese. I push the thoughts of him out of my mind.

Her demeanor changes and I have a bad feeling in my stomach. "What?"

"He's changed a lot, Lace." She looks down at her food. "Xavier, I mean. It's to the point where I don't know if the old Xavier is still in there. I talked to him on Sunday, but he literally threatened to hurt Carlos if I went out with him again. He swears up and down that he doesn't care for me, yet he cares who's in my life."

It sounds like things are getting out of hand. Xavier is clearly a psycho, especially when it comes to Casey.

I can't wrap my head around it, even as I part ways with Casey and walk to English. At first, I've thought Xavier has a soft spot for Casey, but he's coming off as possessive now. It's as if he thinks he's the only guy she is allowed to have in her life.

A hand wraps around my arm, startling me. I whip around to find Dylan's green eyes staring at me. He motions for me to stay outside of class.

"I need to talk to you," he says, running a hand through his hair. "You want to skip this period?"

I chew on my lip nervously. Going with Dylan is a bad and good idea all at once. My heart leaps at the fact that he is talking to me, but it's probably something bad by the sound of his voice. He's changed somehow. His hair is a little longer, and there is a bit of stubble on his face. He looks older somehow.

"Um, sure." I find myself nodding.

Soon enough, we are dodging security as we run through the parking lot to get to his car. The wind makes the air colder, and Dylan cranks up the heat as soon as we are inside.

"Where are we going?" I ask, rubbing my hands together to warm them up.

He turns his body, so he's facing me and reaches out to cover my hands with his. "Just trust me, okay?"

I want to be more nervous than I am, but his words are so reassuring. Not trusting my voice, I nod instead. His hands leave mine, and they're cold again.

As we drive off campus, he doesn't say anything else, seemingly lost in his own head.

At first, I don't recognize where we are heading. Not to Raven's and not to his house nor my apartment. When we turn at a familiar light then down a specific road, my breath catches in my throat.

"Which one?" he asks me, gesturing to the houses around us.

"That one, up there." I point to my old house on the left.

It feels like it's been ages since I've last seen it. I'm expecting to see a "For Sale" sign on the front lawn, but there is nothing but overgrown weeds taking over. The once beautiful gleaming-white three-bedroom house I've called home is completely different. Aged is the right word.

"How did you know where to find it?" I ask Dylan.

He's staring at the house as he answers, "I asked Casey. I couldn't remember the whole address though."

All at once, the memories hit me,—my mom standing by the front door with her hands on her hips and waiting for me to get off the bus, our failed attempts at a family game night, the white Christmas lights my dad always hung on the house, and my dad trying to decide on what tie to wear to work.

Both of my parents worked for banks but different branches. Dad was always in his suits and Mom in her dresses and skirts. I've had a crippling fear at the funeral that I won't be able to remember how they looked like, but the fresh memory of their faces has relief washing over me.

"I'm not sure if now is the right time to bring you here, but I want you to be comfortable either way," Dylan says, looking not at me but at the house. "I have something to tell you."

A million thoughts race in my mind. Is he going to tell me he's going back to Kay? Or join in on whatever Xavier has gotten mixed up in? Both make my stomach upset.

"I was trying to watch Xavier as much as possible for a while now, but he kept avoiding me. I couldn't keep up with him, so I didn't know if he was following Casey still. Then he came to me, almost out of the blue, the other day."

I know where the conversation is heading. "He wants you to get back together with Kay."

He grabs my hands and holds them again. "I don't want her."

Why does Xavier want Dylan to be with Kay so much? Most older brothers don't want their sisters dating. Maybe Kay has him wrapped around her ugly finger and he's willing to do anything for her. But why? Just because they're siblings?

"I'm not good at explaining my feelings," he says. "As much as I respect your alone time, it's been brutal not talking to you."

The more I think about it, the more my alone time makes less sense. I know I wanted time for myself, but I could have made it a couple weeks, not months.

Dylan speaks up again. "I want to be here for you because I know a lot of shit has gone down in your life that I can't fix with just a kiss."

My heart flutters. Dylan's lips look warm and inviting, but the moment isn't right to kiss him. "What about Xavier and Kay?"

He hesitates. I can tell it's something he's been thinking over. "Xavier isn't all talk, and I'm not worried about him coming after me. I can take it," he says and blows out a breath. "I'm afraid something will happen to Casey or even you."

That's scary. I know Xavier doesn't like me, but will he hurt me so Kay can have Dylan? "He wouldn't really hurt me, would he? I mean, Casey is my best friend."

"My theory," he says slowly, "is that he had Casey all to himself while you were with Jacob, and when you two broke up, she left him to help you. Carlos came into the picture, making it worse. Then he has Kay complaining about you, which makes you a target in his mind. He wants me to be with Kay to get her off his back, but I'm not sure what he wants to do about you or Carlos."

Carlos doesn't seem like the type to sit back and take any shit. He'll fight back. If I have to, will I fight back? How did I even get mixed up in all of this?

Dylan probably senses how I'm feeling and smirks. "Are you thinking of an alliance with Carlos? Because he's not one for teams."

"He'll have to be okay with teams if he wants to be with Casey," I say.

Despite his smirk, he looks like he has more to say.

"What else is on your mind?" I ask.

"I hope you're okay with staying friends a little longer," he says, glancing out the window. "We shouldn't rush into anything right now. I don't want Xavier to go after you."

It isn't fair. Why does Xavier get to decide how I spend my life?

"Trust me. If I didn't think he was a threat, then I wouldn't suggest it," he says.

"It's not fair," I say, leaning back in the seat. With my eyes closed, I imagine all the scenarios that can happen. An image of Dylan meeting my parents flashes in my mind. I wish he could've met them.

Part of me feels like pretending that we are getting ready to have dinner with my parents, where they'll meet Dylan for the first time. I wonder what they would think about him. My aunt likes him, so there's a chance my parents would've liked him.

And the memories return, but instead, I replace Jacob with Dylan in all of them. I imagine Dylan shaking hands with my dad and complimenting my mom on the dinner she's made. My dad

261

takes Dylan off to the side and tells him how lucky he is to have me in his life.

Jacob knew what to say to my parents, but I think Dylan would have been more genuine with his words. There was always light when Jacob was around my parents. I imagine that light would have been brighter with Dylan around.

I glance up at the house and sigh. The light is completely gone from it.

"You wanna take off?" Dylan asks.

Nothing will ever be the same. My parents are gone, and getting my old life back is never going to happen. Looking down at my tattoo, I know I have to get it removed or covered up with something else. Maybe I can talk to my Aunt Jade about helping me decide and helping with the cost.

"Yeah."

One memory that keeps popping up is my dad nearly falling off the ladder as he was putting our Christmas lights up.

Or the time Casey slept over and my mom decided to try a new cookie recipe and almost burned down the house because we completely forgot about them in the oven.

Or when I was home alone and got the call from my aunt that she was on her way to pick me up after she found out about the accident.

When Dylan drives us back to campus, it's nearing the end of fourth period. Going into class will be a waste, so we sit in his car.

"Is this a necessary time to skip?" I ask him, nudging his arm.

"It is." He nods. "I hope you didn't mind me taking you to your house."

"It was nice seeing it. I haven't been there since I moved out."

He's staring at me the way the same way he did in his room that day. My heart starts beating at 100 miles per hour. His hand softly touches my cheek, and his thumb ever so gently brushes against my skin. I close my eyes as his thumb traces my lips.

When I open my eyes again, Dylan's green eyes are boring into mine. His face draws closer to me, and just when I think he's going to kiss, he doesn't. Instead, he pulls me in for a hug while his face rests in the crook of my neck.

A sigh escapes him. "That wasn't smart. I'm sorry."

My heart is still beating quickly in my chest, and I sigh too. "It's okay."

When he leans back in his seat, I notice everyone filing out of the school for the end of the day.

"I'll talk to you tonight. I'm going to see what exactly Xavier has on his mind," he says.

"Don't get him riled up. I don't want you to get hurt."

The smirk on his face makes me even more nervous. "I'm not scared of him."

And that's exactly what scares me the most.

While I watch him drive away, Casey appears next to me and watches him go.

She whistles. "I knew you two couldn't stay away from each other."

"We have to be smart," I tell her. "All of us."

If Xavier decides to come after me to tell me to stay out of Kay's way, what should I do? Give them what they want? Give them the satisfaction of everyone making way for their demands?

No way.

I see where Dylan is coming from, but we have to be smart about it.

CHAPTER SEVENTEEN

On Wednesday morning, candy cane grams are being delivered to each class. Casey and I never send one to each other, and Jacob has sent me one once. When a gram has been placed on my desk, my heart flutters. It can't be from anyone else but Dylan. I open the small snowman-shaped card where it says,

Meet me at my car at lunch time. -D

There's a giddy feeling in my stomach but also a nervous one. Dylan knows we can't keep up a relationship with Xavier keeping tabs on us. Maybe he's found a way to make things okay again.

During second period, I can hardly wait for the bell to ring for lunch. When it does, I practically sprint out of the classroom and towards the parking lot. I walk to Dylan's normal spot, but his car is nowhere to be found.

The thought of him skipping out on me crosses my mind, but I know he won't do that. He has probably skipped second period and is going to pick me up, right?

I'm one second away from texting him when a familiar red car pulls up next to me. Kay gets out of her car and stands in front of me with her arms crossed.

"Get in," she says.

Like hell I'll get in the same vehicle as her. "No?" What is she even doing here? She's the last person I want to see.

She lets out a laugh that is anything but sweet. "If you haven't figured it out yet, I'm the one who sent you that stupid candy gram. Now, get in my car. We're going to chat."

I look around frantically, trying to spot Dylan, Casey, any of the boys, or even Jacob. No one is around to get me out of this situation. Part of me is curious to hear what she has to say though, and that drives me to walk to the passenger side of the car.

Her car smells like roses and is spotless. It's newer and way nicer than mine. She puts the car in reverse and zooms out of the parking lot.

"You're going to listen to me, and you're going to listen well, okay?" she asks me, keeping her eyes on the road.

Suddenly, getting in the car with her doesn't seem like the best idea to take.

"Dylan wants to be with me. I know it," she says, sitting up straight. "You're just a distraction."

Her words mirror the boys when I've asked about Dylan and Kay. They've said she's the distraction.

"What do you want from me?" I ask her.

"I want you to break Dylan's heart into a million pieces, so I can swoop in and take care of him." She flashes me a nauseatingly sweet smile.

Her dark hair is straight again with hardly a strand out of place. Her makeup is flawless, and I hate myself for liking the sweater she's wearing.

"How do you know he'll want you after I break his heart? What if he moves on to someone else?" I ask, attempting to make her see the flaws in her plan. There is a flicker of hope that she might move on from him and leave us alone. If she leaves, then maybe Xavier will back off too.

"Sweetie, I knew from the moment I saw him that we were meant to be together. And trust me, I had to fight off a lot of girls to get to him," she says through her glossy lips. "I mean, come on, you think you and I are the only girls chasing after him? Think about it."

My mind flashes to the blonde girl at the football game. Dylan is hot, there's no doubt about it. The girls at school lust after him. I hear the conversations about him. On the other hand, I know better than to listen to what Kay says about other girls. She is trying to drive us apart.

"I don't know. You're the only nuisance I've encountered," I tell her.

She smirks. "I'm only telling you because you've experienced this kind of thing before, right? Couldn't keep your last boyfriend on his leash."

I bite my tongue to stop myself from saying something horrible to her. She's only trying to rile me up, but how does she know about me and Jacob? Dylan didn't tell her, did he?

"Dylan is gorgeous and attracts almost every girl wherever he goes. It's a fact and you know it. You're always going to have girls fawning over him. You can't escape that. I'm just wondering if you can handle it. Your last boyfriend cheating on you couldn't have been easy. What if you lose Dylan the same way?" she asks, taking her eyes off the road for a split second to look at me.

Anger is rising inside me, but that's exactly what she wants. "What about you? Aren't you worried about someone stealing him from you?"

"I can handle it. What do you think I'm doing right now?"

"Right, and having your brother scare Dylan into a relationship is so romantic." I let the sarcasm drip from my tongue.

She smiles. "Xavier will do almost anything for me. I can't help it if I have a good brother."

"And if Dylan refuses you?"

Her smile falters. "He won't."

Having to deal with Kay every moment I'm with Dylan isn't ideal, but I don't want her or Xavier to dictate how I live my life.

"How are you going to keep him around? You can't count on Xavier to watch his every move."

"Where do you think Dylan is right now?" she asks, looking at me to see my reaction. "He's not at school obviously."

Of course she would have Xavier distract Dylan while she deals with me. "So what? You'll have Xavier beat the shit out of him because he doesn't want to be with you? Sounds like a healthy relationship to me."

I'm tempted to text Dylan to see where he is, but it will only amuse her. I'll check on him after I deal with her. I have to tick her off. Make sure she knows that I'm not scared of her. "And how do you know Casey again?"

Her face darkens. "Casey who?"

"Your old neighbor. I heard she got along well with Xavier," I taunt her. I'm not sure how smart this is, but it's my best bet at getting her off my back. "Actually, I heard that he's trying to work things out with Casey."

She rolls her eyes.

"Maybe that's the only reason Xavier is helping you? You'll get the guy and he'll get the girl and you will all be one big happy family."

She slams on the brakes and pulls into the parking lot of an old car dealership that is no longer open.

She puts the car in park and points at me. "Casey is not good enough for my brother. I don't know what he sees in her, but I can't stand it. She was a bitch to me when we lived next to her, and I'm going to make sure he doesn't get her."

"Does Xavier know about this little plan of yours? I bet he won't be too happy to hear that you're trying to keep him from Casey."

"My brother can do much better than that bitch."

Hearing her call Casey a bitch makes the anger inside me boil over. "Don't you see Dylan doesn't want you? He won't choose you, Xavier will choose Casey over you, and you're going to

267

be the pathetic girl standing in the background wondering why no one wants you. It's because you're the bitch."

I have no time to react before the back of her hand slaps against my face. It starts stinging instantly, and I realize she has a ring on. That must be what cut me.

"Get out of my car!" she screams at me. "And stay away from Dylan! He's mine!"

Before she can say anything else, I grab my things and open the door. I slam the door behind me just as she peels out of the parking lot.

My face is warm from embarrassment, anger, and the impact of her hand. On my fingers is small trace of blood coming from the cut that she has opened with her ring. My eyes sting from the tears that want to come out, but I don't let them.

I don't know what to do. Having Dylan in my life has been both a blessing and a curse. He comes into my life and makes me forget about all the crappy things that has happened to me, but he also comes with extra drama that I don't need. It isn't his fault, but I can't find a solution to this.

I'm too far in town to walk back to school, so I have to call someone. I don't want to call Casey, and I can't call Dylan. I'm not sure if my third option will answer, but it's worth a shot.

After I hang up, I wait on the sidewalk and try to keep my face covered. I don't know if it's that bad or just a scratch, but I don't want to draw attention.

Soon enough, Anthony's car pulls up beside me and I rush to get in the passenger side. Once inside, I look at him.

He whistles. "Do I want to know what happened?"

I immediately pull down the visor to look in the mirror. There is a cut the size of a quarter on my face, and the blood is already clotting. A faint hint of a bruise is forming around it.

"Great." I sink into the seat. What am I going to tell Aunt Jade?

"Dylan is going to flip once he sees that," Anthony says.

"I guess getting in the same car as Kay wasn't smart."

"Kay did that to you?"

I nod. "She slapped me when I called her a bitch. Lucky for me, she had a ring on."

"Damn." He shakes his head. "This isn't going to end well."

"Can I get your advice on what to do? Kay clearly doesn't want me and Dylan together, and Xavier doesn't want Carlos with Casey. What solution is going to make everyone happy?" I ask him, though I'm sure he doesn't know the answer either.

"You can't make everyone happy," he says slowly. "I don't even know what to tell Carlos."

"How is he dealing with all of this?"

"He doesn't want to piss off Xavier even more, so he's been staying away from Casey. I don't think she likes it."

"She's pretty upset." I sigh. "I have no idea what to do."

We are both quiet, not knowing what to say in that moment. No solution will please everyone. Someone is going to be hurt. Maybe I should have stayed away from Dylan from the beginning, or maybe I should have stood my ground against Kay.

I pull out my phone and text Dylan to see if he's okay. Kay might've been bluffing, but knowing Dylan, there has to be a good reason he's missing school. I check the time. Anthony and I can get back to school before the end of lunch.

He is still silent, and I feel bad for not being around as much and then just expect him to pick me up after I get in trouble.

"I'm sorry I've been a bad friend. You didn't have to pick me up," I tell him, "but I do appreciate it."

"Don't worry about it, Lacey. I get it." He gives me a warm smile.

Dylan still hasn't texted me back, and that makes me slightly worried. My mind stays on him, and I wonder if I should tell Anthony how I'm feeling.

Things with Dylan are becoming more and more complicated, and I don't know if it's worth it anymore. At a red light, I share my thoughts with Anthony.

"I'm just starting to think things aren't meant to be with Dylan," I say to him.

He shakes his head immediately. "I don't think Dylan has ever liked someone as much as he likes you. Not to be a typical wingman, but he's been acting different ever since you guys have met. I probably shouldn't tell you this, but I'm going to anyway." He smirks. "The night me and the guys met you at Dylan's party, he couldn't take his eyes off you. You walked outside and then it was like we were talking to a wall. It took him a while to go over to you, probably giving himself a pep talk on the inside. When he introduced you to us, we knew he was definitely into you."

The butterflies in my stomach are going crazy.

"I fucking can't stand Kay." He lets out a frustrated sigh. "I told Dylan not to get mixed up with her. We all knew Xavier was going to become a problem if he went after her. Of course, this all happened before he met you. I don't see what he saw in her."

"Why were they only friends with benefits if he liked her?" I ask him.

He gives me a look like I should know. "He met you." He rolls his eyes but smiles. "He definitely has a type, though."

"Are you really grouping me with Kay?" I laugh at the absurdity.

"C'mon. You don't see it? You both have dark hair, brown eyes, about the same height. Her cheekbones are a little better . . ."

"Hey." I nudge his arm. "Watch it." But I think about it. Are Kay and I so similar looking that that's the reason why Dylan likes me? Because I look like her?

We get back to the school campus, and he heads toward the parking lot.

"Can you drop me off at my car? I don't think I want to go to class with my battle wound just yet." Jacob, Sophie, and Seth will definitely ask questions. Will would for sure be nosy about it.

My phone buzzes in my hand, and I eagerly look at it. Dylan's name flashes on the screen.

"Hey," I answer.

"Are you in the cafeteria?" he asks instantly. "I'm actually by your car right now."

Oh no.

Anthony pulls his car in next to mine, which is now next to Dylan's. Dylan turns and sees me, and Anthony drives up. He looks confused, then puts his phone in his back pocket.

"Shit," I swear to Anthony.

"Better think fast," he says before putting his car in park and getting out.

I step out of the car and try to hide the cut behind my hair.

"What are you two up to?" Dylan asks, looking between me and Anthony.

"Just getting some lunch. I haven't seen this guy in forever," I lie. I turn my body towards Anthony, so Dylan can't see my face. "I don't feel good, so I think I'm just going to head home." I dig into my backpack for my keys.

Dylan grabs my arm and twists me, so I'm facing him head on. "What the hell is that?" His face darkens, and he directs his attention to Anthony. "I swear, if you fucking did this to her—"

"He didn't do it," I say quickly before things get out of hand.

Anthony holds up his hands. "I just picked her up, dude."

"Jesus Christ, where were you?" Dylan demand while examining my face.

I bite my lip. No use in lying. "Um, Kay and I went for a drive."

"You were with Kay?" He runs a hand through his hair.

271

The bell rings for lunch to be over and Anthony, lingering, says, "I'm gonna head to class."

"Thanks again, Anthony." I give him a smile. I don't want Dylan to be upset with him.

He waves and takes off, leaving me and Dylan to talk.

"I don't want to go to class like this," I say to him. "I just want to head home."

I still don't know where Dylan was while I was with Kay.

"You wanna come to the apartment with me? So we can talk?" I ask hesitantly. "I'll make us some hot chocolate." Asking him to go over when I needed help with my tire is one thing. We were just friends back then. It's different now that there are clearly feelings between us.

"Sure." He nods.

My heart is ready to leap out of my chest when I open the door to the apartment and have Dylan follow me inside. We need to talk about our situation and how we want to go on. My hands are clammy. I try to discreetly wipe them on my pants.

"My aunt usually gets home around four, so we have until then to talk," I say to him as I toss my backpack into my room. "Do you want a snack or anything to go with the drink?"

"I'm okay," he says, glancing around and not meeting my eyes. He seems distracted while I'm distracted by his choice of clothing. He has a gray zip up over a plain olive green t-shirt and some black pants on.

I walk up to him. "You okay?" Maybe he doesn't want to talk.

"Yeah." He nods. He tilts my chin up. "You should probably clean that cut. Who knows where her hands have been."

With him, perhaps? I don't say it out loud, but I don't think he's forgotten that he's been with her for a little bit.

I make my way to the bathroom and pull out the bottle of peroxide from the cabinet. With a Q-tip, I gently brush some over the wound, where it stings slightly.

272

Dylan leans against the door frame and watches me silently as I work. The bruise isn't as big as I thought it would be, but it is still obvious. I'll have to come up with a good lie for my aunt to believe.

"How did she cut you?" Dylan asks, crossing his arms.

"She had a ring on when she hit me."

"Why did she hit you again?"

I sigh. "She called Casey a bitch, so I called her a bitch too."

"What does she have against Casey?"

"She doesn't like that Xavier and Casey have history together. She also doesn't like that you're spending time with me."

"She's all drama." He rolls his eyes. "This whole thing is turning into a shitshow because, apparently, everything has to revolve around her."

I cap the peroxide and put it back in the cabinet. "What do you want to do?"

"I don't know." He shakes his head. "I want Kay and Xavier to disappear, so I can just be with you with no issues." He stands behind me and stares at me through the mirror. "I thought your dickhead ex was going to be the only problem."

"I did too," I say. I wish Jacob was the only issue we had to deal with. That would've been over with a long time ago. "Let's talk in the living room."

Dylan sits in the middle of the couch while I sit against the couch's arm, ready to figure out how we are going to make everything work. Anthony doesn't think everyone will be happy in the end, but there's no harm in trying.

"Did Kay tell you anything that could help us out somehow?" he asks.

Two things stand out from that conversation. She knew where he was during lunch and I didn't. "Why weren't you in school earlier?"

He hesitates before answering, "I was with Xavier."

273

"Did you guys talk?" From the looks of it, they didn't fight. Or maybe they did and Xavier got the worst of it.

He scratches the back of his neck. "I don't trust Xavier around you, okay? He's got a loose screw in the head, and he's not someone to hang around with freely."

"And that's why you were with him?"

"I told him I'm with Kay again. . ." he trails off and, in the process, leans away from me.

"What? Why?" Why the hell would he do that?

The expression on his face is unreadable, but I know he's trying to choose his words carefully. "He'll leave you alone if he thinks we're not together. As long as he thinks I'm with Kay, we'll be okay."

I knit my brows together. "You convinced Kay that you still like her." It's more a statement than a question. That's why Kay has been so confident that they are going to be together. "You really planned all of this behind my back."

"To prevent you from getting hurt. The less you know, the better. And the less Xavier knows, the better," he snaps. "He'll do anything for Kay, and if that's getting you out of the picture, he'll do it. I don't know how much Casey can help you, but I don't think it'll be a lot." He stares off for a second. "I don't want to make things worse, but I think Casey should really stay away from him."

"What do you mean?" I sit upright.

"He doesn't like Carlos as it is, and I don't know how far he'll go to keep him away from her."

If Casey is in the slightest bit of danger, then both her and Carlos need to know what they are getting themselves into. "I need to tell Casey."

"Don't make her panic or anything. I don't think he'll hurt her physically."

I put my head in my hands. "Why is this happening?"

He's silent.

After taking a deep breath, I look at him. "So, me and you still can't happen?"

"It can. We just have to be sneaky about it," he says. "The thing is . . . I still have to keep up appearances with Kay, but I've got it all planned out."

I urge him to go on.

"I already know what annoys the shit out of her, so hopefully if I play my cards right, I can get her to dump me. I can't go too far, otherwise Xavier will still come after me."

"This situation is so messed up." I shake my head.

"Hey, we can make it work." He nudges me. "Just trust me."

"I do." I nod. I've always trusted Dylan, which is why I've been so open with him since we've first met. He doesn't seem like the double-crossing type.

Which brings me to the second thing that I remember from my conversation with Kay. "I don't think Xavier knows that Kay doesn't like Casey. Maybe we can use that to our advantage."

He taps his chin. "I'll keep that in mind." He hesitates before speaking again. "I know you don't like the idea of me and Kay being together, and I promise things won't go far. If I really have to kiss her, it'll be a peck on the cheek and that's it. Nothing beyond that. I gotta save my best kisses for you."

I can't stop a smile from spreading on my face. "Have our past kisses been your best kisses?"

"Not even close," he teases. "You'll have to wait for the best ones."

Unconsciously, I bite my lip before leaning into him and placing my lips on his. His hand rests on my waist as our mouths move together, causing the same sparks in my head to appear like all the other times we've kissed. When he pulls away, he brushes some hair away from my face.

"I want you to come over to my house this Friday," he says, almost breathlessly.

The way he says it brings tingles to my whole body, and my mind immediately goes to a dirty place, causing my face to go warm.

He chuckles. "That came out the wrong way. I mean for dinner. With my dad."

With his dad? "Really?" I ask, trying to stop my face from blushing further.

"Yeah." He nods. "It'll be the first time in a while that all the Parker boys will be home at the same time."

If Derrick and Ethan are going to be there, then it can't be that bad, can it? "I'd love to." I smile as I say it. My mind sticks to the word "boys." Dylan has never mentioned his mom. I wonder if it's a sore subject for him.

I'll feel horrible if I've only been capable of talking about my own issues and not asking him about his. Did she leave them, or something else?

I decide not to push it. He'll tell me when he's ready.

"Maybe I should get going," he says, glancing at our clock on the wall. "Not to be rude, but I don't want your aunt to see me and have her think I'm trying to corrupt you or something."

"Okay," I say with a chuckle.

As I walk him to the door, he says, "Every time I'm with Kay, I'll let you know."

"Don't stress too much," I tell him. "I trust you."

Sure, it bothers me that they are still going to see each other, but Dylan's actions from the get-go have been nothing but positive when it comes to me. I don't trust Kay, but I trust him more.

After Dylan leaves, I stay on the couch and watch TV, but I'm really staring at it blankly. A million thoughts are running through my mind, and I don't know what to do with all of them. Why does everything have to be a mess? I hate that this has become my life, and instead of fighting back, I'm just accepting it. But what more can I do?

I can't change the fact that my parents are gone, and no matter how much I question why this has happened to me, they won't come back.

And what about Jacob? Why couldn't he just break up with me instead of cheat on me? I could've gotten over a break up easier, but now I have to live with the fact that I wasn't good enough for him that he cheated.

Kay has only made it worse. How do I know Dylan won't cheat? Or any other guy I date if me and Dylan don't work out?

Do I want to fight for him?

My aunt practically rushes inside with a few bags from the grocery store, startling me.

She smiles. "Well, don't you look comfy." She continues to walk past me until she does a double take. "What happened to your face?"

I've completely forgotten to think of a lie for the cut. My mind is racing, trying to come up with a convincing lie. "I—uh, there was a stray cat on the railing by the stairs when I got home. I tried to pet it, and it attacked me . . ." It's a lame excuse, but it's all I can think of.

She set the bags down and strides over to me. Grabbing my face, she examines it. "It's bruising."

"Is it?" I play dumb. "It did have big paws. Grabbed on to my face pretty good."

She eyes me skeptically. "You have the worst luck."

Tell me about it. "Do you need help?" I ask her, standing up and changing the subject.

"No, I got it. I do have to tell you that James is coming over for dinner."

Her genetics professor boyfriend. I haven't seen him since Thanksgiving. "Oh, okay." I nod. "I can see if Casey wants to hang out, so you don't have to worry about me."

"Actually . . ." she says as she walks into the kitchen, with me following her. "I was thinking the three of us could have dinner together, so you could get to know him a little better."

I'm surprised. If she wants me to get to know him more, then that has to be a good sign for them. "Things are going well, then?" I ask.

She's pulling everything from the grocery bags and setting them aside. She lets out a long sigh. "Things are going *too* well. I keep waiting for him to have a flaw." She laughs at herself. "Would you mind cleaning up a little bit? I know it's not filthy, but—"

"I got it," I say. She's nervous, and even though she's trying not to show it, I can see it.

I vacuum the carpeted areas and dust the shelves. While I'm doing all of this, my aunt disappears into her room. When she comes out, she has changed from her black trousers to jeans that match the maroon blazer she has on.

"What time is he coming over?" I ask after I finish cleaning up.

She's at the stove, completely focused on the chicken cooking in the pan. "I told him to come over at six."

Glancing at my phone, I see that it's going to be five-thirty. I go into my room and brush out my hair. I stare at my plain black sweater and decide it's decent enough for dinner. Slipping on my ring from my aunt, I walk out of the room and double check the rest of the apartment. It isn't much, but I hope I've cleaned it enough.

"What are we having?" I ask her.

"Chicken parmesan."

The doorbell rings, and she looks at me. "Can you get that? I don't want to mess anything up over here."

Behind the door is James, who is a tall guy with the beginnings of salt and pepper hair and a trace of a goatee. He has a light-blue button up rolled up to his elbows and some dark jeans. He smiles at me.

278

"Hi Lacey," he greets.

"James." I nod to him before opening the door wider. "Come on in."

In his hand is a tub of ice cream, though I can't tell what flavor it is.

"She's in the kitchen if you want to head in there," I tell him. "I can put that in the freezer for you."

We walk into the kitchen, and she immediately smiles when she sees him. They hug, and he kisses her cheek lightly.

"I brought something for the sweet tooth. You said butter pecan is your favorite, right?" he asks her.

"I did." Her grin widens.

I take it from him and put it in the freezer. My aunt finishes dinner as she talks to him.

Deciding I don't want to be too much of a third wheel, I go to my room and pick my phone up from my bed. I don't have any messages, so I scroll through Instagram before my aunt calls me from the kitchen.

I help set the table before we sit down. I'm at the head, and my aunt and James are sitting across each other.

James, being a genetics professor, is a giant dork. It's not that I don't like him, but the topics of his conversation almost make me lose my appetite.

His other topics are interesting. He tells us how we can see the probability of what traits will carry on in a family based on partners. He's better at teaching this than my sophomore year biology teacher.

"So if you and my aunt have kids, what's the chance they'll have hazel eyes like you?" I can't help but ask. I'm partially teasing, partially not.

My aunt gives me a look, but he chuckles. "Well, there's a chance the dominant trait might be brown eyes since my family has a history of those, and especially since yours are brown," he directs the statement at her. "My mother has dark-green eyes, so I somewhat got a mixture of hers and my dad's brown eyes."

At the mention of green eyes, my mind goes to Dylan and his intoxicating light-green eyes.

"That's a lovely tattoo you have," James suddenly says, his eyes zeroing in on my wrist.

I quickly look at my aunt, and she's almost giving him a "shut up" look. I realize she must've mentioned to him why I have the tattoo, but I'm curious as to where he wants the conversation to head.

"Thanks," I say slowly. "I'm trying to get rid of it."

"Are you thinking removal or cover up?" he asks, looking genuinely interested.

"Um, whatever is cheapest and easiest, I guess."

"Removal is a long process," he says, looking at my aunt. "I had a tattoo removed a couple years back."

"Really?" I ask. My aunt seems like she's heard the story before, but I want to hear it. "How was it?"

"It was a pain. You have to go in intervals until it's completely removed. I didn't want to get another tattoo, so that's why I wanted a removal."

"What was the tattoo of?" I ask.

"Some Chinese inscription I got in college. It didn't mean what I thought it meant, and it was quite embarrassing." He laughs slightly. "The removal is just a little more expensive than what a cover up would have been."

I pick at my food. "At least yours isn't a matching tattoo with your ex-boyfriend." I try to sound light-hearted, but my aunt frowns. I've gotten over the whole thing with Jacob, but she hasn't. And I haven't told her that we're on friendly terms now.

"What would you cover it with?" she asks me.

"I don't know." I shake my head. "I have to come up with some money before I start thinking about it I guess."

James sets his fork down. "I could pay for it."

280

What?

"You really don't have to do that, James," my aunt says to him.

"No, I really mean it." He nods. "I know what it's like to have a tattoo you don't want anymore. I have no problem paying for it."

Excitement is rising in me, but I try not to get ahead of myself. "I'll have to think about it," I say. Covering my tattoo will really allow me to move to a different chapter in my life.

"Well, I can help too," my aunt chimes in. "Anything to help you forget him."

Him meaning Jacob. "We're on good terms now," I tell her. "We've talked through it." And fought and argued, but I don't tell her that.

"In my opinion, a guy who changes your tire and takes you out all the time is a much better guy," she says, a little on the nose. That means she clearly likes Dylan. "Anyway, I think I'm ready for dessert. I'll go pull it out, so it can thaw a bit."

As soon as she leaves, James turns to me again. "I don't want you to think I'm weird for offering help with your tattoo situation. I really care about Jade, and I want to help her any way I can," he says. "I also don't want you to think I'm trying too hard to make you like me."

"I appreciate it, and as long as my aunt is happy, then I'm happy."

He smiles. "If you want that tattoo gone, just let me know. I've heard students talking about the best places in town."

I can only imagine what conversations he hears on a daily basis. "Thanks." I laugh.

I can't wait to tell Casey. She'll help me decide on a cover up. Maybe that can be our small distraction from the Xavier disaster going on.

CHAPTER EIGHTEEN

I'm walking to my first period when I feel a presence to my left. Lauren's long black hair brushes against my arms because she's that close to me. I give her a strange look and she sighs.

"I'm probably the last person you want to talk to right now," she says, looking straight ahead. Her winged eyeliner looks sharp enough to kill.

"Believe it or not, you actually aren't," I admit. Xavier and Kay have taken that spot collectively. "What do you want?"

Lauren sweeps her hair out of her face. "I need your advice."

"My advice?" What can she possibly want advice on?

"Yeah . . . about Jacob."

Oh.

Before I can respond, she speaks up. "You're the perfect yet the worst person to talk to about this. I just don't know what to do about him. Ever since his parents split up, he's been like a hermit. I can't get him to go out anywhere with me. He's not the same person."

Jacob is usually a social butterfly. Always down to go to any party or whatever school function that will allow him a chance to go drink with his friends. I've noticed in class that he isn't as talkative, but I haven't thought he is like that outside of it. She's telling me everything for a reason, and that either means that she wants to help him or she wants to leave him. I hope for his sake, it's the first option.

"Have you talked to him about it?" I ask her. It feels a little strange talking about my ex to his new girlfriend, but it doesn't hurt and I'm glad.

She nods. "He always brushes it off. He just tells me he's tired."

"What exactly are you asking me then?" Is she asking me to talk to him? Or give her advice on how to deal with him?

"Was he ever like this with you?" She tilts her head.

This is weird, so I take a deep breath. "Not really. Then again, his parents were still together and he didn't have to get a job."

"I don't know what to do. Part of me wants to leave him because he's different now, but the other part feels . . . guilty? I guess?" she says, looking at me. "I don't want to leave him when he's feeling down or whatever."

"Honestly, if you're not happy, then leave. Maybe talk to him first though."

"Can you talk to him? I can't get through him. I know this might be weird . . ." She pauses for a few seconds. "Well, really weird, but you'd be helping me a lot, even though I did technically steal him from you."

I haven't had a real conversation with Lauren since the day I've found out Jacob has cheated on me. Maybe I shouldn't open old wounds by doing this, or maybe not. "Yeah, I'll talk to him."

She quickly gives me her number before both of us have to go to class. This only adds another thing on my plate. Involving myself in Jacob's relationship with Lauren might backfire somehow, and I mentally hit myself for not thinking it through.

When lunch comes around, Dylan sits with the guys while Casey and I get our own table. Lauren texts me and asks if I've talked to him yet. As I'm texting her back, Casey takes a peek at my phone. I tilt it, so she can see.

"Does that contact say 'Lauren,' or am I stupid?" she asks.

I sigh. "She wants me to talk to Jacob for her. Apparently, there's trouble in paradise."

"And she wants you to help her?" She scrunches her nose as she asks.

"I'm going to talk to him later in class, so I can be done with this. I don't want to get stuck in the middle. Plus, it'll keep me distracted from the fact that I can't see Dylan." I instantly regret saying that last part out loud because I know Casey blames herself for the trouble with Xavier. "We'll work it out."

She rests her chin on her hand as she glances over at Carlos. "He doesn't even want to talk to me."

Carlos has the tough guy exterior going on, but is he actually scared of Xavier? It sounds like he doesn't even want to fight.

"You guys aren't even trying?" I ask her.

She shakes her head. "He said he doesn't want to risk it."

I haven't told her that Dylan and I are risking it. Maybe I need to keep our relationship a secret from her. The less everyone knows, the better.

"What about you and Dylan?"

I have to lie. "We're done too. He's all Kay's."

"She's such a bitch." She frowns. "Always has been." She gives me a weird look. "What did you do to your face by the way? Don't tell me you were trying to shave your mustache. I told you not try it like that."

I don't want to lie to her about my face too, but if she finds out Kay has done this to me, she'll draw blood. "It's a long story," I say instead. "And I didn't try to shave my mustache."

"Okay," she drawls out.

The rest of lunch is uneventful. Lauren is so impatient. She needs me to talk to Jacob, as if I can do that at the snap of her fingers. I walk into English as I'm still explaining to her how I

285

won't see him until fourth period. Dylan strolls in as I'm concentrated on my phone.

He sits down, but I hear his voice in my ear. "The love of your life just walked in, so you can pay attention to me now."

I roll my eyes and send my message to Lauren. I face Dylan and say, "Someone is needy today."

The way he calls himself the love of my life doesn't feel weird at all. I'm surprised by how comfortable it sounds. It instantly puts me in a better mood.

He chuckles. "You'd think I wouldn't be now that I have two girlfriends."

Being reminded that Kay is still around breaks my good mood, even though he's joking. I try to brush it off. "I don't remember you officially asking me to be your girlfriend."

"You're right." He taps his chin. "Might have to do something about that."

Mrs. Beattie starts talking before I can respond. He winks at me before I turn around to face the front.

After class, Dylan walks me to journalism, kisses me swiftly on the cheek, then heads to his fourth period. I wonder if he really is taking this secret relationship seriously. His nonchalant flirting and kisses make me nervous that someone might know Xavier and tell him what they've seen of us.

I shake those thoughts out as I sit with Vicky and Will, anxiously waiting for Jacob to get to class. He walks in before the bell rings and plops down next to me.

After Mrs. Thomas gives us a rundown of what we need to finish, my group turns to our computers. I glance at Jacob, who is starting to put his earbuds in.

"Hey." I nudge him. "How are you?"

He looks at me suspiciously but smirks. "Are you trying to come on to me? Because we've already tried this."

"What? No." I shake my head. "I'm just wondering how you are."

286

"I'm fine."

"How's your mom? What about your job? And Lauren?"

He frowns at me. "Why do you want to know?"

"I'm a concerned friend." I shrug. "You seem down in the dumps lately."

"So have you, but you don't see me bothering."

Okay, asshole. "What's up your ass?" I provoke him instead. Being friendly won't work, so I have to try another tactic.

"I have an asshole for a dad, and I've been working my ass off to help my mom with the bills. I'm just sick of everything," he snaps, earning looks from Will and Vicky. "I'm not talking to you two."

I give them an apologetic look before looking at him again. "What about Lauren? Isn't she helping?"

"Honestly, I'm sick of her too." He shakes his head.

"You don't mean that . . ." I trail off because I know he does mean it. If these are his real feelings, I'm better off telling Lauren to leave him.

"All she wants to do is party, as if I don't have my mom riding on my back to pick up extra shifts at work. I don't need two needy women bitching at me."

He runs a hand through his hair, and I catch a slight glimpse of his tattoo. I wonder if I should tell him I'm planning on covering mine.

"Can I tell you something?" I ask.

"Sure," he says, even though he's immersed himself in the computer.

"I'm thinking of covering my tattoo."

His head whips to me so quickly, I'm sure he'll end up with whiplash. "Wait, really?"

I nod. "My aunt's boyfriend says he will help pay for it."

His face is unreadable. "Damn. What are you going to get?"

"I'm not sure yet," I say. "Did you ever think of covering yours?"

"I did. It's not really at the top of my priority list right now, though . . ." He lets his words fade. "Would it bother you if I kept it for a while?"

I didn't think the tattoo mean that much to him. I've always thought he secretly hates it, especially since some guys say it's too girly for him. "Does it bother you that I'm covering mine?"

"No. I get why you'd want to."

"Then no, it doesn't bother me," I tell him.

That's the end of our conversation. It's best if I tell Lauren to just break up with him. I can tell the stress is getting to him, and it isn't fair to her. Jacob, I've learned, isn't good at breaking up with someone he doesn't have feelings for anymore.

After school, I'm walking to my car when I pull out my phone to text Lauren. Just as I'm going to hit send, Casey and Lauren walk up to me at the same time.

It's a strange sight. The three of us haven't hung out since middle school.

"I picked up a hitchhiker on my way over here." Casey forces a smile.

"I was going to call you, but I couldn't wait," Lauren explains. "Then I ran into Casey, so I figured I'd just walk over here with her." She bites her lip. "What did Jacob say?"

"Let's walk and talk," I suggest. I give Casey a look to leave us alone, and she walks ahead of me and Lauren.

"It didn't take much to get him to open up. You just have to make him mad."

"And?" she pushes.

A glimpse of red catches my eye; I realize it's Kay's car parked next to Dylan's. He walks up to his car, and she gets out of hers to hug him. While hugging him, she meets my gaze and flashes me a wicked smile, as if to say "I won."

She holds onto him tightly before she taps her cheek. He leans down and kisses her cheek, all while she is looking at me with the same grin slapped on her face.

"You should leave him," I finally say to Lauren, even though I can't tear my eyes away from Kay and Dylan.

"Leave him? Why?" she asks with a frown.

Kay stands on her tip toes and kisses Dylan straight on the mouth. They stay that way until he pushes her slightly.

"He says he can't handle two women in his life right now," I say, just as Dylan happens to look my way. I tear my gaze away and meet Lauren's eyes. "You and his mom, I mean."

Confusion is all over her face, so I say, "If I were you, I'd just leave him. It's only going to hurt you the longer you stay with him, and he isn't going to do it himself. Trust me, I know."

I thought I could handle Dylan being with Kay, but seeing them together hurts like hell. I know he can't completely avoid kissing her full on, but he lingered too long when they did.

Lauren's face is pained. "I guess I should've seen this coming."

I don't know what else to tell her. Jacob is not going to break up with her himself, so she'll have to do it. It's a weird situation. I'm watching the guy I want kiss another girl while giving advice to my ex's girlfriend.

What other weird situation can I be put in?

*   *   *

There's a tap on my shoulder as I walk into the main building on Friday morning. I look over and see Lauren standing by my side. Her hair is curled, and she's light on her makeup.

"I did it," she says.

"Did what?" I didn't sleep well last night. Dylan didn't call or text, and I know it's because he was with Kay. Almost every hour of the night, I kept checking my phone. My mind kept going to the fact that there was a possibility he was with her all night.

He's said he won't let things go far with her, but he still let her kiss him on the lips yesterday—in front of me too—so I feel slightly doubtful, no matter how hard I try not to be.

"Broke up with Jacob." Lauren sighs. "I went over to his house last night and told him it wasn't working anymore. He didn't really seem upset."

She looks upset, however. I can understand why. Jacob is very good at manipulating his image. If he wants you to see him a certain way, he'll make it happen. It has gotten me to go out with him in the first place, and it has driven me mad after we've broken up. He's charming, damn him.

I shake my head. "Don't be upset over him. I might be a little biased, but he's not worth thinking about anymore."

"Do you ever think about the possibility of you two getting back together in the future?" she asks, tilting her head. "Like, in five years you run into him at the supermarket, you both happen to be single, you both look good, and it's like the connection has never been broken? Next thing you know, you're sending out wedding invitations, baby shower invitations, and everything that happened in high school happened because you were stupid kids?"

That is oddly specific. I have the feeling she likes Jacob more than she's letting on. "Are you referring to yourself or me?"

"I don't know." She turns her head. "I guess I was obsessed with you and him. You guys always seemed happy, and he looked like the perfect boyfriend. I wasn't jealous of you, just envious."

"Well, you got a taste of being in a relationship with him anyway," I point out.

"Yeah, but I got the rough patch in his life."

"Then maybe it'll be you who runs into him at the supermarket because I don't have any plans of getting back together with him."

She doesn't seem satisfied with my answer. I'm not sure what she wants me to tell her. That her and Jacob are soulmates and will find each other again in this life or another?

I frown. "Lauren, he's just some dumb boy who needs to grow up and learn how to handle stressful situations. I won't waste my time thinking about him right now," I say to her. It has taken me a while to take my own advice, but I've done it and so can she.

"I guess you're right." She nods slowly. "Can I hang out with you and Casey for lunch today?"

"Yeah, sure." Casey probably won't like it, but she'll have to get over it.

Lunch with Casey and Lauren isn't that bad. Interesting, to say the least, but not bad. Casey still has a grudge against Lauren for stealing Jacob and it shows. She isn't interested in the conversation if Lauren brings up the topic, and she makes snarky comments about her relationship with Jacob.

Casey walks with me to English after Lauren goes down another hallway. "I don't know how you did it."

"Did what?" I ask.

"Forgive her. I mean, think about what she did to you."

"Yeah, but it's not like I still have feelings for him. Plus, she broke up with him. I guess we're just bonding over him now." She makes a face. "She'll probably leave me alone as soon as next week." Lauren will most likely grow bored and go back to whoever she usually hangs out with.

We stop by the classroom door, and her shoulders slump slightly. "I wish I could be like you. More forgiving."

Dylan comes into view down the hall, and my heartbeat speeds up. The plain black hoodie he's wearing hugs his chest, and his jeans cling to his legs in all the right places. Simple but so good on him.

"Being forgiving has its downsides sometimes." I shrug, trying to ignore Dylan. I can't show Casey any hint of our relationship.

He lightly brushes my shoulder as he passes me to go into class.

She raises her eyebrows. "Cold shoulder much?" she asks, referring to him.

"I should get going."

"Wait, are we doing anything tonight?"

I'm about to say yes, until I remember Dylan's dinner proposal with his family. Is that still on? "Um, I'll let you know. I think James is coming over for dinner again."

Lying to her is getting old.

"Okay," she says, believing me.

I take a deep breath before entering the classroom. Dylan is leaned back in his chair when I sit down and face him. "Did you just shoulder bump me back there?" I ask him, frowning.

He smirks. "Why? What are you going to do about it?"

"Assume Kay is rubbing off on you and you're actually starting to hate me now."

His smirk disappears. "She isn't rubbing off on me."

"And that's why you didn't text me last night?"

"I was with her."

"All night?" I'm not being fair, but he isn't either.

"I got home at nine, my dad got home at nine-thirty, and we stayed up talking." He leans forward. "You want to know what time I had my third dream at?"

I give him a flat look. "Not funny."

"Nothing happened," he says. "We went to the movies, ate, then I went home."

Dylan and I haven't even gone to the movies together. Their relationship isn't even real, and she's getting more of the relationship than me. I should have expected it, but it won't have hurt any less.

"You're still coming over tonight, right?" he asks.

I'm tempted to make a comment, but I hold back and nod instead. "What are you going to tell Kay?"

"Me and you have a project to work on for class. She won't like it, but she can't stop me from doing homework."

Meeting Dylan's dad has my heart racing a bit. Ethan and Derrick will be there, so hopefully it won't be so bad. There's still the question about his mom. I wonder if that will be brought up at all.

"Don't be nervous." He cracks a smile. "The Parker men aren't scary, you know. I mean, you've met my brothers."

"Yeah, and the last time I saw Ethan, he caught us kissing in your room." I smirk at the memory.

"That's right." Dylan smirks also before shrugging. "Oh, well."

Mrs. Beattie starts class, and I feel giddy for tonight. Hopefully, it will turn out alright. I wonder what his dad is like. Did Dylan get his personality from his dad? Or does his dad have a personality like Derrick's?

After class, Dylan catches my arm. "Be at my house at six."

"I'll be there," I say, looking into his eyes.

We stare at each other for a moment before a large grin spreads on his face. He shakes his head, then walks away.

I wonder if it's going to be a casual dinner or a nicer one. I have a feeling it'll be casual, but that doesn't mean I can't look nicer than usual.

When I get home, I immediately start rummaging through my closet to find something to wear. The simple blue long sleeve I have on won't cut it.

After pulling out every nice sweater, I still can't find anything that will work. Then I find my off-shoulder, mauve-taupe sweater and hug it.

I pair the sweater with some light wash jeans on my bed, then pull out some tan ankle boots. Once I have everything put together, I realize I might be overthinking it all.

It's only four o'clock, so I focus on some homework. When my aunt gets home, I know I have to lie about where I'm going. Dragging her into this mess isn't a good idea.

"I'm going to Casey's for dinner tonight," I tell her as she steps out of her heels in the living room.

She throws the heels off to the side of the room and lies on the couch. "Oh, yeah?"

I nod. "I won't be home late."

"That's fine." She waves it off.

At five-thirty, I'm putting the finishing touches on my makeup when my aunt walks into my room.

"Someone looks fancy," she points out as she sits on my bed.

"Casey's parents like to make dinner kind of formal." I quickly think of the lie. I'm lying too much to her, and it hurts.

I think she's going to push the subject further, but she doesn't. "Well, James is making us dinner at his house tonight."

It's something they usually do together. "Okay," I say, not thinking much of it.

"Are you staying over at Casey's tonight?" She isn't looking at me. "I'm only asking because I don't know what time I'll be home, or if I'll be back at all."

Well, things have just gotten awkward. "I wasn't planning on spending the night," I say, racking my brain for something else to say. Maybe I can call Casey after I leave Dylan and stay over, or I can just have the apartment to myself.

Either way, my aunt probably won't be home. It's been a couple of months since she and James have started seeing each other, but this is the first time she won't come home from a date.

"I'll be fine by myself if that's what you're worried about," I finally say.

She lets out a laugh that sounds nervous. "I know you don't want to hear about my date, so as long as you'll be okay, my mind will be at ease."

"Don't worry about me," I say, smiling.

On my way to Dylan's, I think about my aunt and James. She's nervous about spending the night with him, and as much as I try not to think about it, it still slips into my mind. But it makes me wonder about my relationship with Dylan.

Jacob and I only slept together once and it wasn't at all what I thought my first time would be like. Things got hot and heavy in his truck after the soccer team had a huge win. It was awkward, rushed, and not romantic at all.

I don't regret our first time, but I've always made excuses for us not to do it again.

Dylan certainly isn't a virgin. I know him and Kay have slept together before we've admitted our feelings for each other. I don't know why I feel jealous that she has that against me.

I know that as long as he's with me, he won't do it with her again. Will he and I get to that level? Part of me feels like we will eventually, and it makes me nervous. My first time with Jacob was lust-driven. I want my next time to be love-driven.

Do I love Dylan yet?

I shake those thoughts from my head as I pull into his driveway. I'm going to meet his dad. I need to put my game face on.

The door opens quickly after I ring the doorbell, revealing a freshly showered Dylan with only a towel around his waist.

I feel my cheeks warm as I try to focus on his face and not his naked torso. "So, you do shower," I tease him to break the awkwardness.

He motions for me to go inside, so I step in. He smirks as he holds on to his towel. "I don't always shower, but when I do, it's for when my girl is meeting my dad for the first time."

My girl. "And yet, I notice the house is strangely quiet.".

"No one is home yet." He shrugs. "Derrick went to pick up Ethan from his friends, and my dad is at the store."

"Why did I need to be here at six then?" I ask him.

295

"Because we have a matter to discuss." He smiles as he says it. "Follow me."

We walk down to his room. Everything is tidier than the last time I've visited. He reaches into his closet and pulls out a black shirt and some jeans. I spent forever trying to pick an outfit, and he just picks out the first thing he sees.

He rummages through some dresser drawers, then announces he's going to change. I try not to follow his figure with my eyes as he leaves up the stairs. The image of him with just a towel is not doing anything to help my hormonal thoughts.

On the small table next to his bed is a copy of the school newspaper. I smile, knowing he has actually grabbed a copy. I wonder if he's read it, though.

He comes back in with combed though still wet hair and the clothes he has picked out.

"I know, I know. You want me in the towel all night, but that won't be appropriate for dinner, okay?" He smirks.

I laugh. "Damn." I snap my fingers before pointing to the paper. "Anything interesting in here?"

His mouth opens, but he doesn't say anything for a few seconds. "As a matter of fact, yes."

I decide to tease him. "I didn't know Dylan Parker liked to read the school newspaper."

"Only for you." He winks at me.

I laugh again before I go back to what he said earlier. "What urgent matter do we need to talk about?"

His hands are on my shoulders, and my heart is racing as he lightly pushes me to sit down on his bed. "Now, close your eyes."

I'm hesitant, but I close them. Though they are closed, I know he's turned the lights off, and I feel like I might pass out.

"This sounds bad, but lay back on the bed and make sure you're staring at the ceiling." I hear him say.

"Are you trying to seduce me?" I can't help but laugh as I ask.

"Not at the moment, no." He let out a laugh.

I do as I'm told and lie back on his bed.

"Open your eyes."

It takes a second for my eyes to adjust to see the lights on his ceiling sparkle. I admire them until I realize they spell out two words.

Be mine?

I immediately sit up and the lights flicker back on. Dylan has a bouquet of red roses in one hand and he smiles.

"I know you said you wanted to take things slow, and now might not be the best time to ask this, but I like taking chances. And I figured I should ask you to be my girlfriend in the spot where you couldn't help but kiss me." The smirk on his face breaks with a smile.

I take the roses. "Well, I couldn't turn you down when you asked to kiss me."

"I mean, if I'm just a charity case, then forget it." He laughs.

Instead of responding, I roll my eyes and lean forward to kiss him. I set the flowers down and wrap my arms around his neck to bring us closer. The kiss is needy and passionate, especially when he lays me back down on his bed. This time, we're not interrupted by Ethan.

Dylan pulls back first and hovers above me. "Is that a yes?"

"It's a yes." I smile.

He pecks my cheek, then proceeds to kiss me all over my face. "Good. Now when I introduce you to my dad, I know what to call you."

"You could have said, 'Hey, dad. This is Lacey,' " I say to him.

"But now I can say, 'Hey, dad. This is Lacey, my girlfriend.' "

There is movement upstairs, and I hear a door shut. The sound of small feet running around confirms that Ethan and Derrick are home.

"Let's head upstairs," Dylan says.

CHAPTER NINETEEN

We greet the other two Parker boys in the kitchen. Derrick is on his phone, and Ethan is scouring through the cabinets.

"Hey, Lacey!" Ethan says as soon as he sees me. He runs up to me, wraps his arms around my legs, and smiles up at me. "Having boy trouble again?"

I cover my mouth to laugh, and Dylan rolls his eyes. "She's not having boy trouble," Dylan answers for me.

"Well, that's debatable," I say. I can't even go out on a real date with him yet because of Kay.

"We'll talk about it later," Ethan says, nodding.

When Ethan walks away, Dylan gives me a flat look. "I just asked you to be my girlfriend. How are you having boy trouble?"

"Your point would be valid if I didn't have to share you." As soon as I say it, he shuts up.

Derrick walks up to us and smiles at me. "Lacey, I hope you're prepared for a night of crazy Parker antics."

"I think I can handle it." Hopefully, I'll be able to. Dylan hasn't mentioned much about his dad, so I don't know what to expect.

Dylan, Ethan, Derrick, and I are all in the living room watching TV when we hear the front door open. The butterflies in my stomach erupt in a frenzy as everyone stands up to greet Mr. Parker. Should I call him Mr. Parker?

Dylan squeezes my hand as we walk into the kitchen, where the other boys are at.

Mr. Parker is slightly taller than Derrick, probably right above six feet. He's pulling items out of grocery bags as he speaks with Derrick. He sees me and stops talking.

"Well, well, who do we have here?" his smooth voice asks.

"Dad, this is Lacey, my girlfriend," Dylan quickly introduces me.

Derrick whistles. "Girlfriend, huh?"

Ethan also jumps in. "Wait, I thought you had a different boyfriend?"

The consecutive questions are overwhelming me, so I focus on Dylan's dad and extend my hand out to him. "It's nice to meet you, Mr. Parker. I hope I'm not intruding dinner with your boys."

Mr. Parker breaks into a huge smile and shakes my hand. "And she's polite! How on earth did you say yes to this guy?" He wraps his arm around Dylan and messes with his hair. "I'm glad you're here. I knew Dylan would get his dad's charm."

Derrick coughs into his hand, and Mr. Parker puts his arm around him too. "In fact, all my boys got my charm."

"Some of us more than others." Dylan nudges Derrick.

Ethan frowns at me. "So, what happened to that other guy?" he asks me.

I'm being put on the spot again. "We broke up a while back. I decided I didn't need him in my life," I tell him.

"Good." He nods approvingly.

"Anyway," Dylan interrupts, "dinner?"

"Yes," Mr. Parker answers. "I picked up some steaks. The potato salad is pre-made since I have absolutely no idea how to make it."

My stomach growls at the mention of steak.

"I hope you're hungry." He turns his attention to me. "These steaks are massive."

While Mr. Parker prepares the steak and turns down my efforts to help with dinner somehow, Ethan suggests the rest of us play a card game, specifically Old Maid. I sit next to Dylan at the table while Ethan and Derrick sit opposite of us. After Ethan deals the cards, I realize I have the Old Maid after taking out my pairs.

"Lacey, go first," Ethan says as he takes out his pairs.

I face Dylan and he rolls his eyes. "Fine," he says, picking a card. He doesn't pick the Old Maid. It's going to be a long game.

Mr. Parker soon has the steaks on the grill outside, and I end up losing the game. While Dylan laughs at me, Ethan shoots up from the table.

"I think I have UNO somewhere!" He runs out of the room as he says it.

Dylan stands up as well. "I'll be right back." He slides behind the glass doors to the backyard where his dad is.

My eyes follow Dylan. It was really sweet of him to ask me to be his girlfriend the way he did. I haven't expected it, plus the roses are a nice touch. All this Parker charm is making me feel giddy inside.

"I knew you guys would go out," Derrick suddenly says, interrupting my thoughts. "I called it."

"You aren't the first to say that." I laugh.

"I think you guys are good together."

I wonder if he knows about the situation with Kay. Getting his perspective will be nice. Has Dylan told him about it? "It's just a little hard right now," I say vaguely. I don't know how much he knows about the Xavier situation or if he knows at all.

He glances at the sliding glass doors before getting up and sitting in Dylan's spot next to me. "Listen, I told Dylan in the beginning not to get involved with Xavier. Now he's dragged you into it, which I'm not happy about."

"Why?"

"Xavier is a psycho. When Dylan got involved with Kay, I was pissed. I honestly thought he was still with her." He eyes me suspiciously.

"We're keeping things a secret," I admit. "Dylan didn't tell you about us?"

"Dylan doesn't tell me anything. I have to get information through Reece." He shakes his head. "Does he know what he's doing?"

I sigh. "I hope so. It's not just him, though. My best friend used to be neighbors with Xavier and Kay, so she got dragged into this too."

Derrick looks at the doors before looking back at me. "I'll give you my number at the end of the night, and we can talk about it more," he quickly says. I'm glad someone knows the truth.

Dylan comes back in and Ethan brings out UNO. Dylan is adamant about winning, but Ethan wins easily.

Mr. Parker then comes in with a plate of steaks in his hands. "Who's hungry?"

After cleaning up the table, we're all served our steaks. "Dig in, everyone," Mr. Parker says, grabbing his knife.

As soon as the steak hits my tongue, I try my best not to shove all the food in at once.

"Tell me about yourself, Lacey. What are your aspirations in life? Any hobbies? Any brothers or sisters?" Mr. Parker asks me.

I swallow the food in my mouth. "Um, no brothers or sisters. I do write for the school newspaper, and I want to be a journalist or an editor."

"You want to write for the local paper? I've got a buddy who works as an editor. He can probably take you on as an intern." He nods.

He'll do that for me? "That would be really great," I admit. "I would love to work for the local paper, but I also want to move up. I want to go to bigger places like TIME or the Post."

"Those are some big dreams," he says. "I like that."

What are Dylan's dreams? Is there something he is passionate about that I don't know? Maybe I don't know Dylan as well as I think, and the reality begins to set in. What will happen after graduation? Does Dylan plan on going to college? What is his dream job?

I've been so wrapped up in the Xavier-Kay drama that I don't know anything about what Dylan wants for his future.

"What about family? Your folks okay with you spending your Friday night here?" Mr. Parker asks, interrupting my thoughts.

It's an innocent question, so I can't be upset. Dylan immediately clears his throat. "Uh, dad." He shakes his head.

"It's okay." I nod at Dylan. "I live with my aunt right now. I lost my parents in a car accident earlier this year." Hearing the words come from my mouth is still foreign.

"Oh," Mr. Parker says. "I'm really sorry."

Things get awkward for a few seconds, and I feel the pity in their looks. I need to break the tension. "This steak is great, Mr. Parker. I haven't had a good steak in a while."

He grins bashfully. "Thank you. And please, call me Dean."

There is a recurring theme in the Parker household, and it's one that Ethan is not a part of. Dean, Derrick, and Dylan all have the same starting letter in their name, but not Ethan.

Dean jokes with the boys about what they've been like when they were younger. Apparently, Dylan liked to run around naked a lot; Derrick liked to break into the cabinets and eat all the peanut butter; Ethan, even now, couldn't go anywhere without making a mess of something.

One thing absent from these memories is their mom, but there isn't a somber feeling about it. It just seems like they share memories that she doesn't happen to be in.

Dylan and I clean up the mess after dinner. The other three sit in the living room while Dylan washes dishes and I dry them.

"I hope you're having a good time," Dylan says.

"You guys are so fun." I nudge him. "I liked hearing the stories about when you were younger."

He shrugs. "What can I say? I've always been a cute kid."

We finish the dishes and go into the living room with the others. Ethan is giggling and Derrick is holding his nose.

"Ethan! What have I told you about farting with girls around? We don't do it!" Dean covers his nose but laughs as he says it.

Dylan and I start to laugh at Ethan, who can't break out of his fit of giggles.

"Get out of here, you stink bug!" Dean pokes Ethan in his stomach, which only makes him laugh harder.

Ethan escapes into his room, and the laughter dies down. Derrick also disappears, leaving me with Dean and Dylan.

"Lacey, can you follow me?" Dean asks, standing up from the couch.

I look at Dylan before nodding. "Yeah, sure."

Dean takes me into the hallway and gestures for me to wait. He emerges from what I assume is his bedroom with a photo in his hands.

"I don't know if Dylan has said anything about his mom, but this is her." He hands me the photo. "Her name is Evelyn."

The photo shows a younger Dean and a woman about the same age with her arms wrapped around his neck. Now I know where Ethan has gotten his 'E' name from.

"She's beautiful," I say.

"The first time I saw her, I knew I wanted to spend the rest of my life with her. She told me right away that she never wanted to commit to anything, but I guess I sort of changed her mind," he says. "We got married, had Derrick, then Dylan. Ethan came soon after, but I knew something was wrong. The boys made her happy, of course, but I think she wanted a different life."

I stare at her picture. They are standing in front of a beach.

304

"She left when Ethan was about five. I knew she was leaving, and I didn't give her a hard time for it. She comes around every now and then. If she's gone for a longer period, she'll send a postcard from wherever she's at. The last one came about a month ago. She was in Boston."

"Is she coming back soon?" I ask.

"I think so." He nods. "The boys had a rough time understanding why she left. She's missed a lot of milestones in their lives."

I hand the photo back to him, and he stares at it. "I take this picture with me everywhere I go."

"It's a nice one," I say.

"I know Dylan isn't really forthcoming with a lot, but he's a good kid. He takes a while to crack, but he will eventually."

"I've seen his good side," I say to him. "I think he's been opening up more."

He nods slowly. "Good. Now, how do you think I tell him he's adopted?"

My jaw almost drops as I try to make sense of what he says.

Then he starts laughing. "I'm kidding," he says through his laughter. "You'll fit just fine here."

We walk back into the living room, and Dylan eyes us suspiciously. "I don't know what you two are plotting, but I'm onto you."

"Should we tell him?" Dean asks me.

"No." I shake my head. "He doesn't need to know."

Dean laughs and leaves the living room again. I hear his voice boom as he yells at Ethan to stop farting again.

Dylan only laughs and shakes his head. "Welcome to the Parker house. Want to go for a drive?"

"Sure."

Dylan tells his dad we'll be right back, and we jump into his car. Dylan drives through town, and I face him.

"I like your dad," I tell him. "He's really nice."

305

"Yeah, he's a pretty good guy." His eyes stay on the road.

I decide to ask him about the future. "Have you applied to any colleges?"

"College?" he asks, looking at me for a split second. "I haven't really thought about it. I know I want to get out of this place. There's nothing here for me, besides you, I mean."

"Where do you want to go?" I ask him.

"Everywhere. With my parents always gone, I was always stuck at home. We never really went on vacations or anything. I just want to see what's out there." He stays quiet. "I'm guessing my dad told you about my mom."

"A little, yeah." He's opening up more, and I'm excited to see it happen.

"My dad thinks one of us will end up like her. Running off while chasing . . . whatever she's chasing. I think it'll be Derrick. He's already making plans to move if him and Jared get signed by that record company."

The way Dylan talks about leaving and seeing everything makes me suspect that he's the one who will end up like his mom, but I keep that thought to myself.

"What if Derrick and Jared end up becoming big celebrities?" I ask him.

He smirks. "The press will realize Derrick has a much cooler younger brother." He stops at a red light. "What if you become some renowned journalist and earn a Nobel Peace Prize?"

"Can you get one in journalism?" I ask, half-teasing. That would be a high accomplishment.

"I'll make it happen, just for you," he says, leaning towards me.

I meet his lips. Suddenly, talking to Dylan about the future feels so right, like we're on the right paths. In my heart, I wish our paths will merge together.

There's a honk behind us, and the light is green. Dylan laughs and starts to drive again.

"Where are we going?" I ask him.

"Wherever you want, babe."

I bite my lip. "Let's go to my apartment."

He gives me a look. "Isn't your aunt home?"

"She's staying with her boyfriend tonight."

He smirks. "If you're trying to seduce me again, it's not working."

I let out a laugh. "Damn," I say teasingly.

We get to the apartment, and I realize I forgot my keys at Dylan's house. We run up the stairs and I pick up the door mat, revealing a silver key. I unlock the door, then put it back under the door mat.

"Don't come breaking in anytime you want," I tease, smiling.

"It would be more romantic if I snuck through your window, wouldn't it?" he teases back as he rests his hands on my waist after I shut the front door and lock it.

My heart is beating quickly in my chest, and I realize I know why I've told him to bring us here.

It's dark in the apartment, and the small sliver of light coming from the outside casts a light on his face. I pull him in for another kiss. We're needy, as he pulls my body closer to his.

I push him towards my room, and he swiftly pushes me onto the bed. He trails wet kisses on my neck, and his hands roam all over me as if he's memorizing everything.

I grab the hem of his shirt and pull it over his head, feeling the curves of the muscles on his back, and an evergreen scent hits my nose. I breathe it in as his hands play with the hem of my own shirt.

I go to pull my shirt off, but he stops my hands. I give him a quizzical look, and he's breathing heavily as he stares at me.

"What's wrong?" I ask him.

"Not now," he says. "I don't want to rush it."

He's right. I got caught up in the moment. If we're going to sleep together, I want it to be perfect. And to make sure Kay isn't breathing down our necks.

We sit up, and he picks up his shirt from the ground. I smirk. "Do you have to put your shirt on?"

He walks up to me before putting it on, getting close enough to my face that we're almost kissing. "You better behave, Lace." Then he pulls back and fixes his shirt.

We walk back out of the apartment. Dylan is holding my hand until we get to his car, where he opens the door for me.

On the way back to his house, I can't help but think that a future with Dylan is something I want.

CHAPTER TWENTY

Dinner with the Parkers has made me realize just how much I miss my parents. My parents and I would joke around at the dinner table, teasing each other. I always asked for a brother or sister from them, but they never seemed interested. I was enough for them, but it wasn't enough for me.

Before I've left the Parker house, Derrick has given me his phone number and has told me to get a hold of him whenever I think Dylan is in trouble or if I want to talk. It's nice knowing someone else knows that we're together. Derrick knows what we're doing is reckless, but he doesn't fight it. He knows it isn't worth it to argue with Dylan about it.

The weekend comes and goes in a flash, mostly with me sitting on my bed with a cup of hot chocolate. Casey is out of town for the weekend, and Dylan is on Kay duty. I come to the conclusion that I need more friends.

On Monday morning, Aunt Jade runs out the door, running late for work. She has stayed over at James's on that Friday and Saturday night. They've also stayed out late last night, hence why she is still putting on her shoes as she runs out the door. I'm happy that she's found someone, but it makes the apartment feel lonelier than ever.

I walk out the apartment door and jog down the stairs. I stop in my tracks when I see a tall figure leaning against my car.

The large build immediately gives away who it is, and my blood runs cold. How does he know where I live?

Xavier turns to look at me and crosses his arms.

I'm not going to let him scare me, but I have to keep my game face on so he can stay in the dark about me and Dylan. "What do you want?" I ask him.

"All I want is your honesty." He puts his hands up. "It seems a lot of people have been lying to me lately, and I'm just asking for the truth."

"The truth about what?"

"You and Parker."

I have the feeling Xavier knows more than Dylan thinks, but now I'm being faced with it. "There is no 'me and Parker,'" I say, putting up air quotes.

"Really?" He tilts his head to the side.

"Really."

"That's funny." He puts his hand on his chin. "I happened to be in his neighborhood last night, and this car was parked outside his house." He gestures to my car.

It scares me that he's keeping tabs on Dylan, but I can't let it show. I have to stand my ground. "So what? You're going to be upset over me and Dylan working on a project for our English class?" Dylan's lie is becoming pretty useful now.

"A project for class?" he scoffs. "How stupid do I look?"

My heart starts to pound. "I don't know what else you want from me. We can't stop our school work because it isn't convenient for you and Kay," I say. "Besides, Dylan likes Kay too much." I throw it in for good measure, hoping he'll believe me.

He narrows his eyes, examining me. "I don't know how much I trust you."

"Why?"

"Casey was ready to give up on you while you were with your little boyfriend. Guess who was there for her when you weren't?"

310

Now it's all coming to the light.

"You'd drop everything for that guy and leave Casey behind. What kind of friend does that?" he ask.

"Do I have to remind you that you're the one she dropped, not me?" It slips out before I can stop it. I need to watch my tongue before I say something that will mess everything up.

"You better watch your mouth, or that pretty lady you're staying with ends up in the ditch over there," he snaps, pointing behind us.

He knows about my aunt and is threatening her. "You're not going to touch her." I point at him. "Dylan and I are not together and never will be, and I can probably say the same about you and Casey."

His tall figure inches closer to me, and I have to look up at him. My heart is ready to come out of my chest, and the tears feel close to coming out, but I calm myself down.

"Casey will come to her senses," he says flatly. "I'll make sure of it."

"Maybe I was a bad friend, but not anymore. I'm not going to let anything happen to her," I say to him.

He lets out a dark laugh, and it makes the anger inside me rise. "Go on. I want to hear all about how you're going to stop me."

The threats against my aunt and Casey are enough to stop me from saying anything else.

"That's exactly what I thought." His eyes turn dark. "Stay away from Parker, and Casey and the pretty lady will be fine."

With that, he walks off. I watch him as he walks around the apartment building and leaves my sight. My eyes start to water, and I'm beginning to question Dylan's plan. Xavier knows too much. He isn't stupid.

I wipe my eyes, get in my car, and leave for school.

The more I think about it, the more I need someone else's advice. During lunch, I text Derrick to see if he's busy. His opinion

311

matters, but I need some other kind of support. Dylan doesn't want anyone to know about us, but it might help to have the other guys know what's going on.

I text Anthony and ask if he's okay with skipping next period with the other guys. I also tell him not to mention anything to Dylan. He and the others agree to meet at Raven's.

Casey needs to be in the dark, so I don't tell her anything. She isn't good at lying, and I know she'll crack under pressure if Xavier catches up with her.

When the bell rings for lunch to be over, I walk with Casey to her class, then quickly leave before Dylan can see me. I hate leaving him out, but he isn't going to listen to me or any of the other's pleas.

I let him know I won't be in class, that something has come up. He wants to know if everything is okay, and I tell him yes, despite the fact that it isn't. His plan is beginning to fall apart, and he isn't going to fix it in time.

When I get to Raven's, I see Anthony's car and a few others in the lot. I walk in and the boys plus Derrick are at a table in the back.

"What's going on?" Derrick asks me right away.

I sit down between Reece and Carlos. "Xavier showed up at my apartment this morning. He threatened to hurt my aunt and Casey if he caught wind of me and Dylan seeing each other."

"You guys aren't together, so what's the problem?" Reece ask, frowning.

"Dylan had the bright idea to pretend to date Kay while he and Lacey actually date," Derrick answers before I can say anything.

Anthony puts his head in his hands. "And you went along with it, Lacey?"

"I don't want Xavier and Kay to dictate who I can and can't date," I say in my defense. "At least I want to fight for someone I care about." Whether Carlos understands my jab or not, I don't know. His face holds no expression.

312

"So, he found out about you and Dylan then?" Derrick asks me.

"He said he saw my car at Dylan's last Friday, and I told him we had a project to work on together."

"So, he suspects it but doesn't know for sure," Derrick theorizes.

"Right." I nod. "I don't know what to do. He threatened to hurt my aunt and Casey, but Dylan isn't going to take it well if I try to break up with him. He'll want Xavier to be dealt with."

All the boys seem lost in thought. Carlos suddenly slams his hands on the table, making me jump.

"Dammit, we told Dylan not to get involved with Kay from the beginning. We told him about Xavier, and he still didn't listen. At this point, he's gonna get what's coming to him," he snaps.

His outburst doesn't appear to settle well with the boys, and it flat out makes me angry. At least Dylan isn't willing to let Xavier run all over him. He's only pretending to be with Kay, so Xavier will stay away from me.

"Dylan is your friend. How can you even say that?" I demand from him.

"Dylan has never given a shit about me. Why am I going to give a shit about him?"

Anthony rolls his eyes. "That's not true. Stop being a bitch, Carlos."

Carlos points at Anthony. "Don't call me a bitch. Everyone has to cater to Dylan's needs all the damn time, and I'm sick of it."

"Just sit down, dude," Reece says.

"No. I'm sick of Dylan and his bullshit." He shakes his head.

His anger is pointless, and he's mad at the wrong person. If he really cares for Casey, he should be pissed that Xavier has threatened to hurt her.

"What about Casey?" I ask him. "You're just going to let Xavier threaten her?"

His eyes meet mine, and there's something behind them I can't quite decipher. "I don't give a shit about Casey. I only dated her to get to you." He lets out a dark laugh. "And then you were never around anyway."

It hasn't clicked to me, until now. Why he was always coming between us, why he'd dance with me to tick Dylan off, and the comment he made after I had kissed Jacob that time.

I've completely looked over it. Now I'm realizing Carlos knows Dylan has offered a room to Jacob, and he's been trying to dangle that in front of me.

And he never cared about Casey in the first place.

"Fuck this. I'm not helping Dylan. He dug himself this deep, he'll have to get himself out," Carlos finishes. He then grabs his jacket and storms out of Raven's.

Derrick doesn't look amused by Carlos's outburst. If someone says that about my brother, I won't be happy either.

"Such a dramatic bitch." Anthony shakes his head before he looks at me. "He probably just wants to hook up with you to make Dylan mad."

This is going to crush Casey. I want to rant about Carlos, but he's not why I'm here right now. "I don't even care," I tell them. "Anyway, I don't know what to do."

No one says anything, and it makes me nervous. Nobody has an immediately solution. The whole thing isn't just going to go away.

"I think," Anthony says slowly, "you need to explain all of this to Dylan and maybe break things off for now."

Breaking up with Dylan will be like letting Xavier and Kay win. And win what? The satisfaction of having Dylan to themselves? What about Casey? Will Xavier leave her alone if I leave Dylan alone for good?

My heart feels heavy in my chest. The people I care about are being put in harm's way, and I can't let it happen. I care about Dylan too, which makes the decision even harder.

I need to talk to Xavier. Alone. I can't let the boys, Dylan, or Casey know that I'm going to do it.

I bite my lip. "I need to think," I say. "Thanks for coming, guys."

We all walk out of Raven's, and Reece leaves with Anthony while Derrick walks me to my car.

"You're not going to do anything crazy, right?" he asks me.

"No," I lie. "It's just a lot to process." Then I ask him, "Do you think I should break up with Dylan?"

He scratches the back of his neck, which reminds me a lot of Dylan. "I don't know. I haven't seen Dylan this happy in a while, but in a way, Carlos is right. He brought this on himself."

"That doesn't answer my question."

He stops and taps on his chin. He looks away for a bit, away from me, Reece, and Anthony. He then turns back to me.

"Yes, I do." He nods solemnly to me. "It sucks, but if he really cares about you, then he will want you to be safe. Your aunt and Casey too."

It's settled. I need to make a deal with the devil.

Getting in touch with Xavier will be a challenge. I can't get Casey or Dylan to ring him up for me, so I have to get crafty.

Kay is always waiting for Dylan after school, so I have to beat him to her. I rush back to school in the middle of our last class. She isn't there when I arrive, but her red car soon pulls into the lot and parks next to Dylan's car.

I take a deep breath and get out to walk towards her. Through her windshield, I can see her smirk before she opens her door.

My mood takes a turn for the worst, and I can feel my attitude shifting. "Do you really miss your last class just to come see Dylan every day?" I ask her.

She crosses her arms. "I have a free period."

A free period?

She must see the confusion on my face because she says, "I'm not stupid, Lacey. I'm actually really good at school. Hence, why I have a free period."

Does she want a gold star? I almost say it out loud, but if I give her too much attitude, she won't give me access to Xavier.

She narrows her eyes slightly. "What do you want?"

"I need to talk to your brother."

She lets out a laugh. "Why? Are you going to tell him you're in love with Dylan and need to be with him?"

That will give her too much satisfaction. I can't do that. "I need to talk to him about Casey, actually."

Her demeanor changes. "So what do you want from me?"

"I just need you to tell Xavier to meet me, so we can talk," I tell her. "Please."

"And why should I help you?" Her perfect brow arches.

This is the part that's going to be extremely hard. "I won't bother you or Dylan ever again." I swallow. "You won."

She doesn't look overjoyed or happy about it. She looks more puzzled than anything. "And I'm supposed to believe that?"

She's testing my patience. "Kay, there are more important things in my life than a relationship with Dylan."

The bell rings in the distance, which means my time is running out quickly.

"Please, just tell Xavier to meet me," I plead.

Kay looks lost in thought, but she nods. I'm not sure if she'll actually tell Xavier, but I can't risk Dylan seeing me with her, so I get back to my car and drive off.

The next day goes by quickly, and English hurts the most because I know I have to end things with Dylan. How can I end things immediately after he has asked me to be his girlfriend? The roses are still in my room, reminding me of how I can't have him.

As we walk out of class, he has his hand on the small of my back, almost in a comforting kind of way, like he knows what's coming. He gives me a small smile before going to his next class.

I sit with Sophie and Seth in journalism class, so we can make executive decisions, as Mrs. Thomas puts it, about the next issue before we print it. Amidst the drama in my life, I can't find any inspiration for an article, so I'm purely focused on editing, which gives more time for Jacob, Vicky, and Will to write articles.

And they've all produced really great pieces. Jacob has written about changes to the cafeteria food for next semester. His reporting is actually pretty good, and it shocks me that he hasn't written about something sports related. Will has focused on what plays the theater class are putting on in the spring, and Vicky has written a piece on confessionals from freshman as their first semester is ending soon.

For a minute, it makes me feel like a proud mother watching her kids grow into prospering reporters for the school paper. They won't have journalism next semester, and a pit of sadness opens inside me. Sophie, Seth, and I, being part of the school paper staff, will have the class again, but with a whole new group of people.

We make some final edits to the paper and send it off to the printing company just as the bell rings. Jacob walks out of the classroom at the same time as me.

"Can you believe this semester is practically over?" he asks me.

I don't even want to think about it. It's been a wild ride.

He pauses before asking, "Are you okay? You seemed quieter in class."

I find it amusing. "You're actually asking me if I'm okay?" He only gives me a look, and I stop myself from smirking. "Things could be better."

"Wanna talk about it?"

Explaining the whole situation will take too long, and dragging Jacob into it will only create more problems. "Not really," I say.

Once we are outside, I see Lauren and Casey actually speaking to each other. Casey making amends with Lauren is a step in the right direction.

"It's freezing balls out here." Jacob crosses his arms over his hoodie. When his eyes travel to Casey and Lauren, his head snaps back to me. "That's a sight to see."

"It really is," I say. Casey seems to have forgiven Lauren. Then I notice Jacob's eyes keep flitting to them. "Lauren told me what happened," I admit to him.

"It's . . . whatever." He shrugs as we cross the parking lot.

Ironic. He cheats on me, and I somehow convince her to break up with him when she asks for my advice. I don't know how he feels toward Lauren anymore, but part of me thinks he's over her.

We head straight for my car, which is also where Jacob is parked near.

"Are you sure it's whatever?" I ask him.

"She couldn't handle me working. It's honestly whatever at this point."

He then looks straight ahead, and I follow his eyes to Dylan and Kay by Dylan's car. "Who's that?" he asks, his eyes not leaving them.

"Dylan's girlfriend, Kay." I don't hide the distaste in my voice. I truly don't want to hate Kay. I've never hated Lauren, and I've found a way to forgive and forget. With Kay, it's different. Lauren hasn't constantly taunted me with her relationship with Jacob like Kay does with Dylan.

I notice Dylan glance at me and Jacob. His eyes stay longer on Jacob before he focuses on Kay.

"You said you didn't want to talk about it, so I wouldn't ask," he says. "I'll see you tomorrow, okay?"

I nod and he walks away to his truck.

As soon as I get home, I see Dylan's name flashing on my screen. He isn't with Kay?

"Hello?" I hesitantly answer. What if it's Kay calling from his phone?

"Hey, real girlfriend," Dylan says, making me smile but also making the pit of sadness inside me grow. "I'm free from Kay's shackles for the night."

"Oh yeah?" I ask him, wandering around my room. I pick up the picture frame with me and my parents in it as he speaks again.

"So if you want to, we can hang out. I can go pick you up, and we can go anywhere you want."

Staring at the picture of me and my parents comes with the realization that I haven't been to the cemetery since the funerals. "Okay," I say.

We make our plans, then hang up. I have a simple long sleeve on, so I throw on another jacket since I know we'll be outside.

I let my aunt know I won't be home for dinner, then run outside when Dylan gets to the apartment. I jump into his car, and he smiles at me.

"Winter looks good on you," he says. He leans over and kisses my cheek. "Where are we going?"

"Is it okay if we go to the cemetery?" I ask.

He looks puzzled but nods. We stop at the dollar store to buy some flowers, then head off.

"Maybe I'm a horrible daughter, but I haven't been to my parents's graves since the funerals," I admit to him.

"That makes you a grieving daughter, not a horrible one," he says.

Once we get there, I tell him where to park and we walk to their headstones. I take a deep breath before kneeling down and placing the flowers on their graves. I know one day I will have to visit their graves, but I haven't expected it to happen too soon.

"Do you want me to wait in the car?" Dylan asks me.

I shake my head. I know it's awkward for him, but I don't want to be alone. "The last time I was here, I was standing with my aunt, my grandparents, and Jacob. We were standing right there when they lowered the caskets," I say pointing to the spot. "I couldn't watch."

Dylan doesn't say anything, and I'm not sure if I want him to. Maybe I can come back and talk to my parents by myself. Would that make me crazy or grieving?

I want to believe that's me grieving. I need their guidance now more than ever, and they can't give me that. Tears come out, and I quickly swipe them away as I stand up. "Anyway, things are different now."

Dylan comes up behind me and wraps his arms around me.

Mom, Dad, this is Dylan. He's amazing, and I can't have him.

"We can go now," I say. "The cold might make my tears come out as hail."

Dylan chuckles and squeezes me tighter before taking my hand and leading us back to his car.

He gets the heater going, and I watch him as he gets settled in. This is the view of Dylan from Kay's point of view when she's with him, and the thought makes me feel like an awful, jealous person. Kay genuinely thinks they're together, but here I am. Suddenly, it feels like I'm the other woman.

"How long will you take a break from school?" I ask him, shaking the thoughts of Kay from my head. It's something I've been curious about after having dinner with his dad. I only know so much about what he wants to do for the rest of his life.

"I don't know yet." He shrugs, not looking at me. "I'll cross that bridge when I get to it."

"You're sure you don't want to go to college?"

That's when he looks at me. "Why do you ask?"

"I'm just wondering," I say.

"Don't do that." He shakes his head.

"Do what?"

"I know you're curious about what I want to do after graduation, and I know it's because you want us to be okay." He shifts, so he's facing me. "I'm going to do me and you're going to do you and we're going to be okay. I promise."

I'm not sure when I'm going to talk to Xavier, but I think I've made my decision. I can't wait until after I talk to Xavier to break up with Dylan. It has to be now.

"You can't promise something like that," I say quietly.

He stares at me before talking again. "Where did you go yesterday? Because I have a feeling that's why you're acting weird now."

I haven't come up with a lie to cover me, and I don't have enough time to think of one. It's time to come clean. "I was at Raven's."

He arches his brow. "By yourself?"

Getting the boys in trouble with him isn't my goal, but I don't want to completely lie to him. The lies are overwhelming at this point. "I was with the boys . . . and Derrick."

"Why were you with them?"

"I needed their opinions. Going behind Xavier and Kay's backs isn't working. I was just asking them what we should do," I say, trying to read his face.

The frown on his face deepens. "You told them about us?"

"I had to. I can't think of a way out of all of this, and I wanted to know what they thought." His anger is evident on his face now, and I'm getting more anxious.

"Everything is fine, Lacey. Kay doesn't suspect anything. Now you told all my friends, who I purposely left out of this secret." His voice raises.

"Everything is not fine," I stress. "Xavier came to my apartment and threatened my aunt and Casey. What am I supposed to do? Just sit back and let him control what we do? And if we don't follow his rules, he hurts someone I care about?" I demand from him. "That's not how I planned on spending my senior year."

He leans forward. "He was at your apartment?"

"He said he drove by your house the other night and saw my car there. I told him we were working on school stuff, but he went to my apartment, Dylan," I say. Talking about this with him is refreshing, but it's still too much.

"I'm going to kill him." Dylan faces forward and grips the steering wheel tightly. "I'm taking you home, and I'm going to deal with him."

"No," I say immediately. "You'll only make him angrier, and what's he going to do then? He'll want to hurt you, so he'll hurt me."

Dylan's whole demeanor is deadly. I'm sure something is ticking in his brain, waiting to be set off. He stays that way for a few minutes, cueing the deafening silence.

"You weren't going to tell me, were you?" he asks me.

I bite my lip. "I just don't want anyone to get hurt—"

"So instead, you were just going to go behind my back and make all these decisions without me?"

"This affects my aunt and Casey, Dylan." My own voice raises as I speak. "You aren't the only person I care about."

Reaching over, he pulls his seatbelt on. "I'm taking you home."

I don't protest, but it makes me nervous for what is to come. Dylan's mood has shifted completely, and I have the feeling he's thinking the same thing I am.

We need to end things.

When he parks in front of my apartment, he doesn't say anything.

My heart is pounding in my chest, and I feel the tears wanting to come out.

"Lacey . . . ," he says.

"I know." My voice cracks as I say it.

"I'll figure it out. I promise," he says, not looking at me.

I can't stand it. I don't want it to be over, but it has to be. Kay and Xavier want everything to revolve around their needs, and I'm sick of it. I want to be done with their world, and I want Dylan to be done with their world.

Before he can say anything else, I open the passenger door and run up the stairs to my apartment. My chest is heavy as I fumble with the keys before letting myself into the dark apartment. My aunt must be with James.

The tears come out as I slide to the ground. I'm about to stand up and go to my room when there's a rapid knocking at the door. I open it hesitantly.

Dylan is standing there with a blank expression, like he hasn't realized he's come to the door. He steps forward and grabs my face. His cold lips touch mine, and it's like an electric bolt shoots through my body.

"Lace," he says breathlessly after backing away. "I'm sorry." He puts his hands on his face.

My head is screwed up, and I'm not thinking straight. Kissing him is a mistake.

His hair, getting a little longer, is sticking up slightly, and I reach out to fix it. He grabs my hand and pulls me towards him. Instead of kissing me again, he wraps his arms around in a hug.

"After this, we can't see each other," he says, his voice muffled by my hair. "And anything you see me and Kay do doesn't mean a damn thing. She doesn't mean anything to me."

Seeing them is going to be even harder. She's going to have him completely this time. "I know."

Dylan doesn't say anything else. He silently walks to the door and shuts it behind him. The heavy feeling returns to my chest, and my breathing becomes ragged as everything settles in me.

I've lost Dylan.

CHAPTER TWENTY-ONE

Luckily, I don't have to wait long to talk to Xavier. When I walk out of my apartment this Wednesday morning, he's next to my car again. Small snowflakes float down from the sky but melt as soon as they hit the ground. I pull my coat tighter to my body as I walk up to him.

"Kay said you wanted to talk to me," he says.

I take a deep breath. "I'll never speak to Dylan again if you leave me, my aunt, and Casey alone."

It's a hard decision to come to, but I don't really have a choice. Nothing else will satisfy him, and I can't put my friends and family in danger just because I want to be with Dylan.

He scratches his chin. "Get Casey to talk to me and you have a deal."

"She doesn't want to talk to you," I stress.

His expression is cold, like it doesn't matter. "That's all I want."

I stare at him. What is his obsession with Casey? It isn't right. "I'll get her to talk to you, but I have to be there with you two."

"You drive a hard bargain," he says. "Fine. As long as Kay wants Dylan, just leave him alone. I'll leave you and your aunt alone once that's done. Get Casey to talk to me, and I'll leave her alone."

"Deal." I nod.

And with that, he walks away.

I instantly get in my car and wipe the sleep from my eyes. I cried myself to sleep and woke up crying. Needless to say, it's a no makeup kind of day.

When I get to school, Dylan's car isn't in the lot yet. I sit in my car and wait for Casey to show up. My heart skips a beat when Dylan's car pulls into the parking lot. I sink into my seat and stop myself from going out there and talking to him. I watch as he tosses his backpack over his shoulder and walks towards the building, not once looking my direction.

His black sweatpants and black hoodie make him look so good, I have to close my eyes and force myself not to watch him.

Casey finally pulls into the spot next to me, and I get out at the same time she does.

"You look sick," she says immediately. "Are you okay?"

"I'm fine." I brush it off. "I have to tell you something."

We start walking towards the main building, and I make the words come out of my mouth. "I talked to Xavier," I say slowly.

Her eyes nearly pop out of her head and her face darkens. "When did you talk to him?"

"We just had a casual run-in." I bite my lip. "I know this might sound crazy, but I think you should talk to him. Not alone, obviously."

"Why?" She frowns as she ask.

"I think he'll leave us alone once you talk to him," I say, trying to make her understand what I can't explicitly say. Casey is smart. I need her to understand. If I tell her he's threatened the people around me, she'll go crazy.

She shakes her head. "No way. I don't want to see him."

The bell rings in the distance, and we don't have time to talk about it further. Once we're inside, we go our separate ways.

Days that drag on aren't my favorite, and today seems to be one of those. Actually, today feels like it's been going on for years.

At lunch, all Casey wants to talk about is her partner in Algebra who she thinks is cute. I don't know how Casey can move on from one guy to the next. It makes me envious. It has taken me forever to get over Jacob. Now I have to find a way to not obsess over Dylan and Kay.

Lauren sits with us at lunch, which makes it easier to stay out of the conversation and in my head. Dylan is eating with the boys in the back of the cafeteria, sans Carlos. I haven't see him at all, and I wonder if Anthony, Reece, or Derrick told Dylan about what he has said.

While Casey and Lauren are talking, I stand up to throw my trash. While walking over to the trash cans, Jacob appears by my side with a tray.

"Is this trash a metaphor?" Jacob asks me. "Maybe trash means something different to everyone. Do you think that would make a good article?"

I roll my eyes. "You don't have to write about everything you think about."

He takes my trash and throws it away for me. "But I do. Journalism has changed my life," he says in his dramatic voice, like he's in a Greek theater. "What are we going to do in class now that the paper is being printed?"

"Probably just have free days until the break." I shrug. Mrs. Thomas always makes the newspaper our final, so we're practically done with that class.

"Speaking of the break," he says, leaning against the wall, "I need to talk to you."

"Aren't you already talking to me?"

"Ha-ha," he says sarcastically. "My mom wants me to invite you and your aunt over for a Christmas dinner."

If this is some scheme by Jacob's mom to get us back together, she can forget it. And my aunt doesn't like Jacob. That dinner is going to be a disaster. "I'll let my aunt know," I tell him, even though I can already see her reaction.

"Cool." He nods. "See you in class."

When I walk back over to the girls, it's quiet. I look at them strangely. "What?"

"You're talking to Jacob again?" Casey asks me.

I look between them and realize they've assumed the worst. "We're friends, I guess."

"I thought we've agreed that isn't healthy?" Casey points out. "Plus, you have all this drama with Dylan now."

Lauren speaks up, "Casey kind of filled me in about Dylan."

They have to be on some kind of drug. "You guys know I would never get back together with Jacob, right?"

They don't look convinced.

I can't believe I have to sit here and explain myself. "I have zero feelings towards Jacob, and he has no feelings for me," I say. "We're talking like old friends right now." I can't help but steal a glance in Dylan's direction.

The root of it all, admittedly, is because Jacob is just more accessible than Dylan right now. It doesn't mean that I care less for Dylan and care more for Jacob. I need more people in my life to talk to, and regardless of what he's done to me, he was my friend before we even dated.

"Well, I just don't want you to get all mixed up in your head again," Casey says thoughtfully.

It's different. I've never imagined my life will come to this stage—me being friends with Lauren and Jacob and pining over Dylan who I can't have. It's not how I've imagined my senior year to go.

English is agony. Dylan walks into class after me and doesn't look at me as he passes by. Feeling his presence behind me has my heart racing as I try to keep it together. Part of me wants the semester to be over already, so I won't have to see him in class.

Journalism is as I expect it to be. Mrs. Thomas gives us a free day to study for other finals or to just keep ourselves busy. I help Vicky study for her English finals. It makes me giddy that she has asked me to help in the first place. It has only taken the whole semester, but she's finally said more than four words to me.

Once she's happy, we sit there and wait for class to be over. Will has his head on the desk; I assume he's asleep.

Ultra-bored, I get up and walk over to Sophie and Seth, who are sitting near the front of the class.

"I have a feeling the rest of this year is going to go by slowly," I say to them.

"Senioritis is a bitch," Seth says.

I want to graduate already, but I'm anxious for college. I've applied to a couple local colleges and some a little further away. I haven't heard back from the one that's out of state. From any of them, really.

"What about you guys?" I ask.

Sophie shrugs. "I'm savoring these last few months of high school. Being an adult just doesn't sound good right now."

When class ends, I stand up to grab my things from the back. Jacob is poking Will, attempting to wake him up.

"He's out." Jacob laughs.

I lean down next to Will and shake his shoulder. He slowly picks his head up. A red spot from where his head was leaning against the table is in the middle of his forehead. Jacob and I stifle our laughs.

"It's time to go," I tell Will as I watch him try to function.

"Right." He nods, his voice still sleepy.

After standing up from the desk, he picks up his backpack and starts walking away. He trips over a desk before walking out of the class.

"I don't think I've ever seen someone actually pass out in class," Jacob says as we walk out behind Will.

I haven't either, then I remember. "Didn't you fall asleep in History during our freshman year?"

He frowns. "You have me confused with someone else."

329

"No, I'm pretty sure it was you. Nathan Pilar even threw a paper airplane at you." I chuckle at the memory.

When we get to the double doors, I stop and hand him my backpack like it's the most natural thing in the world. He takes it, and I slip my jacket on.

"Nathan Pilar is an ass and a shitty soccer player," he grumbles.

"You can't bash your own teammate."

"I'm the captain, of course I can."

As we tread out to the parking lot, Dylan is walking with Anthony nearby. Dylan's eyes meet mine before they snap to Jacob. By the look on his face, he clearly doesn't like that I'm talking to Jacob again.

"He's dogging me, isn't he?" Jacob asks, referring to Dylan.

"I don't know," I lie.

"I thought you guys were done?" He raises his brow.

Jacob doesn't know the half of it, and I can't tell him. "It's complicated right now," I say. It's extremely complicated.

"You want me to tell him something? I mean, he knows we're not dating or anything, right?"

Jacob is acting like his old self again. The reason I fell for him during my freshman year was because he always made me feel wanted. Well, in the beginning anyway. After that, I've been more of a convenience for him.

"Don't bother." Dylan can wonder all he wants about me and Jacob, but if he knows me at all, he'll know I would never get back together with Jacob.

Casey and Lauren are by Casey's car, and they are obviously staring at us. Everyone has their opinions about me hanging out with Jacob again, but it's a matter of who actually knows me.

"I'm not the popular one today," he says, staring back at the girls. "I can't go anywhere with you."

330

"No one wants to see me hurt again," I say honestly. I have people who care for me, and while I'm grateful, it's a little annoying.

"I get it." He shoves his hands in his pockets and looks down. "I'm gonna head out before my ears fall off." He waves before walking to his truck.

It's cold, but it isn't that cold.

I'm surprised by Anthony standing at the front of my car, his arms folded across his hoodie-clad chest. His hair is concealed by the hood.

"Can I help you?" I ask him.

"You're not back with that dude, are you?" he asks me.

What is everyone's obsession with Jacob? "Jesus, do I need to announce to the whole school that I'm not back together with him? We're just friends."

He holds up his hands. "Just asking."

I feel bad for snapping at him. He doesn't deserve it. "Sorry, I've just been annoyed today."

"No worries." He shrugs. "What are you doing this weekend?"

My heart flutters, not because Anthony is asking me but because I have a feeling it has something to do with Dylan. "Why?" I ask. I can't help but be suspicious.

"Reece's birthday is on Monday, so we're heading to his parents's cabin this Saturday and coming back home on Sunday," he says.

A birthday trip for Reece? "Is Dylan going to be there?" It's a dangerous territory. If Xavier finds out I'm going on a trip with Dylan, he'll freak out, especially if Casey doesn't talk to him.

"Yeah, but Kay invited herself . . ." he trails off.

Why the hell would I want to go? To watch Dylan be all loved up with Kay? He's said nothing he does with her mean anything, but it still hurts to watch.

I shake my head. "No way."

331

"It's not going to be totally bad," he says. "Reece's parents are going, and Jared and Derrick will be there too. You can bring Casey if that makes you feel better."

This doesn't sound right. "Why do you want me to go so badly?" If he has some kind of plan, then I'm not comfortable going. Xavier is unpredictable, and going on the trip is too risky.

"You've said it yourself, you don't want Xavier controlling every part of your life. Won't it be fun to just hang out? We can send Dylan and Kay to do their own thing while the rest of us party with Reece."

"I don't know . . . ," I tell him. "Is Carlos going?" That'll be even more uncomfortable if he's there.

He shakes his head. "We haven't talked to him since the other day."

Carlos is a different breed from the rest of the boys. The fact that he's so hateful towards Dylan makes me angry. "I'll think about it, Anthony. I don't even know if my aunt will let me go."

"You have until Saturday to find out."

With that, he walks off.

Going on this trip might be a recipe for disaster, but I have to admit, I'm curious about what will happen if I do go. If everything goes well, it could be a fun weekend to celebrate with Reece. If things go sour with Kay, I'll have everyone else to cheer me up.

I need to talk to my aunt first. If I get the green light from her, then I have to convince Casey to go.

Part of me wants my aunt to say yes, but I also want her to say no.

*   *   *

Friday morning, I have to force myself to get out of bed. My limbs feel like I have the body of an eighty-year-old woman. I wash my face to wake myself up, throw my hair into a bun, put on a black long sleeve and a flannel, and reach for my short boots.

Seeing my appearance in the mirror, I think about swiping on some mascara and lip gloss to make me look less like the walking dead, but I decide against it. I don't care if everyone sees my zombie-like state. I feel like a cold is coming on, and wearing makeup while I'm sick is never a good thing.

When I walk out of my room, my aunt is in her pajamas on the couch with a mug full of coffee. Her classes finished their finals yesterday, so she's in vacation mode.

"Good morning," she says like the morning person she is.

"Morning." I yawn as I say it. "Can I just stay home with you?"

"You're almost done." She laughs. "Get through these last few days. You'll miss them once you're my age."

My aunt doesn't have the body of an eighty-year-old woman either, but she can have the attitude of one. "I'm not counting on my high school years to the best years of my life. I think I'll be fine."

The doorbell rings, and my heart rate shoots up. The first face that pops into mind is Xavier's.

Before my aunt can stand up, I beat her to the door. I'm not sure what I'm going to do if it is him. I've stayed away from Dylan, so he can't use that against me. As far as I know, Casey hasn't talked to him, so it could be because of that.

I open the door and expect the worst.

Instead, I'm met with Casey and Anthony, which is almost just as bad.

"What are you guys doing here?" I ask them. It's unusual to see them together.

"Came to see you obviously." Anthony hugs himself.

They're freezing, so I open the door wider for them and let them inside. After shutting the door behind them, my aunt gives me a quizzical look.

"Hi, Jade," Casey says to her. "Sorry to come unannounced. We thought we'd take Lacey to school today."

At that point, Anthony holds out his hand to my aunt. "I'm Anthony."

She shakes it and pulls her robe closer together. "Nice to meet you. I'm sorry, I still have my bed-head on."

"Why don't we get going then?" I suggest. I'll have to skip breakfast, but I don't want everyone overstaying their welcome.

"Actually, we also came to talk to you," Casey says to my aunt.

She looks between Casey and Anthony, then at me. "Okay."

"Our friend Reece's birthday is on Monday, and his family is having a party for him this weekend at their cabin," Anthony says to her. "We want Lacey to go."

Is Casey going to the cabin? Is Anthony the one who has told her about it? Because I haven't mentioned it. I've been hoping everyone forgets to include me.

"Reece's parents are going to be there, so we won't be unsupervised," Casey explains.

"You're going?" I ask her and she nods in response.

"Well, they said I could go only if you're going . . ." she trails off, glancing at my aunt and giving her best puppy-eyes.

My aunt has an unreadable expression on her face. "How many of you are going?"

Anthony starts counting with his fingers. "Reece, his brother Jared, their parents, my cousins Derrick and Dylan, Dylan's girlfriend, me, and Casey."

"Dylan?" My aunt gives me a look. "Dylan has a girlfriend?"

I know she's sensed there's something going on between us, but she's also sensed that something has happened. There isn't enough time to explain everything, and I can't exactly tell her everything.

"We can talk about this after school when we have more time," I tell her. "I think we should go now."

My aunt gets the picture and nods. "Have fun at school."

Once I have my jacket on, the three of us are out the door. "I can't believe you guys came here and told my aunt about this weekend."

"I knew you weren't going to ask," Anthony says. "I went to Casey, who is a very good planner."

We approach Anthony's car, and I get in the back while Casey sits in the front seat. I feel like a child being scolded by her parents.

"It'll be fun, Lace," Casey says as we pull out of the apartment complex.

I watch the city go by in a blur outside the window. It might be fun if Dylan and Kay aren't going, but it could also be the opposite without Dylan there.

"Reece's parents are super chill. The whole weekend should be fun," Anthony says.

They don't get it. "I'm sorry, I don't want to see Dylan and Kay all over each other the whole weekend." I cross my arms as I say it. "I'll buy Reece a present for Monday and that's that."

They're quiet. I desperately wish I can read minds.

"And what is Kay going to think when she sees me? She's going to make it so much worse," I tell them.

"Kay will have to deal with the fact that while you're not talking to Dylan, you're still friends with the rest of us," Anthony says.

"If she gives you a hard time, then I'll kick her ass myself and drop her off on Xavier's porch. End of story," Casey snaps. "I'm sick of you being afraid of them. I grew up around them. I know what they are and aren't capable of."

While true, I also don't want Dylan to get hurt in the process.

335

We get to school and Anthony parks in his usual spot, which unfortunately is next to Dylan's. Through the window, I can see Dylan talking on the phone in his car. His head is on the headrest, and his fingers are on the bridge of his nose. The phone call looks stressful.

I feel self-conscious getting out of Anthony's car. I can feel Dylan's eyes on me, and I mentally hit myself for not putting on makeup.

Casey walks ahead of me, so Anthony and I take the opportunity to talk alone.

"What if Xavier hears about our trip?" I ask him.

"Everything is going to be fine. Everyone is going to be fine," he says as he stops walking and looks at me. "What happened to you, Lacey? You used to be this cool, confident girl that me and the guys liked to hang out with."

Confident? "I haven't felt confident in a long time." I shake my head. Of course, I've tried to come off as a confident person, but I don't think it ever worked.

"Well, you seemed like you were," he says. "I know you and Dylan are in a weird place right now or whatever, but we didn't like you because you were with him. We like you because you're fun."

It's really sweet of him to say so.

"No one is going to get hurt. Not your aunt, Casey, nor Dylan. I'm going to make sure of that," he concludes.

I don't know what to say, so I hug him instead. It's important to me that he's ready to fight back against Xavier instead of backing off.

It makes me feel ready too.

Dylan is making his way over to Anthony, so I let him go. "Thank you," I say.

Dylan stands silently next to Anthony and I duck down. "I should go." I pull my jacket closer to my body and catch up with Casey.

CHAPTER TWENTY-TWO

Saturday morning, my aunt wakes me up at seven o'clock to take me to Reece's house. Yesterday, he gave me a note with his mom's number, so my aunt could call her and get all the details for this weekend. My aunt thinks the trip might be good for me, despite my efforts to make her see why I don't want to be around Dylan and Kay.

I do some last minute packing before we're off to Reece's. It's another makeup free day, as I can't be bothered to look decent. I'm also blowing my nose constantly, so the makeup would've wiped off anyway.

It's freezing, but there's no snowfall here in town yet. I've made sure to pack for snowy weather at the cabin, which is in the mountains. It's bound to be snowing up there.

While still looking at the road, my aunt speaks up, "Try to have fun this weekend. I don't know what Dylan has done to make you not want to go, but I'm glad you're going."

She's sort of forcing me to go, but I don't say that. "It isn't his fault."

"Don't let his girlfriend get to you either."

"She's a pain, but I'm not trying to fight her for Dylan."

She gives me a knowing smile. "Your mom would like that answer."

Reece's house is in a neighborhood not far from my apartment. All the houses look the same, and they aren't particularly big. I'm not sure why I was expecting something like Dylan's house.

There are a few vehicles in the driveway. I don't see Kay's car or Dylan's, so I hope I beat them there.

My aunt rings the doorbell, and the anxious feeling I've woken up with rises in my chest, so I clutch my duffel bag closer to myself to force that feeling back down. The door swings open, and we come face-to-face with a blonde woman with short curly hair. She smiles at us.

"Good morning, girls," she greets us. "Come inside before you freeze."

We step inside, and I can see Reece, Jared, Derrick, and Casey standing in the kitchen area.

"I'm Jade. We spoke on the phone yesterday." My aunt holds out her hand.

"Delilah." The blonde woman takes her hand before looking at me. "And that must make you Lacey." She continues to smile. Looks like she's also a morning person. "I'm so glad you're here."

They continue to talk about the trip while I wander away to everyone else. Casey hugs me instantly.

"Thank God you're here," she says. "If I have to listen to Reece say it's his birthday one more time, he won't actually make it to his birthday."

Reece laughs. "It's my birthday, be nice to me."

"It's literally not until Monday!"

Derrick stands next to me and flashes me a smile. "You ready to party with the big kids?"

"Sure." I nod, even though I feel ready to blow my brain out of my nose. "Speaking of kids, how is Ethan going to survive the night without you and Dylan?"

He waves it off. "He's staying at his friend's house. He's not going to miss us, trust me."

339

My mind goes to the time Dylan texted me to tell me Ethan and his friends had taken over the house. No doubt, they're going to cause chaos at another house for the weekend. They're like savage little kids.

My aunt comes up to me and smiles. "I'm taking off. You sure you have everything?"

"If she doesn't, I probably have it," Casey answers for me as she puts her arm around my shoulders.

"You girls have fun. Just not too much fun." She hugs me.

My aunt heads for the door after saying goodbye to me. I turn back to the guys, and all three of them are watching her leave.

"Are you guys seriously checking out my aunt?" I ask them after she walks out the door. No shame at all.

Jared and Reece only laugh before Reece holds up his hands.

Derrick shrugs. "Your aunt is hot."

Gross.

We wait a few more minutes before the doorbell rings out. This time, it's Anthony, Dylan, and Kay.

Kay's white leggings are blinding, making them the brightest thing in the house. I hate to admit it, but her red Nike hoodie is really cute.

Dylan is sporting a gray hoodie with a leather jacket over it, jeans, and some dark brown mountain boots. Looking as good as ever. A vision of his arms wrapping around my waist while I fit under his chin comes to mind, and I have to tear my eyes away from him.

"Sorry, we're late. Someone took their time putting makeup on." Anthony narrows his eyes at Kay.

She huffs, "I've already told you I look dead without eyeliner."

Her hair is in a slick high ponytail, and her makeup is flawless. My self-consciousness creeps inside me, and I try to push it aside.

"Well, now that we're all here we should get everything packed in the cars." Delilah nods. "Anthony, you're still okay to drive, right?"

"Yes, ma'am." He gives her a salute. "I can take four others with me."

There is no way I'm going to be in a car with Kay for two hours.

"We can decide in a little bit. Let's just get everything packed for now," Delilah says, opening the front door.

I realize I haven't seen Reece's dad. Aren't both his parents going?

I gravitate towards him. "Where's your dad?"

"He's at the cabin already. He left earlier this morning to get it set up," he explains. "He knew my mom could handle this part."

We all load our bags into the backs of Delilah's SUV and Anthony's car. Kay stands by the front door while the rest of us put the bags in the cars. Casey looks at her, then at me and rolls her eyes.

When Casey and I are alone, she says, "Guess Kay's nails are more important than helping to pack everything."

"It's just rude, honestly," I tell her.

Delilah has the boys help her pack everything else and, quite forcibly, tells us girls to wait inside.

Casey and I sit on the smaller couch while Kay sits on the reclining chair. She's typing away at her phone, clearly ignoring us. When Delilah comes back inside, she tells us everything is ready to go.

She locks up the house behind us, and we all stand in a circle, deciding who will go with who.

I want to have a say in the seating arrangements, but Delilah already has it figured out.

"I'll take my boys and Derrick. Anthony, you can take everyone else, if that's okay," she says.

341

Anthony's eyes flash to me, then back at her. "Yeah, that's fine."

The cabin is two hours away. That'll be four thirty-minute intervals with Kay. I don't know if I can stand being with her for that long. Hell, I don't know if I'll last one night with her.

While walking to the car, I grab Casey's arm and beg her with my eyes to let me sit in the front with Anthony. She nods, understanding.

Anthony opens the passenger side door for me and I step inside, feeling a little better after he gives me a smile. Once he shuts the door, I glance back to find Casey is sitting right behind me, with Kay in the middle and Dylan diagonal from me.

I face forward and pray for the trip to go by quickly.

An hour into the trip, Kay's head is on Dylan's shoulder, seemingly asleep, and Casey is texting me everything she can't say out loud.

Anthony clears his throat and motions to my wrist. "You thinking of getting any other tattoos?"

"I don't know," I say. "I think I'm going to cover this one."

"Your ex has that one, right?" he asks.

Do we have to talk about Jacob? "He told me he might keep his."

"Are you guys really friends now?"

"Seems that way." I shrug. Jacob is not a good topic of conversation, and I don't want to talk about it anymore.

In my peripheral vision, I see Kay moving around. "Are we almost there?" she asks.

"Almost," Dylan says.

It's the first time he's spoken since getting into the car. I grip my seat and focus on the trees we're passing.

"I thought it was only going to be an hour-long trip?" Her voice is annoyingly sleepy.

Casey groans loudly. "Can you just go back to sleep?"

"Can you just shut up?" she tells Casey.

The last thing I want, other than being in the same car with Kay, is hearing her bicker with Casey. "How about we play the quiet game?" I glance back at them like I'm looking at five-year-olds. I give Casey a look before turning to the front.

"Tell me about this ex of yours, Lacey," Kay says, her voice getting to that sickly-sweet tone that I hate from her.

She clearly doesn't know what the quiet game is.

"I'd rather not."

"C'mon," she pushes. "You say you two are friends. What's the harm?"

"I don't feel like spewing my life story to you," I say. A sudden sneeze comes out of me, and I reach into my small bag for my tissue to blow my nose.

Kay, continuing on, says, "Oh no, Lacey is sick. She won't be able to hang out with us."

She shrugs, and it makes my blood boil. It's her way of letting everyone know she doesn't want me to be on this trip in the first place.

Two can play at that game.

"I wouldn't say anything, Kay. We're all going to end up sick if we make fun of her." Anthony nudges me and winks.

She makes a noise like she's disgusted. "I'm already going to end up sick just by being in the same vehicle as her."

I'm fed up. "Keep talking and I'll sneeze in your direction next time."

She stays quiet, and I somewhat relax into the seat. Instead of starting up another conversation, I let myself drift off to sleep.

My eyes peel open just as we're pulling into the driveway. There is a thin layer of snow covering the ground, only softly dusting the trees around the log cabin. The cabin itself is a decent size. It's made with dark wood, with large windows along the side of the house and a pointed peak.

"Nice," Casey says.

343

Anthony parks behind Delilah, and everyone piles out of the vehicles. I pray for warmth when I step out, bringing my jacket closer to stop myself from shivering.

A blond man comes out through the front door, and Jared and Reece instantly wave to him as he jogs down the steps.

"I'm glad the gang got here safely," he says. He holds out his hand to Derrick and they hug.

He says hello to Dylan and Anthony, then he shakes mine, Casey's, and Kay's hands as we introduce ourselves. Instead of calling him Reece's dad, he tells us his name is John. He's a friendly man, and I can see how well he and Delilah fit together.

"Girls, you go on inside. I think us men have the luggage handled," he announces.

I feel bad for not helping, but Delilah motions for us to follow her. Casey, Kay, and I form a duck line behind her.

Once inside, I find a typical log cabin interior. Deer and elk racks frame the walls, and a few family photos are scattered throughout the corridor.

Almost everything is made of wood—the floors, the ceiling, and the doors. It's almost too much, but it's nice. It also smells amazing, like pine.

"I think I have the sleeping arrangements figured out," Delilah says as we walk into the living room area. "There are five bedrooms, two upstairs and three downstairs. I figure Reece, Dylan, and Anthony can take up one room, Derrick and Jared in another, and me and John in the last. You girls get to split the two rooms upstairs, so I'll let you decide that on your own right now."

We thank her and ascend the large wooden stairs. Kay walks ahead of me and Casey, of course.

Kay glances in the first bedroom and makes a face. Then she opens the door to the next one and seems to think.

"It's not a final exam, Kay. Just pick a room," Casey impatiently tells her.

Kay walks into the second room and opens every door inside. "This one has its own bathroom, so I think I'll take this one."

Casey and I shrug and set our things in the other room, which has one bed. Casey and I usually share a bed wherever we end up in anyway, so it works out. We get settled in just as the boys are bringing up our bags.

Anthony groans as he drags Kay's suitcase up the stairs. "Dammit, Kay, what did you pack?"

"Essentials, Anthony. Essentials." She claps her hands as she directs him where to put her bag in her room.

Dylan is holding my bag, and I hesitantly walk up to him to take it.

"Thanks," I manage to mumble.

I can feel Kay's eyes on me as I throw my bag onto the bed.

Delilah jogs up the stairs as the boys go back down. She looks at me and Casey. "The only bathroom up here is in the other bedroom, so you'll have to use the bathroom downstairs. It's a nuisance. Unfortunately, I didn't design the house."

There is a moment of peace after she leaves, and I stare out the window to view the mountains in the distance and the tall pine trees littering the backyard. It's breathtaking.

"I'm so excited," Casey interrupts my thoughts. "John mentioned a trail that starts in the backyard. We can check that out in a bit."

"Okay." I nod. Anything to get away from Dylan and Kay.

"Are we gossiping already?" Anthony's voice comes from behind us, causing us to look at him.

He plops on the bed and rests his head in his hands. "I wanna be included."

"Casey and I are probably going to go walk along the trail outside," I say to him, hoping he doesn't invite himself.

"Hell yeah." He jumps from the bed. "Let me tell Reece and Dylan."

Casey and I exchange the same annoyed look. I can never get girl time with her these days.

Casey goes downstairs to check out the bathroom. I'm about to follow her when Kay grabs my arm. I yank it back from her, and she puts her hands on her hips.

"Why are you even here?" she asks me.

"Reece is my friend. I'm here to celebrate his birthday," I tell her.

She doesn't look convinced. "You better not try anything with Dylan."

"Kay, that hasn't even crossed my mind." I'm sick of her, and she needs to be put in her place. "And you better remind yourself who was actually invited and who invited herself."

Her face shows her displeasure, but she only walks away without saying anything else.

Everyone meets up in the kitchen, and Anthony recruits everyone but Dylan, Kay, and Reece's parents to go on the trail. Everyone is wearing their snow boots, big coats, beanies, and gloves.

Dylan's demeanor has noticeably changed; it's like he's keeping his distance from Kay.

"Make sure you kids stay on the trail," John advises.

We walk out and I can hear Dylan and Kay off to the side bickering about going on the trail.

I ignore them and follow Reece and Jared, who know their way around the trail. Casey holds on to my arm and she squeals.

"Look how beautiful it looks." She glances around us, her eyes filled with awe. "I don't want to leave."

"It's alright." Reece shrugs.

Casey starts asking him questions about the cabin and leaves my side. Derrick drifts from Jared and walks alongside me.

"What do you think?" he ask.

"About the trail, or about the trip itself?"

"Everything."

"The trail is nice," I say. "Being in the same car as Kay for two hours was not so nice. Wanna switch places with me on the way back?"

He shakes his head. "I can't stand her. I've told Dylan not to invite her to our house, ever, because her voice ends up stuck in my head when I hear it."

That's pretty accurate.

"Dylan accidentally mentioned the trip, and she pretty much invited herself, especially when she heard you might come."

"Why does she even care?"

"C'mon, you know the answer to that one." He nudges me. "Everyone knows it's you he cares about. She knows it too."

That sticks in my mind. Dylan isn't the problem. Kay and Xavier are the problems, and I need to remind myself of that every time I want to blame Dylan or be upset with him. His goal, I think, is to keep Xavier away from me. Kay is just insurance to him.

I continue walking and make sure I don't slip on an iced-over rock. Derrick and I have fallen a bit behind the others.

I lean closer to him to stay quiet as I speak, "Do you think it was smart of me to come on this trip?"

He hesitates and my stomach drops. "I get where the doubt is coming from. Who convinced you?"

"Anthony."

"I think Anthony wants to be the hero. I'm glad you're here, but I'd still be careful around Kay."

"What did I miss?" Dylan's voice asks behind us.

We turn around in surprise. Dylan's here without Kay, thankfully.

The look on Derrick's face when he sees Dylan isn't one that I recognize. "Not much." He shrugs. Derrick stays quiet, but I notice him walking a bit faster, almost wanting to catch up with everyone else and leave me and Dylan behind.

Which he does.

"Damn, it's cold," Dylan says, hugging himself.

I only nod in response. Irrational as it is, I keep expecting Xavier to pop out of the woods in an "aha" moment, or he'll find out about me and Dylan even being this close to one another.

"I'm sorry about Kay," Dylan says, keeping his voice low.

He doesn't specify what exactly about her he is apologizing for, but I nod again. "It's fine." Even though it isn't.

He stays quiet but speaks up again, "So what? You can be friendly with your douchebag ex, but not with me?"

That angers me. "Do I have to remind you why we can't see each other right now? Xavier said he'll hurt my aunt and Casey. I can't let anything happen to them."

"You know I won't let Xavier put them in danger—"

"I know you won't. We just have to be smart." This exchange of emotional pleas is heading into dangerous territory, and I know we'll do something stupid if we continue. "Just stick to what you told me the other day." That we can't see each other while he's with Kay.

His lips form a tight line as I walk ahead of him. I can only hope all of this will only be a bump in the road, instead of Dylan taking off in a different direction.

After we get back from the trail, my cold gets worse. Even in the warm cabin, I have to wear my long sleeve with another sweater over it. I even keep a whole tissue pack in my pocket, just for my nose.

Everyone leaves to go skiing around lunch time, except for me and Delilah. She doesn't want me to get sick beyond belief, so she's enforced a strict stay-inside-while-you-get-better rule. I've only gone skiing once, but I've been willing to try again until my body decided to stop me.

Delilah wants to bake some things before everyone gets back, so she's in the kitchen with me sitting at the counter watching

348

her work. She doesn't let me near the goodies, but she hands over small samples to taste.

"The peppermint bark is so good," I tell her after taking a bite. "That's a great recipe."

"It's an old family recipe," she says as she starts the process for pumpkin bread. "My grandmother is a baking legend in my family. She loves being in the kitchen, and since my mom isn't much of a baker, she has passed the recipes to me instead."

The way she speaks about her grandma makes me think of my own grandparents. I haven't seen my grandparents very much since Thanksgiving, and I instantly feel bad for not visiting them more often.

"My grandma is more of a sewing kind of lady. She likes to cook and bake, but ask her to hem your pants and she'll drop everything to do it," I say, smiling as I think about her.

"I wish I knew how. I can't sew to save my life," she says, going to the refrigerator.

I'm not sure if my aunt has mentioned my parents to her, but Delilah doesn't ask about them. I think that's what I like the most about her so far. She isn't looking to know my whole life story. She's just focused on making sure I'm okay for the weekend.

By four o'clock, she's made pumpkin bread, peppermint bark, and a surprise birthday cake for Reece. She takes her time creating the two-tier cake and frosts it to perfection before stashing it away, so Reece won't see it. Everyone arrives soon after, and the cabin is filled with animated chatter.

Casey throws her arm around me and grins.

"How did it go?" I ask her, feeling the cold air come off her body. Her nose is red, and her hair is in a French braid with some strands loose.

"I fell the most out of everyone, but it was fun," she says as she rubs her backside. "I'm definitely going to be sore in the morning."

"I didn't realize Anthony was such a champ at skiing." John pats Anthony on the shoulder. "That was almost Olympic level."

Anthony waves it off. "No way."

Kay and Dylan are noticeably absent. I don't want to be nosy about Dylan, so I glance at Casey and ask, "Where's Kay?"

She rolls her eyes. "She went upstairs to freshen up, I guess. She argued with Dylan most of the time."

Part of me hopes she'll break up with him, so I can have him all to myself and not have to worry about her or her brother again.

Everyone stays in the kitchen and snacks on the goodies while I walk upstairs to put my sweater away. Interacting with everyone has warmed me up.

While in my room, I hear Dylan's voice in Kay's room. I try not to eavesdrop, but curiosity gets the better of me and I stand by the door so I can hear better.

"You're only here because of her," Kay snaps at him. "How about I tell Xavier right now that you're going behind my back talking to her?"

Panic mode strikes inside me.

"Can you stop acting so insane and just have fun?" Dylan demands. "I haven't even spoken to her, so how am I going behind your back?"

I assume they're talking about me. I know Dylan is lying to her. He clearly hasn't told her we've talked on the trail, and he probably doesn't want her to know.

Kay doesn't say anything. I think they're done.

Then Dylan says, "Listen, I won't talk to her, look at her, or even think about her. I don't care about her anymore, okay? I care about you."

The words sting like little knives penetrating my skin. Hearing those words come from his mouth so sincerely hurts worse than the day we've broken up. I'm not sure if he's only saying it, so

350

she won't talk to Xavier, or if our situation is now becoming permanent.

I can't listen anymore. I quietly walk to the stairs and descend into the living room where Casey, Reece, and Anthony are.

It's around six o'clock when John starts to make grilled chicken while Delilah makes a side of pasta. The dining table isn't big enough to fit everyone, so we all eat in the living room while watching Reece's favorite movie, *Die Hard*.

After we finish eating, we all help clean up until Delilah brings out Reece's cake. Reece stands next to me as she places the cake in front of him on the counter.

"She makes a surprise birthday cake every year." He chuckles.

We sing *Happy Birthday* to him, and the boys tease him about what he's wished for as he remains tight-lipped. Delilah starts to cut the cake while Dylan and Kay stand right behind me, making me feel trapped.

My phone buzzes in my pocket, and I think it's my aunt checking in, but Jacob's name pops up on the screen. It's a text message from him.

Hey, you doing anything tonight?

I bite my lip and text him back quickly.

I'm out of town for the night.

It's short and to the point, but I can't help but wonder why he's asking in the first place, so I text him again.

Why?

I feel a presence close to me, so I glance over and find Kay peering down at my phone, obviously being nosy. I lock my phone and stare at her.

She smirks. "Texting your ex-boyfriend?"

Anthony, Dylan, and Casey all look at me since they're within earshot of Kay. I want to hit Kay for saying it loud enough for the others to hear.

"Why are you worried about who I'm texting?" I ask her as my phone buzzes again.

"I just think it's a little pathetic to be texting your ex, that's all." She shrugs.

I feel my eyes narrowing at her. "How about you mind your own damn business?"

She walks away with a smirk that I want to smack off her face. Anthony, Dylan, and Casey are all still looking at me like I've done something wrong. "What?" I ask them, already annoyed.

Casey looks away quickly and Anthony goes back to talking to Reece. Dylan's eyes stay on me a little longer before he goes over to Delilah and takes a piece of cake from her.

I unlock my phone and scan over Jacob's message.

Just wondering.

I don't want to know what he is supposed to ask me to do with him, so I leave him on read.

At the end of the night, Delilah goes to each room to make sure everyone has enough blankets and makes sure I'm drugged up on cold medicine.

The medicine, which is supposed to help me sleep, has been keeping me awake. I lay on the bed and stare out the window. I've thought the curtain-less window will freak me out, but it's soothing. The stars are clearly visible, and the trees are swaying slightly from the wind.

Casey is dead asleep from the sound of her loud snoring.

352

Instead of forcing myself to fall asleep, I decide to get some water. I gently sneak out of the bed, so I don't wake Casey up.

In the kitchen, I fill my glass in the sink and drink it quickly before anyone can hear me. The last thing I want is to wake everyone up or get chewed out by Delilah.

Rounding the corner to go back up the stairs, I run into something solid and let out an oomph. I don't have to look up to know who I've just run into.

"What are you doing?" Dylan whispers to me.

"I can't sleep." I hug myself and back off slightly. "What are you doing?"

"I can't sleep either," he says, staring at me intently. His hair is disheveled, and his long sleeve and plaid pajama pants are perfect on him.

As much as I want to talk to him, it isn't a good idea while under the same roof as Kay. "Well, good night," I say, casting my eyes down to my feet. I'm heading for the stairs when he catches my arm.

"Can we talk?" he asks.

I wring my hands together nervously. "It can't wait until tomorrow?"

"Kay isn't going to be asleep then." His eyes are pleading for me to talk to him.

I can't say no.

He pulls me toward the bathroom in the hallway where he gently pushes me inside, closes the door behind us, and turns the light on.

Wiping the sleep from my eyes, I gaze up at him. He leans against the door before he starts talking.

"I know you heard me and Kay earlier," he says softly. "None of it was true."

"I know." I shrug, even though I don't know for sure. I don't see the point in arguing about it, so I don't say anything else. I only sniffle and avoid his eyes.

He tilts his head. "This trip has been one giant mess." He runs a hand through his hair. "How are you feeling?"

"The medicine didn't kick in, and I currently can't breathe out of my right nostril."

He smirks. "Don't tell me you're that person who gets sick easily."

I cross my arms. "Did you bring me in here to harass me?"

He chews on his bottom lip before saying, "No."

We're going to get in trouble if we keep this up. Kay will wake up and somehow discover I'm missing from my bed. It'll all be over if she barges into the bathroom and catches me with Dylan. I won't be able to protect my aunt and Casey from Xavier.

"I just need to do this." Dylan steps forward and wraps his arms around me in a tight hug.

Feeling his arms around me again has me melting into him. The soft thumping of his heart tickles my ear, causing me to close my eyes and focus on its rhythm.

"I miss you," he says through my hair.

"I miss you too."

I wonder if it's all worth it. Putting my loved ones in jeopardy just because I care for Dylan.

Letting go of him, I take a couple steps back. It isn't fair to Casey and my aunt. Casey wants me to defy Xavier, but I don't want to see how far he'll go to prove his point.

"What are you thinking?" Dylan asks.

My eyes sting from the tears that want to come out. "This isn't smart, Dylan."

"What? Us talking?" He gestures between us. "We're being careful. It's okay."

"It's not okay," I snap. "If anything were to happen to my aunt or Casey, I don't know what I'd do. I can't lose anyone else."

354

He doesn't say anything.

"I thought I could do this, but I couldn't. Anthony and Casey want to go up against Xavier, but for what? For you and me to be together?"

His face hardens. "You don't want to be with me anymore?"

"I do." A tear streams down my cheek as I say it. "We can't be together as long as Kay and Xavier are around. At all."

"You want to give up?" he raises his voice, and we stay silent for a second to hear if there is any stirring in the house.

I take a deep breath and say, "If it means my aunt and Casey will stay safe, then yes, I'm giving up."

He shakes his head, like he can't believe the words coming out of my mouth. "Just promise me you're not planning to get back together with Jacob. That would be some bullshit."

This angers me. "I get that you don't like him, but you should know me better than that. You need to trust that I know what I'm doing. I've trusted you throughout this whole process, and I only want the same from you. The two people you need to worry about are Kay and Xavier."

"I've always trusted you, Lace." His voice sounds annoyed. "You think I trust those two? I don't. I know they'll double-cross me in a heartbeat."

The bathroom feels suffocating all of a sudden.

"You really want to give up on everything we've worked for?" he asks me.

"It shouldn't have to be this hard," I stress to him. "I don't want to keep fighting for you if it's a battle I'm not going to win anyway."

Dylan is breathing hard. He turns his body, so I can't look at him straight on. He runs his hand down his face. "I never would have talked to you if I knew Xavier would ruin everything."

Before I can say anything, he says, "See you around." He opens the door and swiftly walks out of the bathroom.

355

I don't want to go to bed yet, so I shut the door and try to cry my problems away into some tissue.

PART THREE

CHAPTER TWENTY-THREE

The familiar morning sounds of Christmas aren't here anymore. I used to hear my mom in the kitchen making us some hot cocoa and see my dad organizing everyone's gifts and shaking his to see if he can guess what it is before he opens it.

No. I've woken up in the spare bedroom of my grandparent's house to silent moving and shuffling. No chatter from my parents to bless my ears, no hot cocoa being made, and no presents being shaken. I desperately wish I can hear them.

When the time comes to open the presents, I wait for everyone else to open theirs. Aunt Jade receives a pretty sweater and some jewelry from my grandparents. She and I have gotten them a new kitchenware set and some candles.

Everyone urges me to open mine, so I open my grandparents's presents first. Inside the small bag is an even smaller box. Inside the box is a necklace that has a small dainty golden ring with a rose-gold butterfly in the middle.

"It was your mom's when she was young. We thought you should have it," my grandma says.

I hold back my tears and hug them to make sure they know how much I love it.

My aunt holds out a card, and I look at her quizzically. I didn't ask for anything from her, so I assume she's giving me money or something. When I open the card, my heart stops.

She smiles. "I know how much you're dying to get out of here. I thought you could use some adventure."

I stare down at the plane ticket that will take me to New York City, and my hand trembles. Going to a big city has always been on my bucket list, but I've never thought I'll be going this soon. It'll take me out of this town, and I can't be any more grateful for it.

James shows up for our Christmas dinner, where my grandpa has made enough food to feed the entire neighborhood. James, pretty much doing anything to make my aunt happy, gives me five hundred dollars to help fund my end of the school year trip.

After dinner, I sit near the Christmas tree that stands tall. It's decorated in the same red and gold ornaments they've used since I've started high school.

When I tell my aunt about Jacob's mom inviting us for dinner, she lets out a laugh and says there's no way in hell we'll go, which is the response I've been expecting. I text Jacob to tell him we won't make it to their dinner, which he doesn't seem to mind. It probably would've been too awkward for him anyway.

It's strange. In the past week, I've become closer to Lauren and Jacob, even to the point where all of us plus Casey have hung out at school and outside of school since the semester has ended.

It's like waking up and realizing that everything has just been a dream—where Jacob has never cheated on me with Lauren, I've never met Dylan and the guys, and Xavier and Kay are ghosts.

Of course, it isn't all just a dream.

It's the second week of my last semester of high school when it hits me that I'll be graduating and moving on to college in a few months. A certain excitement comes from deep within. I haven't felt excited about something in a long time, and it feels great.

At lunch, I sit next to Jacob while Casey and Lauren sit in front of us. Lauren has made no efforts to get back together with

Jacob. As far as I know, she's talking to another guy from another school and is planning to go out with him tonight. Jacob's still focused on his job and his mom, which has matured him a bit.

Casey cut off contact with Xavier and Kay over the break. I know Xavier is dying to talk to her, and his silence doesn't settle well with me. Either he has something planned or he's truly done with her.

"You're coming over tonight, right?" Lauren asks Casey. "I can't decide what to wear."

"I already have something planned out," Casey assures her. Per usual, she's the stylist for everyone. She's even given Jacob a lesson on what colors look better to bring his eyes out.

While they discuss Lauren's date, I glance over at Jacob, who's been silent for the conversation. "Why so serious?" I ask.

"Just tired." He pokes at his food as he says it.

He's lying, but I don't want to push him too much.

After school, I walk with Jacob to the parking lot. "I think me and Casey are going to catch a movie tonight. You want to come?" I ask him.

"I gotta work tonight," he says, not looking at me.

"You don't work on Fridays." I nudge his shoulder. "What's wrong?"

"My dad is supposed to come over later," he finally says. "He and my mom are having their lawyers meet again."

Jacob's parents have almost settled their divorce, but Jacob's mom has had a sudden burst of confidence and is determined to get more out of the divorce than what has been originally planned. "Well, that's more of a reason to go out with us."

"I don't want my dad and his stupid lawyer to bully my mom."

"I think your mom can handle herself. She's made it this far."

We approach his truck. He unlocks the door, opens it, and tosses his backpack inside. "I guess."

"It'll be fun," I tell him. "We're going to see that new horror movie that's out. We might even grab some ice cream afterwards."

He leans against the truck. "We'll see." He crosses his arms and scans the parking lot, like he usually does.

It's his way of getting himself out of the conversation. He'll find someone to talk about when it comes to talking about his home life or any other aspect about him. His eyes zero in on something, and I steal a glance at what he's looking at.

Dylan is leaning against his car, talking to a blonde girl. His fingers are twirled around her hair, and he's looking at her the way he used to look at Kay before we admitted our feelings to each other. The more I look at her, the more I recognize her. She's the girl he talked to at the football game after Anthony's party at Raven's.

I've only seen him with Anthony around school. Reece and Carlos are never around. I haven't even seen Kay around, and it makes me wonder if they're still together. By his body language, I have a feeling Kay is out of the picture.

My breath gets stuck in my throat, not because he's talking to someone else but because I desperately want to know his situation with Xavier. If Kay isn't around, won't Xavier be going after him for not keeping her happy? And here he is, shamelessly flirting with someone else.

"Let's get out of here," Jacob says.

I know he's seen me watching Dylan. His protective side comes out as he shields me from Dylan and opens the passenger door for me.

On the drive to the apartment, Jacob says, "You don't need that guy."

361

I scoff at the irony. That's something Dylan would've told me about Jacob last semester. How the roles have reversed. "Right."

"I'll go to the movies with you and Casey." He nods. "I don't want to be home when everyone is over."

"Good," I say, my mind still stuck on Dylan and that girl.

Aunt Jade isn't home yet when I walk into the apartment after Jacob drops me off. She doesn't like that Jacob gives me a ride to and from school, but I assure her that it's fine. I don't think she'll ever forgive him, but that's understandable.

After my aunt is settled in the living room and I'm finished with my homework, I get a call from Casey.

"We have a code blue," she says immediately.

"Which is?"

"Lauren's prince charming canceled at the last minute."

I'm beginning to hate all guys. "I'm guessing it'll be an ice cream night only?"

"Probably. She was literally heading out the door when he texted her and canceled. Douchebag, if you ask me." I can practically see her rolling her eyes. "Anyway, we're heading to the ice cream shop."

"I'll call Jacob and see if he wants to go."

"See you there," she says before hanging up.

Jacob is down for ice cream, so I pick him up just in time before the lawyers show up. When we get to the ice cream shop, Lauren is already burying herself in mint-chocolate ice cream.

"It must've been pretty bad," Jacob says immediately. "She did this when we broke up."

"Don't be a jerk now." I shove him.

We sit with Casey and Lauren. Lauren starts to talk about this guy and how he's supposed to be different and nice.

"I honestly think he just wants to get in my pants," she says.

362

"That's what all guys care about." Casey slams her hand on the table. "Not our feelings or anything. They just want sex."

Jacob clears his throat. "That's not true."

"Sorry, Jacob, but I don't think you have a say in this conversation," Lauren tells him, digging deeper into her ice cream.

She isn't wrong, but I keep my mouth shut. I tell myself not to argue with Jacob over the past anymore. It isn't worth it, especially if I want to move on. Plus, it's exhausting at this point.

"Oh shit," Casey says suddenly.

We follow her eyes to the door, where Dylan is walking in with the blonde girl.

It's like déjà vu. I instantly recall the day Casey and I saw Jacob for the first time since I broke up with him and tried to avoid him like the plague.

Dylan has his hand on the small of her back and whispers something in her ear that makes her giggle.

The memory of him taking me to the ice cream shop to cure my Monday blues flashes in my mind. Maybe this is the usual place for him to bring girls, and I feel stupid for thinking things would ever work out with him.

I should've known better.

"It's fine," I say, even though it isn't.

"What an asshole," Casey says, then she tilts her head. "What about Kay?"

"Just forget it and ignore him, please," I beg them. If I try to leave now, it'll show weakness. I need to show Dylan that it doesn't bother me.

I can't help but steal another glance at them. Dylan is smiling at her until his eyes travel to me. His smile drops and I look away before the hurt becomes unbearable.

It's bad enough to go through the whole ordeal with Jacob. It's worse seeing Dylan move on to someone else when I still think there could have been a chance.

Casey, Lauren, and Jacob do as I ask and don't bring him up again, though the conversations are awkward and forced after that.

When it gets late, we decide to leave. I walk behind everyone, and with my luck, we have to walk past Dylan's table to get to the door.

Jacob walks too close to their table, and he ends up kicking Dylan's chair quite purposely.

Dylan has a deadly look on his face. "What the fuck?" he says, standing up and getting in Jacob's face.

Jacob holds up his hands but smirks probably because he's gotten a reaction out of Dylan. "It was an accident, dude. Chill."

It's no accident. Things will only go downhill from here, so I step between them and push Jacob away.

"Let's go," I say to him.

He stares Dylan down before nodding. "Fine."

We're about to leave when Dylan mutters something that sounds like "bitch," which makes Jacob lunge at him. They fall to the ground, knocking over some chairs. Jacob ends up on top of Dylan, his arms swinging back and forth at him.

I frantically look at the blonde girl, who gives me a panicked but confused expression. She has no idea what the hell is going on. Casey is yelling at Dylan and Lauren is yelling at Jacob, making the scene more chaotic.

When the boys get on their feet, I launch myself between them again, with my back against Jacob and my eyes on Dylan. He's staring at me with the most unreadable expression on his face, and I hate it.

"Get the hell out of my store, all of you, before I call the police!" the manager yells at us.

Once we're outside, I shove Jacob, who has a bruise forming on his jaw. "I told you to leave it alone, dammit."

"I'm trying to do the right thing." He motions to Dylan, still frustrated and flustered.

"Come get your ass kicked then!" Dylan shouts at him. He has a bruise on his cheek already.

I'm not sure where the rage from Dylan is coming from, but I'm annoyed by it. He isn't like this. This isn't Dylan. "Will you stop?" I snap at him. "I don't know what your problem is, but this is not you."

He smirks. "Hanging out with Xavier does that to you."

Dylan's been hanging around Xavier? His smirks say it all. It's like the funny, sweet, caring Dylan I've known is gone. His eyes aren't warm anymore.

He wraps his arm around the blonde and waves before walking off into the dark parking lot.

It's a lot to process. Dylan has followed the saying "if you can't beat them, join them." I wonder if that's why he isn't with Kay anymore. More importantly, who broke up with who?

I know it's a horrible idea, but I need to talk to Kay. She probably won't tell me the whole story, but I can try to get it out of her. The issue is getting in touch with her.

On Monday morning, I drive myself to school. I hope I'll catch the right person to put me in touch with Kay. When I park, I see Anthony's car sitting in the lot with him still inside. I pull my scarf tighter around my neck and get out of my car.

He sees me through the windshield and rolls his window down.

"Long time no see," he says. His eyes seem sunken into his face somehow, like he's aged a lot in the past month. "What's up?"

"I need a favor."

"Jump in," he says, motioning to the passenger's side. I run over and hop in with him to find the car nicely warmed.

"Your favors often have something to do with Dylan." He gives me a deadpan look.

I bite my lip. "Please?"

"What is it?"

"I just need to get in touch with Kay."

He frowns. "Why?"

"I need to talk to her."

"I don't know, Lacey." He shakes his head. "I thought you were done with all of this."

He has a point. I've told him over the break that I don't think it is worth trying with Dylan. He's been upset, but he understands where I am coming from.

Part of me wants to stay as far away as possible from this and move on, but there's another part of me that wants to keep checking in on Dylan. Seeing him that Friday night has only made it much more relevant. He's not himself anymore.

"I am," I say. "I just want to ask her something. It's harmless."

Knowing Anthony, he won't give me a way to contact Kay. It's worth a shot though.

"Fine," he says to my surprise. He pulls out his phone and proceeds to write a number down on a ripped piece of paper. "This is her number."

At the same time he's handing me the paper, Dylan pulls into the spot next to him. I grab the paper and say, "Thanks, Anthony. Please don't tell Dylan."

After he nods, I jump out of the car and stalk off towards the main building. The piece of paper feels like it's burning in my hand, and I'm itching to call her already.

CHAPTER TWENTY-FOUR
Part One

DYLAN

Of course, there's no obvious way of moving on. I don't want Kay, and Lacey doesn't want me, so that's the only thing left to do. Move on in a way that will keep everyone away.

After Reece's birthday trip, I've stopped talking to him. It's wrong, but I don't want to involve everyone in my shit, especially if it has to do with Xavier. I can't stand being around Kay anymore, and if there's no hope with Lacey, then there's no reason to keep things up with Kay.

Breaking up with Kay has been hard. Not emotionally. She just doesn't want to accept the fact that I'm leaving her. Besides making it all about her, she makes it about Lacey. She can't understand what's special about Lacey. I don't think she ever will.

In true Kay fashion, she told Xavier about our breakup and he comes after me. Instead of beating the shit out of me, we've made a deal.

Knowing things won't work out with Lacey, I've hit up other girls. Nothing has gone further than making out. It doesn't feel right with them, and it only makes me angrier. I can't be hung up on her forever.

Zoey has been into me since last year, and I've always turned her down. She's a blonde with blue eyes and big boobs. She tends to go from guy to guy, but I'm not judging. Blondes aren't usually my type, but I'm trying to branch out.

I always thought she just wanted to fuck, but when I hit her up, she is down for a few dates. I probably won't ever sleep with her. She looks like the needy type.

For a minute, I'm really into her. Her hair is soft between my fingers, and her eyes remind me of a Dasani water bottle.

I let my eyes wander from her for one second and catch a glimpse of Lacey talking to her douchebag ex. I've seen them together a lot around school. I know Lacey has said she won't ever take him back, but it still makes me curious. They spend a lot of time together, from what I've seen.

Zoey says something, bringing my attention back to her. It's hard to focus on her while Lacey is near me. I steal another glance at Lacey, who is getting into her ex's truck while he holds the door for her.

A snort almost comes out. They look cozy. Too cozy.

I'm not going to think about it anymore. Lacey has given up on me, so I need to give up on her.

It stays out of my mind until Zoey wants to get ice cream later that evening. She wants to go to the ice cream shop I've taken Lacey to. I want to say no because that shop should me mine and Lacey's alone.

Then I remember how miserable Lacey was when she broke up with Jacob, and I don't want to end up like that. Moping over the same shit every day isn't how I want to live.

Walking into the ice cream shop, I can't fucking believe that Lacey is here—with her ex of all people, and not only him but the girl he has cheated on her with.

What the hell is she doing?

I try to ignore them as best as I can. Zoey doesn't know about the whole thing with Lacey, and I want it to stay that way. She doesn't need to know about every person I've dated in the past. She doesn't even know about Kay.

After a while, Lacey's group gets up to leave. I keep my eyes on Zoey, so I'm not tempted to look at Lacey, until that fuckhead passes by and kicks my chair.

I'm not in the mood to deal with his shit. "What the fuck?" I stand up and make sure he knows who he's dealing with. I stare at him until he holds up his hands, trying to act innocent.

"It was an accident, dude. Chill."

Like hell it's an accident.

"Let's go," Lacey says to him, which ticks me off. Of course she's trying to be the peacemaker.

Playing puppet, he nods. "Fine."

He has no idea how much I can't fucking stand him. Everything he's put Lacey through feels personal somehow. I want him to know how much she was hurt at the beginning of the year.

He isn't getting away that easily.

"Fucking bitch," I mutter quietly.

All hell breaks loose. Jacob comes at me, which is what I want, forcing both of us to the ground. I struggle against him for a minute, allowing him to swing at me. He lands a punch on my cheek. I roll over on top of him and get in a good punch to his jaw.

He holds his face and I jump up, forcing him to stand up too. I'm about to take another jab when Lacey wedges her way between us. She's leaning on Jacob while looking at me, and all I can do is stare at her. I don't know if she's trying to protect him or me.

"Get the hell out of my store, all of you, before I call the police!" the manager comes out and yells at us.

I grab Zoey's hand, and we all rush out of the shop. Once outside, Lacey pushes Jacob hard against his chest, saying, "I told you to leave it alone, dammit."

"I'm trying to do the right thing!" Jacob points to me.

Is he trying to prove himself to her? If they aren't together, he's clearly trying to get her back again. "Come get your ass kicked

369

then!" I shout at him. The only dutiful thing he can do is let me beat the shit out of him.

Lacey suddenly whirls around to me, which I don't expect. "Will you stop?" she snaps. "I don't know what your problem is, but this is not you."

I want to piss her off and make her see that I've changed, that I've moved on. "Hanging out with Xavier does that," I say, making sure I look as carefree as possible. She despises Xavier, and knowing I'm on the same side as him will mess with her.

I don't want to feel guilty for moving on. There's nothing wrong with it.

But even as I put my arm around Zoey and feel their eyes on the back of my head, I still feel like a piece of shit.

Zoey asks a whole slew of questions, and I have to answer them honestly. She doesn't like the fact that there is drama behind dating me, but she sticks around after the incident at the ice cream shop.

As I get to school on Monday, I see Anthony's car already in the lot and head straight for it. I slow down once I see Lacey sitting in his car, talking to him.

Angry, I turn away and park quickly. By the time I get out, she's already leaving Anthony's car and walking away.

Watching her, I can't help but look her over. Her long brown hair sways behind her. Her giant scarf over her jacket makes her look cute. Her jeans also fit her perfectly in all the right places, as usual. She never looks out of place, even when she doesn't try hard.

I wonder if she has told Anthony about my fight with Jacob. Has she asked for advice?

One thing that irritates me is her constant advice-seeking from Anthony. He's always the person she goes to. I try not to feel jealous, but I can't help it.

I push it to the back of my mind until lunch. I run into Anthony in the hallway and pull him aside.

"What's up?" he asks, like everything is fine.

"What did Lacey want this morning?"

He smirks, which bothers me. "Is Zoey not interesting enough to keep you busy?"

"Just tell me." The need in my voice is obvious, and I hate it. I don't want to sound hung up on her, but dammit, it's hard.

He shakes his head. "No can do. You've told me not to bring her up in any conversation, and I'm keeping my word."

Shit. I've forgotten I've told him that after Reece's birthday trip. At the time it has seemed like a good idea. "Anthony, c'mon."

"The pizza in the cafeteria is calling my name, so I'm gonna go," he says, pushing past me and heading down the hall.

I let out a frustrated sigh and throw my head back onto the wall behind me. Why can't anything go my way?

My stomach growls, and I figure Zoey is probably in the cafeteria already. Anthony doesn't really like her, so he usually doesn't eat with us. She's not Lacey, so of course he doesn't like her.

On my way to the cafeteria, I notice Lacey's figure standing near the doors. I go to avoid her until I see her talking to Jacob animatedly with her hands going all over the place, as if to emphasize something.

I creep near enough, so I can hear what they're talking about. Jacob is clearly mad because I hear him say, "You're just going to take Dylan's shit?"

I scoff. My shit is nothing compared to his.

"Me and Dylan aren't even together," she says loudly. "What he does is his business. If he wants to rub it in my face, then I'm going to have to put on my big girl panties and get over it. I've done enough moping over you, and I don't want to waste my time moping over him."

She's definitely picked up on the fact that I've wanted to show her how much I'm trying to move on. She says she needs to

371

get over it, which means that she's still serious about moving on from me.

I don't like the sound of that.

Then I feel eyes on me. I stare at Jacob before Lacey turns and meets my eyes. She quickly turns back to Jacob and says, "Look, I can handle things on my own. I appreciate your effort, but I've got this."

Jacob gets the hint and walks in my direction. For a second, I think he's ready to fight again, but he only glares at me before going into the cafeteria.

The way they talk to each other sounds as if they're together again. I wonder if that's why she doesn't want to be with me anymore. Is she in denial and still hung up on him?

She obviously tries to avoid me, but I can't let that happen. I need to talk to her, somehow, some way.

I say, "Don't tell me you two are back together."

If they are, then I really need to move on.

"We're not," she says, crossing her arms. "Not that it's any of your business."

She's trying really hard to appear like she doesn't care. Like she said, she's putting on her big girl panties. To piss her off, I say, "If you're waiting to settle with me, don't bother."

I don't know why I've said such a stupid thing like that. I know I shouldn't be her enemy, but I don't know what else to do. I don't want her in my life because I need to move on.

"I'm not."

Messing with her reminds me of the first time I've met her. I can't believe I've failed to notice her around school, probably because she was with Jacob at the time and I tend not to go after girls in relationships.

I can't help but like her after having English with her. I've been surprised by how much she interests me, even when I was messing around with Kay.

"But I see you're settling nicely with Xavier. Didn't have the balls to stand up to him?"

That snaps me out of my thoughts. "I don't have to explain anything to you," I say automatically.

That's pretty bold for Lacey to say. It sorta throws me off.

"You do realize he's driven everyone away, right? Anthony is going to duck out just like everyone else, and all you're going to have left is Xavier."

She's treading in dangerous territory. I've told her in the beginning that I don't need her looking out for me, that I can take care of myself. I need to get Xavier off her mind. "Was that why you were talking to him this morning? Trying to get into my cousin's pants now or what?"

As soon as those words escape my mouth, I regret saying them.

It has crossed my mind that she could be interested in Anthony, or even Derrick. I don't like how close she is to them, but I don't dive deeper into those thoughts. No matter how much my mind wants to trick me into thinking she'd ever date either of them, I know in my heart she wouldn't.

Her face changes, and I can tell I've touched a nerve. "You're trying to make me into someone I'm not, and I know it's because you know I'm right."

Admitting it is the last thing I'll do.

"I'm not the enemy here, Dylan. I thought you'd be stronger than this," she says, like a slap to the face.

She pushes past me and walks into the cafeteria.

Using my own words against me is one thing. Calling me out on the bullshit that comes out of my mouth is another thing.

The fact that I can't come up with something to say back kills me. Even though it seems like I hurt her, she knows I'm only trying to deflect the truth. And hurting her makes me feel like shit.

As much as I want to move on, it's going to be hard getting away from her. If I can't move on and I can't get her back, then what the fuck am I supposed to do?

I'm not sure if I'm losing my touch or if I'm falling more in love with her.

Part Two

LACEY

I run into Jacob on the way to the cafeteria. He's striding down the hallway like he's in a rush. We haven't talked much after the fiasco at the ice cream shop.

After thinking about it, Jacob had no right to act the way he did. He isn't my boyfriend, and I don't need him to do things like that for me. Granted, Dylan has overreacted too, but that is a whole other situation that needs to be dealt with.

"Hey," Jacob says to me when we are close enough to each other.

I need him to understand why it isn't cool of him to fight Dylan. "We need to talk."

"Why does it sound like you're breaking up with me?" he asks. The look on his face shows that he's joking, but only partly.

I hope he doesn't think we're back together in any way.

"That's exactly it," I huff out. "You shouldn't have started anything with Dylan. You and me aren't together."

The frown on his face deepens. "I know we're not together—"

"Do you?" I ask. "I can fight my own battles, you know. I don't need you to step in."

"Well, maybe I just wanted to make up for being an asshole to you," he says, clearly frustrated.

375

Is he still trying to redeem himself? "You don't have to prove anything anymore, Jacob. Don't be an asshole, and we'll be okay."

"You're just going to take Dylan's shit?"

"Me and Dylan aren't even together." I find myself almost yelling it at him. "What he does is his business. If he wants to rub it in my face, then I'm going to have to put on my big girl panties and get over it. I've done enough moping over you, and I don't want to waste my time moping over him."

Jacob's eyes travel behind me, and I turn to see who he is looking at.

Dylan is standing by the cafeteria doors, watching me and Jacob and clearly trying to eavesdrop. I'm not sure how much he's heard, but I don't care. I meet Jacob's gaze again.

"Look, I can handle things on my own," I say to him. "I appreciate your effort, but I've got this."

He nods. "Fine." He pushes himself off the wall and continues toward the cafeteria. When he passes by Dylan, they share a cold stare before Jacob walks through the doors.

With Jacob, there is always fighting. It wasn't like that when we were together. I think we were lost in our own little bubble and after we broke up, reality set in. Seeing clearly only came when Dylan was around.

My plan is to ignore Dylan and head into the cafeteria, but he speaks up as I'm about to pass him.

"Don't tell me you two are back together."

He sounds more annoyed than hurt, and that's like a knife to the heart.

"We're not. Not that it's any of your business."

His smirk, once flirty and casual, is menacing. He's looking for ways to irritate me. "If you're waiting to settle with me, don't bother."

"I'm not," I shoot back. His smug appearance only makes me angrier. He can dish it out, but I want to see if he can take it too. Two can play this game. "But I see you're settling nicely with Xavier. Didn't have the balls to stand up to him?"

The smirk disappears, and I know I've got him. "I don't have to explain anything to you."

Confident Lacey is finally returning, and it feels *so* good. "You do realize he's driven everyone away, right? Anthony is going to duck out just like everyone else, and all you're going to have left is Xavier."

"Was that why you were talking to him this morning? Trying to get into my cousin's pants now or what?"

What he says only proves my point. It's laughable, but I almost let the words hurt me. I'll never be interested in Anthony. He's a great friend, and that's it. "You're trying to make me into someone I'm not, and I know it's because you know I'm right."

Before he can say anything else, I say, "I'm not the enemy here, Dylan. I thought you'd be stronger than this."

The words he's said to me about Jacob are my only defense against him. I should be more upset by the person he's turning into, but I know the Dylan I care about is in there somewhere. He's suppressing him, and I can tell by the look on his face when I say those words to him.

He doesn't fool me.

At the end of lunch, I text Kay and ask her if she wants to meet me at Raven's after school. She doesn't respond during class, and I start to wonder if Anthony has given me the wrong number.

Finally, after third period, she responds.

4:30. You're late and I'm leaving.

A wave of relief washes over me, and a nervous feeling sticks in my stomach. The last time I've met with Kay, she has slapped me in the face and has left a cut on my cheek. Hopefully, it will go better this time.

After school, I race to the parking lot so I can beat everyone's questions, especially Anthony. He doesn't look so happy about me talking to Kay, but I need to do it.

Driving to Raven's only makes me more anxious. When I pull into the parking lot, Kay's red car is already parked. The time reads four twenty-eight.

Two minutes to spare.

I walk in and pray none of the boys are here. It isn't the smartest idea to meet her at Raven's, but I don't know where else to go. It also isn't smart to go by myself, considering what has happened last time.

Kay is sitting at a table in the back. Her attention is focused on her phone.

I slide into the seat in front of her, which brings her attention to me. Her hair is long and straight, framing her eyes that are almost black.

"What do you want to talk about?" she asks immediately, setting her phone down. "Did you get Dylan back and want to throw it in my face?"

Just like she's done to me when they're dating? As appealing as that sounds, it won't happen. And that answers my first question. They aren't together anymore. "Dating Dylan shouldn't be a contest," I say to her. "And no, we're not together. He's with someone else."

Her eyes turn to slits. "Someone else?"

"Some blonde girl at school. I've seen them around lately," I say.

She's trying to come off as cool, but I know it bothers her that he's with someone else already. "When he broke up with me, I figured he would go back to you."

"I told him I didn't want him."

"You're stupid." She lets out a dark laugh. "Who doesn't want Dylan Parker?"

This topic will never end. She wants Dylan, and if she can't have him, then no one can. "Are you going to make that girl's life hell too?" I demand. "Aren't you sick of being hurt over and over?"

She purses her lips, and I know I've touched a nerve. "You don't know about me and Dylan. I can't just let him go." She plays with her hands before saying, "I think I love him."

Yikes. "Do you really love him, or do you love the idea of him?"

I want her to see that Dylan isn't the only guy in the world who can make her happy, but I don't want to come across as only saying those things just to get her out of the picture. She's stuck to him, and it isn't healthy. I want her to be more open with me, to let me in somehow. I don't want to be Kay's enemy, and I don't want her to be mine.

"I don't know," she says, looking away from me. "Maybe it's just the idea of him."

I can sympathize. Dylan is truly a great guy with only a few flaws. "I felt that way about Jacob."

"Your ex?"

She seems interested. Maybe she's like Dylan. If I open up to her, then maybe she'll open up to me too. "Yeah, it was great with Jacob. He was sweet to me. He showed me off to his friends. I thought we'd be that couple who'd stay together after high school."

She looks down at her hands. "He cheated on you, didn't he?"

I nod in response. "I found out he did it, even after I lost my parents in an accident." I look down at my hands. I can't believe I'm telling Kay everything.

"Shit." She leans back in her seat. She looks uncomfortable when she says, "Sorry about your parents." She looks . . . almost empathetic.

"Thanks," I mumble. Exposing my story to Kay feels weird. I don't know what will come out of our conversation.

"What an asshole," she says about Jacob.

379

"After we broke up, I didn't know if I could trust anyone. I didn't want to get hurt again. Then suddenly, I had Dylan in class. Things just felt so natural with him. He helped me get over Jacob," I say without really thinking. I'm not sure how she'll react when I bring up moments with me and Dylan.

She leans forward again. "Dylan knows exactly what to say. I never knew if he meant what he said or if he was just feeding me bullshit."

That's something I can't relate to. I've always felt like he's completely genuine with me, and that's why I like him. He's someone who's easy to talk to and get along with.

I don't want to continue talking about my history. I steel myself to ask her what I've really wanted to know.

"What is he doing with Xavier?" I ask her. She'll most likely know.

Her eyes narrow, like she's examining me. "You want him back, don't you?"

She's steering the conversation in the wrong direction. "I just care about him, Kay. I mean, I don't want his life to be ruined by Xavier," I say. Her expression reads protective sister, so I quickly say, "Don't tell me you're actually proud of Xavier and what he's done."

The course of our conversation has changed.

"It's not our job to fix Dylan, of course," I continue, "but that doesn't mean we can't try."

Kay isn't looking at me, only at the table, as if she's lost in thought. "I don't know what he's doing with Xavier. I've been left in the dark."

Damn. Maybe I should've talked to Anthony about it first.

"You're in love with him, aren't you?" she suddenly asks me. "I mean, why else would you be doing all of this?"

In love with Dylan? No. "There's a difference between being in love with someone and loving them," I say. "I don't think I'm in love with him."

"But you love him," she says flatly. "You can't deny that."

Maybe I do. I don't want to say it in front of Kay because my feelings are not to be trusted.

"Well, well, what do we have here?"

Our eyes snap to Carlos, who is closing in on our table. I haven't seen him since the day he's blown up on everyone.

"What are we conspiring, ladies?" he asks, pulling a chair up to the table.

"None of your business," Kay shoots at him.

His eyes travel to me. "Something to do with Dylan, right?"

I'm not going to answer his question. Like Kay has said, this is none of his business. "What are you doing here, Carlos?"

"I'm just here." He grins. "Living my bullshit-free life."

Kay rolls her eyes at him. "Leave us alone. You're clearly jealous of Dylan."

She's going to piss him off, and I don't think it will work out well.

He smirks. "Jealous of Dylan? Fuck no."

I don't want to be around him. He's a bad friend, and I don't want to be associated with him anymore. "C'mon, Kay. I think it's time to go," I tell her.

"Kay can leave." He waves her off. "I want to talk to you."

His eyes bore into mine. I look at Kay, wondering what her next move will be.

"I think Lacey has somewhere to be," she says to him, her voice steady.

The fact that she's helping me out has me cheering on the inside. I almost have her won over.

"We're friends, right, Lacey? Let's chat for a minute." He holds up a finger. "Just a minute, then I'll let you get back to your busy life."

Curiosity has killed the cat, but the cat has eight lives left. I'm sure talking with Carlos won't hurt too much.

381

I look at Kay. "Um, I can talk to him."

She looks at me like I'm crazy but nods and stands up. She is about to walk away when she says, "Call me tonight, Lacey."

With that, she takes off. Before I can even comprehend what's happened, Carlos speaks up.

"Making friends with the enemy?" he asks, taking her spot at the table.

"She isn't the enemy." Xavier is. "Now, you have a minute."

"I see things aren't working out with Dylan," he starts, tracing invisible lines on the table. "Why don't you and me go out this Friday?"

I want to laugh. Is he really asking me out? After being a terrible friend to the guys, plus leaving Casey when she needs him? No way. "I don't think so."

"C'mon," he stresses. "You never felt something when we danced or sang together?"

Carlos has gone off the deep end, clearly. "It was fun, but we were just friends." His pressing is making me uncomfortable. I shift in my seat and start to stand up. "I really have to go now."

I walk towards the entrance, but he catches up with me and blocks my way.

"I don't mind if you're not into something serious. We can have a little fun, if that's what you're looking for." He steps closer to me. "What's stopping you?"

His hand makes its to my waist. I know I'm in big trouble. I try pushing him away, but he only comes on stronger.

Then he's abruptly shoved away from me. I look over to find Kay pushing him towards the wall.

"Keep your hands to yourself, asshole," she tells him.

I can't believe my eyes. Kay is really defending me from Carlos.

His face screams anger. "All of a sudden, *you* care about Lacey?"

"When a girl isn't interested in you, take a hint," she spits in his face. "I'll have Xavier come after your ass."

The look Carlos gives me is annoyed and fed up. He bumps shoulders with Kay as he tries to leave.

She isn't done. "Maybe try not being a dick, then there might be some girls who will actually want to date you."

"Maybe Dylan would've actually liked you if you weren't a bitch," he shoots back.

He swings the door open, almost smacking Dylan and Derrick who are just outside. They back up, probably out of surprise, and Dylan stares down Carlos.

I think I'm going to have to mediate yet another fight, but Carlos continues walking.

Kay smirks. "I don't mind being that bitch."

I want to hug her. I'm not sure if we're completely okay, so I don't. "I thought you left," I say to her.

"Carlos always gives me the creeps. As much as I still don't like you, it didn't feel right to just leave you with him."

Well, there it is. Even if she doesn't like me, I'm still grateful for her help.

"Thanks, I think." I laugh.

Things get awkward when Derrick and Dylan walk inside and see the two of us talking. Dylan looks completely confused, while Derrick seems impressed.

"I need to go," she says. "Still, call me tonight."

I nod and she ducks her head as she passes the Parker boys.

Even though things with Carlos have gotten weird, I feel happy and somewhat relieved. I've came in not knowing what would happen with Kay, and I get to leave without a slap to the face.

"Lacey," Derrick acknowledges me as he walks inside Raven's.

Dylan opens his mouth, but nothing comes out. He gapes like a fish for a few seconds until I speak.

"Carlos tried to hit on me and Kay came to the rescue," I summarize.

"What are you even doing here? Were you with Carlos or Kay? And why?" All his questions come out in a rush.

No use in lying. "I met Kay here, so we could talk. Carlos showed up and tried to ask me out. He wouldn't take no for an answer, and that's when she stepped in."

"And she wants you to call her tonight?"

I can tell he's having a hard time understanding what has just happened. My mind is in the same boat. Kay is unpredictable.

"I guess I will." I shrug. She doesn't think the conversation is over, and I want to know what else she has to say.

Dylan is watching me, as if thinking hard about something. This expression of his frustrates me because I want to know what's going on in his mind.

"What?" I ask him.

"I—uh." He stops short and shakes his head. "Nothing."

I hate when he does that. Never finishing a thought that wants to come out. We're both quiet. The thought of throwing myself into his arms and hoping that everything will be all right suddenly comes in my head.

"I should probably get going," I say, avoiding his gaze. During our conversation at lunch, it was hard to see him; only because I was hurt. Seeing him here at Raven's hurts too, but in a way that I know it won't work out.

"Already?" he asks.

His demeanor is different than it was at lunch. The old Dylan is breaking through, and I wish he wouldn't hold back.

"Yeah . . ." I trail off. "I'll see you around."

I take one step before he catches my hand.

He isn't looking at me. He only rubs the back of my hand with his thumb and says, "Get home safe."

My hand turns cold when he lets go.

CHAPTER TWENTY-FIVE
Part One

DYLAN

I'm sprawled out on my bed with my earbuds blasting the loudest song I have on my phone. With my hands behind my head, I stare at the lights above me. I haven't changed them back to their original state. They still read "Be Mine?"

I take a deep breath and roll over, so I'm not staring at them anymore. I'll have to change them eventually, but right now, I don't feel like it.

I've been an asshole to Lacey at lunch today, and she doesn't deserve it. And dammit, she's right. She isn't the enemy. She never has been.

There are quick footsteps down the stairs to my room. The lights flicker on, and I shield my eyes from the sudden brightness. Derrick says something to me, but my music is blocking him out.

I pull one earbud out. "What?"

He rolls his eyes. "Are you still moping?"

"What do you want?" I ask instead of answering his question. So what if I'm moping? I'd rather mope for the night and then get my shit together tomorrow.

"Get up," Derrick says.

"Why?"

"I'm sick of you not doing anything to help yourself. You've been like this since Reece's birthday and it's stupid." Derrick leans against the wall as he says it.

"What the fuck do you know?" I ask.

He crosses his arms. "You're a coward, you know that?"

A coward? I immediately sit up. "How the hell am I a coward?"

"We all told you from the beginning that getting involved with Xavier's shit would only ruin you. You said you weren't scared of him and still went after Kay. Now, he's ruining what you've got with Lacey, and you're just letting him. It's bullshit."

He's never cared this much about something involving me. I feel like I should be suspicious. "Do you have a thing for Lacey or something? You're caring too much about this."

"That's fucking it, Dylan! You're not caring enough!" he shouts at me. He walks over to the small table next to my bed and yanks out the school newspaper I've hidden under a pile of papers.

He throws it at me. "Where's this Dylan? The one who was bragging to dad about what a great editor Lacey is for the paper? Lacey is probably the best thing to happen to you in a long time, and you're just willing to let her go," he says. "I know I haven't been there for you for everything, but I can't let this one slide."

"She told me she doesn't want to be with me anymore," I shoot back. "What am I supposed to do? Force her to be with me?"

"If you two really cared about each other, then you'd tell Xavier to fuck off or beat the fuck out of him."

We're both silent. I know I can kick Xavier's ass, but would that make Lacey want to be with me? Would it be for nothing?

"Come with me to Raven's," Derrick says finally. "I have to talk to Max."

*　　　*　　　*

I'm getting tired of the same old routine. Waking up, going to school, and not seeing Lacey as much, but still seeing girls like Zoey. Not seeing the guys is even starting to get to me. All I have is Anthony, and even he isn't showing his face as much anymore.

I've told Zoey that things aren't going to work out between us after I've seen Lacey at Raven's on Monday. Seeing her with Kay has just confirmed how special she is. She's managed to talk to Kay without getting slapped again, and they're even going to call each other that night.

What the fuck is going on in the world?

When I get to school on Friday, I throw my backpack over my shoulder and saunter into the main building. As I'm walking to class, I see Jacob and Casey standing by a classroom, talking in hushed voices.

This sight is strange to me. Lacey is usually around them, and she isn't this time.

I can't ask them where she is. As much as I'm curious about what she's up to, I don't want to invest myself even more. Admitting to myself that I love her is hard enough knowing it won't work out between us. It hurts too much, and I don't want to feel this pain. This is exactly what I'm afraid of happening.

After my morning classes, I head towards the parking lot. Skipping my next two classes to go home sounds more appealing than spending any more time in hell. I can't wait to graduate.

As I walk out of the main building, I feel my arm being pulled back. I whip around and find Casey with worried eyes.

"Have you seen Lacey?" she asks.

I figure I'm the last person she's asked. "No, why?"

"Dammit." She puts her hands on her hips. "She's not answering her phone."

I glance toward her usual parking spot and see that it's empty. Lacey isn't one to just skip school for no reason.

"Maybe she's sick at home." My suggestion sounds wrong as it comes out. I don't think she'd stay home sick and not let anyone know.

I don't want to get involved if it's not a big deal, but something isn't right. I wonder if it has anything to do with Kay. Lacey's taken up a friendship or something with her. What if Kay has double crossed her and something has happened?

"We can go see if she's at home," I suggest.

Casey hesitates, like she doesn't want to work with me, but she nods. "Let's go."

We're walking to my car when Jacob catches up with us. "Hey, have you guys heard from Lacey?"

Jesus, can this guy be any more irritating?

"We're going to her apartment right now to check on her," Casey answers before I can say anything.

I wish she didn't tell him anything. He'll invite himself, which is the last thing I want.

His eyes meet mine. "Mind if I tag along?"

The urge to tell him to fuck off is on the tip of my tongue, but I bite down on it. This isn't about him. This is about Lacey. "Yeah, whatever."

Lacey and Jacob, for some god forsaken reason, are still close. If I deny him in checking on her, I'll never hear the end of it.

We all jump in my car and speed to her apartment. Casey calls her again, but it goes straight to voicemail.

"I have a bad feeling about this," she says.

"Did you know she hung out with Kay the other day?" I ask her.

She frowns. "Kay?"

"I saw them together at Raven's on Monday." The fact that Casey doesn't know about her rendezvous with Kay makes me wonder what else she hasn't told Casey. What other secrets is Lacey keeping?

389

"Who's Kay?" Jacob asks, leaning forward from the backseat.

"It's a long story." Casey waves it off.

I take a turn into the parking lot of her apartment complex and drive around to her building. When her car comes into view, I don't know how to feel.

"Maybe she's taking a day off for herself," Jacob says. "I think she needed it."

I need this dickhead to shut up before I get too annoyed with him.

"Let's see if she's actually home," I tell them. We can't just assume she's here because her car is.

We get out, and I jog up the stairs ahead of them and start knocking on the door. After a few minutes, I knock again, with no answer.

Something is definitely off. She isn't answering, and I'm beginning to worry.

I meet Casey's eyes. I think we're both thinking the same thing. Casey reaches under the doormat and holds the silver key. "I practically live here too. I'm sure they wouldn't mind us coming in."

"I don't know . . ." Jacob trails off.

"Just do it," I urge her. If Lacey isn't in the apartment, we need to worry.

Unlocking the door, Casey steps inside with us right behind her. Everything appears to be normal. A blanket is casually thrown on the couch, a pair of heels are by the door, and the soft sound of ticking from the clock on the wall fills as background noise.

"Lace?" Casey calls out, jogging to her bedroom. She comes back out and shakes her head. "Something is wrong. I know it."

Jacob scratches his head. "Maybe she's with her aunt. Do you guys have her number?"

I'm beginning to think Kay or Xavier has something to do with Lacey being gone, and that doesn't settle well with me. Kay and I are done, Kay and Lacey seem to be friends, what more do they want with her? Xavier hasn't mentioned any plans with Lacey. But then again, he probably wouldn't tell me if he did.

The look on Casey's face tells me she is thinking the same thing. The worry is clear in her eyes, and it looks like she's about to have a panic attack.

There's only one way to find out if Xavier has her. I take my phone out of my pocket. Lacey could be in Xavier's hands, and that's what I fear most.

Xavier answers the phone after two rings. "I'm a little busy, can this wait?"

"Not if you have Lacey."

He sighs. "Oh, poor Lacey. When is everyone going to give up on her?"

I roll my eyes. He's toying with me. "Cut the shit, Xavier. Do you have her or not?"

"I thought you didn't give a shit about her anymore. At least, that's what I remember you telling me," he says.

"Dammit, Xavier—"

"She's here, sitting pretty."

My eyes flit to Casey, and she throws her head into her hands.

What's happening is my fault. I've gotten too comfortable with Xavier, and now he's taking advantage of that. I let Lacey down.

She's told me Xavier is all I have left, and she's right. I don't have Anthony or Reece or even Carlos around. A wedge has been driven between me, Lacey, and every other person I care about, and it's all my fault.

I was angry when she decided it would never work between us at Reece's cabin. Angry enough to dump Kay and join Xavier in becoming one of his messenger boys. I've made gun trades, gambled on Xavier's behalf, and beat the shit out of those who haven't paid him back.

Most of all, I've been angry enough to tell him I wouldn't care if anything happens to Lacey.

It's selfish, but it has given me a sense of relief that maybe he'd officially leave her alone. That didn't work.

"What are you planning to do with her anyway?" I ask him.

If he's hurt her in any way, he's a dead man. I've said things that I completely regret, but he's stepping over the line. I won't let anything happen to her.

"Well, she's being a stubborn bitch. She won't call Casey for me, so we've had to deal with that."

"Casey?" I ask, looking at her. She freezes up, and her eyes look frantic.

"Do not lay one more finger on her, or I swear to God—"

"Blah, blah, I've heard it before," he says. "This one isn't on you. Casey didn't want to talk to me the other day, and now she's going to pay." His voice echoes and I know where he's at. "Just bring Casey to me."

He hangs up.

I stare at my phone. I shouldn't have underestimated him. I didn't think he'd go this far just to talk to Casey.

"What did he say? He has her? What does he want?" she immediately asks me.

"Wait, wait." Jacob holds up his hands. "Someone kidnapped Lacey? We need to call the police."

Ignoring Jacob, I look at Casey. "He wants to see you after you didn't talk to him the other day."

The color in her face drains.

Before she can respond, Jacob shoves me back against the wall. "What the fuck, man? You know this guy who took her? And you're trying to blame Casey?"

I push him back, angry that he's here in the first place. "You don't know shit. Actually, you shouldn't even be here. Trying to be all buddy-buddy with Lacey, and for what? There's no way in hell she'll get back together with you."

"Fuck you. Me and Casey are going to the police, and we're going to get Lacey back," he says, grabbing her. "Let's go."

We rush out the door, while Casey takes her time locking it and putting the spare key back.

"I did this," she says, her voice cracking. "He wanted to talk to me on Tuesday, and I didn't want to."

I grab Casey's arm. I see the tears in her eyes. I have to make sure she knows I'm being sincere. "Casey, I'm not blaming you. This is all my fault. I don't want you to be put in danger just because that asshole is obsessed with you. We can go to the police, but that will only make it worse. If Xavier sees the cops, he'll run and take Lacey with him."

She wipes her eyes. "I need to see him, and I need to see Lacey safe and sound," she says. "No cops. We're going to him now."

"Hold on," Jacob says. "This is insane. We're definitely getting the cops involved."

"Shut the fuck up for one second, please," I say to him, being one second away from knocking him out.

He points at me. "You shouldn't even be here. I'm not her only fucked-up ex. You've driven her out, and it takes a lot for her to give up."

"I actually kept my dick in my pants, unlike you. You didn't even care that she lost her parents." I get closer to his face. I'm waiting for him to make the first move. One flinch and I'm going to kick his ass.

Casey pushes Jacob away from me and shouts, "Stop it! It's either my way or no way, and I say we go to them without the cops. I can handle Xavier."

I accept it. I can provide back up if Xavier tries anything else. Jacob is the one who doesn't look convinced.

"Now, let's get going," she says.

Part Two

I keep going back to Kay's comment about loving Dylan. Am I in the same boat as her? Do we only love the idea of him, or is there something genuine hidden deep inside?

When I call her that night, I'm anxious to hear what she has to say.

"Hey," she answers quietly. "I can only talk for a minute. Xavier is here."

"What else did you want to tell me?" I ask.

"I lied earlier. I told you I didn't know what Dylan was doing with Xavier, but I kind of do. Over the break, Dylan was meeting up with Xavier almost every day and going somewhere with him. Xavier didn't tell me what they were doing, but I think he's gotten Dylan to do some of his dirty work."

I hope that isn't true, but it explains Dylan's change in attitude. Maybe he is spending too much time with Xavier.

"They haven't met up in a week, so I don't know what's going on," she says.

"Thanks for telling me," I say. "And thanks for getting Carlos away from me." He has never come across as a guy who'd push a girl to an uncomfortable situation. From what I've seen of him when he was with Casey, he seemed really normal. It must've been an act.

It's disappointing to see him this way. I've clearly missed the signs that Kay has been able to read all along. I should've known better when he was always around somehow.

"Well, if I hadn't stayed, Dylan probably would've taken care of him." She sighs. "He didn't even look at me when I left. You're the only person he was looking at."

It's still weird to talk to Kay about Dylan.

"Kay, I'm sorry." I don't know what I'm apologizing for. I just feel like it's my fault that it hasn't worked out between them. I wonder if Dylan would have liked her a lot more if I wasn't in the picture.

"Don't apologize. I've been thinking about what you told me."

"About what?"

"There are more important things to worry about than Dylan."

It's true. As much as I try to think about something else other than him, it's hard. It's hard to take my own advice.

"Anyway, that's what I wanted to say," she says quickly before we hang up.

I stare at my ceiling. What has my life come to?

The rest of the week goes by in a blur. A movie night with Lauren and Casey takes up my Wednesday night, and dinner with Casey's family takes up Thursday's.

Jacob, absent from my plans, hasn't talked to me since we argued. I'm torn with him. He can be the biggest idiot on the planet, but there's something that tells me to keep him around.

It's like a lesson. Learn to move on, but also learn to forgive.

I feel sluggish when I've woken up on Friday. I roll out of bed and go brush my teeth. I throw on some jeans with a thick long-sleeve, then brush out my giant birds nest of hair that I've got after not taking care of it last night.

I swipe on some mascara and lip gloss, then walk out of my room. Aunt Jade is already gone for the day. I make myself some cereal before sitting down on the couch with a blanket.

I want my Friday to go as smoothly as possible. I don't want to think about Dylan, Kay, Carlos, or anyone else. I just want to get through the day without any worries.

When I step out of the apartment, I hug myself and pull my jacket tighter against my body. I adjust my scarf so no cold air gets to my neck. The snow from the night before has settled in a pretty blanket on the ground, sparkling from the little bit of sunshine peeking through the clouds.

What I didn't expect is seeing Xavier standing by my car again. I'm not in the mood for him.

"What now?" I hold up my arms. "What else could you possibly want? You have Dylan all to yourself. What else is there?"

He seems amused, but there's something dark about his presence. "You play the part really well."

"What part?"

"The victim. Poor, helpless Lacey doesn't get to live happily ever after," he says, creeping closer to me. "Boo-hoo."

"What do you want?" I ask him, backing off slightly. I can't let him see that he's scaring me. I won't give him the satisfaction.

"For now, you. We're taking a drive," he says.

My heartbeat speeds up. "I really have to get to school," I say, pulling out my keys. "Maybe we can go another time."

He blocks me as I try to get to my car. "No, we're going now."

I feel myself breathing harder as each second goes by, the scarf feeling like it's tightening around my neck. The expression on his face is serious, but I hope he'll let it go.

"Either you get in my car voluntarily, or we're going to have to do this the hard way."

The hard way? He sounds like a cheesy cartoon villain. "Xavier, I don't have time for this. I need to get to school."

He doesn't block me as I try to open the driver's side door on my car. When I think I'm going to get away, I feel a cold hand cover my mouth and pin my arms.

Panicking, I frantically kick my legs out, trying to pull myself away from whoever has me. Xavier only stands by, waiting.

When I manage my breathing and stop thrashing around, he speaks.

"We're doing this the hard way, I guess. Make one more noise, and we'll cover your head with a plastic bag," he says. "Now, give me your phone. You can thank Casey for this later."

I only stare at him. What has Casey done to him? He's crazy if he thinks I'm giving my phone up.

"Lacey, don't make this harder than it has to be," he says, sounding bored.

I let my anger get the best of me. "Eat shit."

His hard hand across my cheek stings more than the slap Kay has given me.

Shock runs through me, and I don't know why I'm surprised that he hit me.

Xavier grabs my face and forces me to look at him. "I'm done playing games. I've given you too many chances. Now we're playing by my rules. Phone. Now."

One of my arms is released, and I reach into my pocket and shove my phone into his chest.

"Put her in the car."

The hands from his friend wrap around my torso, and the scream that wants to come out doesn't. I'm thrown into the backseat while Xavier and his friend sit up front. Xavier is sitting on the passenger side, glaring out the window. The expression reminds me of Dylan, making me wonder what could possibly go on in this psycho's mind.

"Where are we going?" I ask them, hoping I'll get an answer.

Xavier rubs the bridge of his nose like he's annoyed.

398

He gives his friend a look, and the friend jumps out of the car. He opens the door to the backseat, and my mind goes in a million directions. The duct tape in his hand makes my eyes water. He roughly places a giant piece over my mouth as I struggle to get away from him.

During the drive, I hold my cheek and try not to cry as much. I sit back in the seat as the world seems to blur by outside the window.

*   *   *

It feels like hours since Xavier kidnapped me. He has ripped the duct tape from my mouth and has strapped me to a metal folding chair, with my hands behind me, in the middle of what looks like an abandoned warehouse. Old pipes are exposed at the ceiling, and the ground is covered in muddy water.

I'm the spectacle in the middle of a giant room. My scarf fell off at some point while I was being taken here, and I'm freezing without it. With no heat in the room, I'm mostly getting my warmth from the adrenaline pumping through me. There has to be a way out somehow.

Xavier has been bothering me to call Casey for him, and when I refuse, he slaps me. When he comes to me with a phone call from Casey, I still refuse him. Both cheeks are stinging, but I'm not going to get Casey here for him. He's left me alone for a little bit, and I wonder how I'm going to get out. Will anyone notice I'm gone? Will they help me?

When Xavier comes back in, I take my opportunity to irritate him. As long as I don't call Casey, she won't show up. Anything to keep her away, I'll do.

"What is it with Casey?" I ask him. "You know she doesn't want to talk to you."

"And that's why you're here." He's pacing around me. "I don't get it."

399

"Get what?"

"You left Casey in the dark, yet I'm the one she gave up on," he says, walking behind me. "I was there for her. Keeping her company while you ran off with your pretty-boy boyfriend. She hated him, you know."

I've never sensed hatred from her while I'm dating Jacob.

"How do you know?"

"She'd come over to my house and talk about another one of your dates with him. I think she resented you at one point. Constantly leaving her while you were off having fun."

The guilt is settling inside me, and I hate it. Was I really that bad of a friend to her in the beginning of my relationship with Jacob?

"She'd come to me when she felt left out. She told me she felt like you didn't even want her in your life anymore." He grabs my shoulders from behind and speaks into my ear. "That's what she should have done."

He's trying to wedge us apart, just like he's done with Dylan.

"You disappointed her more than I did," I say through my teeth. "I didn't even know about you until months ago. You clearly aren't that important to her."

The chair is yanked back and my head lands on the cold ground with a thud, causing me to blink away the black spots. Landing on my tied hands has tears coming out of my eyes. Something pulls in my shoulder and my wrist feels twisted.

"Clearly I am because she's on her way now," he says, standing over me. "I always get what I want. I want you out of the picture, and Casey back in my life."

I'm about to talk back, but I bite my tongue and focus on something else other than him and the throbbing pain in my wrist. I close my eyes and let my thoughts wander.

My parents.

I can see them standing on the porch of our house, arms around each other and smiling. They see me and open their arms for a hug. I feel myself being pulled towards them.

They're ripped away when I feel myself being lifted off the ground. I'm sitting upright again, and more tears stream down my warm cheeks.

I was so close to them. It was like they weren't gone and everything was fine.

But everything isn't fine. I'm tied to a chair, Casey is somehow on her way, and I can't protect her.

"No more smartass comments," Xavier says.

At the slightest bit of struggle, a sharp pain is sent up my arm from my wrist. I wince when Xavier has my face in his hand.

He grins. "No more games. I don't want to hear anything else from you until she gets here. That's when the real fun begins."

"Screw you." I spit in his face and he backs off, wiping the saliva off.

He lets out a laugh before he backhands me once more. I don't bother meeting his eyes, instead letting my head hang downwards.

His footsteps trail behind me before a door slams.

I'm alone again.

CHAPTER TWENTY-SIX

My cheeks are warm, swollen from Xavier's slaps. My wrist stings whenever I make any movement. My head is hanging off to the side, with my hair providing as curtains to hide my face.

I'm humiliated.

Xavier's three friends come and go, amused that I'm tied up helplessly. It makes me think of Dylan, and whether he was one of them to some other girl. Did Xavier regularly have girls tied up?

They poke and make crude comments to me. The blond one in particular is laughing especially hard, probably at how weak I must look.

Feeling weak has become a regular part of my life, but this is a different kind of weak. I hate that I need to depend on someone else to help me. I want to save myself, but I don't think it'll happen.

The door opens behind me, and I brace myself for more violence from Xavier, except there are lighter footsteps along with heavier ones. I lift my head just as two figures step into my view.

Xavier has Kay with him, and it feels like she has commited the ultimate betrayal. Of course she has never been on my side. It's her brother after all.

Her hair is curled at the ends, giving her a glossy look. I hate how she always looks put together, especially when I look like I've come from a well.

"You said you were done with this shit," she says to him, avoiding my eyes. "You're going to have the cops on your ass in no time."

"I've got it covered." He crosses his arms, sounding calm.

"I'm sick of this, Xavier. All this for a girl who doesn't give a shit about you. Who cares if Casey comes or not?" Kay demands from him.

"I do. She owes me."

"She doesn't owe you shit!" Kay yells at him. "Just let her go before things get out of hand."

"Shut your mouth! She'll be here—"

The door opens again and more footsteps come rushing in.

"Lacey, oh my god," Casey's voice rings out as she comes to my side. When I meet her gaze, her eyes widen. "What the hell did you do to her, Xavier?"

"Oh, please. She's fine." He walks towards me, watching my reaction. "We were only having fun."

Another figure appears in my peripherals.

"Just let her go," Dylan says.

He's the one who brought Casey? Anger shoots through me, and I glare at him. "You brought Casey to this psychopath?"

Is he so loyal to Xavier that he'll put Casey in harm's way? I don't want to believe it. Dylan isn't that person. He plays tough, but I didn't think he'd actually do anything to hurt anyone.

He avoids my eyes, but Casey sits in front of me. "No, no, no. It was my choice to come."

"Anyway," Xavier interrupts, "let's talk, Casey."

She stands up and faces him. "What do you want from me? You want my forgiveness? My friendship? Because this is a screwed up way of showing you care about me."

"We're not talking in here. Follow me," he says, clearly trying to stay calm. His temper is flaring, judging by the lines on his forehead.

403

"Bullshit. You're not going anywhere with her." Dylan points at Xavier as he stands between him and Casey.

Xavier pushes Dylan back. "This doesn't concern you, Parker. What part are you playing today? Are you my bitch or Lacey's?"

Xavier doesn't have time to react when Dylan punches him square in the jaw. The other two guys topple to the ground, with Xavier landing on top. All three of Xavier's guys swarm into the room—two go to help Xavier while the blond one grabs Casey.

Casey is kicking and screaming as he drags her out of the room. I'm wiggling as much as I can to break out of the chair. A shooting pain comes from my wrist, but I try to ignore it. Casey is out of sight, but I can hear her struggling.

Dylan is on the ground while Xavier throws punches at his face and the other two try to kick him and hold him down.

Then I feel hands on the rope that have me tied. "Go after Casey when I get this thing untied. I'll help Dylan," Kay's voice comes out in a rush.

Soon, I'm free from the rope. I immediately hold my wrist to stifle the pain. Standing up, I glance over Kay's face.

"Go." She points to the door.

I can't believe she's helping me again, but I don't give myself time to think much of it. I sprint to the door and listen for Casey and the guy who has taken her. I hear her cry out down the narrow hallway. My legs can't move fast enough to her.

Every sound echoes off the walls as I check every room, with no luck. In the very last room, I find Casey thrown on the ground while the blond guy who has taken her has another guy against the wall, trying to choke him.

My eyes widen once I realize it's Jacob he's choking.

I run to Casey's side while a small patch of blood on her forehead forms. Thankfully, she's moving and slightly conscious. I sneak behind the blond guy who has Jacob against the wall. He hasn't seen me yet.

With all my might, I kick between his legs and watch him double over in pain. While he's down, Jacob catches his breath and kicks the guy's stomach over and over until it looks like he passed out.

I crouch down next to Casey and help her sit up against the wall. Jacob kneels next to her and moves her so she's more comfortable. I meet Jacob's eyes; all I can think is how the hell he got mixed in with all of this.

"What the hell are you doing here?" I ask.

"Dylan and Casey went looking for you and I tagged along," he says, wiping the blood from his busted lip.

Casey is rubbing her head and groaning, but her eyes are fluttering open.

"I need to go help Dylan. Stay here with her," I tell Jacob.

I run out back into the hallway and slam into a hard figure. Xavier's arms wrap around me before I can fight against him.

"You're coming with me," he says, dragging me back into the room while the other two guys go after Casey and Jacob.

Dylan and Kay are both tied up and sitting on the floor. Kay's head is hanging. Dylan is staring down Xavier as he pushes me into the chair.

Xavier grips my throat and I struggle to breathe. Pain shoots from my wrist as I try to push his hand away. Sounds of Dylan yelling at Xavier and Kay crying for him to stop fill the room.

"Bring them in here," Xavier calls out.

He lets go of my throat and I gasp for air. He pulls out a black gun from his waistband before I can fully catch my breath. My heart feels like it's going into overdrive, like I might pass out at any moment. There's no way Xavier would use the gun, would he?

His guys pull Jacob and Casey into the room with the blond guy trailing slowly behind them.

The blond guy speaks up when he sees Xavier's gun. "I thought we were just going to scare them," he says to Xavier. "You didn't say anything about shooting them."

"Jesus Christ, just shut up," Xavier says sharply, pointing the gun in his direction.

The blond guy holds his hands up. Xavier, switching his attention, waltzes up to Casey and touches her face like she's a porcelain doll. Jacob becomes a statue in his place as he watches.

"Get away from her!" Dylan yells at Xavier.

Xavier ignores him. "See what happens when you don't follow the rules?" he asks Casey. He stares at her without saying anything, and it makes me uncomfortable. It's like he's looking at his last meal. "Why did you give up on me?" he suddenly yells into her face.

Casey doesn't flinch. "You left me!" she screams back.

I'm surprised at her anger, especially since he's holding the gun close to her. She always tells me she wants nothing to do with Xavier, but the hurt in her voice tells me it's more than that.

"I loved you," she tells him, "but when I told you that, you wanted nothing to do with me."

The room is dead silent, and I wish I could make it all go away. Go away for Casey, for Dylan, for Jacob, and for Kay.

"How can you love me and be with other guys? Huh?" he demands.

"I got over you. I knew you were never going to be the same after your dad died. You are not the same person I was in love with," she cries harder than I've ever seen her cry.

I look over at Kay, who is weeping behind her hair. Why didn't she say anything about their dad when I mentioned my parents to her?

"Don't you talk about him," Xavier says, pointing the gun at Casey.

"No!" I scream at him, but I'm too frozen to move. I can't let him hurt Casey.

Kay perks up. Her tears are black from her mascara, ruining her perfect makeup. "Just stop it, Xavier. What would dad say?"

"Shut the fuck up, Kay!" he shouts at her.

Casey isn't done with him yet from the looks of it. With the gun pointed at her, she says, "You're never going to make him proud like this, and I will *never* love you again." Her words drip like venom.

Xavier's eyes are black with rage. I know what he's about to do. I jump from the chair to push Casey out of the way just as a gunshot reverberates throughout the room, stinging my ears.

Time slows down, or at least my perception of it, when people in black swarm into the room. They have guns pointed in all directions, and commands of putting our hands in the air come from every direction.

While laying on the ground, my vision starts blacking out. I hear Casey screaming my name and see blood on her hands after she touches my shoulder. There's shouting all around. Dylan is on my other side, looking panicked.

"Oh, God, Lacey," he says, his hands still tied. "Just relax, okay? Just breathe for me. It's going to be okay."

I try to speak, but then the pain encompasses my body. The burning in my shoulder. Jesus Christ, it hurts like hell.

"Stand back," a gruff voice suddenly says.

Casey and Dylan are being pulled away from me, despite their protests. I make an attempt to sit up, but the man behind the gruff voice holds me down.

"Hold on, hun. The medics will be here soon. Just stay with me."

I feel my body getting colder, especially as more of the liquid drenches my long sleeve. Someone kneels down next to the gruff voice, and I hear the words. Gunshot wound.

Then it all happens so fast. They put me on a stretcher and roll me out of the building. The blanket they put over me does little to stop the cold outside air from hitting me.

Before they put me in the ambulance, I can vaguely see Xavier being shoved into the back of a cruiser. Then I hear my name from Casey and Dylan, but I can't see them. Where did the other guys go? Where's Jacob?

A medic is beginning to wrap my shoulder and the pain makes me cry out.

"Hang on, we're heading to the hospital right now, okay?" Her voice barely registers.

I want to respond, but my voice is stuck in my throat. Spots cloud my vision, and I feel myself drift in and out of consciousness until everything is black.

*   *   *

My body is cold and stiff. My mouth must have cotton in it or something because there's no moisture inside. When I finally open my eyes, I see my aunt sitting next to me.

But we're not in my room or anywhere I recognize.

"Hey," my aunt speaks softly. "How are you feeling?"

Instead of answering, I try to sit up. There's a stinging pain in my right shoulder, and I feel something hard on my right wrist. I can see a cast with a sling wrapped around my entire arm.

"What day is it?" I ask her.

"Sunday," she says, seemingly distracted. "I've only heard bits and pieces of what happened, Lacey. What were you doing there? And with Casey, Dylan, and Jacob? What were you all doing there?" she asks, leaning closer to me, practically on the verge of tears.

It all comes back to me—Xavier kidnapping me; Casey, Dylan, and Jacob being there; and Kay helping me.

Xavier shooting me.

"Where's Casey?" I immediately ask, ignoring her questions. "Is she okay?"

"She's fine," she says softly patting my arm. "Talk to me, Lacey. What happened out there?"

All the things I tried to hide from her have caught up to me. Everything has to come out.

From Dylan and Kay, to Casey and Xavier, to even me and Jacob, I tell her everything. She listens intently, only stopping me to clarify some things. Then, when I finish with the events at the warehouse, she takes a deep breath.

"How did this become your life?" she asks, holding my arm and letting a tear roll down her cheek.

"I thought I was handling it fine."

"I don't even know what to think," she says. "It sounds insane."

Tell me about it. I didn't think it was that crazy until I spewed everything out to her. It's insane, there's no logic behind it all.

"I can't believe all of this was happening and I had no idea." There is a distant look on her face. "Never did I think that something like that would happen to you under my care or that you would end up in the hospital because of something I didn't know about."

She's starting to scare me. Instead of sounding like the aunt I've always known, she sounds like my mom. My mom was always more responsible and a little stricter than my aunt.

More tears come out of her eyes. "I didn't expect to lose my sister so soon or take care of her daughter by myself. And look where you are. In a hospital bed because I didn't take care of you."

"Don't believe that for a second," I tell her. "It's my fault." I'm the one who went behind her back to go through everything. If anything, I abused her trust.

"Your parents would be so disappointed in me." She pulls some tissue out of her purse and wipes her tears.

My mom and I were close to the point where I would usually tell her everything. It's my fault that my aunt is blaming herself because I didn't want to tell her everything. As horrible as it is, the fact that she isn't my mom crosses my mind all the time. Now, she's blaming herself for not taking care of me.

"I didn't mean for any of this to happen," I say softly. "It's on me, and I completely understand if you want to ground me for the next five months."

"You want me to ground you after you've been shot?" She lets out a laugh as she wipes more tears away. "I just want you to talk to me if something like this ever happens, and I pray nothing like this happens to you again."

Hearing the words makes it a little more real. I was shot in the shoulder.

"How bad is it?" I ask her.

"You went into surgery right away. You were bleeding more than they anticipated, but the bullet missed your major arteries thankfully. Your clavicle is broken though. The recovery process might take a while for that. Your wrist is also broken, so that'll need time to heal too."

Great. Just great.

There's movement at the front of the room. Casey is standing at the door with her arms crossed. She's dressed down in sweatpants and a hoodie. With her hair up in a bun, the bandage on her forehead is clearly visible.

My aunt pats my arm. "I'll go get the nurse."

She stands up and puts her hand on Casey's shoulder as she passes her. Casey walks over to my aunt's chair and sits down.

"How are you feeling?" she asks me.

"Could be better. How's your head?"

"It would be better if I didn't have this hideous Band-Aid on." She rolls her eyes. "I can't wear a cute outfit because of it."

I shake my head and laugh. Same old Casey. "You can't make it work?"

"Nothing matches it." She laughs slightly.

"How did it happen?" I never got to ask her how she got the cut in the first place. I'd only walked in after seeing Jacob being pinned by the guy.

She sighs, putting her elbow on the bed and resting her chin in her hand. "That guy pulled me into the room and pushed my head against the wall. I guess that's when Jacob came in and started fighting him."

That brings me to my next thought. "Have you heard from Dylan?"

She shakes her head. "After they brought you here, they took Kay to the police station. She told them Dylan had nothing to do with anything that Xavier did, that it was all him and his friends," she explains. "Kay is the one who called the police right after she untied you."

Kay is the real hero. She called the cops and went against her own brother.

There's still a story there that I'm curious about. Xavier and Kay's dad is apparently dead. It sounds like that's what set Xavier on a warpath and also the fact that Casey wants nothing to do with him. I've probably made things worse too.

Casey remains quiet. She looks down at my sling and starts to cry, putting her head on the edge of the bed.

"Lace, you have no idea how scared I was. I thought Xavier—I thought he killed you."

Tears sting my own eyes as she sobs and I blink mine away.

"You took a bullet for me," she says, meeting my eyes finally. "How can I ever thank you enough?"

I don't know what I would've done if Casey was shot and not me. What if she was killed? I can't even imagine my life without her.

What if I was killed?

The severity of the situation is hitting me. It was dangerous to fight Xavier. I underestimated him. Now, I'll have the scars to remind me for the rest of my life.

CHAPTER TWENTY-SEVEN
Part One

Two Months Later

Prom is never something I get excited for. I never see the point in going, even more so now that I don't have a date. I only went for my junior year mostly because I had Jacob to go with.

Casey manages to convince me that prom will be a nice way of forgetting everything that's happened, and she drags me to go dress shopping with her. I want to go for something simple. The need to dress-to-impress isn't at the top of my priority list. If I can find something plain, then it's perfect.

While Casey is in the dressing room, I see a familiar face shopping nearby. Kay is wearing a t-shirt and some skinny jeans, flicking through the clearance dresses.

Kay has been elusive after the incident with Xavier. I've tried many times to talk to her, but she can never meet up. Either she comes up with excuses or she doesn't respond at all.

Now's my chance to talk to her.

I stride up to her and point to a dress. "That one is nice."

Her eyes meet mine and they widen a bit once she realizes it's me. Her eyes flicker to my shoulder for a split second.

413

"Hey, Lacey," she says, casually going back to the clearance rack.

"Listen, Kay, I want to say—"

"I know. You want to thank me for saving the day, as you've said in your many text messages and voicemails, which makes me want to change my number," she says sharply.

I take a step back and really look at her. Is she trying to go back to the old Kay? She's the one who called the police on Xavier. Why is she being cold to me?

She sighs. "I'm no hero. I called the cops because I knew Xavier was going to do something stupid, and I didn't want to be a part of it. Do you know how that feels? To call the cops on your own brother? My brother is an idiot clearly, but he's still family," she says, gripping on to the dress in her hand.

Xavier would do anything for Kay, and she probably would do the same. It has to be hard to turn your own brother in. I don't know exactly how she's feeling, but I can feel the pain coming off her.

"I don't know what he's going to be like when he gets out, but for now, I just want to buy a damn prom dress and enjoy what I have left of high school," she says.

I just need to drop the subject. She doesn't want to talk about it, and I should've taken the hint after the first two messages I sent her. "Do you want to shop with me and Casey? She's in the dressing room."

She hesitates. "I don't think I can see her right now." She gives me a small smile. "But thanks."

I nod and it seems like she's going to leave, but she stops herself.

"Have you heard from Dylan?" she asks me.

I shake my head.

"I talked to him a couple of weeks ago, and he made it very clear he isn't interested in me." She laughs a bit. "I wasn't trying to get him back. Just wanted to see if he was okay. I know Dylan isn't for me, and I've accepted it already."

"Maybe he isn't for me either." I shrug. "I don't know." Hearing that she talked to Dylan recently has me slightly jealous. He's not into her, but he still talked to her before he talked to me.

"Shut up." She rolls her eyes. "You two actually make me sick from how in love you both are."

Kay throws around the word love like it's plain and simple, but it isn't.

"I'll see you around, Lacey. Don't blow up my phone, and maybe I'll actually want to hang out with you." She smirks before walking off.

Dylan hasn't spoken to me once since the warehouse incident. I've talked to Anthony and Reece, but neither of them let me in on Dylan's business. I've seen him around school, but he avoids me like I'm a walking plague. I don't know why he wants to stay away from me, but it's driving me crazy.

I overheard a conversation between Anthony and Reece that Dylan's mom is in town again. Part of me wants to know how everything is going with her around.

Kay is right. My feelings for Dylan haven't gone away, and they seem to have grown stronger despite not speaking to him for two months. Dylan and I have been separated by Xavier and Kay before, but what's kept us apart for two months? Does he not feel the same anymore?

Casey finally steps out of the dressing room in a long light-pink, almost white gown. The bottom half is an A-line, and the top is similar to a corset but with delicate floral lace lining it. It's almost too simple for her.

"I think this is the one," she says excitedly, clasping her hands together before looking at herself in the long mirror.

"Really?" I ask.

She cocks her head slightly. "You don't like it?"

"I love it," I say quickly. "I was just expecting something, I don't know, more Jessica Rabbit-style."

She twists her face and shakes her head. "I really like the simplicity of this one. I know I always like to go for the show-stoppers, but I think I'll tone it down this time."

She has no desire shopping with the goal of looking like a glowing flower. There's nothing she wants to live up to. It's like she's come in with the same attitude I have, which is whatever at this point. If the simple gown is what she wants, then she's going to get it.

"It's gorgeous on you," I tell her. Any dress she puts on is like it's meant for her, but especially this one.

"However," she holds up her finger, "I do want you to find something outside the box."

How did I know there's going to be a catch? "Casey, that's not—"

"I don't want to hear it." She shakes her head. "You always choose a safe option. I saw something over there that I think you'll like, and it has that wow factor."

She rushes back into the dressing room to change and soon she runs out, setting her dress on the small chair. She heads toward another rack off to the side. The monstrous red thing she's bringing just about consumes her as she hands it to me.

"What the hell is this?" I ask. It's too poofy and not me.

"Trust me, it's going to look great on you." She gives me a thumbs-up.

I don't want to hurt her feelings. I'm not expecting to find one on our first day of shopping, even though prom is in four days. I figure I can find something on the clearance rack that will do just fine.

When I step into the poorly lit dressing room, I glance at myself in the mirror. I've been makeup free since the incident with Xavier. My eyebrows are severely unplucked, something I'll enlist Casey's help for, and my pale face has practically no dimension.

The bun on my head is already loose from walking around, as stray strands are falling on my face.

Then there's the scar on my shoulder. Just last week, I took my sling off. I have to keep my shoulder moving now to determine whether or not I'll need physical therapy. My wrist is free from its cast, so things have been feeling a little more normal.

I shift my attention to the dress, which is actually two pieces made with red satin. I start peeling off my clothes and folding them on the small bench. The scar on my shoulder is still a little fresh and ugly, so I feel a little insecure. I don't really want it on full display, but I push those thoughts out for now.

After slipping on the skirt, which has a flared out A-line, I pull on the top. It's a cropped tank top with a low neckline. There's slight discomfort in my muscle as I fix the top, but I remember I have to keep moving it.

I maneuver the dress, so I can see myself in the mirror again. It's a little overpowering, but Casey is right. It actually looks really nice on me.

Coming out of the dressing room is a little difficult. The dress is longer than me, and I'm trying my best to not trip over the skirt. Casey gasps dramatically when she sees me.

"Holy shit." She puts her hand over her mouth. "You are literally a Disney princess."

I laugh at how ridiculous that sounds. Never in my life have I wanted to look like a princess, but I have to admit, the dress is growing on me the longer I wear it.

"You're crazy if you don't get this one," she says. "If you don't buy it, I'm buying your whole wardrobe for your New York trip."

New York City is creeping up on me, and it's making me nervous—nervous for graduation, nervous for what will come after graduation, and nervous for anything beyond that.

417

"As tempting as that is, I don't know. I feel like I'm cheating or something. I haven't even tried on any other dresses." For now, I need to focus on the prom and not New York.

She leans back in her chair. "By all means, try on other dresses. I don't think they'll be as nice as this one."

Trying on a few more won't hurt. After I change out of the red dress, I pull a few more from the racks and take them into the dressing room. Casey doesn't turn them down when I walk out to show them, but she doesn't have the same reaction as when she saw the first dress.

I take two more dresses into the dressing room and stare at them. The red dress is hanging in the corner, its aura engulfing me. Not how I pictured my prom dress would look for my senior year.

During my junior year, I wore a strapless black dress. The red is more daring somehow, and I'm reminded of what I told myself at the beginning of the year. I told myself I was going to be happier, stronger, and more confident.

The red dress it is.

*   *   *

I came up with a plan for Thursday.

After buying the red prom dress, I decided to follow what I said on the first day of senior year. I'm not going to let any boy ruin anything for me. I've been stuck on a roller coaster of mixed emotions the whole year, and I can't take it any longer.

Waiting for someone, specifically Dylan, to express how they're feeling isn't cutting it. If Dylan is truly in love with me as Kay says, then he needs to own up to those feelings instead of avoiding me.

And I need to face how I feel about him.

After school, Dylan always races to his car and leaves before I even get to mine. I need him alone, so he won't be able to brush me off.

I enlist the help of Anthony, who is all in for my plan. We skip our last periods and rush to the parking lot just before school ends.

He pulls out his wire hanger and says, "Let's do this." He bends the wire, so he can stick it inside Dylan's car to unlock it.

I keep watch, making sure no security guards catch us. It's a serious crime, breaking into someone's car, but it's not like we're trying to steal it. I only need to get in, hide in the back seat, and wait for the right moment to talk and possibly scare Dylan.

After a few minutes, Anthony gets the door open. He gives me a high five before I slip into the back seat. I hide on the floor behind the driver's seat. Anthony says, "Perfect. Dylan won't even see you."

"Thanks, Anthony." I give him a smile. "I really appreciate it."

"Hell yeah." He nods. "Go get your boy."

"You'll give my keys to Casey, right?"

He gives me a thumbs-up before he shuts the door. I quickly lock it from the inside. I put myself back in position and wait. The bell will ring soon, so I calm myself down and rehearse what I want to say in my head.

As I wait, I glance around at Dylan's slightly dirty back seat. It's littered with a couple of water bottles and some receipts. I try not to be too curious, but one receipt catches my eye. It's from a local jewelry store. I move to reach for it, but I hear voices outside of the car.

Dylan and Anthony's voices specifically stand out. Dylan mentions something about going home before I hear the locks moving. The door opens and the car shifts as Dylan sits in the driver's seat. He shuts the door behind him, and the sound of the car turning on makes my heart race.

Suddenly, it's clear that I have to make my move fast. Dylan is a horrible driver when he's by himself. He takes multiple sharp turns out of the parking lot, causing me to be in some

419

uncomfortable positions. I'll have to do this quickly because if I wait any longer, I might actually need that physical therapy. I can't jump out while he's driving. He'll probably freak out and crash the car. I wait until I think we're at a red light.

We finally come to a stop, and I quickly sit up. I crawl up into the back seat and meet Dylan's eyes in the rearview mirror before I can actually say anything.

"What the fuck?" His head snaps toward me. "Lacey, what the fuck are you—how long have you been there?"

His voice is urgent and confused. I smile to myself, knowing that he had no idea I've been in the car this whole time.

"We need to talk," I say to him. "Go. The light is green."

He faces forward again and starts driving. I buckle myself in the backseat and look at him through the rearview mirror again.

"You couldn't just talk to me in the hall like a normal person?" he asks.

"Dylan, you run away from me every time I see you in the hall. This is seriously the last resort," I say, gesturing around me. "I made myself a promise at the beginning of the year that I wasn't going to let a boy ruin my senior year. I thought it was going to be Jacob torturing me, but it's not."

Dylan shifts in his seat and takes his eyes away from me. I lean forward in my own seat, so I can look at him.

"What are you trying to say?" he asks finally.

"I'm saying, I've been waiting this whole time for you to come to me and say you want to be with me, but you haven't. Either you don't want to be with me anymore or you're scared."

He scoffs. "Scared?"

Why is he acting like the confused one? "Maybe you're scared of being in a relationship, or maybe you're still scared of Xavier, I don't know. All I know is Kay and Xavier are no longer a problem, and not talking to you has me wondering if you even like me anymore." I'm starting to rant, so I stop.

420

A long sigh comes out of him, and his eyes stay on the road. I stay quiet as he drives us.

He takes roads that lead to an old park. He pulls into the parking lot and finds a spot away from other cars.

"Come up here," he says, motioning to the passenger side.

I unbuckle and crawl to the front, getting twisted up as I squeeze by. I stretch my arm out, rubbing my shoulder. Planted in the seat, I find Dylan gazing at me with that unreadable expression that I hate.

"Why do you always look at me like that?" I ask him.

"Like what?"

"I don't know. I have no idea what you're thinking whenever you have that face."

He laughs. "And you know what I'm thinking when I'm not making it?"

I shrug. He's getting too invested in what I notice about him.

The small smile disappears, and he drags his hands down his face. "You want to know what I'm thinking?" he asks. He continues without an answer from me. "I'm thinking it's entirely my fault that you were shot and got your wrist broken. You could've died, Lacey, you know that? I wouldn't have been able to live with myself if you—"

He shakes his head like he can't bring himself to say it.

"I'm not dead, Dylan." I look at him straight on. "Also, that bullet wasn't even meant for me. I still would've done it if the gun was pointing at you or Anthony or even Kay."

"But I got you into that whole situation."

I know what he's getting at, but I won't let him blame himself. "You can't change the past. What's done is done."

He shakes his head like he can't believe we're having this conversation. "What else do you need to tell me, or can this wait until tomorrow?"

421

"No, I need to say this now," I say. My heart is pounding so hard in my chest, and I realize how close we are to each other. I haven't felt this way since we talked in the bathroom at Reece's cabin.

This is different.

Seeing Kay has pushed me to really confront how I feel about Dylan. There's never been a time when it felt unnatural or forced with him. It happened so suddenly and beautifully that I never truly processed it. It hurts to see him in the hall, only for him to run off in the opposite direction. It's agony.

I can finally admit it to myself.

"I'm in love with you."

Hearing the words come out of my mouth is like unbuttoning tight pants after eating a shit ton of food. The relief is instant, and it feels great.

I can't stop myself from smiling. Dylan can say whatever he wants, but I'm proud of myself for taking charge. "I've always told myself that I don't need a guy in my life to make me feel whole. I still don't. It's just . . . things fell into place easier when you came along."

Dylan's expression gives no clue as to what he's thinking. Then he says, "Do you really mean that?"

I laugh, despite how nervous I am. "Dylan, I wouldn't have had Anthony help me break into your car if I didn't."

"So that's how you did it." He taps his chin. "I should've known."

"Well, now you're kind of hopping around the subject," I say. I was feeling carefree when I admitted I'm in love with him, but I really care about what his response will be.

Dylan covers his mouth, but I detect a smile underneath. "I think I've been in love with you longer."

My heartbeat speeds up, but I find myself laughing. "Are you trying to make this into a competition?"

"I'm just saying." He finally lets his smile come through.

422

It's been a while since I've seen him smile. Seeing it again, I feel warm and giddy on the inside.

"Well, since you're here," he says, "I need to ask you something."

Part Two

DYLAN

How the hell did I get to a point where I feel like I need someone in my life? I never needed anyone—not the guys, not Anthony, and not even Derrick. Having Kay around wasn't a need, it was more of a want at the time.

I can't be with Lacey knowing I put her in danger. I was the one who got involved with all of Xavier's shit, and Lacey was unlucky enough to be dragged into it when I wanted to avoid that.

The summer before school and before senior year started, I was fine. I had it somewhat good with Xavier, and even though things got a little rocky when I went after Kay, it was all okay. As long as I didn't break Kay's heart, or did anything to intentionally hurt her, I was in good shape.

Then school started, and English suddenly became one of my favorite subjects.

Of course, I was guilty as hell in playing a part of her ex cheating on Lacey. I know I'm not to blame, but I didn't know how to tell her or if telling her was even a good idea.

Helping her get over him was part of my plan to make it easier on her, but it was outright selfish because I knew I wanted her. And she needed to get over that dude anyway.

Having Lacey around the guys and having them actually enjoy having her around was a surprise. They didn't like Kay mostly because of Xavier but also because of her bitch personality. Lacey to them, I think, was a breath of fresh air.

And she is.

Bringing her around the guys was fun for me until it stopped being fun. I was annoyed when Carlos would dance and sing with her, and it felt like he was rubbing it in my face. He was taking it too far, and I know he only wanted to get into her pants.

When Derrick and the guys told me about what Carlos said about me when I wasn't around, it irritated the shit out of me. I confronted him and gave him the chance to step up. He didn't, of course.

I didn't expect to develop feelings for Lacey. Shit, I surprised myself when we became friends. It scares me how everything is so . . . natural? That sounds really weird, but it's true. I'll never admit it, though.

Everything that's gone down with Xavier is in the past. I don't want to think about it, I just want to move on.

A week after the incident and after ignoring Lacey's many messages, I drove to her apartment. I wasn't sure what I wanted to say. If I should apologize for everything or what. When I got there, I couldn't do anything. Her car was there, but seeing it made me uneasy.

I caused so much shit to go down in her life that she didn't need, and I couldn't face her for it. She's been through enough, and adding me to the picture would only make it worse.

So I left. I made the decision to stop talking to her. I couldn't look at her without seeing her bruised face, broken wrist, and bloody shoulder. That image haunts me.

And I've made it worse for myself. I still haven't deleted the text messages we shared before everything went bad I still haven't taken down the "Be Mine?" that is written in the lights above my bed, and I'm left staring at them every night when I turn them on.

Of course I had to tell my dad what happened with Xavier, and I had to tell Ethan that things aren't going to work out with Lacey. Derrick only shakes his head; he knows the truth. We've argued about it plenty of times, with him saying I'm not trying hard enough.

Then, as if the universe is trying to tell me something, my mom came home.

I guess Dad told her what happened with me, and it prompted her to make another visit. As much as I want to hate her for being gone, I can't.

I know I should be upset when she leaves. Ethan would cry for her to stay, while Derrick tries to be understanding to her. Me, I'm left in the middle. I know if she tries be a full-time mom, everything will be different. The house has a dynamic that was able to survive without her.

She's in the living room, helping Ethan with his homework while Dad and Derrick went to look at guitars.

I walk up the stairs to the kitchen to get some water. She sees me and stands up from her spot with Ethan at the table.

"How you feeling?" she asks.

"Fine."

I don't want to tell her everything because what will she do? Retain the information then leave like I can solve it myself?

She purses her lips and crosses her arms. Her short black hair hangs by her face before she tucks some of it behind her ear. "You want to talk about it?"

Ethan suddenly barges in and goes straight to the fridge for a water bottle. He stands between me and mom as he gulps it all down before burping.

"Don't burp in front of girls," I scold him.

"It's just Mom," he says. Then he looks away. "I bet Lacey would've laughed."

Before I can say anything, he rushes back into the living room. Mom gives me a look.

426

"I keep hearing about this Lacey, but not from you. It sounds like everyone in the house likes her," she says.

"Yeah," I say. It's hard not to like Lacey.

She grabs my hand. "Sit with me for a minute."

Instead of yanking my hand back, I let her lead me to the dining table. She sits at the head of the table, where Dad usually sits, and I plop down next to her.

"I met your dad in college and thought he was a clown at first." She chuckles. "But he grew on me, even though I wasn't looking to date anyone at the time. Then things happened so quickly. We had Derrick, we had you, then Ethan came along. You are the best kids a mom can ever ask for."

I bite down on my tongue to stop myself from asking why she's always leaving if we're really the best kids.

She hesitates before talking again. "I know this will sound awful, but there's no other way to put it. I felt like I was missing out on life. I didn't travel. I didn't have a chance to see other places like I planned before I met your dad."

I guess I never thought to ask why she leaves. I was too busy being pissed off that she was gone all the time.

"And he understood that. Leaving was hard, and it still is, but I want something to tell my grandkids about when I'm older. I don't want to say I stayed home and did nothing. I want to tell them about the time I went to Boston or New York or even Alabama. And now that you're older, I want you to understand why."

I don't say anything. How do you respond to something like that?

"I see Derrick thriving with Jared and their band, and I know they're going places." She nods as she says it. "I want to know if you want to get out of here too."

"What are you asking me?" I ask her.

"I'm staying for your graduation and as a present, I'll take you anywhere you want. I've talked to your dad and he's fine with it. I've got money saved up, so you choose where you want to go and I'll take you there."

It's a lot to process. She's really giving me the option to take off with her after graduation? Getting out of town would be perfect, but where would I go?

It feels like news I want to share. I want to tell Lacey, but I can't just tell her I'm going to leave after not speaking to her for a whole two months. That doesn't sit right with me.

What's my excuse? If I love Lacey so much, why am I staying away from her?

"Okay," I agree. "But can you help me with something first?"

*　　*　　*

I have everything planned out. I'll go home, get the box with her necklace, and surprise her at home, telling her how I feel about her. I'll ask her to be my prom date, then ask her to be my girlfriend.

Again.

I jump into my car, and my heart is racing. I don't know why I'm so nervous. I've asked Lacey to be my girlfriend before. I mean I'm really in love with her, so maybe that's the difference. At a stop light, I can't help but imagine what her reaction will be. Will she like the necklace?

Then it's like I'm really looking at her.

Her face is in my rearview mirror, and I'm just about to shit my pants. "What the fuck? Lacey, what the fuck are you—how long have you been there?"

I listen to her talk about what went down with Xavier and how she's been feeling for the past few months. I feel somewhat relieved to know that her feelings haven't gone away either.

I can't help but state the obvious that I played a huge part in her getting shot and getting her wrist broken. I still have nightmares about that day. I never want to see her like that again.

And teasing her comes naturally, of course. I don't like it when things get too serious. She climbs to the front seat after I park the car. I can't believe she's here in the first place.

"What else did you need to tell me, or can this wait until tomorrow?" I ask her, knowing she'll get impatient with me.

"No, I need to say this now."

Whatever she has to say, she can't beat what I'm going to tell her.

"I'm in love with you."

Okay, she beat me to it.

Hearing the words come out of her mouth has my heart pounding in my chest.I'm not going to tell her I love her until the perfect moment. It surprises me that she's so ready to say it, considering the year she's had with Jacob.

Then she starts talking again. "I've always told myself that I don't need a guy in my life to make me feel whole. I still don't. It's just . . . things fell into place easier when you came along."

It's like she's reading my mind of what I want to say to her. Things have just fallen into place perfectly and kind of quickly. "Do you really mean that?" I ask. I don't want her to feel like she's forcing any feelings.

She laughs, and I feel a little more at ease. "Dylan, I wouldn't have had Anthony help me break into your car if I didn't."

Damn it, Anthony. "So that's how you did it. I should've known." I should have told him my plan, so this situation wouldn't have happened. I mean, I didn't expect her to break into my car and say she loves me. It's pretty bold, and I love it.

"Well, now you're kind of hopping around the subject," she says as she tucks a piece of hair behind her ear, clearly getting nervous.

I have to stop myself from smiling like an idiot. "I think I've been in love with you longer."

When I see the smirk on her face, I know I have her.

A laugh comes out of her and she asks, "Are you trying to make this into a competition?"

"I'm just saying," I say. I still have to go along with my plan, but I'll have to make some adjustments now that she's here. If I ask her to prom, I need the necklace, which is at my house. Bringing her to the house will work out okay, but my mom is probably there.

I've met her aunt. She's met my dad. I'm sure she won't mind meeting my mom, especially if I plan on leaving with her after graduation.

"Well, since you're here, I need to ask you something."

Her face shows her eagerness with her cute lip bite.

I take a deep breath before asking, "Do you want to meet my mom?"

She looks relieved, but I can tell she isn't happy with my lack of emotional response. She's spilled her heart out to me, and I'll do the same. I just need it to be perfect.

But she smiles anyway. "Yeah, I'd love to."

After making sure her car situation is okay, I drive us to my house, with the palms of my hands getting sweatier the closer we get there. Asking her to be my girlfriend is one thing. Asking her to be my girlfriend, then telling her I'm leaving after graduation is another thing.

She's also going to have college to focus on. I don't have a plan. I figure I can take a year off, get my head together while working.

"How long has your mom been in town?" she asks, breaking my train of thought.

"Almost three weeks," I tell her.

She stays silent, and I wonder what's going on in her head. She's a heavy thinker, someone who gets wrapped up in their thoughts too much. There's a certain face she makes when the gears in her head are hard at work; that's the face she has right now.

"I have to talk to you about something else too," she says.

It has me a little worried, but I shake my head. "Don't think about anything else. I have a feeling we need to talk about the same thing, so just let it happen."

She nods and noticeably chews on her lip.

I want to take her in my arms and say everything right then and there, but I have a plan. Sticking to it will probably have better results. I can't talk about her going off to college or me leaving or anything else that can bring the mood down.

When I park in front of my house, I get out quickly and jog to Lacey's side of the car, but she's already opened the door before I can do it for her.

The rental car my mom is using is in the driveway, so I brace myself. I have tell my mom what my plan is in brief, so she'll be in for a surprise too.

I open the front door and wait for Ethan to bolt to me like a dog.

His footsteps carry through the house, and instead of running to me, he runs into Lacey's arms while screaming her name.

"I thought you'd never come back!" he says, holding her tightly.

I worry about her shoulder and wrist, so I nudge him away. "Careful, dude."

"I'm so glad you're back," he tells her, stepping back. "Dylan has been moping around the house without you."

I'm going to kill him.

"Oh, has he now?" Lacey asks as she gives me a look.

"Ethan is exaggerating." I can't tell her I really was moping the entire time.

My mom appears at the end of the hallway and makes her way towards us. "I was wondering what all the commotion was in

431

here," she says, glancing over Lacey then looking at me for an explanation.

Before I can say anything, Ethan says, "Mom, this is Lacey."

The realization of who she's looking at is all over her face, and she smiles at Lacey. "So you're the famous Lacey I keep hearing about. It's so nice to meet you."

She takes Lacey in her arms and hugs her while Lacey hugs back.

"Good things, I hope," Lacey says, sounding a little concerned.

"Of course," my mom says. "What brings you kids here?"

The question is directed at me. I can't have her ruin the surprise, so I have to subtly let her know I haven't gone through with the plan yet.

"Um, Lacey and I have a lot to talk about, so we're going to be in my room," I say, moving Lacey slowly towards my bedroom door.

My mom seems to get the hint, so she nods.

"Can I hang out with you guys?" Ethan asks, giving Lacey puppy dog eyes.

Before she can say anything, my mom grabs his shoulders. "Actually, honey, you can help me decide what we're having for dinner."

I pull Lacey into my room before anything else can be said. I'll have to thank my mom for getting Ethan out of my hair.

My room isn't ready for people to be over. I have clothes and homework on the floor, my bed isn't made, and the little box with the necklace is in plain sight.

I turn Lacey around, so she's facing the stairs instead of my room, and I pray she didn't see the box. "Can you face this way for a second while I clean my room?"

She smirks. "I've seen a dirty room before, Dylan. It's nothing new."

432

"Just, please don't turn around," I practically beg her. She's going to ruin even more of my plan, and it's just my luck to have everything not fall in place like I want it to.

"Okay, okay." She laughs.

I rush to shove my clothes in my laundry hamper in the corner and throw my covers over the bed, so they are somewhat presentable. I take the box and shove it in the small gift bag that I bought. Once I'm finished, I say, "Okay, you can turn around."

The bag is in my hands behind my back, so when she turns around, her attention is immediately on me. "What are you hiding?"

A laugh escapes my mouth before I take a deep breath. "You're seriously making this impossible."

She raises a brow and steps towards me. "What are you talking about?"

My heart pounds in my chest again, and I calm myself. I have to be cool about it. "I was going to go to your apartment later today, but you kind of showed up, so now I'm improvising."

"I'm listening," she says, visibly trying to hold back a smile.

It's now or never. "I know I've been an asshole the past few months, and I wasn't doing it to purposely hurt you. I thought taking myself out of your life would make things better because of all the shit I've caused."

"Dylan—"

"Let me finish," I say as I hold a hand up. "I know you're over it, and I want to be over it too. That's why I'm asking if you'll go to prom with me."

Lacey's smile gives me hope that everything will be okay in the end. "Okay," she says, continuing to smile.

I take her in my arms and hug her tightly. "Here." I hold the bag out to her when I let her go.

"You didn't have to get me anything," she says.

I just shrug and watch her open the bag. She pulls out the small, black box and gives me a look. She slowly opens the box and I can't tell what she's thinking.

433

"Dylan, this is beautiful." She takes the necklace from the box.

It's a simple silver necklace with three little diamonds, fake because that's all I can afford, in a row.

She starts reading the little message that comes with the necklace. "Three wishes. Imagine being given three wishes. Place this necklace close to your heart, close your eyes, wish big, and believe."

"Let's just pretend I'm the one who came up with that," I say with a laugh.

She quickly clasps it around her neck. "I love it."

It's time. "I'm glad you like it. I wanted to give it to you at your apartment, but here we are." I scratch the back of my neck.

Shit, what else do I want to say? I had all this rehearsed earlier, and now my brain can't form a simple sentence. "If you don't want to think of them as three wishes, you can always think of them as three words. Any three words, really. Mostly from me to you though. And I don't want you to think I blew you off earlier. I wanted to wait until I gave you the necklace. I'm trying to say the words you can think of are 'I love you,' which is also what I'm trying to tell you, but I fucking suck at this."

That was rough.

But Lacey's lips on mine and her arms around my neck tell me I got it right.

It's been so long since I've held her this close. I can actually enjoy my time with her without worrying about Xavier and Kay. I don't want this moment to end, but I know we'll have plenty of moments like this.

Then the realization hits that I haven't told her I'm leaving.

I let go of her and tuck a piece of hair behind her ear. "I want you to know I really mean every word."

The look on her face is unreadable. I can tell she is slightly skeptical, but she doesn't know why she has to be.

434

"I have to tell you something else," I say, preparing myself. She has something to tell me too, but I'm not sure what it is. "My mom is back to watch me graduate. As a graduation present, she's taking me with her when she leaves."

She tilts her head. "Where are you going?"

"I don't know yet. It's up to me to decide where and for how long."

Instantly, she grabs the necklace and moves it between her fingers. Without looking at me, she says, "I'm leaving after graduation too. Just for the summer though."

"Where to?"

"New York City."

New York City?

Part of me jumps to the conclusion that I can go to New York at the same time as her, but I'm not sure if she wants that. Maybe this is a trip she needs for herself.

"Why there?" I ask instead.

She shrugs. "My aunt picked the place. I think it'll be nice to get out of here for a while." She doesn't meet my eyes, and I can understand.

While I really want to meet her in New York for my trip, it doesn't seem like a good idea. She needs some time for herself.

"Don't feel guilty for wanting this trip to be your own," I say, making sure she knows I'm not mad about it. "You do your thing, I'll do mine, and in the Fall, you can go to school and I can work."

"You're really taking some time off from school?"

I'm guessing she remembers our conversation from a few months ago.

"School isn't exactly at the top of my priority list right now," I say nervously.

"I'll stick with you through whatever, if you'll do the same with me," she says assuringly.

"Always."

I place my lips on hers, and my whole body feels like it's on fire. No other girl has made me feel like this, and I'm glad Lacey is the one who makes me feel this way. I know everything will be okay from this point on. No more pains in the ass like Kay or Xavier.

It's only me and her.

CHAPTER TWENTY-EIGHT

Since Casey and I got ready at her house for homecoming, we're getting ready at my apartment for prom. It doesn't feel real that senior year is coming to an end. It's been a whole journey from the beginning of the year to this moment; where I'm looking at myself in the mirror, dressed up and finally feeling confident in myself.

There is nothing to fake. I don't have to force myself to feel this way. I set a resolution for myself in the beginning, and I've fulfilled it. Feeling completely content with myself and my life is all I've wanted after my parents's accident. They wouldn't want me to wallow in my own self-pity for the rest of my life, and I know my mom would always wants me to feel my best.

My hair is in an elegant updo. I'm wearing some dainty silver earrings that match perfectly with the necklace Dylan has given me. My black heels contrast with the red dress, pulling the look together.

I take a deep breath as Casey walks back into my room from the kitchen. As soon as she checks herself in the mirror, the doorbell rings.

My heart races in my chest, and I pick up my skirt so it doesn't drag as much. I quickly unplug the lights Dylan gave me for my birthday and follow Casey into the living room, where Dylan and Anthony's voices are.

Anthony, who is wearing a black suit, white shirt, and light pink bowtie and vest, whistles when he sees Casey. "You look great," he says, glancing over her.

They look happy together, and I'm not sure if it's a romantic happy or relief now that Xavier is gone.

My thoughts are interrupted by Dylan, who is dressed in an all-black ensemble besides his red tie. My mouth is watering, and I feel utterly embarrassed for it.

He smiles when he sees me. "You are stunning," he says. It's like there's a sheen of amazement over his eyes.

My aunt holds her hand over her heart. "You all look so amazing and so grown up." She scrambles to grab her phone from the kitchen. "Picture time!"

She takes every photo combination possible before she says, "Okay, okay. That's enough from me. You kids go have fun."

Anthony and Casey walk ahead of me and Dylan on the stairs outside of the front door. Dylan puts his hand on the small of my back and leans over to me.

"I did say I love you in red, right?" he whispers in my ear.

"You might've mentioned it." I give him a smile. That didn't influence my decision to get the dress. It occurred to me after buying it that Dylan had mentioned he liked red on me.

Anthony steers Casey towards his car, and I start to walk that way until I see Dylan's car next to it. "We're going separately?" I ask him.

"If you're okay with that."

I nod and wave to Casey before Dylan opens the passenger door for me. Once I have my dress settled, he shuts the door and hops in the driver's side.

"I really love that dress on you," he says to me, grabbing my hand and kissing it.

I feel my stomach tingle. I prepare myself for what I'm about to say, "How would you feel about taking it off of me later?"

I was never overtly sexual with Jacob. He always hinted at doing it again, but I always blew him off because the first and only time we had sex wasn't how I pictured my first time to go. It didn't feel right with him.

With Dylan, since everything else is so natural, I figure sex will be too. I'm ready to try again.

His eyebrows raise, clearly taken off guard by my comment.

I bite my lip and wait for his response. I don't want to say anything else to ruin the mood.

Dylan gapes at me like a fish for a few seconds, before he smirks and lets out a little laugh. "Let's get this damn dance over with then," he says, backing out of the parking lot quickly.

The prom is being held in a hotel ballroom. Dylan finds a parking spot next to Anthony, and we all walk inside together. Everyone is wearing elegant gowns and fancy suits.

We run into Lauren, who is wearing a sapphire number with a high slit. She greets me and Casey before disappearing with another guy. Sophie and Seth are also lingering around the entrance, and I give them both a hug.

The ballroom is decorated with black and white decorations. I can't remember what the theme is, but it looks really sophisticated.

"I give decorations a ten out of ten," Casey says to me. "Better than homecoming."

"Will the music be as good, that's the real question," Anthony points out. "And remind me to stay away from the snack table."

We all laugh at him before finding a table to claim as our own. People are still gathering in the room and meeting up with other friends. Reece finds our table and immediately sits down.

"I feel like a fucking loser without a date," he grumbles.

"You should've asked that blondie in your first period like I told you to," Dylan says, reclining in his seat while putting his arm around me.

"In my defense, she's really intimidating," Reece says.

"You won't ever find a date if you think every girl is intimidating." I laugh at him.

"True." He taps his chin as he says it. He glances around the room before standing up again. "I'll be back."

As he vanishes, Casey grabs my elbow and motions toward the drink table. Understanding she wants to get away for a moment, I say, "We'll go get some drinks."

Dylan sits upright. "Me and Anthony can do it."

"No, we got it." I smile at him before taking Casey away from the table.

While at the drink table, I spot a familiar face.

Jacob is standing off to the side, holding a drink against his chest. He's talking to a pretty brunette. When he sees me, he says something to the girl and walks over.

Disappointment fills me. That girl looked interested in him, and he just left her to talk to me.

"Hey," he says, putting on a bright smile. "You look great."

"Thanks, so do you." He is wearing a simple black suit with no tie, but he does have a silver pocket square. "Who is that?"

"Oh, she's in my Trig class." He waves it off.

I recall the conversation I had with him the day after I got out of the hospital. He was confused by the whole situation, and I felt bad that he got dragged into it all. He should've stayed out of it.

"She's into you," I tell him, escaping my thoughts.

He glances back at her before looking at me. "I know what you're doing."

"What do you mean?"

"You think I haven't moved on yet."

Kind of. "I just want to see you happy."

440

He tips his cup to me. "I'll see you later." He looks at Casey. "Nice seeing you too, Casey."

He walks off, and Casey gives me a look.

"What?" I ask her.

"I don't know what to think about that boy." She shakes her head.

We take the drinks back to the table and talk for a bit as the music gets better. Dylan stands up and grabs my hand.

"Dance with me," he says, smiling.

On the dance floor, we dance to an upbeat song with Anthony and Casey joining us. I feel Dylan behind me, with his hands on my waist. We move to the fast rhythm and I laugh when Anthony busts out some weird moves.

When I look at Dylan, he has possibly the biggest smile ever on his face. I've never seen him so happy and it makes me giddy inside.

A slower song starts playing, and Dylan spins me around so I'm facing him. I wrap my arms around his neck and he does the same around my hips. His lips gently brush against mine, and I feel fireworks in my stomach.

His hands grip onto my waist tightly and they feel like fire against me.

We stay on the dance floor for what feels like forever. It's the first time since my parents's accident that I feel truly happy. Surrounded by my favorite people, I couldn't have asked for a better night.

Once we grow tired of dancing, we sit back down. Anthony, Reece, and Dylan start talking to each other, so I turn to Casey.

"Thanks for sticking by me," I tell her. "This year was rough, and I didn't mean to cast you out."

She grabs my hand. "I'll always be here. I'll be here for your college graduation, your wedding, all three births of your kids—"

441

"Who says I'm having three kids?" I interrupt while laughing.

"Well, I'm not having kids, so you have to have one for me. I'll be the cool aunt, like your Aunt Jade." She shrugs.

I can't argue with that. "She is pretty cool." I have to give her more credit for taking care of me for the past year. She could've shipped me off to my grandparents, but she didn't. While she's been strong on her own, James is helping her too. He makes her light up, and that's all I want for her.

I haven't told Dylan that I'm going to cover my tattoo before graduation with James's help. I don't want to walk across the stage with something that doesn't mean anything to me anymore. Something else needs to cover it.

The night draws on. We dance and laugh some more. Reece is convinced he can sneak in a bottle, but Anthony and Dylan manage to change his mind. There will have to be an after party for that.

Dylan places his hand on my knee. "No one is going to be home, so I'm going to invite some people over. We'll have to leave a little earlier, so I can clean up a bit."

Dylan sure does like to throw parties. I wonder if his dad or even his mom knows that he throws parties regularly.

Things slow down, and word gets out about the party at Dylan's house. We leave the hotel earlier than everyone else, so we can prepare the house.

"Where is everyone tonight?" I ask Dylan once we walk through his front door.

"My mom wanted to take Ethan camping, so that's where they're at now. My dad's tagging along with them. Derrick should be with Jared."

"So we're alone?"

He gives me a wicked grin and slides his arm around my waist before he plants a kiss on my cheek. "I know you want to, you know. Don't get me wrong, I want to do it too, but I don't

442

have any condoms, and I don't want you to be the cliché girl who gets pregnant on prom night."

As disappointed as I feel, I know he's right.

"Let's just enjoy one more high school party before the real world comes creeping up on us," he says before kissing my forehead.

There is no longer a feeling inside me that feels like Xavier will pop out at any moment. The only thing I have to be afraid of is adulthood. I can't allow myself to worry about my future with Dylan. Things have to happen naturally, as they always have with him. Forcing ourselves to think about what's next won't work out. If it's meant to be, then it will be.

*   *   *

I stare at my wrist and let my thoughts wander as the speaker's voice vibrates in my ears. My original infinity-heart tattoo is now covered with two detailed sunflowers to represent my parents.

The original will always be a part of me, being the first time ink ever touched my skin, and I accept that. The sunflowers stand as a reminder that no one is forever, no matter how much I want them to be.

How silly it was to think Jacob and I would stay together forever, and how silly it was to think that I would have my parents forever.

And here I am, crossing the stage as the speaker says my name to receive my diploma. Here I am, after the ink, growing into myself and accepting everything that comes my way. I can hear the cheers from my aunt over everyone else, and I know for the rest of my life that I want to make her and only her proud.

In the sea of students, I know Dylan is cheering me on. I know that as long as he's around, he'll push me to be a better version of myself, and I'll do the same for him. If not forever, then for the small moment of time given to us.

EPILOGUE

My dad once took me to work with him. He was pretty popular among his coworkers, talking to nearly everyone we passed by. He taught me what he did in the bank and why it was important. I realized that day that growing up and having to deal with bankers like Dad and Mom was not as simple as I thought.

When I entered high school, I couldn't see a future for myself. It was hard to imagine what I would be doing in the next ten or fifteen years. I had no idea what I wanted to do because I knew becoming a banker was not what I wanted. I never told my parents flat out that it wasn't the job for me, and I wish I had the chance to do so.

Taking journalism in high school was the best decision I had ever made. My burning curiosity was fueled by that class. Suddenly, I could picture myself working for a larger paper. Somewhere where news matters and deserves to be reported. Where I could be a trustworthy source for the public.

I dabbled in the editorial part of it, but the reporting was fun. I wanted to know why things are the way they are and why we should question them. I felt like I should be able to question everything.

Curiosity nearly got me killed by Xavier, but it also brought me closer to Dylan. When we met, I wasn't sure what his life plan was. As I got to know him, I felt like I knew where he was heading.

He expressed that he didn't know what his life would be like in the next five years, but he wasn't too worried about it. I instantly knew how Dean felt when Evelyn left. She had a wandering spirit, and it's been passed on to Dylan.

He left with her after graduation, as planned. He and his mom left for Arizona to see the Grand Canyon. They decided to explore the desert more when they got there.

I left for New York City, and everything seemed fine. We talked every day, keeping each other updated on what we did, exchanging adventures.

After two weeks in the city, I realized how much I missed him. I asked him if he could visit me. We spent two weeks together, and it's the most magical thing to ever happen to me. To be with the love of my life in a city I loved, I couldn't ask for anything better.

He left after the two weeks were up. He met his mom in Philadelphia.

When I got back home in time for school in Greenwell to start, he still wasn't here. He said he would be back the week after me, so I waited. One week turned to two, then three. Before I knew it, a whole month had passed with no word from him.

Dylan's words from those last few months of senior year rang in my ears constantly. In my heart, I knew he would never hurt me on purpose. I knew he's charmed by the sights he's seeing. What sane person would come back after adventures such as those?

I saw myself as a Dean Parker, someone whose love had a wandering spirit. I visited the other Parker boys as much as I could, and it hurt when I found out Dylan had talked to them but not me.

I couldn't be angry with him. Dylan didn't have a plan for the future, and I couldn't force him to plan it out. I also couldn't force him to have a future with me. He needed to see it himself.

That didn't mean it hurt any less though.

Dean could see the pain I was feeling, and I could almost feel the pity radiating off of Derrick whenever I was around.

Another month later, I finally got a call from Dylan.

He apologized for leaving me in the dark and for not coming back. The hurt in his voice was clear, and I knew he's sincere about everything he said.

I knew what's coming though. He didn't know when he would come back home. He didn't say it explicitly, but I knew he wanted to say he didn't think he would come back home at all.

He also implied that I could go along with him, but I couldn't. School came first. That's all my parents wanted me to do. Graduate high school, then graduate college. I couldn't put it on the back burner of my mind.

Then he came back. He had so many stories to tell that I couldn't be mad at him for not coming back on time. He's so excited to tell me about what he'd seen and what he'd experienced.

I tried picturing what life would be like with Dylan by my side. Now that he's back, I pictured us being a normal couple, with no psychos following us and nothing separating us. I could picture it up until I graduated college.

Would Dylan want to travel again? Would he come back at all? Maybe the trouble we went through in the past was a sign for things to come. Maybe the hurt would never end.

I wondered how my decision would choose our path. If I chose to stay with Dylan, how would I know that things would work out in the end? I didn't know, and that's what scared me.

Then I recalled Lauren's words about Jacob. She figured Jacob and I would run into each other at the supermarket in a few years and would find that the connection was never broken. She predicted we'd get married, have kids, and live happily ever after.

I didn't want to see Jacob in the supermarket. I wanted to see Dylan.

Do you like YA stories?
Here are samples of other stories
you might enjoy!

CHAPTER ONE

The worst part about losing someone is losing them when you least expect it. It's not every day you have your parents break the news to you that your best friend has committed suicide. It's one of those days where I just have that gut feeling that something is bound to go wrong—and trust me, I've had more than one of those days—but never in my life could I have imagined something going this wrong.

The memory of hearing of my best friend's death is as fresh in my mind as ink on a sheet of paper. The days after hearing of her death are a blur of tears and locking myself in my room all day, convincing myself that this is all just some cruel joke. I soon learned this to be the first stage of grieving—denial. I'm not ready to move on, but I know I have to try because even if she isn't here to live her life with me, I know that she will want me to live mine for the both of us. Even if I'm still angry and confused about why hers ended.

*   *   *

I sit in my car and stare up at my high school. The lawn is littered with teens conversing about what they did over break, going on as if absolutely nothing has changed when it feels like my whole world has changed. Taking a deep breath, I grab my things before opening the car door and stepping out. Putting my head down, I try to walk briskly into the building without having to run into anyone.

"Alexa!" *Just my luck.*

"Paige, hi." I force some enthusiasm into my voice, but it just ends up falling flat. "I heard what happened, and the girls and I just wanted to say sorry for your loss. If you ever need anything, I will be happy to help," she says with what I can obviously tell is fake sincerity. I look at her and the rest of the girls sitting at a table a few feet away.

"Thanks for your concern, Paige," I say, forcing down any hint of anger. "But I'm fine." I abruptly turn around and walk away before she can get a chance to reply.

Walking through the crowded hallway, I glance at the place where my best friend's locker used to be. The place where I would meet with her every day to complain about how awful our mornings were as we headed to our first class together. The place I will no longer be going to every morning. I trudge through the halls with memories surging my mind as I try hard not to break down right here and now. It's hard enough waking up this morning and driving past her house on my way here, but this . . . this just adds salt to the wound. The shrill ringing of the bell breaks me out of my trance, and I hurry to my locker before heading off to my first class of the day.

I can't seem to focus as Ms. Anderson promptly starts the lesson. I can't stop hearing her voice at the back of my head or picturing her next to me, not paying attention to the lesson at all as she makes snarky comments about how awful Ms. Anderson's outfit choice is that day.

"Alexa? Ms. Parker, are you with us?" The sound of Ms. Anderson's saccharine voice interrupts any further thoughts, and I try to clear my head.

"Yes. Sorry," I say quickly. She gives me a sympathetic look before continuing with the lesson, a lump forming in my throat. Time seems to be moving agonizingly slow as my next few classes go by; it doesn't help that every few minutes, I am approached by people saying how sorry they are for my loss and how she was such an amazing person. Half of them don't even know her. It infuriates me that these people didn't give her a second thought when she was alive, but now that she's dead, she suddenly matters to them.

When lunch finally comes around, I sit at a table towards the back. I'm relieved to get a break and a chance to sort my thoughts. My break is short-lived as I'm joined by company.

"Hi, Alexa. How are you?" Alison greets timidly as she and Madison sit down with their lunch trays. Alison and Madison are twins and probably the sweetest girls you will ever meet, but right now, I just wish they will get up and leave. I'm tired of people coming up to me with their pity and condolences, which only reminds me more of my loss.

"I'm fine," I reply half-heartedly, not having it in me to ask them to leave. "What brings you guys here?"

"Can't we have lunch with our captain?" Madison says with that bright smile that can light up any room.

"We just want to check on you, and the team wants to know if you'll be at cheer practice today." *Right. There's practice.*

"Yeah, totally." I flash them a smile. I can't let them see my weakness, and if moving on means that I have to resume the role of the girl I was before that day, then so be it. As lunch progresses and they make no move to leave, I struggle to stay focused. Everything reminds me of her.

The table near the center of the room used to be our table. The table we would sit at every day and talk about boys while also discussing our future. She would always talk about how we would attend the same college and become roommates and then rent an apartment together in a different city after graduation. It all just keeps leading me back to the question of 'why?'. I can feel my eyes start to blur with tears, and I stand up suddenly. The twins look up at me with concern-filled eyes.

"I-I'm going to go. I just remembered I have to go to the library and check out a book for my next class," I say while grabbing my things.

"Oh okay. I guess we'll see you at practice?" Alison asks.

"I'll be there," I promise her.

I emerge from the cafeteria and make my way to the bathroom with my eyes locked on the ground so no one can see the tears ready to fall.

"Sorry," I say after accidentally bumping into someone, not even bothering to look at them as I start to sprint to the bathroom in my frantic state. After making sure it's empty, I slide against the wall and do the one thing I promised myself I wouldn't do today— I cry. The tears pour out like a waterfall, the confusion and anger and pain with them. I cry until my vision is blurry and my eyes are red. I cry until I know that I can't be in here any longer because someone is bound to walk in, and I'm not sure I can handle confrontation in this state. It's been a month since she's been gone, and instead of things getting easier with time, everything seems to be getting harder. I wish that I can just go back in time and stop any of this from happening.

It's taking me some time to compose myself. I missed the remainder of my classes for the day, and I can't even bring myself to care. I end up leaving cheer practice early at the suggestion of the team. I can't focus on the routine, and I was messing everything up. Pushing through the double doors of the gym, I let out a frustrated sigh as I lean against the wall and pinch the bridge of my nose. I eventually head to the school's parking lot, which is mostly empty with the exception of a few cars.

"Alexa?" I hear my name being called and I go rigid. *Why can't I be left alone?*

"Hey, Matt." I turn to look at him and his friends surrounding his truck with sweat and dirt running down their faces. Matt Carpenter is the quarterback of our school's football team. I don't really recall having any real interactions with him other than at football games.

"It's been awhile since I've seen you," he says.

"I have a lot going on at the moment." I unlock my car door, not caring to continue this conversation after the crap day I've had.

"Wait," he says as I'm about to make my escape. I look at him expectantly, feeling annoyed that I'm being delayed from leaving.

"I'm sorry but I need to go." I shut my car door and leave, not allowing myself to feel bad for how harsh that probably sounded. When I finally enter my house, I'm greeted by the smell of my mother's cooking.

Before, I would be rushing into the kitchen, anxious to get a bite of whatever was on the stove. Now, I barely have an appetite.

"How was school?" she inquires with a smile as I throw my keys down on to the table.

"It was okay." Sighing, I watch as she dumps some pasta into the pot of boiling water.

"You know you can talk to me, Alexa. What happened isn't something you can easily recover from," she starts with a soft gaze in her eyes as she looks at me. "I know you both were close but—" I clench my hands into fists at her words.

We weren't *just* close; she was all I had. She's the only person that understood me, and now, she's gone. No explanation, no warning, and no apology.

"Mom, I know you're trying to help me and I appreciate it; I really do, but I just need time and space. She's my best friend and I don't want to think about the fact that she's gone." She looks taken aback by my words but she nods anyway.

"Okay. Well, I'm here if you need anything. I just want you to know that you're not alone," she replies with a sad smile, and I give her a quick hug before heading upstairs to my room. I lock the door and collapse on to my bed as I stare up at the ceiling. I grab my journal from the nightstand and open it up to a clean page but I freeze as a picture falls out.

It's of her and I at a party. We were holding red solo cups—which were filled with ginger ale—and smiling like there was no tomorrow.

"I can't believe you did that!" I exclaim as we both stumble into my room, hunched over in fits of laughter. "The look on her face was priceless!"

"It was definitely an accident," Cam says with a smirk.

"I think Paige knows you spilling that drink on her wasn't an accident."

I shut the journal and hold it tightly to my chest. It isn't fair. It isn't fair that Cam is gone, and I'm expected to just move on. How can I when most of my happiest memories are with her? How can I when all I can think about is her day in and day out? The tears fall down my cheeks for what feels like the thousandth time today. I curl into a ball with the picture clenched against my chest. I don't know how long I stayed like that, but before I know it, I'm asleep.

If you enjoyed this sample, look for
Say You Won't Let Go
on Amazon.

SOME ONE LIKE YOU

JENNISE K

PROLOGUE

When I met him on a rainy afternoon, the air smelt like gardenias.

My black Oxford pumps were soaked from accidentally stepping on a puddle, and the tiny yellow umbrella I held up barely saved me from the chilly rain.

When I met him on a rainy afternoon, the sky was pink and blue. I was starving and almost craving to smell the stuffy scent of my closed-up home's small living room.

When I met him on a rainy afternoon, his son held my feet out of the blue and called me 'mum'. He rushed out of the restaurant only seconds later, his cheeks a pale flushed hue.

When I met him one day on a rainy afternoon, he looked into my eyes and apologized. And inside my head, I thought to myself . . . what a lovely way to meet a lovely man on such a lovely rainy afternoon.

CHAPTER ONE
One Rainy Afternoon

She rushes through the crowd in the pouring rain.
She rushes soaking wet, closer to the scent of lilies.
Closer to his heart.

As I walk out the front door, the light showers of rain continue to drizzle over the healthy green and prettily blossomed foliage that surrounds my plain home. The flowers I've spent hours nursing almost every weekend since I've inherited this home from a distant aunt are luckily all in bloom at the same time, and every inch of the garden is looking well-groomed.

I smile. The corner of my eyes crinkles with pleasure as I glance around my front yard while standing at the edge of my front porch, opening my bright yellow umbrella. I quickly pull it over me. It doesn't help to keep out much of the rain, but it's convenient.

Quickly, I step out on to the driveway and begin rushing towards the front gate. The quicker I get to the bus stop, the better. I really need to hand over the hard copy of the manuscripts I've just completed proofreading and editing last night. Thankfully, I still have almost four hours until the deadline.

"Where are you rushing off to, Gemma?" Mrs. Red yells as I slide the gate to a close and lock it as quickly as I can. Turning around, I smile at the old woman. My small feet hurriedly shuffle along the sidewalk. Her blatant need to pry doesn't surprise me—as much as it used to—anymore. I've just come to accept that with age comes the need to satisfy one's curiosity about one's family members, neighbours, and everyone else's personal lives.

"Going to submit these manuscripts, Magenta! See you around!" I yell back, putting my hand up in a quick wave as I almost fly past her house. I'm only three blocks away from the bus stop now, and I can almost see the bus driving its way towards the stop quicker than my two tiny feet can carry me.

Magenta Red.

I have always thought that it is a beautiful name—if not particularly hilarious in its unity. Sometimes though, I couldn't help but wonder if Mrs. Red's parents ever thought that their daughter would go on and marry a man with the surname Red when they named her Magenta. I could only laugh thinking about her parent's reactions when they first heard of their daughter's new surname.

"Oh no!" I gasp as I feel my feet step into a puddle.

Looking down, I frown as I notice that my black Oxford shoes are completely soaked. Sadly, I do not have the tiniest bit of time to stop. Instead, I push forward until I'm at the bus stop and then quickly begin shaking off the leg that had stepped into the puddle.

My eyes meet a strange woman's, and I instantly smile, embarrassed at being caught in this situation.

"Even such a beautiful day like this has its disadvantages, doesn't it?" She speaks quite clearly. Her tone is brisk but I can hear a hint of humour. I nod back sheepishly.

"You're right. It's such a shame."

Soon enough, the bus reaches the stop. After letting the current passengers get off, I join in the line for getting in.

Stepping on the bus, I look at the empty seats as I assess the best spot to sit. It doesn't take too long to realize that my usual seat is empty, and I quickly make a beeline towards it. I grin happily as I settle myself into the seat and place my bag on my lap.

The rain outside splashes against the bus's window. The bus begins to move, and I smile as I try to see through the foggy glass out into the world outside. The usual feeling of content settles into my chest as I pull my jacket closer to my neck and place on my earplugs, tapping play on my usual playlist.

I love taking bus rides, especially when it rains like this.

Sitting here, almost near the back as it rains outside, a whole new world seems to be created in the large vehicle. A whole new world that feels safe despite being so uncertain of its passengers, that feels warm despite it raining so hard outside. It's a system that works well enough, loving bus rides and not having a car of my own.

I am not a girl from a . . . particularly rich family. In fact, my family is quite the middle class. Ever since I can remember, my mother has worked as an accountant in a large firm, and my father has been a professor for the Faculty of Agriculture in a local university back home. Their jobs never changed and neither did our financial standing.

I was always aware of the bills and expenditures of the house. Despite having a single maid that came by five days a week, I remember we would always budget and be aware of our spending. Regardless, I was always quite content with my life. I loved my moderately sized home, and it didn't matter that I didn't get a car gifted on my sixteenth birthday like the other kids or a credit card to spend my parents's money with.

Breaking me out of my thoughts, the bus comes to a stop. I check that all my manuscripts are safely placed in a plastic bag inside my bag before pulling out my umbrella and getting up. Quickly, I begin making my way towards the exit. Today is a more important day than usual. Apart from having to submit these manuscripts, it's also payday, and that means it's the day I do my grocery shopping and pay the bills.

Being a twenty-four-year-old girl taking care of my own house and expenses and doing my master's part-time at the university while working full-time as an editor for a very popular publishing company is not exactly what I had initially thought adult life to be. I had been a dreamer; in my dreams, everything was pastel and Instagram-worthy. I was living a beautiful life filled with magical multitasking and a prince charming who always stood by my side, supporting me.

Reality isn't like that though. I figured that out the very first day I moved into this house alone. Although I know my parents would love to help me out, asking them for money is probably the hardest thing I have had to do in quite a while, and so, I try to keep that off as the absolute last option. So far, it has been working well. Sometimes, in the moment of solitude, I even admit to myself how proud I am of this little world I have created for myself.

Stepping off the bus, I turn in the direction of the publishing company.

Despite life's realities, however, I still do try to find the beauty in things. I try keeping my home and garden just as I used to dream it would be. I reckon, as long as I can get one thing right, the rest won't matter too much.

Prince Charming looks way better in my imagination anyway.

Turning around the street's corner, my eyes spot the publishing company. I let out a huff of exhausted breath, already dreading having to go up five floors of stairs. Being claustrophobic isn't exactly a quirk to celebrate sometimes.

The rain begins to get stronger, and my feet don't carry me as quick as I want them to. I tighten my grasp on the small yellow umbrella as I angle it against the direction of the pelting rain and grimace when it barely does anything to hold the icy shower of water off.

As I pass the large brightly painted building, I've come to appreciate over the past years working at the publishing company the rich scent of beef stir-fry that wafts out of the Chinese restaurant and out into the rainy street. Had it been some other time, I would have given in; however, this month, I am tight on the money and have to buy other things for the house, so Chinese take-outs will have to wait for a while.

"Gemma! It's good to finally see you in the office! Have you been well?" Alicia, the chief editor of our publishing company, smiles up at me as I enter the office and walk over, knocking on the door. I open it when she gives the green signal.

I try to ignore the secret jibe she holds in her sweet greeting and smile back at her as brightly as I can. "Hello, Alicia. Yes! I've been well. As you must know, since we report to each other every day one way or another . . ." Instantly, I smile brighter and push the sealed and tagged envelopes towards her on the table. "I've just brought over the finished editing for the three hard copies you wanted to get done."

Alicia's smile turns into a grin. I can't help but wish I had just mailed the manuscripts instead. "Thanks, Gemma, I'll get through the rest of the processes."

"How are your studies going?" Alicia asks as she always does, carefully putting the envelopes to the side. She's trying to seem like she's just showing concern and care, but I know better. Alicia only holds a post-grad. Soon, I'll hold a master's. This specific thing has caused a lot of the most boring manuscripts coming my way to edit for the past few months, and that too, most of them the old-fashioned hard copies.

"It's going really well." I chuckle awkwardly as I shuffle on my feet, trying to think of how I can keep myself from coming off as a show-off. In the end, I give up. Anything I do will seem like a slap in her face. Alicia has always been very brutally competitive. The main reason why she's the chief editor and so many of the rest of us are not.

"That's great." Alicia nods, turning back to her large desktop screen.

"I just hope it doesn't affect your work efficiency, Gemma. I'd hate to let you go."

*   *   *

The strong smell of the rain and traffic hits me straight in my senses as I step out of the building and on to the now slightly drizzling street. Despite the rain, the skies have turned into the colour of pale pink blush, and I glance around the sky with affection before opening my umbrella and stepping out into the light drizzle.

"Take care on your way home." One of the graphic designers in our company, Jason, waves at me as he sticks his head out of the front door and then sticks it back in.

"Thanks, Jace!" I smile at the man's antique and dumbly wave back. Knowing the silent clash between Alicia and I very well, I always appreciate it when Jason sneaks out of the office just to come down five floors and wave me goodbye, just to make me smile after the harsh encounters.

My black Oxfords tap against the sidewalk, and I smile as I begin making my way towards the mall. After dealing with Alicia, I'm glad to be having an outlet for distraction. It's even more stressful on days I do desk duty. Those are the worst.

My gaze roams around the somewhat busy downtown street, and I realize that the heavy rain has slowly calmed down during the time I was at the company. *It's better this way*, I think to myself as I begin to pass the Chinese restaurant. *I mean, after all, I do have shopping to do and bills to—*

"Mum-mmy!"

I freeze. My eyes snap down to my legs where two tiny pale arms are now wrapped around my calves. Immediately twisting around slightly and kneeling down, my eyes find two large bright ones staring back at me.

Despite my shock, I smile at the little boy. I wrap my right hand around the small boy's waist, and I craftily pull him under the protection of the umbrella.

"What's your mummy's name, little man? Have you lost her?"

"Mummy!" The child's small grubby fingers find my hair as he tries to climb on to me. I flinch awkwardly, thinking of how to handle this.

Flustered, I re-adjust my shoulder bag and pull the very mistaken, climbing boy into my arms.

Before today, I've never been quite good with kids. It's not like I dislike them. On the contrary, I love babies. It's just that they hate me. My nieces and nephews, and even random babies on buses. Well . . . maybe not this child.

A quick look into his eyes and I notice how tear-stricken his cheeks look. His large, wide eyes are staring at me in wonder and with love I don't really deserve. I can't help but envy his mother though. To have this child look at her with such devotion and love all the time, she must be a very happy woman.

I frown slowly, suddenly realising that his parents are nowhere to be seen. "Where is your mum, sweetie?"

"Mum-mmy! Have you forgot me?" the boy sobs out loudly as he begins pulling at my hair, trying his best to stick his slightly wet self closer to me.

This isn't going to work out. I sigh as I look around for an adult looking for this child.

"Okay! Okay!" I blurt out, making up my mind as I tighten my hold on the child. I've begun to notice how awkwardly the security guards at the restaurant have begun to look at me. "Where's your dad?"

"I'm so sorry!" The smooth liquid-like voice flows smoothly through the air and into my ears. Something about this soft boyish voice sends a ripple of awareness through me. I almost flinch with the awkwardness of these feelings.

My eyes snap up and my breath hitches in my throat as I stare at a man rushing towards us with a large black umbrella over his head. My eyes run over his perfectly styled hair that has fallen a bit askew with clear signs of distress as I notice him run his fingers through his hair nervously.

Reaching us, he also drops to kneel before us and our eyes meet. Something in my chest bursts and I can only blink.

Breathe, Gemma! Breathing is important! It gives carbon dioxide to plants. Plants are very important. They give oxygen to us. Basically, breathing is very, very important.

Inhale. Exhale. Inhale!

"I'm so sorry," he says, moving his eyes from his child to me. My eyes, however, are focused on the pale pink hue on his cheeks. They remind me of the sky and I smile.

Exhale, damnit!

"Pa! Mum-mmy!" The little boy suddenly jumps in my arms. Surprised, I almost tumble back when two strong hands wrap around me, stopping me from falling on my arse. Immediately, I tighten my arms around the boys in return.

"I'm so sorry about that. Isaac is usually more well-behaved." The man coughs, removing his hands from me as if he has been burnt.

"It's no problem." I shake my head awkwardly. "I'm afraid he's gotten a bit wet. You should change him out of his clothes in case he gets sick."

The man bristles at my words but still smiles and nods.

His arms begin to reach forward towards his child when, suddenly, the kid begins pulling at my hair, trying to get closer to me. Despite my pain, I grit my teeth together to stop myself from yelping and, instead, hold the boy close. It's time to take a different approach.

For a second, I glance at the man awkwardly, hoping he doesn't hate me too much for this, then I turn back towards the frantic child.

"It's okay, sweetie. Mummy is going to be here," I mumble into the tiny boy's ears. I notice the man before me stiffen. I avoid his eyes, caressing the boy instead while I continue to talk to the child. "Mummy needs to grab something from the supermarket. Why don't you go to Dad for a bit?"

"No! Mummy liar!" young Isaac whines as his tiny fingers find the material of my jacket and curls around it tightly.

My eyes snap to the man's, and I fight the urge to just stare into the deep brown eyes that seem to penetrate into my soul.

"Your . . . your mother's right, Isaac. She needs to grab something from the store. We'll wait for her in the restaurant with Grandma and Grandpa. Come." The man reaches for the child again, and I lean forward, allowing him easier access.

"No!" Isaac screams out in the—thankfully—almost empty sidewalk. My eyes avoid the passersby as I decide to pay attention to the child before me instead. He moves his small arm to my neck and tightens.

"Don't let me go, Mummy. Pa is a liar," he whispers into my ear, and I almost feel my heartbreak for the little guy. He moves his head back to look at me with pleading eyes. I purse my lips together, knowing exactly well that I am losing to the child. He has his father's eyes—eyes that make me feel like they are looking into my soul.

"Don't you trust Mummy?" I gulp and quickly whisper back, remembering to smile warmly at the child in my arms. His father stays kneeled before us, watching us quietly.

"You do, don't you?" I can only imagine what a scene the three of us must be to the other people walking around us. Still, I keep my focus on the strong little bundle in my arms. Slowly, the child nods and my smile widens.

"Then go to Daddy. Mummy will find you both, okay?" I whisper in the child's ears. The man stays kneeled before us, still quiet. Still observing us.

"Promise?" the child whispers as his fingers tighten around my neck.

I almost push him into his father's arms and bolt away from this place. In my life, there are many things that I have done. I've lied. I've stolen from my mum's makeup collection. I've skipped school once or twice too. I've even snuck out of my home once just to go meet my then best friend who had just broken up with her stupid boyfriend.

Despite all these reckless things I've done, I've never cheated on someone, and I've never given someone a fake promise.

"Promise?" Isaac whispers again and I turn to his father. I feel my heart jump in my chest when I see the man's quiet eyes already watching me. The pink hue that was present only in his cheeks has now spread all over his face. Instead of looking embarrassed, he looks upset now. Still, the man watches me, waiting for what I'm about to say to the boy.

"I promise." I smile at the big sad-eyed boy as I take my free hand away from him and quickly push it into my bag. Quickly pulling out one of the many cards I was made to make, I put one into the now relaxed child's hand. "And in the meantime, if you miss Mummy, then you can always call me, okay?"

"Okay, Mummy," Isaac whispers softly as he closes his small fingers around the card. My eyes turn to the man's once again and I smile.

"If Isaac misses me, please let him talk to me," I tell the silent man as I lean forward and let him take the child into his arms.

Immediately, both of us get up on our feet, and I realize just how tall the man is compared to me.

"Again, I'm very sorry." The man nods again, looking slightly embarrassed and grateful.

"Let him call me if he wants," I reply instead. Something about the man makes me think that this will be the last thing he will do in case Isaac misses his mother.

Waving at both the teary-eyed boy and the tall man, I turn around to leave.

I don't know what it is that I'm feeling in my chest, but suddenly, something feels heavy. Is it possible to get so attached to a strange child I've never met before . . . so quickly?

"Wait! Mummy!"

I stop. Turning around, I watch the boy extending his arms towards me. I walk closer towards little Isaac with a bright smile. "Yes, sweetie?"

"I miss you," the boy whispers as if he doesn't want his father to hear.

"Isaac," the man warns. "Your mother has somewhere to go."

I glance at the man and then at the child. For a second, I just stand there under my umbrella, watching the father-and-son pair in front of me.

"I'll miss you too, Isaac," I respond finally and then on impulse and my embarrassment, I lean forward and place a kiss on both of his cheeks. "Now, be good, okay?" I smile, waving as I begin turning around and walking. The further I get, the quicker my feet begin to move.

"I miss you, Mummy!" I hear a distant yell. I feel my heart constrict. Rain begins to pour down on the city again. I quicken my steps, hoping that the distance will make me feel less of a loss for a child that isn't even mine.

Still, under the thunderous rain, I let myself have a moment of weakness. I let myself act because of my emotions. I don't think I'll ever forget this afternoon, this situation, and this child. This rainy afternoon will always be something that I'll remember every time it rains.

"I'll miss you too, Isaac. Take care of yourself. Please don't go running out of restaurants during rainy afternoons. It's dangerous. Please don't call strange girls 'mummy'. Please be healthy and well. Maybe one day we will meet again."

If you enjoyed this sample, look for
Someone Like You
on Amazon.

Caffeine

LIVIA HALTEH

CHAPTER ONE
Café Latte

"Morning, Aspen. Your usual?"

My tired eyes drifted up to the perky bartender, Vivienne. Her black hair was tied into a high ponytail as her pale fingers rested above the cash register. I gave a weary smile in return.

"You know me too well."

She flashed her pearly teeth at me, typing in the order and accepting my money, then returning my exact change. I made my drowsy way towards an empty table. While Café de Fleur was a gorgeous little café that made the best soy lattes in town, it wasn't the most popular, so finding a table was easy for me.

As I took my seat, I couldn't help but let my eyes drift over to the table beside me, hidden in the very furthest corner of the café. Isaac Hensick sat alone at his usual table, his long tanned fingers slid a graphite pencil across a small sketchpad, about the size of his palm, hidden from my sight.

Beside his muscular arm sat an untouched cup. His soft green eyes fluttered across the page, one step ahead of his hand as he marked the paper with his pencil.

Isaac is a classmate of mine, although he was barely seen in class. To be completely honest, my morning visits to the café were the most I had seen of him all day. He was a popular boy, well-liked—if not loved—across the entire school, but he was definitely not the studious type.

Every morning for the past two years he'd sit on that chair, too focused on his drawings to notice me, and too absorbed in his own world to even sip the coffee he always ordered.

Black coffee, three sugars.

"You're staring again, Aspen." Vivienne's booming voice woke me from my thoughts. "Here's your latte."

I looked up to see Vivienne in front of me, her arms extended with a takeout coffee cup in one hand and a small brown bag containing my usual biscotti in the other.

I flashed an embarrassed smile, taking my order from her hand.

"Thanks Viv," I mumbled gratefully, taking a long sip from my coffee. Almost instantly, my pounding headache was relieved. I let out a sigh in relief as the burning coffee slid down my throat and scalded my tongue.

I grinned up at Vivienne and she sent me a knowing smile.

"Have a good day at school," she said before returning to her counter, busying herself by tidying up the cake display.

"You take care," I replied, my eyes subconsciously moving back to Isaac.

He was in my French class, meaning he'd have to leave now to get there before the bell, but he made no effort to move from his seat. Instead, he stayed occupied with whatever he was drawing. His coffee remained untouched beside his scribbling hand, the steam long gone.

Turning away from him, I opened the door to exit the café and make my way to school. He could miss class as much as he wanted to, but I was going to turn up on time.

As I began my walk to school, I watched the people on the street with familiar faces of neighbors and classmates who probably didn't even know of my existence.

I guess I was what you'd call a wallflower. I was never involved with any school dramas or the subject of the grade's daily gossip. It's not like I minded it, though. It was always fun to observe, to not get caught up in all the drama, even if it made my life completely uneventful.

"Aspen, Aspen!"

At least I had my friends.

I turned to see my best friend Riley bounding through the hallway to reach me at my locker, her little blonde ponytail flying around the back of her head. For a such tiny person, she was always filled with nothing but energy, the exact opposite of me.

We've been friends since the fourth grade, when she stabbed Billy Johnson's hand with a pencil after he spent all lunch pestering me. She received a week's suspension and was forced to begrudgingly write an apology letter to Billy and his family. Ever since then, she was my closest and oldest friend.

"Good morning, Riley." I sighed, closing my locker and turning towards her with an exhausted, lopsided grin.

"Aspen, guess what!" she squealed, not even pausing for me to guess. "Arthur Andrews got a haircut!"

My grin turned into a sarcastic smile.

"Great."

"I know right!"

I chuckled at my best friend before turning to the sudden sound of a horde of teenage girls's squeals.

What do you know, Arthur Andrews really did get a haircut. Riley let out a sigh of admiration, leaning against my shoulder with a dreamy grin.

Her eyes followed Arthur Andrews in all his muscular, tanned glory; his cropped brown waves sitting neatly atop his head. He was the soccer team's captain, and Riley had been crushing on him for months.

"He's so cute. I'd love to go out with him."

I snorted at her, shoving her off my shoulder. "You and a hundred other girls."

"I can dream!"

A laugh spurt from my lips when a hand gently tapped my back. Turning, my eyes met with our other best friend, William.

William was a lanky boy with black hair that fell just above his brown eyes. We had become friends in our first year of high school, when Riley had dragged him out of his introverted bubble to sit with us at lunch.

"Aspen." He inhaled hard. He reached a thin arm out to loop around my shoulders.

"Ew, you're sweating!" I exclaimed, shoving his hand away as he panted frantically.

"I had to run for the bus," he explained, leaning against the lockers as he struggled to catch his breath. His face was all red, and a bead of sweat traced its way down from his forehead. He wiped it off, still wheezing.

"Yeesh, how far did you run for it?" Riley joked, nudging me with an amused look.

He gulped air down hungrily, his cheeks still flaming red.

"Well, I missed the bus," he continued, out of breath. "So I had to walk to school."

We stared at him in silence as I took a sip of my coffee. His story itself was tiring me out and I was already on the verge of collapsing from exhaustion. It had been a long week of minimal sleep, as most could probably tell from the purple bags lining my bloodshot eyes.

"But I saw Mitch on the way," William paused to turn to me, "that's my mom's dag of a boyfriend." He faced Riley again to continue, "So I went the long way behind Picasso's and since it's so long I had to run."

I stifled a giggle with a final sip of my coffee. I wrinkled my nose at the taste—it already turned cold from the short walk to school.

"You're an idiot," Riley scoffed, rolling her eyes at William. "You know, you're going to have to speak to him *sometime*."

"Over my dead body!" William spat, causing Riley and I to laugh in unison.

"William," I began, resting a hand on his arm. "It's not so bad. Give him a chance. I refused to talk to Sabrina's boyfriend for half a year, and now they're planning on getting engaged."

William's face contorted into an expression of horror.

"If my mother marries that buffoon . . ." He took a sharp breath through his nose. "I'm moving to Canada."

Riley found this hilarious, evident through her loud, high-pitched laugh. She squealed in short giggles, slapping William on his back. He fell forward, his lanky body no match for Riley's enthusiasm.

William smiled, clearly proud he had been able to make Riley laugh so hard, and I rolled my eyes at the pair. The warning bell soon rang throughout the hallway, alerting us to start making our way to our classes.

"I'm going to go work on that runaway plan," William muttered, turning to follow the trail of students trudging to their classrooms. "See you at lunch?"

I nodded, and Riley started walking with me towards our French class. William had chosen to take Spanish this year, claiming girls loved a Spanish speaking man which earned the silent treatment from Riley for a week for "betraying our friendship."

I took a step in the opposite direction, my shoes squeaking against the floor and causing her to pause in her tracks.

"I'll meet you there," I said to Riley, holding up my empty coffee cup.

She sent me a curt nod, turning to walk towards our class alone as I headed towards a nearby bin.

Before I knew it, the hallways were cleared, with me being the only person left as I made my way towards the closest rubbish bin. I quickly tossed the empty cardboard cup into the trash can before making my way back to Riley before Mrs. Dubois arrived.

My legs felt heavy as I dragged myself across the hallway. The sound of my shoes squeaking against the linoleum rang through my ears, contributing to the throbbing headache that had returned just behind my eyes.

I pressed my eyes shut, wishing I had gotten a second coffee to get me through first period. My body ached with fatigue, and my arms felt heavy by my side.

Six hours to go.

The sound of running footsteps snapped me out of my self-pitying daze. I peeled my eyes open a second too late when I collided with a sudden well-clothed wall, causing me to shout and trip backwards. Before I could fall, an arm snaked around my back to hold me back from the impact.

I squinted my eyes open, blinking through the confusion the collision caused, only to see the dazzling green eyes of none other than Isaac Hensick, who was studying my face with concern.

His hand gripped my waist tightly, his hair falling in messy locks over his forehead as he leaned forward to hold me. His brow furrowed as he watched me.

"Are you okay?" he asked, his voice raspy.

I nodded, speechless, stumbling out of his arms and on to my own two feet. His eyes sent shivers down my spine, preventing me from looking away. I felt locked, frozen in place, and quickly forgot about my fatigue and the pain coursing through my head.

How did he get to school so fast?

His perfectly pink lips parted once more, letting out that gorgeously raspy voice that I had only heard from a distance in Café de Fleur. His cheeks imprinted with those famous dimples as he spoke.

"Do I know you?"

My heart fluttered from nervousness. I never thought I'd see him this close before. I watched with fear as he narrowed his eyes, scanning my face, a hint of familiarity and confusion lingering behind them.

He was even more gorgeous up close.

Up close, I could see the brown lining in his eyes, blending with the green as it glittered beneath the fluorescents. I could also see the grooves of his dimples in the corners of his grin.

Silence settled between us. I swallowed thickly, my chest swelling with anxiety as I realised I had left an awkwardly long pause since he asked the question.

My throat felt tight and, unable to speak, I shook my head wildly, causing him to frown and wrinkle his brow at me. It felt so strange seeing him up close rather than our usual encounters at the café, if they could even be called that.

"Are you sure? I swear I've seen you before. Are you new here?"

I chewed on my bottom lip anxiously, shaking my head once more and clearing my throat.

How could he not recognise me? Despite being a wallflower, I expected him to at least be aware of my existence from the English class we share. Or the French class; or the art class; or literally from just walking around the same school for the past four years.

"No, I'm sure," I squeaked out, desperate for this awkward encounter to end and my heart to stop pounding so hard.

I clenched my fists, my nails biting into the skin of my palms.

He opened his mouth, ready to speak, when the final bell sounded. My heart began to race as I took the chance to escape.

"Well, that's the bell, better get going!" I rushed, stepping around him as I began to power walk towards my class. "Don't want to be late!"

Mrs. Dubois was way past retirement age, meaning she often turned up to class a little late, but I didn't want to be with Isaac for a moment longer.

I sent a thin-lipped smile and began taking long strides, sliding down the hallway as fast as possible.

His brows rose, and his mouth fell open—ready to speak, but with no words to voice. I kept walking, feeling incredibly awkward and watched as I moved through the halls, rushing to get to my French class nearby.

Nevertheless, I could feel his eyes on my back, tempting me to turn back.

Sending one last glance behind me, I noticed him still staring at me as I sped away from him just as I had suspected.

But I didn't expect his wide eyes to be swimming with one emotion.

Recognition.

If you enjoyed this sample, look for
Caffeine
on Amazon.

ACKNOWLEDGEMENTS

First, I'd like to thank my parents for supporting me through this journey and listening to my many rants about the writing process. You both make my life so wonderful. I love you so much.

To Serena, Emery, and Tony, I don't know what I'd do without you all in my life. You make me laugh every single day and I wouldn't want anyone else as my siblings. You guys will always have my support.

To all of my extended family who have patiently waited for this book to come out, I want to say thank you for having my back and loving what I do. I appreciate every single one of you. It's all about family!

Finally, a huge thank you to everyone at Typewriter Pub who worked on this book with me. Thank you for giving me this incredible opportunity once again.

AUTHOR'S NOTE

Thank you so much for reading *After the Ink*! I can't express how grateful I am for reading something that was once just a thought inside my head.

I'd love to hear your thoughts on the book. Please leave a review on Amazon or Goodreads because I just love reading your comments and getting to know you!

Can't wait to hear from you!

B.D. Fresquez

ABOUT THE AUTHOR

Brianna Fresquez was born and raised in Las Cruces, New Mexico. An early love of books led to a love of writing at the age of thirteen. She is a New Mexico State University graduate with a Bachelor's degree in English with an emphasis in Creative writing. When she's not writing romance, reading romance, or eating chocolate, she's spending time with friends and family, or listening to movie soundtracks.